# EARTH AND HEAVEN

Sue Gee

# EARTH AND HEAVEN

Typeset by Letterpart Ltd
Reigate, Surrey

Printed and bound in Great Britain by
Clays Ltd, St Ives plc.

Headline Book Publishing
A division of Hodder Headline
338 Euston Road
London NW1 3BH
www.reviewbooks.co.uk
www.hodderheadline.com

For Marek and Jamie

To integrate bed and board, home and school, the small farm and workshop, earth and heaven.

Eric Gill

The transience of experience and the permanence of painting.

Nicholas Watkins, *Bonnard*

# Prologue

When Walter painted his family at evening, a towering angel stood at the door with folded wings.

The fire was lit: it just took the chill off. Sarah, at the bedside, with its slippery mounds of quilt and eiderdown, had turned from the window's starry sky, the winter stretch of fields, and was looking towards the door, very still. And Meredith, perched on the blanket chest, tugging off long woollen stockings, had looked up also, towards the shivery gap in the landing, and seen, startled, the figure in the shadows, the full strong rising curve of wings, the door about to open further.

She shrank, her face illumined.

The painting marked a turning point, for Walter had not known, when he began it, that an angel would descend upon the canvas – no, not descend: would walk, barefooted, along the creaking landing, his presence colder than the winter air, brushing against the torn patch of paper above the dado, and stand, full of severity and power, outside the plain square bedroom, waiting.

'Like *The Light of the World*,' said Meredith's lover, years later, looking up at the great framed canvas.

They were walking through a London gallery. Around them people came and went, turning the pages of catalogues.

'You know that isn't true,' said Meredith.

1

# I

## In Kent and London

# 1910

An early summer morning: the first liquid light, the first starling and blackbird, out in the orchard round to the side of the cottage, where the geese were sleeping. The sky was milky and soft as the sun rose; the grass in the orchard and garden shone with the dew. On the path up to the back door the flagstones were silvered with the night's slow progress of snails. A snail was climbing the water butt, up towards the overhanging planks on the top, where thrushes had their vantage point.

Half a mile away, from the farm beyond the hopfields, came the three hoarse notes of the cock. Walter stirred, and woke. He turned, and the bedsprings squeaked beneath him; his brother's nightshirted back was warm and still. Walter, the youngest, was often the first awake, the first of them all out of bed and down the stairs for breakfast. This morning he did not want to get up. He lay in the warmth, watching the curtains move dreamily at the open window, listening to the birds.

This was the first true morning of summer: Walter sensed it. Days had led up to this day, this daybreak, and the light at the gap in the faded cotton curtains touched everything in the room like a gift, as if to reveal, for now, for ever, the true and lasting shape of every object – this text hanging aslant on the yellowing wall; this stub of candle; this chamber pot; this full round jug in its bowl; the grain on the drawer of the washstand, running from west to east like a river.

Walter lay in the rumpled sheets and blankets, listening to the breathing of his brother and sisters, and the broken cry of the cock. How still and full the room in the tender light. How quiet the cottage, and the lane beyond the gate.

At length, the door of his parents' bedroom clicked. Footsteps came creaking along the landing; the children's door was pushed open. Walter closed his eyes, holding fast to the peace and stillness. His mother lifted the jug from the bowl: he could hear how carefully she did this, so as to leave them sleeping.

Down the bare treads of the stairs. The gush of water into the kettle, splashing into the stone sink, then the bang and the hiss on the range. He heard the back door opened, the enquiry from the geese beneath the trees. Clank of a pail. The chain pulled in the spidery privy. Back to the kitchen, the door left open to the fresh cool air. Another gush of water: into the white china jug.

The creaking return up the stairs. His mother came into the room again. Still as a bird on the nest, he watched her through half-closed eyes, tipping the jug on the edge of the bowl and pouring.

All that water, all that light.

Walter lay looking and looking.

She set the jug down: roundness against rim, the chink of china. As she crossed the floorboards dust danced after her. She drew the cotton curtains, and the room stirred.

'Good morning, children. Time to get up.'

No one answered.

She went quietly out again, down to the kitchen. Walter heard the kettle lifted, the tin taken down off the shelf. Soon she would be up again, with his father's tea in his mug. Up and down, up and down, starting the day.

Walter looked at the wall as his brother grunted. In the white china bowl on the washstand, the water was moving. The early sun streamed in through the open window and glanced off the surface: on the yellowing wall across the room from his bed, a tiny reflected patch of light was leaping, up and down, up and down, full of life and quickness.

Walter watched it.

The summer morning spread over the fields of Kent, the strings of hops, the deep quiet woods. Walter lay watching the leaping pulse of light, listening to his waking family, suspended between earth and heaven.

This is the story of art. Of Walter's art, which stretched back and back. Of a corner of English art, in the years between the wars, when waves of European modernism broke upon the shore.

Walter was too young to fight in the First World War, which he and his generation called the Great War, but the brother who shared his bed was killed: Private John William Cox, of the First Battalion of the East Kent Regiment – The Buffs, blown to pieces on the Somme on 16 September 1916, in the Battle of Flers-Courcelette.

When the telegram came on the squeaking bicycle, Walter was helping his father saw up the last of the elm which had come down the previous winter. His mother came out to the field without speaking. Walter had stacked all the logs in a barrow. The air was full of the sweet fresh smell of sawdust. They looked up, and saw her face.

Mr Burridge from Hobbs Farm rang the passing bell that Sunday, though John William's body never came home for burial.

They were not the only family in the village.

Lengthening shadows: name after name after name.

A corner of England, a grave in France.

In the winter of 1910, Sarah Lewis was taken by her parents to the Grafton Galleries. It was a Sunday afternoon; they walked through St James's Park and watched the waterbirds. The outlines of the shrubs on the curving islands were soft and dense in the thin grey London light; black railings bordered the reeds. Leaves dropped from an overhanging willow and drifted amongst mallard and mandarin and teal, out on the silvery lake. It began to rain. Sarah's father put up his great umbrella and they all stood under it, watching the needle-sharp splash of water upon water, and the pleasure of the ducks. The rain fell harder: they hurried across the grass, and into Green Park, where they sheltered beneath the plane trees. All along Piccadilly, black umbrellas were up. When the rain eased off, they made their way across the thoroughfare, and down into Grafton Street.

The gallery blinds were dripping on to the pavement; people came out of doorways, avoiding the puddles. Sarah's father shook out his umbrella and held open the gallery door. They stepped inside.

All her life, Sarah remembered that afternoon. After the rain, and the winter monochrome of the park, the London streets and buildings she had known all her childhood – here, with the shining drops of water sliding down the window, was a deep rich light, great flat planes of it, spilling from heavy frames. She was too young to call it Mediterranean. She knew where Paris was on the map, but had never been there; nor to Dieppe, or Provence. She had never heard of Tahiti. But she stood in her damp boots in the middle of the murmuring rooms and something in her leapt.

*Manet and the Post-Impressionists.* She let ochre and umber and amber wash over her. Half-naked women with great dark plaits of hair lay watchful in empty bedrooms. They leaned against doorways as night fell, squatted beneath luxuriant trees; half-wrapped in crimson and emerald cottons, they brushed out their hair by pools and waterfalls.

Sarah saw her mother on one of the button-backed couches, turning the pages of the catalogue. She heard her father, talking to his friends from the New English Art Club, people who came to the house every week, bringing their sketches and canvases, drinking and smoking upstairs in the studio, keeping her awake. Had they seen her looking at the undressed women, with their strange, watchful eyes?

Some of the conversation in the room was growing heated.

'Have you seen the Van Goghs? As for Cézanne – the man is nothing but an amateur. It's a disgrace.'

The catalogue was waved about.

' "The pictures collected together in the present Exhibition are the work of a group of artists who cannot be defined by any single term . . ." If there were no ladies present I am sure I should be able to think of one. What on earth does Fry think he's up to?'

' "The Post-Impressionists consider the Impressionists too naturalistic." '

'Do they indeed?'

' "The Post-Impressionists"! Is that what they are? "Too naturalistic"! Have you ever heard such—'

'Ah, Tonks, my dear fellow. What do you make of all this?'

'I fear we are at the summit of a very slippery and dangerous slope. What we see here is crude, brash, unfinished—'

'I fear you are absolutely right.'

'But think of Whistler,' Sarah heard her father put in. 'A picture is an arrangement of line and form and colour – that before anything else.'

'Forgive me, Lewis, but painting is about more than arrangement. What is to become of the man who abandons nature? The representation of nature?'

'Well?' asked her father. 'What is to become of him?'

'Lewis, why are you speaking for the defence? What we see here is grotesque!'

'Have you seen the Picassos?'

'Fearful, fearful.'

Sarah walked into the next room. A dirty domed skylight filtered a watery sun. Pigeons walked up and down on the wet glass. Sarah took herself to yellow stone houses in France, baking on long afternoons. She gazed at the distant mountain, observed the geometry of the terracotta rooftops, square-patched with trees. Bitter cypress reached to a starry sky.

The light above the dome of glass drew dark again: the rain began to fall.

'Sarah?'

She stood before a different London: a stippled yellow sky and yellow river, racing past the sweep of a pink Embankment. The skyline of churches and factories was a heavenly blue; clouds of steam puffed from tugboats on the water, streamed from a train on the long straight bridge. How bright, how alive!

Colour meant something in 1910.

They took a crowded omnibus to Waterloo, huddled together on top beneath the black umbrellas, mackintoshes over their knees. Sarah shivered, and sneezed.

'You've caught a chill.' Her mother drew her close; Sarah rested her cheek on damp alpaca.

'You enjoyed the paintings?' Her father turned up his collar. Sarah nodded.

'Why?'

How to begin?

The omnibus rumbled over the river. Lights from barges shone through Whistler's dusk. They caught the five o'clock train to Wimbledon, walking hand in gloved hand past wet laurels. Sarah was put to bed, and had a fire in her room.

She returned to the life of the suburbs: the schoolroom, the windy Common, old ladies with little dogs on leashes, the clop of the milkman's horse. She took up the routines of an ordered girlhood: hockey and homework and Sunday lunch. Her father taught and painted, and had his visitors. Occasionally she sat for them, and was made into someone pretty. Her mother ran the house and read. Nothing ever happened.

The suburbs had their own subjects, and poetry. Later, Sarah knew that: growing up, leaving home, looking back.

But by then the war had taken half of London.

9

# 1918

Walter, too young to go to France, enlisted with John William's regiment. He spent the last months of the war marching out beyond Dover, up to Pegwell Bay, marching back to Dungeness. Gunfire sounded from across the Channel. The wind stung the faces of the young recruits and blew over Romney Marsh; they tramped over shingle and long damp sands. Seals barked on the rocks, dark groynes stretched to the edge of the incoming tide, the sky was limitless. When they had time off, Walter made sketches in a flapping notebook: the seals, the fishing smacks, the shrieking gulls; the long clean sweep of the shore, a tanker, far out. Sand blew into the pages, he spat it out of his mouth. He put his sketchpad and pens and pencils back in his kitbag and set off back for the mess. When he thought about John William the emptiness felt like the drop from the edge of a cliff. Back in the mess he sketched the men: playing cards, mending kit, polishing patched boots, snoring on their beds.

Once, given leave, he went home to Asham's Mill. It was right at the end of the summer: people were talking about the war ending soon. He painted his mother, out in the orchard, mending his shirts, and his father's shirts, under the apple trees. His father had propped a ladder against the Bramleys, but it would be a couple of months, yet: he just liked to get up there once in a while, and see how they were doing.

Walter stood in the uncut grass and watched his mother, drawing up thread, snipping and patching in the warmth of the late summer sun. He could smell the hops on their bines, the dusty stubble in the cornfields stretching away beyond the hedge to the horizon; he could feel the sun on his back. The geese were sleeping, down at the far end, next to their muddy tin dish; bees sailed in and out of the hives. He stood at the easel he'd borrowed from the school, and framed his mother: deep within the orchard, the sunlit stretch of rough ground leading to her chair, her basket in the grass, the blue and khaki heaps of cotton shirts, the white of a pillow case. The smell of turpentine mingled with the corn, the grass, the lavender along the path behind him. Bees droned as he worked at the patches of light and shade in the leaves of the apple trees, at the sun on his mother's faded hair, her troubled face, so intent upon her mending. For a long time after John William's death, she had laid his place at the table, counting the knives and forks, and stopping. She had done it this morning.

All afternoon he painted, as the light deepened and the geese woke, and came honking over the grass towards them.

He finished as much as he could of the picture next day; then he went back to the mess. He left the canvas up on the easel in the empty bedroom, drying in its own home, waiting for the end of the war.

Then he came back, and took a good long look at it.

Now what was going to happen? He didn't know what to do with himself. He helped his father out on the farms. People were being demobbed: his old headmaster came over, to offer condolences. He didn't talk much about his own time in the war, just said he was glad to be back. Walter's mother mentioned the painting: he asked to see it.

He and Walter stood in the little square room. It was mid-morning, a cold December day. Mr Hawthorn stood back, and bumped into the end of the iron bedstead. He crossed over, picked up the canvas, held it up to the cold winter light at the window.

'This shows a lot of promise.'

'Do you think so?' Walter fetched out the sketchbooks.

'I remember you so well,' said Mr Hawthorn. 'You and John William and the girls.' He sat on the edge of the bed, turning the pages. 'What are they doing these days?'

'Annie's in service. Over near Canterbury. Ellie's nursing, up at the Hall. You know it's a Convalescent Home now. For officers.'

'Yes, of course, I remember. Your mother must miss them.'

'She does.'

'Let's see another sketchbook.'

Walter leaned over his shoulder. Mr Hawthorn ran a finger over the long, pure, pen-and-ink line of the coast; he touched the distant outline of the tanker, the plume of smoke rising, dissolving in the clouds. He looked at the men in the mess, the open mouths against lumpy pillows, the pots and pans and tins of polish, a boot brush left in a corner.

'We had an artist attached to our regiment,' he said.

'Did you, sir?'

'Yes. A fine man –' Mr Hawthorn closed the sketchbook abruptly and handed it back to Walter. 'Well, now.' He got up from the bedstead: the springs creaked back. 'What are you going to do with yourself?'

'That's what I don't know, sir. It makes me feel an awful fool.'

'Helping out your father?'

'Yes, but . . .'

'I know, I know.' Mr Hawthorn took another look at the painting.

'I borrowed the easel,' said Walter. 'I must fetch it back.'

'I wouldn't worry too much about that. You must go to classes, that's the thing. The Technical Institute in Ashford – that'll start you off. Why don't you get over there in the New Year? They'll open up again then, I expect.' He made for the doorway, bent his head. 'I'll give you a letter.'

'Thank you, sir.' He followed him down the stairs.

His mother came to see the headmaster out. Leaves blew about at the open door.

'Come and get the letter tomorrow,' he said to Walter. 'I'll write it with my memory fresh.' He shook their hands. 'I'm so sorry,' he said again.

# 1919

Walter took the bus to Ashford on Tuesday afternoons and Wednesday evenings. Women clambered on and off with shopping bags, farm boys tramped to the back for a smoke and left bits of straw and muck on the floor. The fields stretched away behind untrimmed hedges: too many men away for too long and too few coming back. In the town, the gas lamps on street corners came on at six, flickering over faded brick, tin plate advertisements for Benger's Food, Bird's Custard, Kenilworth cigarettes. The recruitment posters outside the Drill Hall in Newtown Road had been covered over with warnings about influenza; the Union Jack run up for the Armistice was stiff with the cold. Walter got off the bus by the cattle market, and cut across the square to the Technical Institute in Elwick Road.

The college had been closed soon after the outbreak of war. Re-opened now by the Board of Education, it offered new classes in rooms done up with a couple of coats of distemper but the same old desks and tables. The art classes were poorly attended at first. Mr Wicks, the tutor, had studied in Canterbury before the war and served with The Buffs: invalided out with wounds to the shoulder, sent back again, sent home with a medal. He started them off with natural history watercolours: on the first afternoon there was a Kilner jar of hazel and catkins, set on a table between the windows.

The refraction of the twigs, and the way they darkened below the waterline, reminded Walter of hours spent looking down into the stream, when they were all children. He sat next to a girl he hadn't seen since elementary school, and told her about Mr Hawthorn's visit. She was shocked to hear about John William. She asked if he'd heard about Eddie Pierce, and that shocked him. He saw her to the bus stop, and they travelled together out as far as Otham. Then she got off, the evening drawing in and the sheep ghostly beneath the

15

trees, and he went on to Asham's Mill, the bus almost empty and freezing.

On Wednesday it was already dusk, and the rooks settling, when he set out, taking a packet of sandwiches and a flask. Edna, the girl from their schooldays, wasn't in the class: she'd said she'd only be coming on the Tuesdays, when it was light. This evening Mr Wicks had rearranged the tables and put a still life in the middle: three-quarters of a loaf, with a couple of slices and the breadknife on the board, two apples. He wanted them to draw it, to concentrate on a variety of texture and shading. He'd pinned up yesterday's jars of twigs on the wall. There were sighs as the class got settled, keeping their coats on. The porter came in, letting in the draught from the corridor, and lit an oil stove, supplementing lukewarm radiators.

'This is the best I can do with the rations,' he said, fastening the catch and getting up stiffly. 'Even paraffin's still a job to come by.' He went out, letting the draught in again.

Everyone blew on their fingers and made jokes about it. 'This is what you need,' said Mr Wicks, showing them his fingerless knitted gloves. They all agreed they were a good idea. 'This bread's making me hungry,' said Miss Whiteley from the post office, who'd been here yesterday, because it was early closing. In the break, they all huddled round the paraffin stove eating sandwiches, drinking from their flasks. Mr Wicks said the canteen should be opening in the spring. 'Not much good to us now, then, is it?' They took a look at each other's watercolours, pinned up on either side of the map. 'I like yours,' someone said to Walter.

'What do you enjoy painting?' someone else asked Mr Wicks. He said he feared his painting days were over – the wound had been in the right shoulder, and damaged the nerves to his hand. He was glad of the teaching.

'Can't be the same, though.'

He didn't answer.

After the break, he walked along behind the chairs, and had a look at how everyone was getting on. He stopped behind Walter and made a few suggestions. Walter could see what he meant. Mr Wicks asked him to bring in anything he had at home: he'd seen the letter from Mr Hawthorn.

Walter went back on the bus in the dark and thought about the loaf of bread, the crusty bulk of it beside the smooth apples, the scattering of crumbs, the serrations of the blade of the breadknife, made in Sheffield.

Next week, he took in his sketchbooks. Mr Wicks looked at them during the class. He had set up a new arrangement: a bird's nest and different kinds of moss.

'That's a warbler's nest,' said Ernest Deacon. 'You're right,' said Mr Wicks. 'I know I'm right.' 'That's a star moss,' said Walter, thinking of the stream in the woods. 'And that's a common moss,' said Edna. 'We've got that on our porch.'

The afternoon was sunny. Mr Wicks asked them to enjoy themselves, to use the watercolour to show the essentials. He indicated the deep soft cup of the nest, the curve of the rim, the lichen here and there on the twigs, the different greens in the different mosses.

'That nest makes me want to put an egg in it,' said Phyllis Whiteley.

Chink of the brushes in jars of water, the search for greens in a choice of three.

'You'll have to mix them, won't you?'

The afternoon sun of early spring poured in. Mr Wicks turned the pages of Walter's sketchbooks. Walter dipped his brush and wiped it. After a while he forgot about the turning pages. The nest was a hollowed sphere: he thought for a moment that you might show it only as that, and tried a little sketch in the corner, with the broken clumps of moss beside it only as squares, or patches. He narrowed his eyes for the effect, then found it meaningless, then saw a pattern you might repeat. He repeated it. He looked back at the nest, so small and dense and beautiful. He set to work. The wall clock ticked, Miss Whiteley went to change her water at the sink.

'The moment I like best,' she said, bringing the clean jar back, 'is when you dip your brush with the paint on it for the first time – when the water goes cloudy.'

Everyone agreed. Children coming out of the school up the street ran past.

'My goodness, is that the time?'

'Hasn't it flown?'

'I must get Molly to come, it'd do her good.'

They started packing up. Mr Wicks came round. He thought they'd all done very well.

'Mr Cox? Have you a moment?'

'Yes, of course.'

Mr Wicks went over to the desk; he picked up the sketchbooks. 'I should hold on to these,' he said, giving them back. He crossed to Walter's place at the table, looked at the watercolour nest, the greys and pinks and browns, the feather; he asked about the little essays at something, up in the corner. Walter explained. He nodded.

He said, 'You'll go on to something, after this.'

'Will I?'

The sun was slipping away with the end of the afternoon.

'You're an artist,' said Mr Wicks. 'You do realise that.'

Doors swung out in the corridor. People were arriving for the next classes.

'Well,' said Walter. 'Well, I –' Then something in him which had been restless and uncertain, ever since the war began, ever since the telegram, steadied, and settled, into the right place. 'Yes.'

But it wasn't then that I knew, he said, years later, holding his love in his arms. That was when I felt confirmed. I knew long before, really.

– When?

– When I was a boy. Just looking at things. Messing about with a pencil. Everything made sense, then.

– When did it stop making sense?

– When John William died. Nothing felt right for years after that.

– Until?

The curtains stirred at the open window.

He lifted her over, to lie on top of him.

– You know when that was.

'There's an exhibition, up at the Royal Academy. War paintings. It ends next week.'

'In London?'

'Yes. I was wondering if you'd like to go. There's some good people – Wyndham Lewis, Christopher Nevinson, Paul Nash, Henry Tonks . . .'

Walter had never heard of any of them.

'Tonks is the head of the Slade,' said Mr Wicks, packing paints into a cupboard. 'Professor of Painting. The Slade School of Art,' he said, closing the doors. 'It's part of University College. That's where I think you should aim for. You'd need a scholarship, but we can look into that.' He winced as he got to his feet.

'Oh. Are you all right, sir?'

'Fine. Will you come?'

In May 1918, Paul Nash held his first one-man show, *Void of War*, at the Leicester Galleries, just off Leicester Square. Walter had had no one to tell him about this. Years later, looking at the catalogue of drawings and oils from Nash's months on the Flanders battlefields, he wished he had gone. In those days he never went up to London.

Now, in the winter of 1919, he sat in a second-class compartment travelling up from Ashford to Victoria. 'We can take the omnibus from there,' said Mr Wicks, settling into the opposite corner. 'Down to Piccadilly.' The train gave a chuff; they began to move. 'You comfortable?'

'Fine, thanks.'

Mr Wicks pulled out the *Morning Post*. Walter looked out of the window. They gathered speed. He looked out on the familiar fields seen from an unfamiliar place: on the Great Stour, gleaming in the sun of a bright March morning, on the clumps of woodland, the scattering of Romney sheep. People got on and off but they still had the carriage to themselves. They went through a tunnel. They stopped at Tonbridge. Mr Wicks looked at his watch, and put away the paper.

'Tell me about your family.'

They pulled out of Clapham Junction and approached Victoria. 'This is where I left for France,' said Mr Wicks, as the platforms came into view. 'Came back here, too, on a stretcher—' He broke off, shaking his head.

'I'm sorry,' said Walter. He looked at the crowded platform as the train hissed to a halt.

'Well. Here we are,' said Mr Wicks.

'Yes,' said Walter, as the doors began to slam. And then, 'I'm glad you came back.'

Victoria Station was busy and full, and pretty filthy. They came out on to the forecourt, where hansom cabs waited outside the hotel. A man with medals on his chest leaned on crutches and rattled a tin. A woman took delivery of a basket of laundry and heaved it indoors; paper boys shouted, pigeons flew up.

'This way.'

They walked past a flower-seller and waited for a gap in the traffic, then came out on to Buckingham Palace Road. Omnibuses roared past; they could hear the squeal of trams; the buildings were covered in grime and soot. For the first time, walking beside his tutor as they crossed the road and made their way along the crowded pavement, Walter noticed the effect of the wound to the shoulder: Mr Wicks lurched as he walked – only a little, but it was noticeable. Once he put out his arms to steady himself as a boy ran past.

They caught the omnibus and climbed to the open top, Mr Wicks holding tight to the rail. The morning was windy and bright: Walter looked out on the bare trees in Green Park, and the traffic round Hyde Park Corner.

'I've only seen London in books.'

'Is that so? I must try to show you a bit of it.'

They got off in Piccadilly. Mr Wicks pointed out Fortnum & Mason. Women in furs were coming out of the plate-glass doors with parcels; they met men with cigars. Walter looked at them. Not everyone had suffered in the war, it seemed.

'And here we are,' said Mr Wicks.

Flags were blowing on the roof of the Royal Academy, but the courtyard was sheltered. People were queuing, reading the papers. Pigeons walked in and out amongst them.

'It's a good thing I sent off for tickets,' said Mr Wicks, reaching into his breast pocket.

Following him, Walter noticed a girl in the queue. He didn't know quite why she drew his attention, whether it was the wiriness of her hair beneath the little hat, the gloved hand on her father's arm – yes, it must be her father – as she looked at the paper he was reading, or just that she had an air: poised, unhurried, serious. Perhaps that was it. After the noise of the traffic, the pushing about on the street, here they were, in a quiet courtyard, going to look at paintings, and she was – she was . . .

He stopped, and looked at her. She must have sensed his gaze, for she turned, and looked up from the morning paper, and for a moment her eyes met his: clear, thoughtful, unperturbed. Then her father said something, and she turned back to him, and the moment passed.

☆

But that was you, they said to one another, years – not so many years – later, she spread beneath him, he cradling her head.

– That was you.


'Coming?' said Mr Wicks, turning back to look for him.

'Sorry,' said Walter.

They climbed the steps.

He hadn't known what to expect. Outside, in the courtyard, people were talking amongst themselves: in here, once they had climbed the broad staircase and come into the galleries, they fell silent.

He fell silent.

Men sat slumped by the roadside, their heads bowed. They groaned in the trenches, stumbled through the rain with stretchers, fell into abandoned craters; they died without a blanket to cover them, arms outstretched and mouths wide open. Wyndham Lewis, Muirhead Bone, Henry Tonks; Christopher Nevinson, Stanley Spencer, Philip Wilson Steer; Paul Nash. Walter stood before a little drawing, a chalk and ink: *Landscape – The Year of Our Lord, 1917*. Coils of wire rolled across heavy mud, blackened trees stood beyond endless water. He walked on and in painting after painting the graves stretched away, away.

'Walter?'

Shells roared, and the animals were screaming.

He could not look at any more of it.

The sun rose, behind a blood-red mountain, striking the tree trunks, hallowing the mud.

*We Are Making A New World.*

'Walter –'

'Do you mind if we go?'


'I'm sorry,' said Wicks, over lunch in the basement restaurant. 'I should have realised.'

'But you were there,' said Walter, drinking London water. 'You were there.' He put down his glass. He thought of Mr Hawthorn, last December, come to give his condolences, looking at the sketchbooks, in the bare cold bedroom, saying nothing about his time in France. Not really.

'It makes me feel a fool,' he said. 'Not being there, not knowing –' He knew if he said John William's name he would make a proper fool of himself. He swallowed. 'And you were – you must have – I'm glad you came back,' he said again.

'So am I.' Wicks picked up his knife and fork. 'I know what will make us feel a bit better.'

'What's that?'

They walked down to Trafalgar Square, and spent the afternoon at the National Gallery, looking at Constable and Vermeer and the Dutch masters. The Gallery had not long re-opened; some of the rooms were still shut up, with notices. Walter pictured the ghostliness of dust sheets. They went where they could.

Sun slanted in on to chequered floors, young women stood at the virginals, held necklaces up to the light, poured milk, poured water. He thought of the girl in the queue. The stillness of the Dutch interior filled him; he gazed at tranquil courtyards, arches in red brick, women in black and white.

They went to look at the Constables. One had hung on the wall of the schoolroom, in an engraving: he remembered Mr Hawthorn talking about it, one morning after assembly, pointing out the sky, the tumultuousness of the clouds, the glancing sun, the tumbling water, and the boy.

'We should go, if we want to catch our train.'

They caught it with moments to spare, puffing back through the darkening fields.

Spring came properly, wet and full, the trees moist green, the blossom thick in the orchards then blowing away into heaps in the long grass. Lambs raced over the fields, the cows were let out, the thrush in Walter's garden at evening sang as if there had never been a war.

He went back to the classes after Easter.

'I think you should try for the Slade,' said Wicks once more. 'For the autumn.'

'What do I have to do?'

'Tonks needs to look at your work. I'll see if I can get you an interview.'

With the spring, there was more to do on the farms, and fewer men to do it. Walter went out with his father every day, except for the Tuesday afternoon of the class. They chopped wood, mended tools and machinery, patched up barns and mucked out piggeries.

They drove lambs to market in Wye. He helped out with the milking on Hobbs Farm most mornings, at Mill Farm most evenings, except for the class on Wednesdays. At Mill Farm she'd lost both husband and son: there was a brother, but he wasn't quite all there. Walter drove the herd in with his father: Friesians and Shorthorns and a couple of Jerseys. One day she'd start a new herd with those two, she told them, bringing their mugs of tea out. When she felt more up to things. They leaned against the muddy warm flanks, listening. The milk hissed into the pails, the sun seeped through gaps in the brick, the cows licked the feed pellets round the metal bowls. When the evenings grew lighter, Walter took his sketchbook down there. He drew the cows chewing the cud, and once his father, milking the last one, his sleeves rolled up and his boots planted square on either side of the stool, sinewy hands beneath soft full udder, fingers on the wet teat. Walter drew the empty stalls when the herd had swayed back to the big field, and his father's cap on the nail in the door.

His father turned the pages, looking at it all.

They walked back down the lane to the cottage, the sun sinking, the rooks making a racket in the elms.

'You were always the dreamer,' said his father, stopping to light his pipe. 'It was John William wanted to farm.'

The girls came home on Sundays when they could. Annie said she'd had enough of being in service. Ellie said she should come up to the hospital, up at the Hall. They were taking the overspill of wounded and convalescent from London, they always needed more nurses.

'Mind you, you need a strong stomach.'

Annie said she would think about it.

'Listen to that thrush.'

'Time I got back, I suppose.'

A letter came for Walter from the Slade.

'Where's that, then?'

'You don't want to go and live in London.'

'Mother? You don't want him to go and live in London, do you?'

The interview was at the end of May. Wicks travelled up with him, for moral support. They took the omnibus to Piccadilly again, and then the 19 tram up Tottenham Court Road, getting off opposite Heal's. They cut through to Gower Street, arriving at the university gates with half an hour to spare. They'd planned this journey the previous evening, having a drink after class.

'Better early than late.'

'More time to be nervous, I'm afraid.'

'You'll be all right.'

The towering façade of the university faced them across the quad.

Walter shifted his portfolio from right hand to left. 'Where are we going?'

'Let's ask at the lodge.'

'The Slade, sir? That's it, over there on the left.'

They looked across the quad to the elegance of a pillared portico, railings and shallow steps. The door was open. It was early afternoon, people sitting out on the grass beneath the trees, smoking on the benches. One or two easels were up. Walter began to sweat. They walked round the quad. Grey stone, broad paths, clipped squares of lawn. They walked round again.

'What's the time?'

They looked at their watches as the clock on the roof of the lodge struck the half-hour.

'Come on.'

Up the broad shallow steps. A staircase right in front of them, a beadle in a booth to the left.

'Yes, sir?'

Walter told him his business. The beadle pointed out the office. Wicks said he'd wait on the steps.

'Well?'

'I'm in. I'm pretty sure, anyway. He said there'd be a letter.' Walter was shaking. He took Wicks's arm, they walked up and down on the path. 'Not until January, though. He said he was giving priority to men coming back from the Front – men he knew, who'd been students before the war.'

The lodge clock struck three.

'I can't have been in there for half an hour.'

'But he liked your work?'

'I think so.'

'He must have done. What did he say?'

'I can't remember.' It was true. He could hardly remember a word. A dry quiet voice, a long endless body unfolding itself from the chair

24

behind the desk, a beaky nose. Long fingers, going through the portfolio.

Himself so nervous he could hardly think.

Some talk about the war, the Professor's own service, his medical background. Pages turned. A murmur of, 'Yes . . . yes, I think so –'

A handshake at the door.

'I'm sure he said yes.'

'Did you ask about a scholarship?'

Walter was crestfallen. 'I'm such a fool.'

'Do you want to go back?'

'I'd look a worse fool.'

'You do want to come here?'

'Oh, yes.' It was true.

They went for a drink.

The letter of acceptance came in the following week. Walter took it into the class. Everyone cheered. He showed it to his parents that evening. The garden was full of birdsong and the hum of bees. His mother got up and kissed him, hard. Then she went out to the orchard, where the washing was strung beneath the trees. The geese came over: she took no notice. She unpegged the sheets one by one, her back to them, working slowly.

'Mother?'

'Best to leave her for now.' His father tapped out his pipe. 'Time I was off for the milking.'

'I'll come with you.'

'I'll manage.'

He wrote back to the Slade, accepting the offer. He asked, with great diffidence, about the possibility of a scholarship. He spent the summer working and saving. People were selling off land where they could, cutting back on the livestock. There wasn't as much work as there had been. He heard from the Slade again. Yes, there would be some financial assistance. He was talented; he had served, albeit briefly, in the Army.

'All that money, just to be a student,' said Annie.

'It's got to last.'

'I should think so.'

He helped out on Hobbs Farm with the ploughing. When the

evenings drew in, Wicks lent him books. He spent hours with the oil lamp at the kitchen table, looking at engravings of the Old Masters, reading articles in *Studio* and reviews in *The Times* of English painters he'd never heard of. The New English Art Club. Roger Fry, Duncan Grant, the Omega Workshops. Wyndham Lewis, and the Rebel Art Centre. Sickert and the Fitzroy Street Group, the Camden Town Group, the London Group. Gilman and Ginner and Gore. Every time he turned a page, he found something else he didn't know.

Winter came. Men were still missing. No swinging of the lantern across the yard, no tugging off boots at the back door. No click of the latch.

At Mill Farm she hanged herself, out in the barn, from the crossbeam, kicking the chair away. It was the brother who found her. It took them a long time to understand what he was on about.

Everything was overshadowed by this.

Walter left home in the first week of January. He didn't want anyone to come to see him off: he knew what would happen. He took the bus to Ashford, and he went to say goodbye to David Wicks. Even that was difficult.

Then he caught the train, leaving it until the last moment on purpose. Waiting around was no good. He found a seat by the window – that was a piece of good luck. The whistle blew, the train gave a couple of chuffs, then they were off.

Kent on a winter afternoon. The second winter after the end of the war. In November they'd held the first Two Minutes' Silence. The girls came over. They all stood in the parlour, listening to the tick of the clock. The bells rang out from the church. Then the silence began.

He couldn't bear to think of it.

He couldn't bear to think of John William, dying without any of them. He couldn't bear to think of his mother's face, in the silence. His father's. He thought, as the train gathered speed, of saying goodbye to them all at the door, walking out with his bag and portfolio, not looking back. He thought of her, up at Mill Farm, her husband and son still missing, her climbing up on to the chair in the dark.

Kent in winter. The fields of his childhood stretched away, frosty, speckled with Romney sheep, bordered by clumps of bare trees. He saw a man lead a horse down a lane, he saw the empty strings of the hops, he saw smoke here and there from farms near and distant, a crow flapping over ploughed land.

The telegraph wires rose and fell along the track. This was the fast train. They came to the tunnel, the whistle blew. For a few moments they were plunged into darkness, the carriage swaying, steam everywhere. Then they were out again, picking up speed, the wheels in a rhythm he held deep inside him, making words he was hardly conscious of: far-away-far-away-far-away-far-away.

Clots of soot streamed back and hit the window. The landscape of his childhood flew past him, on either side of the track. Then it was gone.

# II

## In London

# 1920

January, mid-afternoon in a cold city. The hour before the lamps were lit: a sinking sun, a smoky sky.

In Flanders and in northern France, rain splashed off pools in abandoned shell-holes. It dripped from white crosses. The mud had frozen.

The men had come back from the Front: war artists without a war; soldiers without battalions.

In the wake of the war, an evil influenza.

*Unreal City . . .*

*I had not thought death had undone so many . . .*

*We are making a new world . . .*

Walter took lodgings in Camden Town. Soot from the unswept chimney fell into the fireplace every time he crossed the room. He paced out the distance between iron bedstead and washstand. Between them, at the rattling casement, was just enough room for an easel.

'I don't want any mess,' said his landlady. 'Nor visitors.'

'I wonder if you would ever sit for me?' ventured Walter.

'Sit? I haven't got time to sit.'

Walter stood at the window and looked out on Sickert's streets. Unswept leaves blew along the pavement; pigeons beat through a melancholy sky, over slate rooftops and broken chimney pots. He could hear the squeal of a tram from the High Street, the clank of goods trains. He had walked from the station, past men in doorways, leaning on crutches, holding out their hands.

'Anything for an old soldier?'

He gave one a threepenny bit, then hurried away.

Now he unpacked, and hung up his clothes in the towering wardrobe. He pushed his bag under the iron bed, and the buckles chinked against the chamber pot; he hung his jacket on the back of the door and piled his loose change on the empty mantelpiece. The room held not a single picture, nor ornament. He laid his portfolio flat on the bed and opened it carefully. The smoky city light made everything different. He picked up the small canvas of his mother, sewing out in the orchard in Asham's Mill beneath the apple trees, and propped it on the mantelpiece, next to the photograph of John William, in his uniform, taken in 1916. He stepped back on the worn green rug before the hearth; soot pattered into the grate, where last week's *Daily Graphic* had been crumpled and laid with a little heap of kindling. The London sky was darkening: he gazed at the dappled orchard grass of Kent and at his mother, so intent upon her mending.

Doors banged out in the street. People were coming home from work. The room was freezing. Walter put his hand to his mother's face, and bent to the box of coal.

Dusk settled over the parks and squares and gardens. Gaslight hissed in the streets. In her rented room in Fitzroy Square, Nina Frith lit oil lamps and stood before her mirror. She held up crumpled velvet, unpressed silk; chiffon drifted over her bobbed fair hair; she stepped out of lace and taffeta. All these pretty things, spilling out of her open suitcase. Was she really going to wear them again?

The room was vast and chilly. A faded paper of yellowing ferns and parakeets lined the walls; the heat of the fire was lost in the cavernous ceiling. Nina shivered, smoothing a beaded black dress to her little pale breasts. Jet and silver, the beads flashed in the firelight.

Someone in the house was playing the gramophone: *After you've gone*, so fast, so sorrowful, filtered through the floorboards.

Nina frowned, rubbed her bare arms, and flung the dress over a screen. She pulled on her dressing gown, made tea, lit a Turkish cigarette. Mr Schnecburger had given her the cigarettes, pressing a small wrapped packet into her hands on her return to the house.

'My favourite tenant. Happy New Year.'

'Happy New Year,' said Nina, stepping back as he stepped forward. The door stood ajar to his own apartment, down at the end of the hall. She could hear the canary.

'You will come and have a glass of sherry?'

'Another time, thank you.'

'I can help with your suitcase.' He stretched out a little fat hand.

'No, it's quite light. I can manage perfectly.' She heaved it up the staircase.

'But you have not been well.' His voice followed mournfully; he hung on the balustrade.

'I'm quite recovered, thank you.'

'People have died from this influenza.'

'But I have not,' said Nina crisply, and set down her suitcase with a thump. The odours of the lodging house hung along the landing: cheap scent, stale smoke, the unwashed plate and unwashed glass of gin. She took out her key, unlocked her door.

Well. Here she was again.

Nina sipped her tea, and drew on her cigarette. She caught sight of herself in the long mottled glass, a hollow-eyed convalescent in a dressing gown, and turned away; she sat at the table by the balcony window, looking through worn muslin curtains across the square at evening.

Numbers 34 and 35 held the Swiss House for Foreign Governesses: two young women were hurrying home in the cold. The square was full of hostels and hospitals, of single people in dim rooms and studios. On her arrival last year, Nina had walked round examining the doorplates of milliners, dressmakers, artists' colourmen. At number 25 was a Japanese flower-maker; in the basement of number 30, Miss Rose Millauro made artificial eyes.

At number 33, on the corner of Conway Street, a peeling hand-painted signboard, a blue arum lily, announced the Omega Work-shops. Duncan Grant had painted that once-radiant lily: Nina had read all about the Omega, and seen their designs in magazines. Such fabrics! Such painted plates and high-backed chairs! And the houses all round the square, so tall and well proportioned, held such a sense of Edwardian elegance: of maids, and parties, and chandeliers, cabs rolling up to the iron railings, deep rooms filled with candlelight, the rustle of an evening dress, the scent of a cigar . . .

Oh, how I used to love parties and dancing, thought Nina, smoking her Turkish cigarette.

Now, the houses were all run down by the long neglect of the war, the stucco flaking and the railings chipped with rust; the beautiful deep rooms were rented, one by one. Nina had rung the doorbell of the Omega Workshops and had no answer. She peered through the letterbox on to closed studio doors and a heap of envelopes: the war had stopped everything.

But now the war was over!

Now illness and misery were behind her, and her life could start again. It will start again, thought Nina, setting down her teacup with a decisive little chink.

*After You've Gone* had ended. There was a pause, and then a dance band, light and quick and tuneful, struck up *Havanola*. Nina's feet began to tap. She stubbed out her cigarette, took down the beaded black dress, and held it against her narrow hips. She did a little two-step, all round the room, brushing past the screens round her bed, and round her makeshift kitchen.

The record from another room wound down, and started up again. Nina, breathing fast, and feeling a fever rising, danced it all through, and sank into the chair by the fire. Gaslight burned through the darkening square. Tomorrow the term began.

The morning was bitter. Sun filtered through heavy cloud and the rooftops glistened; shreds of fog hung in Walter's street and the worn stone steps were dark with moisture. He caught his breath as he came out, feeling the raw air go straight to the windpipe, and he pulled up his scarf as he set off, past greying lace curtains and grimy doors.

At the junction with King Street an old horse clopped over the cobbles, pulling a milk cart; outside the Victoria, a waiting char-woman moved from foot to foot. A boy was stacking shelves at the back of West's General Stores; across the street in the bakery, girls in turbans were setting out trays. Walter walked up to Camden High Street and waited for the tram.

The man in front of him lit up a Woodbine and coughed; Walter ventured a remark about the weather and was ignored. He didn't know if this was because he had not been heard or because, slight and muffled up and hesitant, he was not worth noticing. He stood looking at the patched tones of brickwork, as errand boys rode past: at the muddy pinks and browns and greys, the shabby paint and worn lettering on the shopfronts. Then the rails hummed and he saw the lights of the tram.

Inside, on the upper deck, he leaned against the unwashed window pane, looking out on to the endless streets of Camden and Mornington Crescent, a fog-grey impression lit here and there by a shining rail, moisture on a dark coat, the dull gleam of pawnbrokers' gold.

The tram slowed; a woman in a dressing gown drew back bedroom curtains: he caught a glimpse of tired face, bare arm, a vase, a mirror on a mantelpiece. Sickert's streets and Sickert's bleak interiors – he felt himself move through lives he knew only through paintings: ennui in shuttered rooms, the tick of a clock through a silent marriage, violation on an iron bedstead. The tram whined, and picked up speed again: the woman and that moment in her life were gone. And as he travelled, watching the patches of fog roll away in the headlights, Walter had a dreamy but intense sensation of the hour, the fleeting moment: of himself living on in a present which should have belonged to his brother, too, and which, even as he lived it, was becoming his past, his children's past. The time before they were born: that all was this morning would one day be to them.

And then they swung out into the busy Euston Road and his throat tightened. Someone had rung the bell, the tram squealed to a halt and Walter climbed down the curving stair, his portfolio bumping against the rail. People were pushing on to the boarding platform; he squeezed through them, and was out, making his way along the crowded pavement, turning into Gower Street.

He walked a few yards and stopped, hollow with nerves. The sun was rising, watery and pale, above the buildings of University College. The fog was drifting in and out through the railings and the branches of the soot-blackened trees, away up the length of the street. The clock in the tower above the porter's lodge was striking nine; a rush of starlings dipped and rose around it. Other students were arriving, walking in ones and twos through the gates; a boy went whistling past on a bicycle.

Walter stood on the London pavement, shifting his portfolio from hand to hand, his life before him and his life behind him, an arc between that time and this time: a winter morning and a winter city light, which he noted, stepping off the broken flagstone, crossing the street to the open gates.

The patchy grass and the paths and the broad shallow steps were swept and empty, the stone glittering in the cold. He walked up to the high double doors beneath the portico, and turned the handle.

He was early. He realised this as soon as he stepped inside, wiped his feet and then heard his footsteps loud on the tiled floor. He looked about him: he heard a cough.

'Classes begin at nine-thirty, sir.'

A large man in top hat and wine-coloured uniform came walking with measured tread towards a booth by the door.

'Oh, yes,' said Walter. 'Yes, of course.'

The beadle entered his booth.

'If you would like to sign yourself in, sir.'

Walter was handed a heavy foolscap ledger, bound in green leather. He felt in his inside pocket.

The beadle opened the covers. The end-papers were marbled, the colour of flame. There were columns of pre-war signatures: page after page after page. Some of the names he recognised, from all the reading he had done at home last year: Augustus John, Wyndham Lewis, Gwen John, Dora Carrington, Stanley Spencer, David Bomberg . . . And he was following this company. He turned the pages. The columns grew shorter. 1914, 1915 – they shrank to half a page, a dozen lines. 1916. Conscription. Then most of the men were gone and the columns of women signing in grew longer; the surnames adorned with Lilian, Laura, Daphne and Winifred and Marjorie. Beatrice. Walter's eye ran over the turning pages.

'Here we are, sir.'

1919. The men were coming back from the Front: name after name. Few he had heard of, here.

He unscrewed the fountain pen his father had given him, a handsome Osmoroid.

*Walter Cox.* Blue-black ink, and a neat hand. Others above it flowed and flourished.

'Thank you, sir.' The beadle drew the book towards him, and blotted it. 'Classes begin at nine-thirty.' He nodded towards a door to the right of the entrance. 'Professor Tonks will receive new students in his office.'

'Thank you. I wonder, could you tell me where the lavatories are?'

'The door at the far end of the hall, sir.'

Walter gazed at the cuts he had made while shaving, and washed with gritty soap. The hall was filling by the time he came out, and two or three women were leaning against the radiators, taking off hats and gloves. Walter walked past them, as casually as he could, and took his place amongst a knot of others waiting outside the office with its gilt-painted board: *Professor Henry Tonks.*

If the war had broken down barriers, and made conversation easier, he did not feel it, searching with sudden anxiety for his cheque book, waiting for the door to open.

'As you know, you will begin your studies in the Antique Room, and proceed to the Life Class only when you are considered to be satisfactorily advanced. You will attend weekly lectures on Anatomy and the History of Art.'

Tonks placed Walter's papers beneath a blotter, leaned back in his chair and put his hands together, as if in prayer. His gaze across the desk was level and cool and appraising.

'Yes, sir.' Walter forced himself to return the gaze, and was almost imperceptibly acknowledged.

'I recall your work. You show some promise – if this were not so, I should not have admitted you, nor granted you a scholarship, despite our circumstances. We are reassembling ourselves . . .'

Tonks paused, rubbing his thin lips and great hooked nose. He pushed back his chair, and strode to the window.

'I fear we have lost a great many men, both on the staff and amongst our students. The School, like the University, has been half-empty.'

Walter watched him, gazing out over the quad. Long-backed, long-legged, grey-suited, he was a waterbird, a wader, a priest upon the shores of the lake, surveying his territory.

'I myself have recently been engaged in critically important work. You recall, I am sure, that I am originally a medical man – a surgeon. My training has enabled me to be of some service, in drawings of the wounded – to help in the plastic reconstruction of faces. It is a chamber of horrors, but I am quite content to draw them. It is excellent practice, though I fear we shall see for a long time to come dreadful cases of ruined minds. Far more difficult to treat than wounds.'

There was a silence. He turned to Walter. 'You are of course too young, thankfully. You have been spared such suffering.'

Walter gazed at the panelling behind the heavy desk. 'I am afraid my brother –' he said at length.

'Ah.' Tonks crossed the room again, and put a hand on Walter's shoulder. 'You are hardly alone, of course. However – my condolences. I am very sorry.' There was a pat, a moment's rest of the hand,

and then he was walking up and down again.

'But you have a gift, you must concentrate on that. So far it seems but a small one, but we shall see how you develop. You must cultivate this gift, you must be unswerving – I say this to all my young artists. And as to whether or not you have served your country, there are a great number of men to whom I have had to say quite bluntly, "Just because you've been through the war, don't think you have a place at the Slade." Our standards now must be higher than ever. And you are following a great generation.' He stopped by the door, gesturing to Walter to rise. 'So. There we are.' He held out his hand. 'Welcome to the Slade, Mr Cox. You may go straight to your class.'

'Yes, sir. Thank you.'

He was out in the hall again, now crowded and full of conversation.

'Excuse me.' He approached the beadle in his booth once more. 'Could you direct me to the Antique Room?'

'Straight up the stairs and turn left, sir.'

'I'll take you, if you like,' said a voice behind him.

Walter turned. A slight girl, in a long straight jacket, held out her hand. 'Frith,' she said coolly. 'Nina Frith.' The jacket was the colour of milky coffee, the fair hair cut in a bob.

'Walter Cox.' He cleared his throat.

'How do you do?' Her gaze and her skin were as clear as water. She led him towards the staircase. People were setting up easels, all along the balcony. 'You're on the first floor. You're new,' she said, as they climbed the stairs.

'Yes. And you?'

'Oh, I've been here for ever. They've only just let me into the Life Class – I was ill last term, and missed lectures.'

'I'm sorry to hear that.'

'Oh, it was nothing *serious*.' Her hand was on the banister, slender and white. 'Just a terrible bore.' Walter followed her quick light steps, as they reached the crowded balcony and went down a narrow high-ceilinged corridor. She stopped outside a panelled door. 'Here you are. Prepare for months of boredom.'

He hesitated. 'Where is your class?'

She nodded towards the other end of the corridor. 'In the women's Life Room – that's a bore, too, there's only one, so we have to use it on alternate days.'

'I don't quite understand.'

'Men and women – we couldn't be in there *together*, could we? Tonks would have a fit.'

'Is he very –'

'He and I don't get on,' said Nina lightly. 'Well, I'm late, I must go.' She turned, and in the narrow corridor brushed past him, just a touch.

'Miss Frith –'

'No need to be so stuffy. Frith will do.'

'Thank you so much for –'

'It's nothing to make a fuss about.' And she was walking quickly away, narrow feet clicking along the floorboards, right to the far end. She did not look back.


The Antique Room was large and crowded. It smelled of plaster and dust and pencil shavings and, in the close warmth from monumental radiators, of the human body. Casts stood on plinths amongst the easels, potted palms were in corners, drawings pinned up all along the walls.

No one looked up as Walter entered. He hung his jacket on a row of pegs and stood wondering what to do.

'Ah, good morning, you're new to us, I think.' A thin, faded man approached him with a notebook. He held out a hand from a fraying cuff. 'Bevan-Petman. Assistant Lecturer in Drawing. And you are?'

'Cox,' said Walter. 'I have a registration card.' He pulled it out of his pocket.

'Ah, yes, very good. You will need your ticket of admission to the class . . .'

Formalities were completed. 'Now, then, let's find you a place.' They squeezed amongst donkey-stools and easels; dust tickled the back of Walter's throat. 'Here,' said Petman, finding a gap before a limbless torso. 'I'll leave you to get on.'

Walter, amidst the murmur of voices, drew a deep breath and sat down. He unfastened his canvas bag and took out the box of pencils the girls had given him for Christmas; he tried them out, down in the corner of the cartridge paper roughly pinned to the easel; he set them carefully on the ledge, with his eraser. He looked up at the limbless torso. It was chipped here and there; dust lay in the creases of the muscles. Pectoral and abdominal: weekly Anatomy lectures were to come. 'Drawing is the foundation of art.' He could hear Tonks's dry, insistent tones as he took up a pencil, and as he looked again at the dusty torso he was filled with nerves. What did he know of Anatomy? How had he thought he could draw?

Around him was muted conversation, the sound of pencils being sharpened, pencils on the page. Now and then the door was opened, to admit another new arrival; now and then someone walked across the room, and pinned up a drawing. The sky had brightened.

Walter steadied himself. He looked with half-closed eyes at the object before him, and back at the paper. And again, and again, beginning to map out the space, the place which neck and chest and belly might occupy, and fill. As in Ashford, he set his pencil in different places, measuring, considering. *Take your time*, said Wicks. He made a mark, rubbed it out, and made another. He sketched out the whole in a sudden rapid motion, looking quickly from cast to paper, up and down, up and down, absorbed now only in these two things: a plaster cast of a part of the human body; a rectangle of white. How to translate – how to represent – the one upon the other.

It was mid-morning. The room was full of a calm unclouded light.

Days passed. Tonks came stalking round. Walter grew to recognise the particular click of the door, followed by the entrance of the tall grey figure, the quiet 'May I?' to the lecturer. Most of the Professor's time was spent in the painting classes, but he looked in on everyone once or twice a week, and the atmosphere in the Antique Room changed as soon as he entered.

'May I?' He came and stood by a chosen student, who struggled to remain oblivious. Most of those in the Antique Room were women. On his first day, Walter had been so anxious that he was barely aware of this: now he was beginning to notice individuals. Sometimes Tonks passed on without speaking, and this could leave people devastated: was their work unworthy of a single remark? The first time it happened to him, Walter was forced to deduce this, and spent the rest of the class in an almost blind anxiety. He had completed preliminary drawings of the torso – his torso, as he had begun to think of it – and had been invited by Bevan-Petman to pin them up, with largely encouraging remarks. But if Tonks did not like them . . .

He sat before the easel, turning his worn ball of rubber in his hands. Beside him, a pencil fell to the floor and rolled along the boards. He bent to retrieve and return it.

'Thanks.' The fellow next to him glanced towards the long grey-suited body, now bent over the work of a girl in glasses, and gave Walter a wink. Walter winked back, feeling the first glimmer of friendship.

Generally, Tonks drew up a stool. This was done without preliminaries. He took a pencil from his pocket, he leaned towards the work. 'Now, then.' With rapid glances from cast to paper he made a little sketch alongside the student's drawing: a detail of a limb, a fold of drapery. The sketches were detailed and exquisite.

'Now, then.' The stool was drawn up alongside Walter, scraping the boards. The endless body folded itself downwards. 'Mmm.' He was thoughtful, taking in the whole of Walter's new model: the angle of the head on the slender neck, the dreamy face, the eyes cast downwards, the missing arm, the long straight fall of the robe from the shoulder, except where, with a lift of the hand, a swathe of fabric was lifted to reveal a narrow foot.

'When I was at school,' said Tonks, taking out his pencil, 'I was continually learning from books. As a medical student at the London Hospital I began to *observe*. This is the heart of it all, is it not?

'Now, then.' He pointed to the hand, lifting the swathe of fabric. 'Observe the curve of the finger here ... and here. Think of the joints, the tendons. Perhaps you do not yet see how with every articulation, each muscle of this young woman's hand will articulate another. This is not a hand at rest, Mr Cox, this is a hand grasping something, holding up heavy drapery, is it not?' Long graceful fingers appeared on a corner of Walter's drawing, the shading as fine as Dürer. There was the merest indication of linen, held and falling away.

'You see?' Walter nodded. 'You must look, and look, and think of the bones beneath the skin. Without drawing – *real* drawing, real understanding of the body, the artist has no depth. He has no soul. How can you understand what this young woman is thinking, if you do not even understand how she uses her hands?' He pulled out a handkerchief and blew his nose violently. 'Carry on.' He pushed back the stool, and stood up.

Walter sat before his drawing, and before the hand which Tonks had left him. He opened out his own hand, and examined its likeness to his father's: square, practical, with blunted nails. He thought of Nina Frith, her pale fingers on the polished banister. He had not seen her since.

'And what, pray, is this supposed to represent?'

Walter looked up. Tonks was across the room, towering over a girl in a smock. He had not raised his voice but each syllable cut the air. 'You have before you the head of a fine young man. I believe he is possessed of the full complement of features?' The girl was silent. Tonks leaned over her drawing. 'This is a nose? This has some relationship to the cheek? The brow? The sockets of the eyes on either side of it?' The girl gazed at her work, and even at this distance Walter could see her flushing scarlet.

'How long have you been in this class?' The room was hushed. She shook her head, and tears fell on to the smock. 'Quite some considerable time, I believe,' Tonks continued relentlessly. 'Quite some time. I find it hard to account for this lazy drawing, this uncomprehending –' He strode towards the door.

The room, when he had gone, was shocked and silent. Walter found he was sweating profusely: he wiped his hands on his trousers. Someone said quickly, getting up from her work, 'Don't cry, he doesn't mean it,' but the girl had risen, tipping her stool back, and fled, sobbing, out into the corridor.

'Bastard,' muttered the young man next to Walter.

Tonks was the Slade and the Slade was Tonks. It was his predecessor, Frederick Brown, and it was his contemporaries, photographed in charabancs, on picnics in the summers before the war. It had been briefly Sickert, who left to work for Whistler, and then went to live in Dieppe. It was Philip Wilson Steer, the heir to Constable, master of English Impressionism, a man who had managed to spend two years of his youth in Paris and return without a word of French, who taught alongside Tonks for almost forty years, and who, like Tonks, never married.

The Slade was the starry generation of pre-war students: Augustus John, whom Tonks revered; his sister Gwen John, who became Rodin's lover, was cast aside and died in a street in Dieppe; it was Wyndham Lewis, who blasted Roger Fry and founded the Rebel Art Centre; it was Carrington, who shot herself when Strachey died, and Gertler, her ex-husband, the Jew from Whitechapel who also killed himself. It was Stanley Spencer and, briefly and uncomfortably, Paul Nash; it was Nash's friend Ben Nicholson, who lasted at the Slade for just one term; it was David Bomberg, briefly fêted, enduring long post-war years of neglect.

But above all it was Henry Tonks, Professor from 1918–30, the atheist who saw painting as a holy craft, who was loved and feared and, in the end, left a long, long way behind; the surgeon turned artist who had never been trained in France, who admired Proust, and Eliot, but who mocked Cézanne and implored his students to turn their backs on Post-Impressionism, Cubism, Futurism – on everything that was new, and unsettling, and bold – and return to the study of nature.

And, for a while, it was Walter Cox, who met all the important people in his adult life there, one of a generation of young men whose lives were lived beneath the war's long shadow: all those who had been bereaved; all those who had gone, and come back, and were trying to recover.

Walter came down the stairs at lunchtime and saw Nina, crossing the hall with a friend. He stopped and watched them, walking past the beadle and round to the basement stairs. He hesitated. The basement held the women's retreat – a tea room, the ladies' lavatory, the models' washroom: this much he had gathered from overhearing conversation amongst the women in the class. He would have liked to lean casually over the banister, and call to Nina, to address her as plenty of the other men seemed able to address the women – 'Frith! I say, Frith!' – but he knew he couldn't, and so he went on down with everyone else and followed her, giving a cough, which was, amongst all the coming and going, quite unnoticed. She reached the top of the basement stairs, and he stopped, for surely it would be indelicate to approach her there. He turned away and banged straight into someone else, a woman from the class whom he liked: Sarah Lewis. He'd had lunch with her once or twice, in a group, although they'd hardly spoken beyond the pleasantries. She now looked quite taken aback.

'I say, I'm terribly sorry.' He was overcome with embarrassment. Following someone, hanging about near the top of the women's stairs, crashing into people. 'Are you all right?'

'Yes, yes, of course.' She was recovering from their collision, putting a hand to her hair. Looking down at the floor, he saw a wavy hairpin. He bent to retrieve it, just as she did.

'Sorry.'

'Please –' She rose with a half-smile, blew dust off the pin and was gone, away down the stairs and greeting a friend and laughing.

Walter was mortified. He made his way back through the throng, and out of the front door. People were hurrying across the quad in the cold, and he followed them, making for the College refectory.

The refectory was cheap and crowded. He stood in the queue amongst law students in suits, and white-coated medics, as clouds of steam rose above the counter and the girls in turbans wiped their faces with the backs of their hands and ladled out varieties of unrationed cubed soup, mutton stew with boiled potatoes, corned beef and pale blancmange.

'Next! Yes, sir?'

Walter stood behind a man with a beard, whose fingers trembled. He wore overalls flecked with plaster, and his hands, too, were spattered with white. When he felt in his pocket for change he took time to get it out, and count it. The girl on the till sighed impatiently.

Walter followed him away from the counter, looking for someone he knew. Amongst the University population the students from the Slade stood out. They were scruffy, or stylish: they had an air. Today he saw no one he recognised, and the tables were filling up fast. Ahead, the man in overalls was looking about him. He was tall and well made; his tray shook dangerously.

They took two of the last places left, beneath an oil painting of an elderly Professor of Mathematics. Walter set his own tray down and felt in his pocket. No book – no Hardy, for solace amongst strangers. They sat down. Across the table, the man in overalls struggled to break a roll, and crumbs flew everywhere. Walter drank thin pea soup and left his own roll untouched. Across the room, the door banged open and shut; amongst the clatter of tin lids from the counter, the hiss of the tea urn, and the rise and fall of voices, they made a little pool of silence: two men whose lives were to intertwine for decades but who, at their first encounter, barely spoke.

Walter cut the gristle off his meat. Everyone seemed to have someone to talk to. He looked at his watch, calculating the time before his next class. He thought of his ineptness with women; he tried not to observe the sight of a tall, well-made man having difficulty eating his lunch.

☆

It was the beginning of February, and very cold. People were going down with flu again: it was said to be serious. The papers carried advertisements for Kruschen salts, Formamint tablets, phenatecin; Walter's landlady believed in Navy rum, last thing at night in a basin of gruel. His mother sent a thick blue jersey, wrapped in layers of newspaper and brown paper; pinned to the sleeve was an envelope with a postal order for 2/6d for extra coal.

He was wearing the jersey on the filthy wet morning he walked into the Antique Room and found Sarah Lewis leaning on the brown-painted radiator, gloved hands outstretched, her unlaced ankle boots perched upon it, drying out at either end.

'Oh. Hello. You're early.'

'So are you.' She shifted in her stockinged feet, putting them up in turn against the bars. Behind her, the high windows were streaming.

Walter hung up his jacket and cap. He had left his greatcoat in the cloakroom downstairs. In the warmth of the room, after the cold and wet outside, both their cheeks were burning.

'Do you have far to come?' asked Sarah, taking her gloves off.

'Just Camden Town. I've taken a room there. And you?'

'Just Wimbledon.' She smiled, and turned to lay her gloves beside her boots. The room was filling with the smell of wet leather; the floorboards where she had been standing bore the imprint of her stockinged feet. 'I'm hoping to move into Hall in the spring, but my parents wanted to keep me at home for the first term.'

'I expect that's best.' Walter stood looking at her for a moment, only half-aware that he was doing so. There was something about her which had always felt familiar, as if he'd known her a long time ago, but he couldn't place when.

'What?' she asked him. 'What are you thinking about?'

'Sorry.' He pulled himself together, went across to his easel, pinning up fresh paper.

'Oh tell me, please.'

He stood looking at his blank paper. 'Have you ever had that feeling about someone – you dream about them, and see them soon afterwards, and they look like someone you know very well, and you can't remember why.' He stopped, feeling himself sounding far too familiar.

45

'How strange,' said Sarah. 'Does that mean you've been dreaming about me?'

He blushed. 'I don't know.' He went over to look at the drawings, pinned up on the wall.

'What are you working on?' She came over, and stood beside him. 'Which one is yours?'

He nodded towards the cast of the woman lifting her robe at the hip.

Sarah looked at his drawings, but did not comment. Were they really so poor? He felt himself flush deeper. 'I'm starting something new today. Petman said I was to move on to this chap.' He indicated the half-crouched figure of a discus-thrower, on a plinth in the centre of the room. 'What about you?'

'I'm – where am I? Down here, I think.'

He followed her towards the windows, and stood next to her, looking at four or five studies of bare feet, sandalled feet; a foot arched, and ready to run; a winged foot, ready to soar.

'They're beautiful.' He turned to her, noticing loose strands of her piled-up hair drying out, straying over her forehead. Behind them the door was pushed open, and people came in chattering.

'Morning.'

'Morning. Filthy day.'

'Foul.'

He stood beside Sarah, feeling a part of things, in the casual exchange of greetings. He said, as though he were quite used to asking girls out, 'Will you have lunch with me?' And Sarah said yes, she would like to, walking back to the radiator, lifting down her boots.

They crossed the dripping quad, stepping over the puddles. Walter had said, as they came down the stairs, 'We could go out, perhaps,' recently aware that people spent long afternoons in the pubs and cafés of Cumberland Market, in the nearby Express Dairy, or down in Grafton Way.

'Another time, don't you think? We'll only get soaked.'

And indeed the sky was darkening again. He held open the door of the refectory. It was packed, everyone else, also, clearly wanting to stay close to home.

'Let's get a place first,' said Walter, seeing the endless queue at the counter.

'Look,' said Sarah, pointing to a wildly waving hand, 'we can join the gang.'

Walter looked. He saw people from the class: Gwen Taylor, the girl whom Tonks had goaded until she wept; Henry Marsh, who'd called Tonks a bastard under his breath, and a couple of others he knew well by sight. And Nina Frith, sitting opposite a willowy young man in a waistcoat and yellow kerchief, who was making her laugh.

'Isn't there . . .' Walter looked quickly about the room. Surely there must be a couple of places somewhere. But Sarah was already waving back to the others, at Henry Marsh leaning exaggeratedly across the table, arms outstretched to save the last two chairs.

'Is this all right?' she said, as he followed her between the tables.

'Of course.' And he hung his jacket on the back of the chair and greeted everyone, nodding to Nina, who returned the nod and leaned across to her companion, reaching her slender hand to his.

Walter turned back to Sarah. 'What can I get you?'

'Oh, I'll come with you,' she said, putting her chair in, and they pushed through the narrow gap between the tables, through the din, and stood in the queue, making conversation about what to eat, and about the rain, pelting down outside.

Walter glanced across at Nina. The rain fell, the noise rose, and she and her companion in the yellow kerchief sat talking and laughing. Walter, sitting next to Sarah on their return to the table, ate tepid shepherd's pie and listened to Henry Marsh going on about the place where he was living, a run-down mansion block in Primrose Hill, and how it was overrun with mice, and had no bath.

'You're doing rather well,' said Bevan-Petman, working round the classroom on Monday afternoon. He paused by Walter's easel and stood looking over his shoulder. He stared at the discus-thrower with half-closed eyes, he stood back and put his head on one side. 'He's coming to something, don't you think?'

'I hope so.'

'You have the shoulder – yes, you have the whole, I believe. The shading here, and here –' he indicated the bulging muscles of the thigh, the straining tendons in the neck '– this isn't quite right yet. I am sure you can see that.'

Walter held up his pencil, measuring distances. Two places away there was an absence. Sarah was ill.

'But essentially,' Bevan-Petman continued, 'you are making good progress. I shall be happy to recommend you to Professor Tonks for the Life Class in the summer term, if that would suit you.'

'It would. Thank you.'

On Mondays, at a quarter to four, they broke for tea, and then went to the Anatomy lecture. Walter, arriving early with Henry Marsh, seated himself in the theatre and watched the entrance of a group of students whom he had not noticed before.

'That's the sculpture chaps,' said Henry, looking up from a doodle in his notebook. 'Do you know any of them?'

'No, not really.' But he saw the tall overalled figure of the man with whom he had once shared a table, coming in and taking his place with the others, and thought, You're someone I'd like to get to know.

'Where are the sculpture studios?'

'Down in the basement. They used to be in an annexe over Warren Street Station, but they came back last year, I think.'

'The basement?' Walter frowned. 'But that's where the women's rooms are.'

'Other side – different staircase.' Henry looked at his watch. 'Come on, let's get this over with.'

People were filing in. Walter knew that Nina would be amongst them, but did not turn to look. A porter was drawing the blinds down. Then the white-coated figure of Professor Elliot Smith was on the podium, hanging a chart up, and the model was standing behind a chair, and the chatter in the room died down.

'Good afternoon, ladies and gentlemen. Today we shall be examining the structure and anatomy of the joints and muscles relating to the knee . . .'

Henry yawned. Walter flattened the pages of his notebook. An hour passed.

When they came out, it was cold and dark. People were hurrying across the quad for evening classes.

'Come and have a drink,' said Henry. 'Do you know the Orange Tree?' They fetched their coats and crossed the road. The pub was on the corner of Euston Road; firelight flickered through leaded windows.

'What'll you have?'

'Just a half. Thanks.'

Walter sat in a corner while Henry went up to the bar, and watched the place fill up. He saw the sculpture students come in, and heard the man he liked the look of addressed as Euan, and saw his hands shake, and slop beer on the floor as they made their way to a nearby table.

'Cheers,' said Henry, returning. 'How are you getting on?'

'All right, I think.' Walter raised his glass, and told him about the prospect of the Life Room.

'Good show,' said Henry, offering him a Player's. 'No? Well done. I don't know how I'd have survived the bloody war without them.'

'Where were you?'

'Here and there.' Henry shook his match out. 'With the Fusiliers. Best not to think about it, don't you find? It's either that or bore the pants off everyone.' He drew the smoke down deep. 'I don't find my people are very good at hearing much about it – perhaps they're right. What about yours?'

'I lost my brother,' said Walter. 'You're right – let's not speak about it now.' Across on the table of sculptors there was laughter. He saw Euan leaning back in a corner, smoking a pipe. The fire glowed, the door swung open and shut, the place was building up a good fug. Walter thought, This is London, and I am a part of it, as others from the class came in, and joined them, and he bought the next round, barely able to afford it, but none of them could, and it didn't matter. He heard someone say there was going to be a dance, and who was buying tickets, and he bought one, and caught the tram home in a daze, shivering as he hurried up his street, and shivering in his room after supper, with the unlit fire and wavering jet of gas.

In the narrow iron bedstead he lay with his feet on the stone hot water bottle brought from home. He read for a while, then he turned out the gas and lay listening to the trains clanking out of Camden Station, puffing away towards local London districts he knew only by name from the map: Chalk Farm, Hampstead Heath and Brondesbury, Highbury and Dalston and Haggerston, stretching east and west to the outer limits of the city, houses built along the track and lives he could only guess at. He thought of his bedroom in Asham's Mill, the lamp blown out, the darkness of the countryside deep around the cottage, the soughing trees, the silent fields. No one about.

He turned over. He drew down the pillow, into his arms. A long time ago, he'd slept next to his brother. How strange, said Sarah now, stockinged feet damp on the floorboards, the windows of the Antique Room streaming with the rain. Did you dream about me? He drew her close. He slept.

He woke, and knew he had dreamed of Nina, naked. He had never seen a naked woman. The girls had moved out of the bedroom even before the war, his mother turning out the lumber room, getting him and John William and his father to take all the trunks and boxes which had been there since Lord knows when, and carry them on the cart to her sister's, for storage. Buckets and distemper, a real turn-out.

'The girls need their privacy now.'

'Why?'

She didn't answer.

'Why?'

'Because I say so.'

That had been that. He had never seen a naked woman, he knew nothing at all about women, though he and John William used to make guesses. Now he lay in the thin light of the London dawn and wondered. He closed his eyes again, saw Nina as he had seen her in the dream, her skin so white and her hair so silky.

He lay in the narrow bed, trying to imagine it all.

He tried to put all this to the back of his mind.

It grew colder. Snow fell. In Kent the fields under snow would be pure and still. Here, trams pushed through the slush. Walter went in and found the class half-empty. No Sarah.

'I'm afraid she is probably ill, sir,' said the beadle in his booth.

Walter gave back the signing-in book. 'I wonder – have you an address?'

'I'm afraid we are not permitted –'

'No, no, of course not.'

'Let's hope it is not a return of the influenza. For all our sakes.'

'Oh, I hope not.'

More snow fell. Classes were cancelled. A leaden sky hung over Camden, where Walter kept to his lodgings, and wrote to Sarah, huddled over the fire, pressing on a blotter.

*33 Arlington Street*
*Camden Town, NW*

*21st February, 1920*

*Dear Sarah,*
*I hope you are well, though I fear you may not be. The School has been pretty much shut down these last two days. I have decided to hole up here for a bit. When the weather clears, and you are feeling up to it, will you come with me for a walk one day? I have a fancy to see something beyond these grey streets. I have yet to visit even Regent's Park, though at night when it is quiet I sometimes hear the lions roar in the Zoo. Nor have I visited Hampstead Heath, nor anywhere beyond. I am reading and working and trying to keep warm. No doubt you are doing much the same?*

*My respects to your parents. I hope to hear you are well.*

*Yours ever,*
*Walter Cox*

He pressed the page to the blotter, then re-read it. How dull, how ordinary. For a moment he read it as he thought Nina might read it: skimming, alighting on awkward phrasing. Then he reminded himself that he was not writing to Nina. He thought to add a decoration: a lion from the Zoo, asleep at the foot of the page. He addressed the letter care of the Slade, and marked it: *Kindly Forward*.

He caught the three o'clock post at the corner pillar box and slipped as he hurried back across the street, coming down hard in the path of an errand boy, who swore and swerved and turned back to shout at him. Walter limped back to the house and was pleased to accept his landlady's offer of tea in the kitchen, where he sat beneath a line of damp washing above the range and watched the kettle hiss.

His landlady folded shirts and talked of the harshness of the war, the losses, the rationing, and then the influenza. And now men out of work. She made tea in a brown pot and let Walter go up to his room and bring down his sketchbook and draw her: leaning on the oilcloth, spreading dripping from a cracked white bowl, lifting the teapot. He could feel Tonks there in the kitchen, watching. He didn't know if this was having a good or a bad effect, but his landlady asked if she might keep the one where she was slicing bread. She lit the oil lamp and hoped they would soon be on the electric, as the street outside grew darker, and children ran home from school in the cold, and front doors banged open and shut.

More snow fell. This time it settled. The rooftops of Camden glittered. Walter had a letter from Sarah.

*WIM 4327*                                          *Wimbledon, SW*
                                                   *3rd March, 1920*

*Dear Walter,*
*Thank you for writing. I have indeed been ill with the influenza – not as badly as last year, but still unpleasant. Your letter came from the Slade yesterday afternoon: it has done much to cheer me up.*

*I like your suggestion of a walk. I am still not up to travelling much, but perhaps we might go to Norwood, which isn't far from here. Pissarro used to paint there – the son – I expect you know that – in the 1890s. Winter scenes. I could meet you at Gipsy Hill Station: perhaps you could telephone me?*

*I hope you yourself are keeping well.*

                                                   *Sincerely,*
                                                   *Sarah*


*PS I liked the lion.*


It was mid-morning when he arrived, handing in his ticket to a collector who quickly went back inside to his stove. Sarah was waiting in the ante-room. She rose to greet him, pale and wan.

'I hope I haven't kept you?'

'Not at all.'

He held the door open for two elderly ladies, walking arm in arm. Outside the station, the snow lay thick. The elderly ladies stepped carefully towards a waiting bus. When it had gone, the road was empty. They could hear someone scraping a shovel.

Snow in the suburbs.

'Which way?'

They walked away from Gipsy Hill towards Norwood Park, along streets which had been Pissarro's lanes, bordered by fields and hedgerows. There were still untouched acres. Their breath streamed out before them. Sarah's galoshes crunched in the snow.

'His place,' she said. 'Pissarro made this his place. I can only think of him when I come here.' They walked on. 'That's what I want to do.'

'What's that?'

'Make somewhere my place. I haven't found it yet. My father says I will.'

'Is he an artist?'

'Yes. He trained at the Slade, as well. Forty years ago, under Legros.' She saw Walter's expression. 'I am the child of elderly parents,' she said drily. 'The only child,' she added. 'I grew up with painting and painters – sometimes it felt as if the New English Art Club almost lived in our house. And you?'

'No painters. Two sisters.'

Snow lay thickly on tiled rooftops. Someone was chopping wood.

'That makes me think of my father.'

Someone was whistling.

'That makes me think of my brother.'

'You said –'

'We lost him in the war.'

'Oh, Walter.' Sarah touched his arm. 'I'm so sorry.'

They came to a gate in a hedge. Walter wiped the snow off the top with his sleeve and they leaned on it, looking out over the whiteness. A cattle trough stood in a corner, thick with ice.

'This makes me think of home.'

'Where's that?'

'Down in Kent.'

'I've never been to Kent.'

'No?' He looked across the field, thinking of it. Snow on the oasthouse cowls. The frozen banks of the Stour. 'That's my place.'

# Spring

The snow melted, classes were resumed. Walter bought a bicycle from Petty & Sharp in Kentish Town, reconditioned but service-able. He bicycled down to the Slade. Camden Town. Mornington Crescent. He began to feel a part of the early morning street life, getting to know the shops. Blinds up, doors unbolted, lights coming on. Miss Minnie Bartlett, Miss Victoria Dayes. Provisions and provisions. Lamps set down on doorsteps.

'Morning.'

'Morning.'

Smog and the mist dispersing.

Past the bath house, the lodging house, passing the laundry van, slowing down for the drayhorses brought to a halt outside the Victoria, the Mornington Arms, the Cricketers. Steaming coats, clink of the bit. Barrels clanging down on the pavement. Coal carts, with miserable ponies; chutes opened up for the rush of the delivery. Road gangs setting up for the day. Ironmongers, bakeries, holes in the road. Market stalls in side streets.

The first leaves appeared on the blackened lime trees, the birds began to sing. Walter could sense a raising of spirits as he wheeled his bicycle out of the hall each day and set off. Front doors opened, the milk taken in, buckets brought out and a lot of scrubbing. Rugs hung out of upper windows. Here and there a whistle. Out in the High Street he rang the bell, weaved in and out of the traffic, timing himself against the trams.

He rode on, down busy Hampstead Road, through busier Euston, past the drunks, crossing over to Gower Street on foot, cycling up to the tall iron gates and the lodge, greeting the porters.

'Morning, Frederick.'

'Morning, Mr Cox.'

55

He wheeled the bicycle across the quad to the railings, and got out his padlock. When he walked back to the shallow steps he no longer felt quite so self-conscious, pushing open the heavy door, nodding to the girls ranged along the radiators, chattering, trying on each other's earrings, eyeing each new arrival of the day. He greeted Sarah, Gwen Taylor; he managed, on the rare occasions she was there, to nod to Nina.

'There's Steer,' Henry Marsh said suddenly, as he and Walter were reading the notices one morning.

'Where?'

'There – going into the office.' He nodded towards a big man with a stoop, shuffling through the throng towards Tonks's door. 'I haven't seen him for weeks.'

'Is he good?'

'As a teacher? He's only here once a week, in the painting class. People say he leaves you to get on with it. He doesn't attack you, unlike Tonks.'

They climbed the stairs to the class and took their places. Walter was working from a bust now. After weeks of limbs and torsos it felt both liberating and strange to spend his time studying a human face, a female face: to measure the proportions of hairline to brow, and brow to cheekbone; to draw the sweet and subtle curve of the lips. The model was Athenian, her gaze intent but distant. Walter spent hours upon her. Left profile, right profile; studies of the ear, the tendrils of hair, the dreaming eyes.

'You are a classicist,' said Petman, standing beside him. 'You understand her.'

Walter did not know how this was so, but he cut short his lunch-hour that day and came back to her, pacing back and forth in the empty room, reconsidering her beauty, taking a new sheet of paper, moving his easel so that he saw her from the back, her head at an angle, as if she had heard him and knew he was there, and would, when she was ready, turn to face him.

On Saturdays classes stopped at one.

'You should go to the British Museum,' said Petman, pulling his jacket on. 'We like all our students to go, now that the Greek and Roman rooms are reopening. The Elgin Marbles are coming back in bits, I think, and of course there's the Parthenon frieze. It's all been kept in underground shelters.' He felt in his pockets. 'Have I got my keys? Yes, here we are.' He held the door open. 'Perhaps you are visiting the galleries already?'

'I'm afraid I haven't, yet.'

'Fifteen minutes on foot. The beadle has a Bartholomew's if you ever need it. Have a good weekend.'

The sky was overcast and the quad was windy and cold. Walter unlocked his bicycle and wheeled it towards the gates. He saw Sarah, talking to Nina and Henry. His stomach turned over.

'We're going for lunch in the Dairy,' Henry said. 'Coming?'

'I'm broke.' It was true.

'I'll treat you,' said Henry. 'I'm flush.'

He hesitated. 'I was going to go down to the British Museum.'

'How *earnest*,' said Nina. Henry laughed.

Walter turned his bicycle aside. 'I think I'll stick to my plan.'

'Oh, don't be so stuffy.' Henry put out a friendly hand. 'Come on.'

'No, really. I'll see you on Monday.'

'Oh, well – toodle-pip. Come along, girls.'

Walter cycled up Gower Street, feeling the first drops of rain on his face, feeling a fool. It should have been so easy to join them, but he flushed at the thought of Nina's cool voice; he flushed at the thought of her sitting near Sarah, making him awkward with her, too. The rain began to fall faster: he turned into Great Russell Street. Umbrellas were up, and people were taking shelter in doorways, hurrying into the shops. He drew up at the gates, where a man was selling chestnuts. Rain dripped from his cap. Walter bought a quarter and wheeled the bike in through the wet. He padlocked it to the railings and ran across the forecourt, shielding his bag as it began to pour. Up on the steps he stood with a handful of others beneath the portico, eating the chestnuts and watching the rain soak into the gravel and grass. Pigeons approached him: he dropped bits of hot skin, and more followed. A uniformed attendant appeared from the doorway: Walter screwed up his paper bag and dropped it into a bin. He walked through the massive doorway.

The hall was enormous and echoing. An old lady took off her gloves and put on her glasses. She peered at a plan on the wall. Walter stood beside her. She turned to look at him.

'And what are you after?'

'The Greek and Roman rooms, I think.'

'Here we are.' She pointed to the plan's ground floor. 'Down in the basement.'

'Thank you. That's very helpful.'

She gave him a dazzling smile. 'So wonderful to see you young men coming back.'

He didn't know how to answer, made a little bow, and backed towards the cloakroom, leaving his damp jacket and scarf there. Then he walked over the cold tiled floor and down to the Graeco-Roman rooms.

Plinths stretched the length of a gallery, dusty and hushed. The rain was trickling down a fanlight; the light was muted; pale marble heads offered noble profiles. Walter took out his sketchbook; he felt for his box of pencils. He moved along the rows of emperors, philosophers, athletes, youths and maidens, hearing his own quiet footfall, the trickle of rain, a cough. He saw a tall figure at the far end; a man standing back from a head with a laurel crown, considering, taking out a notebook, starting to draw.

The sculptor. For a moment Walter could not remember his name, overheard in the pub one evening weeks ago. Then it came back. He considered approaching, decided against it: observing the man's absorption, feeling his own shyness well up like blood. He chose a young athlete, crouched and tense before the race, looking across the gallery from beneath Hellenic skies, hearing the roar of the crowd, smelling dust from the track, and thyme from the baking hills . . .

Tales from the village school. Walter took out a pencil.

The natural light was fading: dim electric lights came on. Shadows fell upon the athlete. The fanlight with its leaded panes went dark.

Footsteps approached him. 'Care for a drink?'

The sculptor was beside him, a massive presence in the low-watt light. He held out his hand: it trembled. 'Euan Harrison. We had lunch together once, I think. After a fashion.'

Walter shook his hand. 'I remember.' He introduced himself, then picked up his canvas bag from the floor. 'Yes, I'd like that. Where shall we go?'

'There's the Museum Tavern, just over the road.'

They walked up the long flight of stairs towards the attendant, stifling a yawn at the gallery entrance, the last to leave, their footsteps distinct on the stone.

☆

Years later, up in his Kent studio, the window open on to the churchyard, entirely unable to work, Walter looked back and saw them: two men meeting just after the war, coming out of the British Museum on a cold spring evening, beginning the most important friendship of their lives.

And now? Fred Eaves was mowing the grass in the churchyard; a fine spray of cuttings leapt up from the blades. Walter put his head in his hands.

They came down the steps to the forecourt. Dusk had fallen; the chestnut stove glowed beyond the gates. Walter's bicycle ticked between them as he wheeled it across the street.

'I haven't got any money,' he said suddenly, remembering, as he propped up the bicycle outside the pub.

'This is on me.' Euan held open the door.

The Tavern was filling up. Walter, keeping a place in the corner, watched Euan make his way to the bar through knots of clerks and shop girls, students, attendants from the Museum having a drink after work. A few older men were playing chess in a corner, but the men in their twenties and early thirties were missing, a swathe cut out of society, and up at the bar Euan's tall figure was distinctive. He was young, though older than Walter, and he had come back. But it was more than this: he was his own man, he knew what he was about. Watching him, Walter knew he had sensed this the first time he saw him, making his way across the refectory, finding a place, not caring whether or not he had someone to talk to.

And now he had approached him.

Euan came back, and put down the glasses. Beer spilled on to the table. He pulled out a chair.

'Cheers.'

'Cheers.' Walter raised his glass. 'Thanks.'

Euan nodded, taking out pipe and matches, struggling to light up with trembling fingers before the match went out, and he had to struggle again.

'So.' He succeeded, and sat back. 'How are you getting on?'

'All right, I think.'

'Do you feel you're a Slade man?'

Walter considered. 'It's early days, but yes, I'm happy there. When

I'm working. It's my first formal training – I'm beginning to see the point of it all.'

'Not everyone does. Some people leave – Nash left, after a term. Sickert left, twenty years ago. Said he didn't want to spend his whole life copying.'

'Well . . .' Walter thought of the Antique Room, its smell of dust and plaster, his lunch-hours spent in an absorbed forgetting of everything else: only the page, the woman's head, her dreamy, contemplative gaze, and the pleasure he took in trying to capture it. 'I think I'm learning a lot.'

'You're a Slade man, then. There have been many great Slade men. And where are you from? You're not a Londoner.'

Was it so obvious? 'I'm from Kent,' said Walter. 'A little hamlet no one's ever heard of, on the Stour. Near Denham – that's where I went to school.'

'And what is your ambition, now you're here?'

Walter thought about it, drinking tepid beer. 'I've just fulfilled one – I've got this scholarship.' He told Euan about the modest, post-war classes in Ashford; how Wicks had encouraged him. 'All this is more than I've ever dreamed of.' He put down his glass. 'And you? Where are you from?'

'Cornwall,' said Euan, smoking. 'Stony ground,' he added drily. 'That's where it all began. I spent a lot of my boyhood out on the moors, or the beach. Me and my dog.'

'And have you brothers and sisters?'

'No.'

Walter found it hard to imagine this. He had scarcely a moment to himself when he was a boy. He hesitated. 'Is it as lonely as they say?'

'It made me self-reliant.' Euan reached for his glass. 'My father died when I was very young – I have no memories of him at all. He worked in the quarries and went down with a lung disease. So – it was always just my mother and me. And the dog.' He gave a little smile.

'And you went walking,' said Walter, not knowing what else to say.

'I did – we used to go for miles. All that cold and wind, and those standing stones on Bodmin – they made a deep impression. I used to draw them, and I used to bring home pebbles from the beach and spend hours arranging and rearranging them – all that sort of thing. I always felt I knew what I was doing, that this was my material.'

'I know what you mean,' said Walter. It was just how he felt with a pencil or brush. 'But I don't know anything about stone, or sculpture. I've never had anything to do with it – only looked at the carvings in church, I suppose.'

'That's a good place to start. You didn't see the Epstein show last month?'

Walter shook his head. He hadn't even known it was on.

'There was a lot of fuss about it in the papers. The scandal of *The Risen Christ* – people called it barbaric.' Euan sat drinking. 'I thought it was magnificent, I must say. What about Eric Gill? Do you know his work at all?'

Walter shook his head. 'You must think me very lame,' he said, turning his glass on the table.

'Not in the least. Gill's pretty new, still. He's just done *The Stations of the Cross* in Westminster Cathedral. We could go and see them one day, if you like.'

Walter said that he would. He sat listening to Euan talk about Epstein and Gill, and about the galleries in the British Museum showing sculpture from early civilisations, Negro and Inca and Aztec, which Roger Fry was urging everyone to visit. Fry used to lecture at the Slade before the war, before he and Tonks fell out. Euan had heard him once.

'I was there two years before call-up,' he said, finishing his pint. 'Coming back feels like coming home, in a way.'

'And what is *your* ambition?' Walter asked him.

Euan put down his glass. He spread his hands above the table. They were large, capable, the fingers long and blunt, and their tremor was painful to see. Walter glanced away.

'Don't. This is something I'm living with – the after-effects of shell-shock. It's mild: I'm lucky.'

Walter looked at him. There was a pause.

'I was at Passchendaele,' Euan said slowly. 'With the Artists' Rifles. I lost half my men. They come back and visit me, every night.'

Walter did not know what to say. 'I'm sorry. It feels hopeless, not having been there. Sometimes I wish—'

'No. Don't wish it.' Euan looked at him gravely. 'We're here. There's a life to be lived. Now I have to get better: that is my ambition. Then – I never want to stop working.' He picked up his pipe and it shook in his hand. 'So,' he said, drawing on it again. 'Here we are, in the aftermath. Where are you living?'

'I've got digs in Camden. I lead a pretty quiet life, I suppose.'

'What about women?'

Walter flushed. 'I haven't really had time to think about all that.'

'You must have been busy.'

They laughed.

'Well,' said Walter, feeling more relaxed than he had done for weeks. 'You know how it is. One or two people I like the look of, but nothing's happened yet. What about you?'

'I like women,' said Euan, 'but I've got to recover my health before I can even think of it. I'm not in a hurry, there's plenty of time.'

'Quite,' said Walter, as if he had always thought this. 'And where are you living?'

'In a lodging house in Euston. Cheap and not very clean, but it'll do.'

'Do you ever go home? To Cornwall?'

Euan shook his head. 'Not for a long time. My mother died – I have no real reason to go back now.' He puffed on his pipe. 'Besides, everything it gave me, I carry inside. That kind of childhood lasts for ever, if you understand me.'

'Yes,' said Walter, thinking of his own. 'I understand that very well.' He felt liking and affinity grow between them, stronger and steadier than anything he'd felt since he'd come to London.

'Have another.' Euan got to his feet.

'I will. It's on me next time.' Walter watched him move through the crush. He thought, This will last. I can feel it.

'What about your family?' Euan asked, when he came back. 'What do they think of it all?'

'Me in London? They're pleased, but we miss each other. Sometimes I'm so homesick I don't know how to manage.' He hadn't realised how true this was until he said it. Did it make him sound a fool?

'Who's at home?'

'My mother and father. I've two sisters, but they've left too, now: one's in service, the other's nursing.' Walter looked at Euan, listening attentively. He said, beginning to realise the place that this friendship could fill, 'I lost my elder brother. It feels like half my body, still.'

Sharp flurries of rain shook the city windows. Then the tight cold days of early spring opened out in a rush. Daffodils swayed in the parks, the sooty streets of Camden were lit by piercing shafts of sun, glancing off slate and chimney. The trees in the squares near the Slade were in leaf overnight; the quad was full of birdsong. Tonks strode along the paths and took the steps briskly.

'Good morning, Mr Cox.'

'Good morning, sir.'

Walter was always early. Nina was often late. Thus he managed hardly to see her. But he felt compelled to see her. He was aware of her everywhere: light footsteps crossing the hall, or running upstairs to the Life Room. He caught glimpses – pale hair like a gleam of spring sun in an unlit corridor, the swing of her skirt. He heard her: talking to Henry, to Gwen, to any number of people whose names he did not know yet. Casually, one afternoon, he asked Sarah where she lived.

'Nina? In Fitzroy Square. Why? Has she asked you to one of her parties?'

'No. No, she hasn't.'

'Walter?'

'Yes?'

'Nothing.'

Ducks beat across the skies in Camden, making for Regent's Park. The afternoons grew longer, mornings brighter. Walter, some days later, followed Nina home.

He pushed his bicycle all along the pavement in Grafton Street, apologising to nurses and medics walking swiftly to and from the hospital, steadfastly keeping in view a slender straight back in a belted jacket, little buttoned shoes. In Tottenham Court Road he lost her: one omnibus slowed down behind another, stopping outside Maples. When they moved on, she had vanished. He pushed his bike out amongst the traffic; brakes squealed and a driver shouted – he was panting as he reached the other side. Where had she gone?

She came out of a tobacconists on the corner of Fitzroy Street. He stopped and waited. She turned into the square; he followed, his hands slippery on the handlebars, dreading lest she turn and see him. The sky was filled with a fresh spring wind; a dancing, impatient light came and went upon tall windows, in and out of the trees. He waited on the corner, his heart pounding, his whole being concentrated into this moment, counting the houses until she reached her house, not far down on the south side, stopping on the steps to take keys from a slim brown bag, and quickly going inside.

It was just after four o'clock. A signboard creaked on the corner, a door banged to and pigeons rose, startled, from the pavement. Walter steadied himself, and mounted the bicycle. He rode round the square, to get the feel of it: the notices offering rooms to let, the Home for Working Girls in London, the Clergy Nursing Home on the north side, the signs for music lessons, sewing and alterations. Someone in an upper room was playing the piano badly: Walter heard the same chords again and again, and the clap of hands at an open window. 'Stop! Stop!' There were any number of bell plates for artists: decorative, stained-glass, artists' colourmen.

And Nina lived here.

And Sickert, he remembered from a book, or a lecture, had taken a studio nearby, in the years before the war: at 19, Fitzroy Street.

Walter cycled out of the square. He stopped, and stood before Sickert's railings. On Saturday afternoons, there had been open house here: visitors climbing the stairs from the street smelled cigarettes, heard teacups handed, and conversation. Canvases were stacked against the wall. You took your time, looking through markets and music-halls, railway stations, suburban sunsets, afternoon tea in dim bedsitters. Sickert and Ginner and Gilman and Gore, the founders of the Camden Town Group, putting up work on an easel if you liked the look of it. Around you they were talking of Degas and Dieppe, Van Gogh and Arles, the Paris dealers, Cézanne, Picasso, Cork Street . . . Walter, leaning on his bicycle, could see it all, hear the chink of cups, the voices insisting that English art must find its own subjects, and English artists their own community.

And where was the avant-garde in that community?

In the Omega Workshops, behind the sign of the blue arum lily, Roger Fry was employing impoverished young artists to make chairs and screens and pottery. 'That handbag and pincushion factory in Fitzroy Square,' sneered Wyndham Lewis from the Rebel Art Centre, down the road in Great Ormond Street. He drank with Marinetti, visiting from Rome; he pasted up the Italian Futurist Manifesto, spent hours with Ezra Pound in the Cave of the Golden Calf in Percy Street. If you weren't a Futurist, you were a Vorticist: this was the age of the machine! Lewis put out two issues of *Blast!* on thick cheap paper. Blast England! Curse its climate, curse the Aesthete, curse the man Tonks!

And then the war came, and machines went into action. And the war, said Lewis, stopped art dead.

But the war made English art great, thought Walter, buttoning his jacket as the fresh spring wind blew colder, thinking of Nevinson, Nash and Spencer: men who found great themes and turned away from sentiment. He recalled the afternoon he had spent with Wicks in the Royal Academy, this time a year ago – Wicks making light of his shoulder wound, his awkward movement through the throng, himself overcome by the power of the paintings: the bitter, angular figures waiting in driving rain for orders, the skeletal trees and flooded trenches, the sun rising over the dead, the dying.

And now? War artists without a war – and what is my own ambition? Walter asked himself, as Euan had asked him, standing at the rusting railings of 19, Fitzroy Street. It was sixteen months after the war had ended; he was still bereaved, uncertain. Am I to become a decorative artist, and put up a notice in my window? I am copying Antique heads. It is months since I painted. I am a stranger on the streets of London, still. I am making friends, but . . .

What about women? Euan had asked him, drawing on his pipe.

*I have followed a girl without daring to speak.*

*I cannot approach and conquer the woman I long for.*

Yes. He had allowed himself to think it.

He turned his bicycle back towards the square. He would walk up the worn shallow steps to her door, and ring—

He turned away again, took a corner, found himself in Charlotte Street, cycling into the end of the afternoon past Belgian pastry-cooks, Italian confectioners, Bertorelli's Refreshment Rooms. I will bring Nina to these places, Walter thought. I will ring upon her doorbell – not today but another day, soon. I will get to know her, I will invite her out. I will take her to dances and teas, I will hold her and hold her.

He did none of these things. He went with Euan to look at Gill's *Stations of the Cross*. Around them, footsteps came and went. Coins dropped into wooden boxes. Candles flickered. The air smelled of wax and stone and incense. Every now and then the door of the cathedral swung open, and light flooded the aisle and pillars. Walter walked back, and began again, taking in once more the long progression from dignity to humiliation. How pure the stylised line, how cruel the death. What drama in the placing of cross and spear and outstretched arms.

'What do you think?'

He thought of the sound of chisel on stone, something he knew nothing about. These carvings felt classical – timeless, yet very modern. Perhaps he might start all over again with his heads from the Antique. What should he do? He tried to say all this, as they walked up and down on the smooth worn flagstones.

'I want to come and see your work,' he said to Euan.

Euan had his hands in his pockets, listening. 'I admire this, I find it beautiful. The purity – everything is essential, everything belongs.'

Yes, thought Walter. Yes – exactly that.

'But I want something entirely of itself, perhaps not figurative at all.' He looked at Walter. 'Do you see what I'm driving at?'

'I'm not sure.'

'Nor am I. Anyway, one has to be practical, I suppose. I might do a lettering course at City & Guilds, when I leave. Learn a bit more about Gill. Or something. Shall we go?'


'Walter?'

'Yes?'

'Will you – would you like to come and have lunch this weekend? I mean with my parents. Sunday lunch.' Sarah made a little face. 'Not very exciting, but perhaps you're busy?'

Walter looked at her. Now that the weather was warm, people spent their lunchtimes out beneath the trees, spreading rugs on the grass, taking off their jackets. They lit cigarettes, and planned parties. Sarah, in a blue linen shirt, all the paleness of winter gone, had her legs tucked beneath her on the rug. She looked back at Walter.

'What? Have I said the wrong thing?'

'Not in the least.' He touched her arm. 'I was thinking how nice you look. I'd love to come – thank you.'

She smiled. 'This Sunday. Let me give you our address.' She reached for the bag beside her. 'I'll write it down.'

Nina came out on to the steps. Walter somehow knew she was there, and he turned and saw her: framed in the doorway, shading her eyes, looking out. He felt the moment fill with her, the whole of the quad come alive with her presence.

'Or I could meet you,' said Sarah. 'Walter? Would that be easier?'

☆

Sunday came. The train drew into the station. The hiss, the slam of the doors, the walk along the platform, the whistle of the guard, the bright green waving flag – ordinary, orderly, comforting. Trains have gone, and trains will come again, and how good it felt to be out of the soot and grime of Camden, away from his room and the prospect of a Sunday spent reading or walking alone. Somewhere new. He stood on the platform watching the train puff away down the track, between banks of wild buddleia and willowherb.

One day perhaps I will paint a station, he thought, turning back to the exit. Geraniums stood in a pot, beneath the fire bucket. The ticket collector was whistling.

'Thank you, sir.'

But not just the station, not just the train puffing off. The painting must stand for more than that. It must mean something, say something.

Or should it just stand for itself? Plain, unadorned. A station.

This station.

He came out on to the street.

The house was Edwardian, double-fronted, and substantial. The path, laid with black and white tiles, was lined with wallflowers; art nouveau lilies filled the stained-glass panels framing the front door. Walter stood in the porch and knocked. He brushed his jacket, suddenly noticing how worn his shoes were, and nervous as he had not thought to be, walking up Wimbledon Hill from the station, seeing a magnolia, white and full, getting hungry.

A marmalade cat came round the side of the house. Footsteps approached the front door: he knew they were Sarah's. She opened it and the cat made a little sound, brushing past him, tail held high as he trotted down the hall.

'I wasn't answering the door to you,' Sarah told him. She smiled at Walter. 'You found it, well done. Come in.'

The hall was broad and deep and tiled in mosaic. Light fell from a tall window halfway up the stairs. He could smell roast beef, polish, cigar smoke.

'We're all in here,' she told him, and he followed her into the drawing room. Paintings, a piano, French windows, a fire. Her father sorting magazines on a table, his cigar beside him; her mother putting aside her book.

'This is Walter Cox,' said Sarah.

He hesitated, then felt himself give a little bow, something he had never done in his life. Everyone laughed.

'Come, come.' Geoffrey Lewis crossed the room. They shook hands, he introduced his wife. 'Will you have a glass of sherry?'

They stood at the open French windows and admired the tulip tree. Or was it a magnolia? Walter said he'd seen a fine example, walking up here, and they speculated on whose it might be. The cat leapt into the chair vacated by Sarah's mother, and was chided but not removed. Walter learned his name, and then forgot it. Also his age. He was offered a cigar and refused politely; he stood with his glass of sherry, something he couldn't remember ever drinking, and answered questions about the Slade, and how he was finding it: they had heard so much about him. Sarah bent to the strap of her shoe. And about the class, of course, said her mother. They all took a turn round the garden. The daffodils were over, the bluebells just in bud.

'I should like to hear about your days at the Slade, sir,' Walter said to Sarah's father.

'Oh, you will,' said her mother.

Clouds blew over the tulip tree, a blackbird sang; inside, a carriage clock chimed the quarter-hour.

'If you'll excuse me,' said Sarah's mother. 'Lunch won't be long.'

'Perhaps you would like to see my studio?' asked Mr Lewis.

'After lunch,' said Sarah.

'Won't you young people want a walk after lunch?'

Walter and Sarah looked at one another.

'It's very pleasant on the Common,' she said.

'Come on up,' said her father. 'I'd like to have a young eye.'

Sarah went to lend a hand in the kitchen. Walter and her father climbed the stairs. Everything felt solid and well cared for. The chest beneath a window on the landing shone, and tulips stood in a jug upon it; rugs were thick and curtains generous.

'What a lovely house.' He could not think that he had ever been anywhere like it.

'You must thank my wife for that. Now then.' They had come to the top of the small second flight, and Sarah's father was leaning against the banister to catch his breath. 'Come in and see what you think.'

Two sash windows overlooked the street, a cluttered table between them. The studio was large, but it was workmanlike and plain, the boards bare, the walls unpapered, with canvases stacked against them, a few hung in frames here and there. An easel stood at either end: he looked from one to the other.

'You see, I like to be able to move about a bit – turn to something else. I don't like to get stale.'

Walter nodded. He looked at an interior in blue and grey: the corner of the drawing room, he realised, with the fall of curtain to the garden, the mantelpiece and clock, the chair with the sleeping cat. He walked over to the further easel: a little still life, of fruit in a bowl. They were gentle and accomplished pieces, and no one would have known that the war had ever happened.

'What do you think?'

'I like them,' said Walter carefully. He moved back, moved closer.

'Have a look round, don't be shy. Put things up on here if you like.' He began to clear a space on the table, dropping tubes of oils into the lid of a box.

Walter bent down and looked through the unframed paintings propped against the wall. Smoke rose from bonfires in suburban gardens, a young girl played the piano, cornflowers stood in a jug. Then he saw the portrait.

He lifted it out, and held it before him. Sarah looked back at him – no, beyond him, away and out of the picture. She was in evening dress – midnight blue, a string of pearls, her hair piled high.

'Ah, yes. I'm putting that in for the winter show at the RA. I showed it at the last New English – bring it over here, why don't you?'

Walter propped it on the table and stood back.

'It's very good.'

And why? Because the midnight blue was so deep and satiny, so rich against skin and glistening pearls.

'After Sargent, of course,' said her father beside him, 'but still – I hope I've done justice to his influence.'

'I like it very much.'

And why? Because the portrait showed more of Sarah than he knew of her, and more, perhaps, than she knew of herself: distinctive, dreaming – of what?

The gong sounded, deep within the house.

'By the way,' said Geoffrey Lewis, touching his arm as they made their way out, 'Sarah has told us about your brother. We're so sorry.'

'Thank you.'

'We needn't speak of it again.'

He and Sarah walked over Wimbledon Common. Sunday afternoon in a London suburb, the second spring after the war. Nurses pushed perambulators on the paths beneath the chestnut trees; a father pushed his son in a bath chair. Young women strolled arm in arm; young men lurched past without an arm, the jacket pinned across the chest; they hopped on crutches with half a leg missing, the trouser pinned above the knee. Walter and Sarah looked, and looked away. They passed a couple wrapped in each other's arms on a bench: her face beneath a little hat pressed against his jacket, his brilliantined head bent low. Children pulled toys on leashes, the wind blew in and out of the trees.

'Walter?'

'Yes?'

'Nothing.'

He drew her hand through his arm; briefly her head inclined against his shoulder. He remembered descending the stairs for lunch, his head full of the portrait – dark eyes, glistening necklace, the deep blue folds of satin – and of seeing her waiting for them in the hall, looking up, her eyes meeting his, and looking away again.

Her hand was warm in the crook of his arm. They walked on, taking the sun. He thought of the way his mind had been filled with Nina, how his days at the Slade had begun to revolve around whether he might or might not see her, how he had followed her, dreamed of a strand of pale hair on his cheek, her hands in his, her mouth receiving, at last, his kiss.

'Walter? You're very quiet.'

'I'm sorry. You must think me rude.'

'Not at all. Do you want to tell me what you're thinking about?'

He flushed. 'No. Forgive me, that must seem –'

'It's all right. Was lunch very dull?'

He turned to look at her. 'No, no, of course not. It was so kind of your parents to invite me, and you seem so close. It makes for very pleasant company.'

'We are close,' said Sarah, 'but it's time I left home, don't you think? I've applied for a place in Hall next term. And I want to change my course.'

'Change your course? Why? What do you want to do?'

'I don't think I'm a painter, not really. I can draw – that's my only gift. That's why Tonks puts up with me. And I don't know, but perhaps after being amongst painters all my life, I just want to do something different. There's a very good wood-engraving course at the School, did you know?'

He shook his head.

'It's run by Mr White. I've been to see him and he's going to let me try my hand, give me one or two lessons, to see how I like it. I think I shall. Just being in the class with all the tools and the wood, and the press – I loved it. I haven't told my parents yet, but I keep looking at all my old childhood books, all the illustrations. And Bewick, of course, and Lucien Pissarro. I feel quite excited.' She broke off. 'I'm talking too much.'

'Not in the least – it all sounds marvellous. It's something I've never known anything about.'

'Well, perhaps I can show you, once I get going.'

'I'd like that,' said Walter. 'But leaving your home – do you really want to do that? You're so cherished, everything's so comfortable. Why should you want to leave?'

'Oh, Walter! Exactly for those reasons. I love my parents dearly, but . . .'

'Yes, of course,' he said. 'Of course. It's only that I am sometimes so homesick myself. My landlady is very kind, but – that's why it's so nice being here now.'

'Having a good lunch.'

'Not just that, you goose. Being part of a family.' He stepped aside as a child ran past them. Sarah's hand in his arm briefly tightened. 'Anyway,' he said, as they walked on, 'of course I understand. You want to be with people your own age.' How pompous that sounded.

'I want to be with you,' said Sarah.

For a moment he thought he had not heard this: then he saw her colour, and look away. He stopped on the path and unknown feelings flooded him.

'Oh, Sarah.'

Years later, up in his studio, entirely unable to work, listening to the whirr of the mower on the churchyard grass, Fred Eaves heaving

71

the machine in and out amongst the graves, this was another occasion on which Walter looked back, his head in his hands.

Two men coming out of the British Museum on a cold spring evening, beginning the most important friendship of their lives.

He and Sarah, on a warm spring afternoon, people walking past them, on the path beneath the chestnuts, the stretch of the Common on either side of them, dogs racing over the grass and barking, and the moment entirely filled with the tension between them: her declaration, his rush of longing, possibilities of everything he might dream of opening up before him. The image of Nina, who would not be relinquished.

Sarah was scarlet. She took her hand from his arm. 'I shouldn't have said that.'

'No – no – don't think that, please.' He took her hand again, drew her to face him. He said, 'I am honoured. I am – you are so beautiful. It's only that – we're so young. And I'm quite inexperienced – I don't know my mind in these things. Forgive me.'

'Please,' said Sarah. 'Please – forget what I said. Let's talk about something else.' Her hand in his was trembling. He raised it to his lips, and brushed it, and released it. Her eyes filled.

'Forgive me,' he said again.

'There is nothing to forgive.' She swallowed. She wiped her cheek. 'I think perhaps we should be getting home.'

'Of course.'

They walked back, taking the path to the hill. Someone was flying a kite, and they talked about that for a while.

Lies by omission. Am I a fool? Walter asked himself, as the train puffed out of the station. He had said goodbye to Sarah at the garden gate, after tea by the fire – 'No, please, you must stay for tea. My parents will think it strange if you don't,' she had said, when they came back from the Common. So they all talked about the price of coal and how good the Madeira cake was, as the sky beyond the French windows darkened, the curtains were drawn and the room, beyond the small reach of the fire, grew chilly.

Sarah put her jacket on, to see Walter down the path; she shivered as they came to the gate.

'Please don't catch cold,' he said, as she clicked it open. He took her hand. 'May I see you again?'

'Oh, I'm sure we shall see each other,' she said, and he knew that the moments of longing and fear in the sunlit afternoon were over, and that he had lost her.

The gate clicked shut, she walked back to the house. Lozenges of light from the stained-glass doorway fell on to the tiles in the porch: he watched her go quickly inside and close the door, and he pictured her, the only child of elderly parents, going back to the drawing room, taking up her book. Was it like that? He walked down the hill in the dusk. Inside the station waiting room he pulled out his own book, but could not read it. The stove was unlit, a Sunday evening economy: he rubbed his hands. A couple of other fellows came in and sat smoking; he heard the bells for Evensong. By the time the train came in his spirits were lower than he could remember for months.

Am I a fool? He leaned back against the grimy upholstery and thought of his mean little room in Camden, with the painting of his mother, sewing in the orchard beneath the apple trees, propped above the fire. He thought of his sisters, his sisters' friends, girls he'd been to school with. None of them was in the least like Sarah. Or Nina.

They went through suburban stations, gardens fenced off from the track. At Waterloo, where long trains of men setting off for the Front had pulled out, and long trains of wounded pulled in. He walked across the concourse to the windswept steps and almost turned back, to ask for the next stopping train to Ashford. If he'd missed the last bus out to the villages, he could walk.

I want to go home, he thought miserably, as rain began to slant across the steps. He stepped back beneath the portico, hearing the low notes of riverboats, sounding from the Thames, and the hiss of the trains in the station behind him. He saw himself getting out at Ashford, the bus gone from the market square, the long walk out to Asham's Mill, with every turning known to him, every stile and gate.

Then the sharp slant of April rain had gone again, and the gaslit street below him shone in the wet. He saw an omnibus approach on the far side and hurried down towards it. If it went to Euston he would call on Euan. Pipe smoke and a pint. He dashed across the wet street, waving.

*Camden, NW*
*25th April, 1920*

*Dear Mr and Mrs Lewis,*
*I write to thank you for your kindness today. It was a great pleasure to*

*meet you, and luncheon was quite delicious. I was also very glad to have the opportunity to see some of your work, Mr Lewis: thank you for that honour. I much admire the portrait of Sarah.*

    *The journey home was uneventful. Thank you once again for your hospitality.*

*Yours very sincerely,*
*Walter Cox*

He blotted and sealed it and set it aside.

    *Dear Sarah,*

What could he say?

    *Dear Sarah,*

The last of the coal had gone; he had bought none from his landlady since the end of March. Euan had not been at home, and the wait for a tram up from Euston had chilled him.

    *Dear Sarah,*
    *The last of the coal has gone. I remind myself that it is spring, and should not feel like winter, but it does. The house is cold, and the street is dark, and I fear that I distressed you today, and that distresses me . . .*

Should he say these things? Didn't that make it worse?

    *Dear Sarah,*
    *Thank you for a lovely afternoon . . .*

    *Dear Sarah,*
    *Thank you so much for inviting me today. I hope very much that our friendship, which I have enjoyed and valued, may continue . . .*

Pompous fool. He tore each sheet up, and stood at the window, drawing back the curtains. The rooftops of Camden stretched away, street after narrow street.

*Dear Sarah,*
*I don't want to lose you . . .*

In the end he sent nothing, dropping the letter to her parents into the box on his way out the next morning and cycling away down the street. After last night's showers the air felt clean and fresh. He would see her – he would try to put things right.

And how was he to do that? he wondered, as he caught up with her on the stairs between classes, and she said only, 'Please – it was nothing. I've forgotten all about it,' and caught sight of Henry and called him, and went off to lunch without a backward glance.

# Summer

Summer came. Walter moved into the Life Class. Sarah moved, too, to her wood-engraving, he supposed. The classes were on different days, and though both were held down in the rambling basement, he hardly ever saw her.

For the first time since his days with The Buffs, Walter now found himself entirely amongst men. As demobilisation had proceeded, the School had filled up: suddenly there were far more men than women. Most, like Henry Marsh, had attended public schools: unlike Henry – who would follow him to the Life Class 'when Lord God Almighty gives the word' – many were standoffish and cool. They all shared the same, pre-war references – to London clubs and restaurants, to Rugby and Latin and Greek; they'd shared, more recently and importantly, life in dugouts, action, responsibility, fear. They were bonded by class, education and the experience of war, and every time Walter opened his mouth he felt how set apart he was.

For all that, he liked the atmosphere in the Life Class, which was serious and intent. Like Euan, a number of the men had attended the Slade before the war – something else which they shared and which excluded Walter. They had lost time, and were keen to make up for it. If Walter could not share jokes or take part in much conversation in the breaks, he gradually found he was able to lose himself in the work. Besides, he longed to be painting again, and to paint you had to be able to draw, as Tonks continually reminded them.

'I fear I am a hurdy-gurdy with only two tunes,' he announced to the class one afternoon. 'Construction and proportion.' He paced up and down amongst the easels. Walter had last seen him just before Easter: casting a cool eye over his drawings from the Antique, offered for admission to the Life Class, eliciting the thin response, 'You'll do.'

Walter gathered the drawings up again, and replaced them in his portfolio. 'Thank you, sir.' He made for the office door.

'We'll make an artist of you yet,' said Tonks, looking up from his blotting pad. 'Of course, a good artist is someone who would distinguish himself in any profession. Don't you agree?'

'Yes, sir,' said Walter, and closed the door behind him. He had no idea what other profession he might have followed, and now, hearing the quiet clipped voice in the class, he felt as nervous as in his first weeks.

On the dais, the model sat motionless, a thin girl on a stool, with her legs crossed and her gown draped on the screen behind her. Her arms were loosely clasped at the wrists, her hands upon her knees: small-breasted and narrow-shouldered, her head carefully placed at an angle, she looked frail and vulnerable, and Walter's drawing, in response to his sense of this unclothed girl, was light and delicate.

Footsteps came down the boards towards him.

'May I?' Tonks stood beside the easel, his eyes narrowed. 'Please, Mr Cox.' He made a gesture for Walter to continue. He continued. Her head was so, and the slender neck was so . . .

'Very nice,' said Tonks coolly. 'And how do you suppose this young lady is to walk, when she so chooses?'

'Sir?' Walter glanced from model to paper, back to the model, as still as marble.

'I am talking about her legs, Mr Cox, and the weight she is to place upon them. She is slender, but you have made her a wraith, have you not? Think of Degas, think of those dancers! Construction.' He pointed to the hips. 'And proportion.' He sketched out the length between hip and knee, knee and ankle. 'Is this a human body or a doll?'

Walter nodded. He could see it all: the weakness, the insubstantial frame. Had he learned nothing?

'The hands, however,' said Tonks, his pencil upon them, 'the hands are rather good.' He glanced at his watch. 'Rest, model!'

The girl on the dais reached up for her gown. Naked, she was a model, someone whom Walter somehow regarded with detachment. He sensed that for Tonks this impersonality was complete. But for him, in her dark patterned gown, and little slippers, she was a woman, now, and he blushed as she slipped past him, and out to the door. Along the corridor was the women's tea room, the models' bathroom and retreat. You could hear the hiss of the urn, and running water bang in the pipes, as the door swung to and fro. He looked at his work, and around him the murmur of conversation grew to a buzz, as Tonks walked out again. No Henry to wink at him. No Gwen to comfort, for far worse treatment. No Sarah.

The break was for fifteen minutes, taken every hour. In the mornings, or early afternoon, few people bothered to leave the room – perhaps a quick visit to the lavatory, or a cigarette out in the quad. But by late afternoon they were tiring, and there was often a general exodus. And now it was summer, the trees full and the grass cut, and talk of picnics. Once you were in the Life Class, the breaks and lunch-hours were also the only chance you had to speak to the opposite sex, though woe betide you if Tonks saw a man and a woman talking in the corridors. A cough, a stiff nod – that was enough to have his feelings made plain.

Walter stayed behind, as the others went out with their friends. He looked at the two-dimensional girl on his sheet of paper and felt how weak she was, what a poor weak thing when set against the grace and depth of the head in the Antique Room, which he had grown to understand, and cherish. Was that because the model was flesh and blood, and he, in his innocence, was more confident with marble?

How feeble, how pitiful, if that were so.

The door had been left open, and he could hear, from the women's rooms along the corridor, the chink of cups and a burst of laughter. He pictured them all: the provider of tea, as everyone called her, stirring a vast enamel pot; the urn with its clouds of steam; the cakes on the oilcloth; gossip and confidences. Henry had said once that that was where the shy ones went, to get away from the men and feel safe. That was where they took refuge with their tears, when Tonks was at his vilest. Did Sarah go there now, to avoid him after lectures? Did Nina share secrets, and try on clothes?

Who knew?

More laughter came along the corridor.

Walter got up from his easel. He said aloud, 'The next time I see her, I shall ask her out.' Good. Very well, then. He strode to the door and flung it wide. Nina, passing it, gave a little gasp. Walter went scarlet.

'You quite startled me,' she said, collecting herself, and then, seeing his colour, gave her cool smile. 'It seems I startled you, too.'

'I was – I was hoping to see you,' Walter stammered.

'Really?' She raised her eyebrow. 'Why was that?'

Footsteps came clattering down the stairs. Everyone was coming back to the class, and here was Tonks, his hand on the banister, his glance raking the corridor, sweeping them all along.

'Miss Frith? Has something detained you?' His tone was glacial. 'Mr Cox – I believe that the class has reconvened.'

He held the door open, the model reappeared from the tea room, everyone trooped inside. 'Shall we proceed?' The model climbed on to the dais, the door was closed with a click.

Walter cycled round Fitzroy Square. A warm May evening, with people out and about, taking a turn in the gardens, smoking and reading the evening papers. Windows open, a gramophone playing *Missouri Waltz* – you heard it everywhere, tinny and bright.

Walter dismounted. He wheeled the bicycle up to Nina's house and leaned it against the railings. Someone looked out of the basement window; he heard a canary chirrup. He cleared his throat, he walked up the three stone steps to the door. Faded nameplates, some more recent. Miss Nina Frith. He rang, he waited, wiping his hands on his trousers, his heart thumping.

Across the square the record had wound right down. Above him a voice called out quickly, 'Hello?'

Walter stepped back. He looked up, saw Nina on the balcony, gazing down at him. She was wearing a dressing gown, dark and silky, tied at the waist. Against it her hair was like moonlight on a lake. He swallowed.

'I hope I'm not disturbing you.' He cleared his throat. 'I was passing – I wondered if you were free.'

He looked up at her, she looked down at him. He stepped back again, saw her tall narrow windows open to the summer evening, the fall of muslin, the darkness of the room beyond.

'Well . . . could you wait a moment?'

'Of course.'

She moved inside; he saw the muslin curtains part and fall back. He turned to look out over the square again, filling with deep shadow as the sun began to sink. Someone was laughing beneath the trees in the gardens, beyond the dark curve of railing. He saw the glow of a cigarette.

*I am here. She is coming down to meet me.* He could not think beyond this, and he stood at the foot of the stone steps watching the sudden arrival of a flock of starlings, swooping down into the trees and settling, until the door opened behind him and he turned and saw her.

She had changed into a dress and jacket, she carried a little black bag.

'Where are we going?'

'Well, I –'

'And how do you know my address?' She came down the steps towards him. 'Perhaps I should have asked that before I came down, only it seems rather unbecoming, somehow, talking from the balcony to someone one hardly knows.'

'I – yes, yes, of course. Forgive me, I've been unpardonably rude.'

'Oh, I wouldn't say that. Not unpardonably.' She glanced at his bicycle. 'What are you going to do with that?'

'Well . . .'

'If you leave it out here someone will steal it. Would you like to put it in the hall?'

He nodded dumbly. She unlocked the door again, and he bumped it up the steps. 'Of course,' said Nina, standing well back, 'someone may steal it from here, too, but perhaps there's a little less chance. Just prop it up there, that's it.'

He leaned it against the dado, feeling a fool. The hall was enormous, and not very clean. A door at the far end was opened.

'Ah, Miss Frith. You have a visitor?'

'Yes,' said Nina. 'Goodbye.'

She closed the front door smartly, almost on Walter's heels.

'My landlord. A terrible bore. Now, then – where are you taking me?'

Visions of Charlotte Street swam before him. He had no idea.

'Bertorelli's,' he said suddenly, recalling it. 'Would that suit you?'

'Very nice. Have you booked?'

'You have a reservation, sir?'

He lied, as he had lied to Nina, professing surprise that his name was not in the book; he glanced up at full tables, candlelight, hurrying waiters.

'Are you sure? Is there no room at all?'

The manager looked at his jacket and fraying cuffs.

'Two poor young artists?' Nina pleaded. 'One day we'll be famous.'

'I'll see what I can do.'

He squeezed them into a corner at the back, brought a rose and a candle.

'Angelic man.' She looked up at him with a dazzling smile. 'All we need now is a supper for sixpence.'

He pressed his hands together. 'Liver and bacon? Mushrooms? Half a bottle of claret?'

'Perfect.' She looked at Walter. 'Do you agree?'

'Entirely,' said Walter. 'You are extraordinary,' he added, when the manager had left them.

Nina unfolded her napkin. 'You still haven't explained how you know where I live.'

He hesitated. 'Someone told me.'

'Who?'

He paused again. 'Sarah Lewis.'

'Sarah? Why? Did you ask her?'

'Yes.'

'And she gave you my address? That rather surprises me.'

Walter flushed, uncomfortable because he was evading the truth, uncomfortable because he was implicating Sarah.

'No, not exactly. She told me you lived in Fitzroy Square, but that was all. And then – then I followed you.'

Nina frowned. 'I don't think I like that.'

'I know,' said Walter. 'It sounds dreadful. It's only that –'

Liver and bacon and mushrooms arrived, set down with a flourish.

'Only that –' Nina persisted.

What could he say?

'Well, you know what it's like at the School. You see people, and they're busy, or in another class, or you get interrupted.'

The room was full of conversation, the clinking of china, the smell of good food.

'Tonks is a bully,' said Nina, spearing a mushroom.

'Do you really think so?'

'Don't you?'

'Yes, I suppose so. He's much worse with women, it seems.'

'I wonder why,' Nina said coolly. 'And it isn't just that – he's so dated, so out of touch.' She put her hand to her brow. ' "All this talk of Cubism is killing me – I shall resign." '

Walter laughed. 'Does he say that?'

'He's always saying it. "I'd rather be damned with Steer and Turner than go to heaven with Matisse and Picasso." Such rot. Such nonsense. Does he want us to paint young girls trying on hats for ever? Can't he see that Matisse and Picasso are gods?'

'Is that what you think? Do you really admire them?'

Nina gave him a look. 'Perhaps to the provincial eye they may seem rather advanced.'

Walter flushed. 'I wouldn't call Tonks provincial.'

'But he didn't train in Paris. He came to painting late. He's a dyed-in-the-wool conservative surgeon, Walter. He doesn't understand modern thinking. Or modern women. Sometimes I think he should have stayed a surgeon, and left us all in peace.'

Walter knew he was out of his depth: something in him, too, was being challenged. What did he know of Paris? Or of women at all?

He said carefully, 'It isn't just girls in hat shops, is it?' He poured her another glass of wine. Did he look like a man of the world? 'Tonks did some fine war paintings – I went to see them last year. And his drawings of the wounded . . .'

'Oh, please don't start talking about the bloody war!'

Walter was shocked. Nina saw it.

'Sorry,' she said quickly. 'Perhaps I shouldn't have said that. But really, it's time to get on now, isn't it? We're young, we're alive. I want to *be* alive!' For a moment a shadow crossed her lovely face. 'I want to think about the future,' she said, and the shadow was gone in an enquiring smile. 'Surely you must, too?'

'Yes,' said Walter. 'Yes, of course. It's just that . . .' But he couldn't tell her that the past was always with him. Instead, he asked her, as Euan had asked him, 'And what is your ambition?'

'Ambition?' Nina gave a little laugh, and at once he felt a fool. 'That sounds frightfully serious.'

'But you're talented,' he said. 'I'm sure you are.'

'Tonks doesn't think so. He wants me out.'

He didn't know what to say to that.

'I have an eye,' said Nina. 'I don't know if I have a gift. Anyway,' she dabbed at her mouth with a snowy napkin, 'that's quite enough questions for now. You still haven't told me why you were following me.' She darted a mischievous glance above the napkin. 'A girl could quite take against that, you know.'

Had she forgiven him, or was she making up for callousness? To speak of the war as she had done –

She reached across the table, touched his hand. He had a sudden memory of seeing her do so, in just the same manner, to a fellow in a yellow scarf one lunch-hour in the refectory. Months ago. How hard he had found it to observe that gesture then. And now –

'It's only that . . .' He knew that if he made a declaration he was lost. He knew, too, in a chilling moment, that there was something about Nina that he didn't even like. And yet – hadn't he thought about her for months? Hadn't she turned his heart quite over, seeing her stand on the steps of the School, glimpsing her run up the stairs, hearing her footsteps? Shouldn't he seize the moment, embrace the future boldly? Take a risk?

'I think you're so lovely,' he heard himself say, and knew, even as he spoke it, that this was not entirely true. He looked at her, gazing at him across the table through the candlelight, her expression softening. 'I think of you all the time.' That was true.

'Silly boy.' Her hand was in his. He lifted it to his lips. He thought of Sarah, on the path beneath the trees, the spring wind rippling the grass across the Common, her serious face, her sadness. He thought, This isn't right, and yet – this is the moment I've dreamed of.

'Dear silly boy,' said Nina, pressing his hand in hers.

They walked along Charlotte Street, their arms about each other. Candles glowed in café windows, people came laughing out on to the pavement, piled into taxis. The air smelt of scent and cigars.

'You see?' said Nina. 'People are happy now.'

'I know.' His hand on her waist tightened beneath the little jacket. 'Are you happy?'

'Yes. And you?'

'Oh, yes.'

The moon hung high above Fitzroy Square. Dance tunes floated out of upper windows: *That Naughty Waltz*, *Three O'clock in the Morning*.

'I shan't ask you in,' said Nina.

'No, no, of course not.' It hadn't occurred to him that she might.

But the gates to the garden were still unlocked, and shadowy figures moved amongst the trees.

'Will you come and sit with me for a moment?' Walter asked.

'Only a moment?'

They found a bench on the north side; they could see Nina's house beyond the shrubbery, the glow of the fanlights all along the street.

'Aren't you going to kiss me?'

His arms went round her, he drew her to him; his mouth on her mouth, silken hair against his face, in his fingers, her lips parting, unknown sensations, everything else forgotten.

Nina wanted a life that was vivid and urgent. She leaned on her balcony in Fitzroy Square, watching the bruise-coloured clouds of a summer storm gather above the trees, and the bright hard spatter of the first drops on the pavement. She held out bare arms, and the rain fell faster, pattering on to the dusty leaves. The clouds burst open. Thunder rolled. Nina lifted her face to it all, her arms held wide and her hair soaking. Below, people raced for doorways, slammed down windows, but she, as the rain beat down and down, threw her head back, let it drench her. Behind her, the double doors of her window swung back and forth, and the rain swept through the muslin curtains.

A clap of thunder, gooseflesh all along her bare arms, the square lit up by lightning. Nina returned to her room, stood at the long narrow windows in her dressing gown, wet muslin curtains draped over a chair to dry. She watched the storm shake the trees, heard casements rattle, saw lights go down. Gradually it lessened. The thunder rolled away, the rain diminished: doors were opened, puddles shone. Nina, in her dark silky dressing gown, felt in her purse for a shilling, and went to feed the meter on the landing. She gathered her sponge bag and towel and went out along the corridor. One or two doors were half-open: she heard the hiss of a gas ring, caught sight of Lily Barnes taking her hair down.

The bathroom was cold and high, with cracked linoleum, and too many people shared it. Nina shook in the scouring powder, and scrubbed at worn enamel. When you turned on the mildewed taps it sounded as if the room was going to explode. The geyser roared, hot water spurted and gushed, and the pipes banged for an hour afterwards. Nina, after the storm, lay in the great plain masculine bath, swishing her legs, making ripples. She could hear the last of the rain in the drainpipes, the drip of the trees.

I am a water creature, she told herself. I am a mermaid now: naked to the waist and cold cold silver all beneath. When Walter comes, I shall tease him and tease him.

She dried herself, and left a trail of scented powder, all the way back to her room.

Tinny little waltzes from someone else's gramophone, the shadowy romance of lacquered screens. One hid Nina's makeshift kitchen, and one her bed: sitting with her on his lap in the worn leather armchair, Walter could make out the softness of a pillow, the tasselled edge of a silken shawl. A painting, were he calm enough to paint it: just that corner, the vertical of the screen, the glimpse of square white pillow, the softening fall of tassels and silk, the promise of an intimate embrace –

He drew her to him again, parting her lips with a finger, as she had taught him to do, slipping it between them, feeling the sharp little press of her teeth, closing his eyes, swept away on a tide of longing.

'Please, please . . .'

Her midnight-blue dressing gown hung from a corner of the screen beside her bed. He longed for her to wear it again, as she had done when she leaned out to him from her balcony; he lay in his own narrow bed in Camden and dreamed of her silken hair falling like moonlight upon its darkness, his hands running over the slippery fall of satin, slowly untying the sash, revealing her pale and perfect nakedness.

'Oh, Nina, Nina . . .'

On lengthening May evenings, the doors to the balcony open, the muslin curtains stirring in the breeze, they danced to the strains of love songs, drifting out over the square, and as the records wound slowly down Nina laid her head on Walter's shoulder and let him lead her to the deep recess of the chair and embrace her, as if it were all she had ever wanted. She opened her mouth like a flower beneath his own, she leaned back in his arms like a stem in the wind.

'You're perfect,' Walter whispered, feeling hard little nipples, and soft little breasts. He unfastened tiny buttons, slipped his fingers inside scalloped lace, drew down a satin strap and cupped her, feeling himself grow hard with longing. 'Let me kiss you there . . . and there . . . Is this what you like?'

'Yes,' said Nina, but her voice was suddenly cool, and she moved to sit up in his arms, and slipped off his lap. She stood up, straightening her dress, fastening the row of buttons.

'What's happened? What's wrong?' He was shocked and unsettled.
'Nothing.'

'But—'

'You mustn't get carried away,' said Nina lightly, and reached to
the mantelpiece for her cigarette box. She opened and offered it; he
shook his head, watching her strike a match sharply, and flick it into
the empty grate. 'That's better.' She inhaled deeply, leaning against
black marble. Invitation cards stood upon it: the pleasure of her
company was requested here and there all over London, but Walter
was not invited to accompany her.

He leaned back in the armchair, trying to calm himself. Smoke
curled into the last of the evening sun streaming in through dusty
glass and muslin; Nina's long mirror reflected the depths of the
room, its fading fern paper, and crumbling cornice. She stood before
the glass. She licked a finger and smoothed each eyebrow; she
reached for her brush and ran it through her hair.

'There.' She turned to smile at him. 'Shall we have something to
eat?'

Walter shook his head, and closed his eyes. What had he done
wrong?

He felt her light touch on his brow, and a swift soft kiss, opened
his eyes again and reached for her, but she had already moved away.

'You're a dear sweet boy,' she said, picking up her cigarette again,
'but you mustn't be too serious.'

He got to his feet. 'But now that we're courting—'

'Courting!' Nina was laughing at him. 'Is that what you call it?'

He was bemused. Courting was how his sisters had always spoken
of it, hadn't they? Courting or walking out. 'What would you call it,
then?' he asked her, hearing his voice sound sharper than he wanted.

'I'd call it having fun,' said Nina.

He took her hand. 'And are you never serious?'

For a moment Nina's face clouded. Then she said, 'No, not unless
I have to be.' She drew on her cigarette. 'That's quite enough
questions. I think you should go.'

Walter walked home in the summer dusk. London churches chimed
the quarter-hours: in Euston, in Mornington Crescent, in Camden
Town. He watched cloud gathering over spire and rooftop and
thought of the steady, unanswered notes which rang from the church

tower at home, in Asham's Mill, where he had never known such turmoil might be possible. He thought, I shall not call on her again.

But at home in the cheerless little room he undressed and fell into bed with a groan, feeling Nina's hair brush his face, and her lovely mouth open so willingly beneath his touch. He heard her sigh and move closer, closer – surely she wanted him? Surely she would not invite him up to her room if she did not want him? He dreamed of her naked beneath him, in her soft white bed behind the lacquered screen, and he came, then, alone on his own iron bedstead, and felt relief and shame wash through him.

Afterwards, he lay quite still, hearing the trains come and go, re-living the evening more calmly. The little portrait of his mother gleamed softly in the light of the rising moon, seeping through thin curtains. He lay there looking at it, and at the framed photograph of John William, thinking: I came to London to learn to be an artist. I'm losing all sense of that. He turned the lumpy pillow and slept at last, dreaming all night of Nina and coming again in his sleep.

Next morning, when he saw her at the School, crossing the quad as he arrived, he stopped, and waited until she had climbed the steps and gone inside. Then he wheeled his bicycle up the path between the trees. The air was alive with birds, it was going to be a beautiful day. And I shall keep to the Life Room, thought Walter, and stay there working until the light goes, and I need never see her at all. He dropped the padlock in his pocket and walked back to the entrance, his heart pounding.

Nina was waiting for him, just inside. She touched his arm, and he leapt.

'Silly boy.' She kissed his cheek with affection. 'Are you cross with me?'

'No, of course not.' People were coming and going all round them; he caught sight of Sarah, books beneath her arm, and flushed.

'I'm sure you must be,' said Nina. 'I was horrid, asking you to go. Sometimes I just get into a mood, that's all. Can you forgive me?'

'Yes, yes, of course.'

'And shall we see each other again?'

He looked at her, and her gaze, at this early hour of the morning, with everyone making their way to the studios, was as intimate as if they lay in bed in each other's arms.

'Yes,' said Walter. 'Yes, of course we will.'

☆

Of course, of course . . . He would take her to tea after classes, to supper in candlelit cafés, and walk her home, and kiss her on the doorstep, the square behind them full of courting couples, laughing beneath the trees. Was that not what they were, a courting couple?

'Would you like to come in?' asked Nina, not every time, but sometimes.

'You know I would.'

Into the echoing hall, up the unswept staircase, watching her unlock the door to her room and taking her into his arms almost before she had closed it, kissing and kissing her, everything sweet and familiar between them again, until . . .

'That's enough. Walter – I said that's enough.'

Was she seeing anyone else? Why? Would he mind? Of course he would mind. Did she not want him to mind?

'I've told you – I want to have fun.'

May slipped into June. Nina left her balcony windows open all day, came home from the School to change before going out again, walked up the baking steps and entered the shadowy hall. She took off her straw hat and fanned herself.

'Miss Frith. You're looking so well these days.' Out came Mr Schnecburger, the damn bird chirping behind him.

'I have put his cage in the garden now, he is enjoying the sun – like you. I was so anxious for you last year, but now . . .'

'Yes,' said Nina. 'Now I'm enjoying life again.'

'You have a young man, I think. Sometimes I hear you dancing.' He was moving towards her, smiling. 'I used to like dancing myself, when my wife and I were young. Now it is lonely without her.'

'I'm so sorry,' said Nina. 'I must go now, do excuse me.' She ran up the stairs.

The gramophone was starting up in Number 11 – crackling 'Margie', then 'The Wang Wang Blues'. Heavenly bright little tune, tap tap tapping, everything fast and bright, London tap tap tapping into the Twenties, with dances at the Slade, Tonks lending out the models' skirts for the summer ball, layers of taffeta, little tasselled slippers and a Turkish cigarette . . .

Nina slipped her clothes off, slipped into her satin dressing gown. She made tea on her sputtering gas ring and lay in her armchair, smoking. Walter's face, so intent and yearning, swam before her, and swam away again. Let him lose his heart if he will, thought Nina, blowing soft clouds of smoke into the room.

Hot days, and endless summer nights, dancing in the quad beneath the silver moon, Tonks smoking on the steps, being nice to her for once; foxtrots from the open windows, champagne corks rolling down the paths, kissing and kissing beneath the trees – Henry and somebody else she couldn't remember, and a man she had always wanted to ask her, and Walter cross with her, turning his back, silly boy. It was summer, it was the *ball* –

Dew on the grass at four in the morning and home holding hands with a nice young medic, kissing on the doorstep, dawn light breaking, leaning on the doorway, hands all over her – no no no – drunk and laughing – come on, come on – stubble grazing her, breath all over her – no, that's enough – please, please – fumble for the keys – come on, Nina . . .

*No.*

Slam of the door.

Door at the end unchained and opened. Schnecburger in his dressing gown, hair sticking up and without his glasses.

– Miss Frith? Miss Frith? Something has happened?

– Nothing at all. I'm so sorry.

Carpet slippers – Are you quite sure?

– Certain, thank you. Making for the stairs, clasping the banister.

– A sigh. Chirrup of the canary. The door closed to with a click.

Fall into bed and sleep all morning.

Heartless. Heartless.

– Please, Nina, please.

– Oh, Walter.

– Please, *please*.

– You're being tiresome.

Walking home in the small hours, the moon so calm and himself so wretched. Howl of a cat, clatter of a dustbin.

– Got a light?

– No.

Women in doorways, women under the streetlamps.

– You're out late.

– You're up early.

– Fancy a quick one?

– Be like that, then.

Footsteps echoing up the street. His street, his footsteps. Trains in the goods yard, clanking through the dawn. The first lamps lit in the terraced houses. Grimy little houses. Sickert's bleak interiors.

Leaning against the door: complete exhaustion. Key in the lock.

– Mr Cox?

– Yes. Sorry.

Creeping out down the back passage. Pissing in the privy. Back across the sour little garden. Creeping up the stairs. Flinging himself on the iron bedstead.

I shall go mad if I can't have her.

# Autumn

In mid-October 1920, the miners went on strike. London transport workers joined them. A march filled Whitehall, held back by police. Lloyd George declared a state of National Emergency.

For two weeks in London it was as though the war had returned. There were no lights in shop windows, minimum lighting at night. The streets were almost empty of traffic and Walter, cycling into the School after another miserable weekend, felt as if he were riding through a ghost city. Once again, he found classes half-empty: those students or tutors who lived nearby had walked or cycled in, but those further afield were stranded without Tube or tram or omnibus. Next day, cycling up windy Gower Street, he saw Nina, holding her hat to her head as she crossed. He braked, and pulled into the pavement, his heart thumping. With the School so sparsely attended, he knew it would be impossible to avoid her, and he knew now that he must avoid her. When she disappeared through the gates, he turned and wheeled his bicycle over the road. For the first time since his arrival at the Slade, he had deliberately cut classes. As he rode away, and back towards Euston Road and Camden, and an empty day, he felt frustrated and ashamed.

Coal was rationed and expensive. People were urged to save on water. Emergency lorries brought milk in from the country, to a depot set up in Hyde Park. It grew colder. Walter, in his fireless room in Camden, wrote a letter to Nina and tore it up. He made a drawing of her room, from memory: the verticals of window and screen and fireplace, the half-hidden heap of the bed, the fall of heavy curtains framing the softness of the muslin which blew in and out at her balcony, the curve of the table where she sat smoking, looking out over the square.

*Walter, it's time you went home.*

He tore up the drawing, too. He pulled on his coat and scarf and went walking, restless and without direction. Many of the shops were closed. People looked pinched and low. He walked up towards Regent's Park. It began to rain.

The strike ended. London came back to life. Walter took Nina to tea in the Café-Bass in Charlotte Street. They ate macaroons in silence. A light shower fell and blew away; the street was lit by a vaporous autumn sun. Walter took Nina's hand. She leaned her face against their clasped fingers. Anyone seeing them would have supposed them quietly content. For a few moments it felt as if they were.

'What is to become of us?' he asked her.

She let him walk her home, as the watery afternoon slipped away into dusk. In her room she lit candles, and slipped her shoes off. They danced once again, to the sound of somebody else's gramophone.

'You need one of your own,' said Walter, holding her close.

'For Christmas?' asked Nina.

*Wyoming Lullaby* played over and over again. He kissed her lifted face.

'Where have you been?' she asked. 'I missed you.'

'Did you really?'

'A little.' She rested her head on his shoulder. The record was changed: *Three O'clock in the Morning* came through the floor-boards.

He wanted to say, 'But you have tormented me. It's easier never to see you.' He wanted to be able to say these things and be honest, and for that to be right, for things to be right between them. He wanted to ask her why she was as she was with him, and whether she cared for him at all. With someone so unpredictable, he didn't know how to go about any of this.

He said, 'I think of you all the time.'

'Still?'

She drew him to the armchair by the fireplace. Nobody had any coal, and the fire was unlit, but the candles gave the illusion of warmth. She sat on his lap and let him kiss her, deeper and deeper. He felt himself lost in the darkness of the room, the darkness of her wet wet mouth, opening and opening beneath his, their tongues exquisite together, like a dance.

He thought, This is how it should be. This is how it must always be between us.

She said, 'That's enough now,' planting a light little kiss on his cheek, twisting out of his arms.

'Nina –' He felt himself breaking.

'What?'

Walter went to see Euan. It was a cold November day, a week after the Armistice. The Unknown Soldier had been brought from France, for interment at Westminster Abbey. The streets were lined, the papers were full of it. Walter knew he should have gone home for the Armistice. He thought that if he did so he might never come back. He wrote a long letter, all about public events.

The leaves had been swept into heaps on street corners. They blew in and out of the traffic along the Euston Road. Soot and smoke from the two stations hung in the air. Walter rested his bicycle against the wall of Euan's lodgings and lifted the knocker. A window came up on the second floor. Walter stepped back. Euan looked out.

'Are you working?'

'Trying to.'

Walter hesitated. 'I'm in trouble.'

'I'll come down.'

Walter padlocked the bicycle, hearing the clock from King's Cross striking midday above the traffic. A train hooted, the front door opened. Euan stood in the dark entrance, wearing a filthy old collarless shirt and an apron covered in clay.

'Forgive me,' said Walter, dropping the padlock key in his pocket.

'No matter. I could do with a break. Come in.'

Walter followed him down the hall, past a pram and Euan's own bicycle, and up the narrow, unlit stairs. Nailed-down linoleum was coming away from the treads, the smell of boiled cabbage hung about. On the first landing a tiny window filtered dull light through a sooty pane. They went on up.

Euan had left his door open. Walter glimpsed a low fire and a lot of mess.

'Make yourself at home.'

He hung his jacket on a nail on the door, on top of Euan's. Chilled by the ride down from Camden, and with weeks of misery welling up inside him, he sank into a wicker chair on its last legs. Euan filled a tin kettle at the sink in the corner and lit the gas ring. He rinsed out a tin teapot and took down a couple of mugs from a shelf. Walter sat looking at this activity and at the room, with its old bed in the corner, the pigeon walking up and down on the windowsill, the table covered in newspaper and lumps of clay. Postcards and sketches were pinned here and there on the wall, shirts were stuffed into open drawers, Euan's pipe lay in a saucer of burned-out matches.

Walter thought of his own neat room, much smaller, which had become a place to dread.

'Well?' asked Euan, leaning against the window.

Trains hooted, leaves and smoke blew past. Walter, desolate, sat in the creaking wicker chair and didn't know where to begin.

'I see you've got coal,' he said.

'Yes.' Euan reached for his pipe. 'I take it you haven't come here to talk about the strike.'

'No.'

Euan waited. 'A woman,' he said, tamping down tobacco. 'Yes?'

'Yes.' Walter let the small warmth of the fire and the rising hiss of the kettle seep into him.

'Tell me about her.'

He tried. Euan listened.

'What shall I do?' Walter asked, as they drank strong tea with rationed sugar. 'Should I give up?'

'Probably. It doesn't sound much fun.'

'But she's . . .'

He thought of her, held in his arms, so close, so close, his mouth on hers, her heart beating hard beneath his urgent fingers –

*No.*

Slipping off his lap without warning, slipping her shoes on. Picking up her hairbrush, looking in the mirror, fastening an earring.

*Don't look so miserable, Walter.*

He put his head in his hands.

'Do you love her?'

'Sometimes I think I hate her.' Beside him a coal shifted in the ash and fell. 'What shall I do?' he said again.

'Are you working?'

'Not as I should be. Or want to. During the strike I cut classes, just so I needn't see her.'

'I thought I hadn't seen you.' Euan drew on his pipe. 'I'd give it a rest. Don't you think? She has her reasons. But it sounds to me as if you've had enough.'

Walter said nothing. Then he felt the slow tide of relief wash through him.

He said, 'I'm a virgin. Nobody ever told me – I've never been involved with a woman before. I think I thought of sex as something holy.'

There was no response to this.

'Euan? Do you – have you ever?'

Euan was tapping his pipe out, reaching for the tin of Woodbine. 'I don't think the time is right,' he said. 'I'm still recovering – I still don't sleep much.' He prised the tin open, his fingers shook, the lid flew across the room. Tobacco was everywhere. 'Look at me,' he said. 'What use am I to anyone?' And then, more seriously, 'The truth is, I want to wait. Not just because I'm trying to get better, but because it has to be the right person. And that is someone I certainly haven't found yet.'

No, thought Walter. Nor I.

He watched Euan picking up strands of tobacco, packing his pipe again. 'What are you working on?'

'I'm just messing about. Trying things out.'

'May I see?'

A pause. 'If you like.'

Walter got up and went to look at the table. Headlines from the *Chronicle* were visible amongst smears and lumps of clay: the strike, the Armistice, a picture of Stella Pankhurst. Two or three rough little figures, which he'd been in too much of a state to notice, rested here and there, dwarfed by the block of clay. He frowned, and looked at them more closely.

A man stood with arms upraised; another was crouched, as if to fire, though his hands were empty; another lay sprawled on his belly, his arms flung out. Walter saw the beginnings of another, a man on his back with his hands to his face. And he saw, lying as casually amongst the figures as a scattering of marbles, something else: dismembered limbs, a hand, two feet at right angles to one another.

There was a silence between him and Euan as he took all this in.

Then Euan said, 'My memorial.'

'Yes,' said Walter. And, unbidden, the memory of the day the telegram had come to Asham's Mill assailed him, in endless slow motion: his mother coming out to the field, he and his father sawing the fallen elm, the air sweet with sawdust. The sudden sharp glimpse of a square of yellow –

He gazed at the fallen figures.

'You're thinking of your brother,' said Euan.

'Yes,' said Walter again. And then, 'You're thinking of your men.'

'I'm always thinking of them.'

They looked at one another. Had they been women, they might have embraced. Walter thought this later, back in his room. Then the church clock on the corner struck the hour, and Euan said, 'I must go. I've a class at two.'

'So have I.'

'Come along to the studios afterwards. We'll go for a drink.'

Down in the murky light of the hall, Euan pulled the pram away from his bicycle. Banging about came from the kitchen, and the sounds of a fretful baby. Walter opened the front door; they stood on the windswept pavement.

'I'm feeling better,' he said. 'Thank you.'

'I haven't done anything.' Euan swung his leg over the crossbar and waited while Walter unfastened his own bike.

They set off up the street, gathering speed. The trees were almost bare, the air smoky, the buildings the dull brick colours of brown and pink and grey – London colours, thought Walter, knowing that they had begun to sink into him, to mean something to him. Euan, much taller, was taking the lead. He watched him, approaching Hampstead Road and slowing before he swung out into the traffic. He thought of the fallen figures, dwarfed by the great mound of clay, he thought of John William, and of the intensity and torment of his time with Nina. The wind was in his face and his eyes streamed. He stopped at the corner and stood there, flooded with feeling, one foot on the pavement, weeping.

'Are you all right, love?'

He nodded blindly to whoever was asking, willing her to go away. He fumbled for his handkerchief, blew his nose, recovered, gave a weak smile to a woman with a shopping bag and rode out towards the Euston Road, the Slade, his class.

By four the light had begun to go. Walter packed up his pencils and made his way to the sculpture studios. Down here, in the basement near the women's rooms, was where he had bumped into Nina, early in the summer: Tonks above them glacial and disapproving, he stammering and overcome.

He felt his hands begin to sweat at the possibility of meeting her again, now, after his turmoil and decision, but he did not meet her, and as he pushed open the door of the sculpture room and closed it behind him, he knew the purest relief. And in the quickening of interest which followed, hearing the chipping of stone, smelling plaster and clay, entering a territory quite unknown to him, turmoil and exhaustion were forgotten.

The last of the autumnal light was fading beyond small windows; lamps flickered between them. Plaster heads in varying stages of progress stood on plinths here and there on a dusty floor; none of the students at work upon them turned as Walter came quietly into the room, and the model on the dais was motionless: a young lad with sloping shoulders and a thin, sallow face – someone who'd been through the war and now was in need of a job. The School took on allcomers, Walter had heard, and was probably saving some from destitution. He looked around him, seeking Euan's height and presence. When he did not see him, he moved down the room towards a couple of whitewashed screens. Hammering came from beyond them. There was a silence. He stepped through the gap.

Euan was standing before a monumental piece of stone. Walter stopped dead. He felt as though he had entered a room in a museum of natural history, expecting to find fossils, or the careful arrangement of bones, and come upon a unicorn. The stone towered above him, the lights burned. Euan, in complete absorption, stood back a step or two, considering. He looked up and down, he moved forward again, he took up the chisel and hammer. He began to chip away at the stone once more, in steady rhythmical movement which Walter was still too young and inexperienced to recognise as having a sexual power but which he later realised had this profoundly. Stone chips fell to the floor. A rough-hewn shape, already in progress, began to reveal itself further: a limb, carved deep from the body of the stone.

Watching, Walter felt all disquietude vanish. This was the real thing. He knew it without framing the words: a marriage between man and material which felt entire, complete.

What need of more?

Euan stopped work, and his hands trembled. He put down the hammer and chisel, turned, and saw Walter watching him.

'Ah.' He wiped his hands on his apron. Unhurried, unstartled, accepting. 'There you are.'

Walter stepped into a circle of light.

That night, in his room, he lay and considered all this. He traced the day's long progress from despair to elation; he traced the course of his months at the Slade, and the arc of his life, still rising, still rooted in brotherhood and bereavement. He felt again the awe of watching an act of creation and he asked himself, How long is it since I was lost and absorbed in that way? He could not remember. He thought of a still quiet afternoon in an empty studio, himself and a young Greek girl in marble, his tracing of her fine grave features, his turning her this way and that.

And since then?

Sarah, serious and true – he knew it. Nina, whom he no longer wanted – all that longing, all that misery – swept away, something he did not even want to think about.

The longing to work again, to lose and to find himself.

Trains puffed out of Camden Station, smoke and steam and autumn passing.

Walter turned in his iron bed and slept.

Looking back, years later, how long that first year seemed.

# 1921

Early in February, Walter moved into the Painting Class. The University was building new Chemistry laboratories: sometimes a workman's face appeared at a studio window, as he strode along the planks of scaffolding outside.

'At least some people are getting jobs,' said Henry Marsh, greeting Walter on the steps one morning. 'How are you these days?'

'I'm fine, thanks.'

'You seemed rather to drop from view last year. Looked a bit peaky, as my mother would say.'

Walter smiled. 'I'm feeling less peaky now.'

'Good. Let's have a drink one day.'

The morning was fine. They stood talking on the steps, watching people arrive.

'Are you painting?' asked Henry, lighting a cigarette.

'Just started. And you?'

'Likewise.' He threw down the match. 'Have you had a class with Steer?'

'Not yet. He was supposed to come last week, but he was ill.'

Walter saw Nina, briskly approaching along the path. He looked at the lodge clock.

'Oh, Steer's always got some filthy cough or cold,' said Henry, 'but he's a dear old boy – you'll love him. Good morning, Frith.'

'Good morning, Henry.' Nina brushed past Walter without a glance. Henry raised an eyebrow. Walter ignored it.

'I'd better get to class.'

'Good man. Nice to see you. I'll just finish my cig.'

'There is no interest in painting unless one is out on a new discovery.' Tonks, on the first morning of the new term, paced up

101

and down. They all sat listening. 'You must open yourselves as young artists – you must dedicate yourselves entirely. You must remember that the business of the artist is the representation of nature.' He cleared his throat, he strode, the floorboards creaking, the room hushed. 'Modernism be damned!'

' "*All this talk of Cubism is killing me! I shall resign!*" It's only because *he* never trained in France, and doesn't understand modern thinking. He just wants us all to go on painting girls in hats.' Walter, listening, heard Nina's quick light voice, saw her face in the candlelight at Bertorelli's, the first evening they had spent together. 'Oh, the bloody war!'

Each week they had a chilly little brush with one another.

'Are you avoiding me, Walter?' she had asked him lightly, at the end of last term.

They were coming out of the building, the last of the wintry afternoon sun diffuse behind the trees. He had not wanted to see her. He knew that someone stronger would have made a proper end to it all, maintained some dignity, allowed her to do the same. He did not know how to do this.

'Walter? It feels as if you are.'

People came past them down the steps. It was very cold.

'Yes,' said Walter. 'I am.'

'But why? What on earth have I done?'

What could he say, out here in public?

'Nothing.'

'Well, then – what's wrong?'

'Nothing,' he said again, and then, abruptly, 'Excuse me.' He went over to the railings where his bicycle was padlocked, and felt for his key. When he looked up, she had gone. Now, they never spoke. At first, he had dreaded seeing her again. Now, he no longer cared. Perhaps this was what London did to you. Well: there was more to London than Nina.

'Unless one regards painting as a holy craft, in which one is a humble practitioner, nothing comes,' said Tonks. 'I believe all great men have felt this.' He looked at his watch. 'So – to work.'

Walter stood before his easel.

*The candidate must submit a series of six works, including two paintings of the head, two paintings of the figure, and two compositions, certified by the teacher. Subjects for composition will be given by the Professor once a month.*

He knew the prospectus by heart.
He had not found his subject.

For now, this did not matter. His subjects were before him, as directed by the School: a succession of models from whom he was to paint – and painting preoccupied him entirely. What was done yesterday must be undone today: he came in at nine, and sometimes earlier, and wondered that yesterday he had thought to place a shadow here, and here, when now he could see that what was required was highlight, there on the brow, there upon the cheek.

He took out his palette knife and scraped it all away.

He was absorbed by the light of a studio interior, he was absorbed by paint itself. To enter the class and smell oil and turpentine, primer and varnish, to squeeze out colour, to work with colour, to mess about and play with it, to seek within his palette the smoke and brick and rain of London, the glance of winter sun on canvas, on flesh . . .

He thought of the classes in Ashford – for the first time in months he really thought of them, the way Wicks had taught them to look, and to look; the freedom he had begun to feel: to do it all just as he wanted, trying things out on the edge of the paper, losing himself in the colours of twigs beneath water, moss upon moss. Now he thought, I am rediscovering that. 'That' had been watercolours, 'that' had been still life – nothing grand, quite the opposite – everyday things. Things that meant something – to local people, to people coming out of a war.

Walter mixed oil, mixed flesh tint with flake white, mixed ochre and grey. He thought of the contentment of those Ashford afternoons, the long fresh look at what was familiar and loved. Where did he stand in relation to Tonks, and his fear of the new? I have not been to France, he thought. I have barely been to the galleries. I have been to Slade lectures on Florence and Greece – what am I going to make mine?

'Well, now. How are you getting on?'
Steer had recovered. Steer had come back.

Walter put facts about Philip Wilson Steer together, bit by bit. He had taught here for twenty years. Each week he came up from his house in Chelsea, where he lived with his cats, and his coin collection, and Mrs Raynes, who had looked after him since he was two, when he almost died of bronchitis. In those far-off days the family had lived on the River Wye, and Steer had gone to school in Hereford. As a young man, he'd spent two years in Paris, at the École des Beaux Arts.

'Never learned a word of French, mind you. Damnably difficult.'

But he'd seen something of the Impressionists, and taken them to heart. Now, almost sixty, he was a name. Some said a great name. He spent his days painting, he spent his evenings with Tonks, and a couple of cronies, the critics Moore and MacColl. They played chess, they played Patience, they kept a good whisky. Tonks and the others talked for hours. Steer nodded off.

Some of the class remembered him from before the war. Tonks had gone out to the battlefields with Sargent. Steer, on commission for the British War Memorials Committee, painted Navy ships in Dover Harbour, found the wartime hotel and the wind from the sea pretty trying. Of painting itself he said little: Steer was not a talker. It was said that he'd walked all round the Post-Impressionist show of 1910 in silence, murmuring only at the end, 'Well, I suppose they all have private incomes.'

When Henry told Walter this, they doubled up. But as Henry had said, Steer was a dear old boy, and his students loved him. When Tonks came into the studio, they were on guard. When Steer came in, they rushed to close the windows: his fear of a draught was a legend.

'Good morning, good morning. Carry on.'

Perhaps, in his younger days, he had been more voluble. They doubted it. The whole point of Steer was his presence: massive, kindly, somnolent. He made most of his points with his brush. He came up behind you, he drew up a stool, he said nothing. At first, Walter found this disconcerting. What was the great man thinking, settling himself down, observing your apprenticeship?

A glance, a nod.

'Carry on.'

Walter picked up his brush again, returned his gaze to the model. In early spring the light was ever-changing. The skin of the model, on the dais by the window, reflected all this. Walter struggled, and ended up with a mess.

Steer leaned forward. He fumbled amongst the brushes on the easel's ledge. When he'd found the one he wanted, he heaved himself to his feet. Walter stood aside and watched. Steer's manner was all at once alert, intent. He glanced at the canvas and back at the girl, he dabbed at the palette. The brush in his hand was a thing alive; a few strokes and the girl, too, was alive, not a painting of flesh but flesh itself, the light playing over it, as light was wont to do.

'Carry on.'

The brush was set down, the lumbering figure moved on to another easel.

That was a good day. Looking back, Walter thought it exceptional. A lot of the time you'd spend hoping Steer would reach you in his rounds; if not, that was another week gone. Or he'd come up behind you, and settle himself, the stool creaking alarmingly.

'How are you getting on?'

'I'm in a muddle.' He could never have said this to Tonks.

There was a silence. 'Well, muddle along, then.'

He tried to. When he turned round for guidance, Steer was fast asleep.

He realised that before he came into the Painting Class what had been preoccupying him – when he was not aching for Nina – was composition. The vertical of a screen, and how close to the frame of the picture to place it. The contrast of this with a fall of silk, a square of white cotton. The edge of the square of white cotton. He thought, Well, I was reducing a picture to its elements. I thought I was thinking of surface, and materials – satin and cotton and billowing muslin – but no. I was thinking about line, and composition. And I was drawing, not painting.

He breathed in the smell of the oils.

He thought, I might have considered skin, and flesh. I did consider them, but to touch, to hold.

Now he considered them in paint.

He thought of these two short periods in his life as quite distinct from one another: man and painter, each seeing things differently, and with different needs.

He began to keep notes, not just on the light, and the weather, but on all this.

Spring came. He went out to the galleries with his stool and canvas bag, on his own, and quite content, for a while, to be so. He spent long hours on Saturdays in the British School rooms of the National

Gallery, copying Crome and Constable and Turner, making notes, losing himself in mills and water-meadows, under windy skies; in the drama of *Rain, Steam and Speed* and the misty stillness of *Evening Star*. He studied the Whistler bequests: *The Little White Girl* reflected in a looking glass, the *Nocturne – Black and Gold* with its firewheel of golden sparks, above shadowy crowds, amongst dark trees, and the *Nocturne – Blue and Silver*, pale and cloudless, a boat moving softly amongst the reeds.

He went to the Dutch School rooms, first visited with David Wicks, on his first trip up to London. He looked at the girl at the virginals, with her calm clear gaze, and found himself thinking of Sarah, and went out again, to eat an apple in Trafalgar Square, watching the fountains play. Sometimes he cycled along Piccadilly, to the West End galleries in Cork Street and Grafton Street, but he found their sleekness intimidating, looking through plate glass on to oils set against draped velvet. Hard to imagine that he, or anyone he knew, might one day show there.

He bicycled down to Zwemmer's, in Litchfield Street, just off Leicester Square, and browsed in the bookshop, looking at all the French art books and magazines, buying blurred postcard reproductions of Monet and Van Gogh and Matisse. Matisse, even in reproduction, thrilled him. Perhaps this was someone whose spell might work its magic – not London brick but Mediterranean light, streaming through open shutters. But he should be painting London: this was where he was living, after all.

He tried doing a little oil of the view from his room in Camden, and knew that Sickert had done it better. He squared up the drawing done of his landlady, pouring tea from the big brown pot in her kitchen, on a winter afternoon, in preparation for another oil. He knew that Gilman had done it better.

He was in a muddle. He had better carry on.

The School provided essentials: an easel, a stool, and clay for modelling. Students were expected to purchase everything else. In the Painting Class, social gulfs now revealed themselves. If Walter, in the Life Class, had felt himself isolated from the shared conversation of ex-public schoolboys, ex-servicemen, he now felt acutely aware of a limited income. Around him, people spoke of shopping in Winsor & Newton in Rathbone Place, and Cornelissen's, in Great Queen

Street, as if it were nothing to spend two or three pounds on paints or brushes, or to purchase a larger canvas just because you felt a particular composition required it. There was some swapping about, of course, but not a great deal: almost never of brushes, which became, after time, like a part of you, worn in with your weight, your handling. Walter, at Christmas, had received enough money for a range of flat and round hog-hair brushes and a half-dozen colours. The girls had given a palette. He gave them each a drawing.

'You're looking ever so thin, Walter. Isn't he? Don't you think he looks thin?'

'Glad I'm not living in London.'

'I don't know. At least there'd be a bit of life.'

'You wouldn't like it.'

'How would you know?'

He met up with Wicks: they walked down the long leafless lanes. 'How is it?'

He talked about Antique heads, and drawing from life, and Tonks. 'But do you feel it was right? Are you learning something?'

'I learned a lot from you.'

He did not talk about Nina. Or Sarah. He mentioned Euan.

'Bring him home, then,' said Annie, cutting the last of the Christmas cake.

'He might be married.'

'He isn't.'

'What about you, Mr Wicks?'

'Annie!'

'I only want to offer him a slice of cake.'

Everyone in stitches, the wood fire blazing.

Spring had come in earnest. Blossom blew over the grass in Regent's Park, where Walter went walking in the Easter break. He took his sketchbook and sat on a bench and drew the buildings of the Zoo against the softening outlines of the trees, listening to the roar of the lions and the shrieks of birds and monkeys. He couldn't afford to go in. He drew the long sweep of Regency terrace, beneath high clouds; he drew the lake, the island and waterbirds, the narrow canal, as bushes and shrubs became greener, denser. He made notes on colours: he felt like Constable, or like an Impressionist, working out in the open, but he needed more money for paints, and he was living in a Post-Impressionist age. He looked at his drawings and felt they were timid. How could you be bold, with pictures of a park? Should it matter what the pictures were about? Were they about the subject, or themselves?

At the School, people were reading the new Roger Fry. Euan was reading him, a copy of *Vision and Design* taken out of the library, marking passages in pencil.

'To me it is of no significance whether I paint Christ or a saucepan – it is only the underlying form which matters.'

Walter did not feel he would ever be a person for whom subject was without significance. He held out his sketchbook, he narrowed his eyes, he turned to a fresh page and started again.

Walking home down Park Street, past people coming in and out of the pawnbroker, the young women emerging from Mrs Herbert's Employment Agency, he saw the men in the doorways, with their tins and their trays of bootlaces, their medals, their sewn-up trouser legs. It wasn't just the wounded, and it wasn't just the ranks: outside the Hippodrome each Saturday a man in a bowler hat, his medals on a pre-war, once good coat, offered matches to the picture-goers.

'How kind. Thank you so much. Bryant & May, Bryant & May . . .'

The wound-up music-hall tunes of the hurdy gurdy came and went through the traffic, over and over again. '*Boiled beef and carrots, boiled beef and carrots* . . .' The tunes were bright, but the effect was melancholy, a downtrodden man turning the wheel, an ill-fed dog beside him. Last spring, cycling off to the School, Walter had felt that London looked like a city pulling itself together again: building works, roadworks, repairing the Zeppelin damage, taking down the boarding-up. Now, in the wake of a second miners' strike, a four-day State of Emergency, rationed coal, and unemployment, Camden, in the back streets, felt pinched and bitter. Even in Park Street there was a pawnbroker, and Mrs Herbert's Employment Agency, but there were also bookshops and confectioners, and Perugini's Tea Rooms, the kind of place where he might once have taken Nina.

Well. He wasn't taking her out to tea now.

The weather grew warmer, the summer term began, easels were set up in the quad. Walter went down to the sculpture studios, now and then, at the end of the day. Euan was working for the Diploma. With a year at the Slade behind him, before the war, he would graduate a year ahead, this summer. Already, Walter knew he would find this difficult.

'What will you do when you leave?'

'Pretty much the same, I should think. I'll have to find somewhere to work.'

'You won't move out of London?'

'I don't know. I don't think so. I might.'

Reading Fry had sent Euan back to the British Museum. He spent every Sunday there – not in the Greek and Roman rooms any longer, but in the galleries of early civilisations. Sometimes Walter went with him. They climbed the sweep of stone stairs and walked through Africa, Aztec America, Ancient Mexico, Peru. The dreaming gaze of the Athenian maiden Walter had drawn so obsessively last spring slipped away: here were grimacing masks, enormous pregnant bellies, tiny figures with their own still gaze cut from a single line in stone.

'Back to the bone,' said Euan, drawing.

They looked at tools, weapons, cooking pots; they looked at Saxon tools and vessels, row upon row in glass cases. Walter could connect with these. They were functional, domestic, essential. He and John William had once found an arrow head, turned up by ploughing – what had happened to that? He'd once found a coin which he'd hoped might be Roman. His father had had a good look at it, washing off the earth in the sink, putting it into a drawer in the parlour.

'You can take it to a museum one day.'

They'd forgotten all about it.

He wandered back down to the Greeks and found the young athlete he'd worked on the day he and Euan met here that spring. He remembered the way he'd been lost in the whole idea of Greece, all based on elementary schoolbooks, but even so . . .

'*You are a classicist.*'

He didn't know what he was.

He thought, If I had a studio, and a bit more money, I could get on more. His room was so cramped. He never had a bean.

'I thought I'd find you here,' said Euan.

In Euan's studio, Walter felt again the sense of coming upon something magnificent, entirely unexpected.

The Diploma in Sculpture required three figures: one from the Antique, and two from the Life. Euan, working all through the Easter break, had brought the two together. Walter walked in and stood silent. Where before there had been an unhewn mass of stone, and a limb emerging, now two figures had revealed themselves: reaching towards each other, one fallen, one inclined. The carving was plain and the figures featureless: they had a mythic, timeless quality and the relationship between them was ambiguous. One fallen, one inclined: Walter saw soldier and saviour, lovers, brothers, mother and child –

He stood in the corner, watching Euan hammer at limb and head and torso. Stone flew in chips: he wore overalls and a mask. Many of the sculpture students were modelling, not carving, and there was a great deal of talk about measurement, and accuracy. Walter sensed that Euan was unusual: not the only one to be carving, but almost.

'Let's have a drink.' The hammer and chisel laid down, sweat pouring.

They went to the Orange Tree, where medics crowded the pavement outside, and then on to the Devonshire, on the corner of Euan's street in Euston, where people played darts and dominoes. As the evenings grew lighter, they took to cycling much further, down to the river, along the Embankment. London was opening up. Walter had hardly known the river – only from glimpses on the journey to and from Ashford, and from paintings. Now, in Chelsea, they locked up their bikes and went walking: down to Battersea and back, and sometimes further, watching the sun sink, the smoke rise, the effects upon water and sky. Turner's Thames. Turner and Monet, visiting Whistler. And Steer, who lived in the Vale, off the King's Road – not far away. Near Tonks. Perhaps they should call. Perhaps not.

They walked up and down on the broad worn pavement, leaned on the stone balustrade, witnessed sunset and dusk and darkness. Riverboats hooted, lights came on.

Walter wanted to paint it all.

He thought about finding digs down here. 'What do you think?'

'You couldn't afford it.'

'Perhaps if I shared?'

'You wouldn't want to live with me,' said Euan.

'Is that a question?'

'No.'

Cycling home one evening, they made a detour, rode along the Strand and stopped to look across at the Epstein statues, set in niches high on the façade of the British Medical Association Headquarters in the years before the war. The figures were muscular, naked, huge and symbolic: a man with a newborn child, the Goddess of Medicine holding cup and serpent, lovers reaching out towards each other.

'They're getting damaged,' said Euan, gazing up. 'Some kind of erosion. No doubt that'll please a few.'

'Why?'

'They caused a terrible fuss. Clergymen were outraged. The usual thing.'

Walter had a crick in his neck. It was very hot. 'Let's have a drink.'

They rode down into Covent Garden. The stalls were mostly empty, and few of the country lorries had arrived. Children were scavenging for bruised apples, cabbage leaves and potatoes; men stood about outside the pubs in their caps and shirt sleeves, smoking and waiting for the night's work to begin. The air was rich with the smell of fruit and vegetables, beer and cigarettes; a few bright young things on their way from the Adelphi or the Drury Lane Theatre were having a look at it all, arm in arm in evening dress, talking of *Heartbreak House* and supper in Henrietta Street. Dusk fell. Outside the Opera House, the crowds spilled on to the pavement, cigars were lit and taxis hailed and a little snatch of Puccini sung by a chap on an orange box.

'*Che gelida manina . . .*'

'Oh, Charles, you're such an ass.'

'Where's Ralph? Anyone seen Ralph?'

'Taxi!'

Walter stood with Euan outside a pub on the corner of Bow Street, taking all this in. Amongst the throng, he saw a familiar figure walking along the pavement towards them, a good-looking chap with a girl on either arm: Henry Marsh, with Nina, in scarves and a long string of beads, leaning against him, laughing. And, on the other side, Sarah. He turned quickly to Euan.

'I'm going to the gents – back in a minute.'

Inside the pub he felt himself hot with nerves and embarrassment.

In the gents he stood beside an old boy with a wheeze and a tremor so bad he could hardly undo his buttons. Bloodshot eyes and years of drinking. He smiled in a watery way at the basins and Walter smiled weakly back, washing his hands elaborately, playing for time. When he went to the door, he saw them all there on the pavement, talking. He made to retreat, but Henry had seen him.

'Walter. Just buying a round. What'll you have?'

'Oh, just a half, thanks.' He nodded to Nina.

'Hello, you horrid boy,' she said, her hand on Henry's arm.

'Hello, Walter,' said Sarah.

They stood with their drinks amongst the passers-by: Henry and Euan, and Nina, flirting with both of them. Walter and Sarah. He did not know how to begin.

'How are you?'

'I'm very well, thanks.'

How should he move on?

'Where are you living now? Did you move into Hall?'

'Just for a couple of terms. Now I'm renting a little flat.'

'Near the School?'

'No, near here. We've all been having a drink.'

'Oh.' He felt himself quite tongue-tied by this.

'What about you? Still in Camden?'

'Yes.' Nina was laughing at something. He glanced at her, remembered long walks in the small hours, up into Camden, drunk with misery. Sarah noted the glance. He realised that as he looked back at her.

'Sarah . . .' Somehow he must act.

'Yes?' He could feel how veiled she was now, how guarded.

'May I see you?'

'Perhaps.'

Amidst polite exchanges, the single word felt honest.

The summer night had darkened, the air smelled of scent and cigars. He could see musicians coming out at the back of the Opera House, with horn and cello cases. Stars hung over the rooftops.

'I'll write to you,' he said to Sarah. 'May I?'

'If you like.'

'We're thinking of supper,' said Henry, turning to them both. 'Any ideas?'

Walter could not contemplate it. He and Nina. He and Sarah. Euan, smoking his pipe, knowing so much about Nina.

No.

His bicycle leaned against the wall. He pulled it away and bumped into a girl going past. 'Sorry – I'm so sorry.' He turned to the others. 'I'm afraid I've got to get back.' He nodded to them all, said to Euan, 'I'll see you tomorrow.'

'If you're broke . . .' said Henry, reaching for his wallet.

'No, no, it's not that.' He swung his leg over the crossbar, not looking at any of them.

'Lights,' said Euan drily.

'What? Oh, yes.' He reached to switch them on.

Nina said, 'God, you're a bore,' so lightly and humorously that you might have taken it for the friendliest teasing.

'See you all soon,' said Walter, flushing like a girl. He rode away from all of them, weaving in and out of the traffic, wishing himself anywhere but here.

He was writing a letter to Sarah out in the park.

It was a Sunday afternoon in summer, boats out on the lake, the trees full beneath a clear sky. It had not rained for weeks, and the grass was parched and browning. People lay in deckchairs, a brass band played old songs from the war: *It's a Long Way to Tipperary, Roses of Picardy, Keep the Home Fires Burning*.

Ex-servicemen without a job sat tapping out the beat. The grass was littered with Woodbines. Someone was flying a kite.

A kite had been flying the day he and Sarah went walking on Wimbledon Common last spring. They'd watched it because they could not look at one another.

He had been a fool.

*15th May, 1921*

*Dear Sarah,*

*I hope you are well. I am writing this in Regent's Park, where I often come and draw. I am enclosing a little picture which I hope you will like. May I see you before the end of term? May I take you somewhere nice? Since I never have any money, perhaps we could go for a walk again? But I am determined to try to find some work in London. I look forward to hearing from you.*

*Yours ever,*
*Walter*

He signed it, he looked through his sketchbook. What should he send? The pages were bone dry in the heat, the corners curling. After a while he moved away from the lake and into the shade. He made a drawing there and then, especially for her, much more to the point: two old men asleep in the sun with their hats pulled down over their faces, a baby in a pram beneath the trees, the nurse knitting on the bench. He looked up and down as he drew, saw a fellow come limping along, lay down his crutches and pull out his pipe. He went into the picture, too, the crutches leaning against the bench, a pigeon or two picking up crumbs beside them, the pipe-smoke dissolving into the summer air.

*Pack up your troubles in your old kitbag*: trumpet and cornet sounded in the heat as the band finished off with a flourish. Walter saw the face of the man across the path, the tune so bright and the truth so dreadful.

Next morning, he slipped the letter into the pigeonholes, alongside the beadle's booth. Then he went outside again. A few people had set up easels on the dried-up grass. The University disapproved of this – why should the Slade take over the lawns? – but the bolder students took no notice.

Steer, on his weekly visits, looked fearfully hot, mopping his face with a large bandana, seeking the shade. He took off a battered straw hat and fanned himself; he slipped his cotton jacket over the back of a chair and sank into it as if he might never rise again.

'Carry on.'

Often he fell asleep in the heat, but he woke refreshed, and was affable when people brought him drinks.

'Very kind. Now, then – how are you getting on?'

Sometimes he set up his own easel, underneath a tree, and took out his paints. People came over to watch him working, his shirt adrift beneath his comfortable belly, his head and his hands too small for his great big bulk, but the gaze still keen as he leaned towards the canvas, the movement of the brush still sure. In a morning, the fullness of the trees, the broken light within them, shadows on the grass and the solid sunlit stone beyond, all took shape and being.

'But really, y'know, I like to be further afield. Can't get the sky right here. Not enough of it, for one thing.'

In the right mood, he talked of his trips to Walberswick, back in the 1890s, painting amongst reed beds on the Suffolk coast, painting girls on the pier. Blue cotton dresses and panama hats, the morning sun and wind, limitless sea and sky, Monet in every brushstroke.

'Do you know that part of the world?'

Walter said the only coast he knew was the coast of Kent, just a little, from a wartime billeting. How long ago it seemed. Steer half-listened. He looked at Walter's canvas.

'You seem more sure of yourself out here. Better than from the life, I think. If it's you I'm thinking of. Is that right?'

Walter said that he believed it was. He thought of the painting of his mother, sewing in the orchard, grieving; the grass and the bees and the smell of it all. He told Steer he'd spent most of his boyhood out of doors, down in Kent.

'Is that so? I spent some of my boyhood on the River Wye. Herefordshire. D'you know that part of the world?'

Walter said that he didn't.

'Good, unspoilt place – you'd like it.' Steer dabbed at Chinese blue. 'Kent, now, Kent, you say . . . old student of mine down there, now. Nash – Paul Nash. D'you know his work at all?'

*We are making a new world . . .*

Walter remembered mud, and wire, dead trees and desolation. 'Yes.'

'Had a breakdown,' said Steer, wiping his brush. 'Bad business – don't know much about it, but perhaps Kent's doing him good. Lot of chaps getting out of town these days, bit of peace and quiet after the war. Of course, the country's not as it was – too many damned trippers, too many damned cars. Might as well stay in London a lot of the time. Down by the river, that's the thing.'

Walter said he went down to Chelsea sometimes, cycling in the evenings. He wondered if Steer might suggest a visit, but he didn't.

'Think you might do well in watercolours,' he said, considering a patch of green. 'Not quite the thing at the Slade, but it's giving me a lot of pleasure as I get older. Well, now, I must be getting on.' He looked at his watch. 'Time for a spot of lunch.' He heaved himself up, wiped his brow and replaced the battered hat, walking slowly across the quad to where Tonks was painting. Walter watched them: a heron and a – what kind of creature was Steer? Tonks was so beaky and certain and brisk. Steer was more like an intelligent wombat. Or dormouse. Sleepy and fat but bright-eyed when he woke. He thought he might make a drawing of him, for Sarah, if she ever spoke to him again. She was not working out on the grass with the others, and she had not answered his letter. He checked her pigeonhole, feeling shifty. The letter had been taken. It was over a week. He didn't know what to do next.

Watercolours might not be quite the thing, but would be more affordable. They brought back memories of Ashford. Walter went without lunch for a week, living on his landlady's breakfasts, which had always been decent, and a loaf of bread and cheese for supper. He did not go to the pub, where in any case his consumption was generally modest. Euan was working most evenings, the Diploma examinations only weeks away. With three shillings saved and his trousers hanging off him, Walter cycled down to Cornelissen's.

He went early, to avoid the heat, and arrived in Great Queen Street before the shop had opened. He locked up the bike and took off his jacket and went for a walk. He thought of the evening a couple of weeks ago, watching the theatre- and opera-goers – evening dress on a summer night, another world from his, and then the awful encounter, Nina so cutting and Sarah so reserved, himself cycling away like an idiot.

Still no letter.

He came to the market. A man in overalls was hosing the ground. Spray and puddles glinted in the light from the high glass roof; pigeons fluttered up to the girders. It was cool and dim – a painting in a muted palette by one of the Camden Town Group, Gilman or Ginner or Gore, showing at Sickert's open house in Fitzroy Street, on Saturdays before the war. Walter walked round in the quietness, his jacket hung over his shoulder, listening to the hiss of the spray, the beat of wings. He took out his notebook, and made a little drawing, dating it, noting the heat in the city, still: *30th May, 1921*.

That was the day when we knew, they said to one another, years later, looking back on their time at the Slade.

– I knew long before then.

– So did I, in my heart.

– You never said so.

– I was a fool. Let me kiss you.

Walter walked out of the market and back to Great Queen Street. Awnings were out, the pavement deep in shadow. A van was pulled up outside Cornelissen's, and a panel in the basement doors had been opened. At first Walter thought his bike had been stolen, but then he saw it had just been moved along, so the driver could send down the delivery. He stood for a minute watching bags of gums and pigments slide down the chute, as clerks and shop assistants hurried along to work. Then he went into the shop.

The bell rang, the man behind the counter looked up.

'Good morning, sir.'

'Good morning.' Walter closed the door behind him, and walked in on polished boards. He looked at the gleaming, glass-topped counter, where the man, in a blue serge apron, was wrapping a brown paper parcel. He looked at the shining jars: brushes, quills, pigments high on a shelf. On this, his first acquaintance, and for years afterwards, coming up to London long after he had left it, he found a visit to Cornelissen's entirely satisfying.

He breathed in the smell of oils and glues and varnishes, saw shelf upon shelf of tins and tubes, columns of little oak drawers with gilt numbers. A wall clock ticked. Mud-brown stairs wound up from a door at the back. Later, Walter learned that this was where Mr Thoms, now wrapping the brown paper parcel, stretched canvas. 'You can't have an art shop without making peculiar canvases' – that was what he said. Now he taped down the corners of the parcel, and tied it up with string. He reached for a pair of good strong scissors and snipped off the ends. The way in which he set about all this, and the flat square shape of the parcel, were wholly pleasing.

'Yes, sir?'

Dozens of boxes of pastels and pencils and tubes of gouache lay beneath the polished glass.

'Watercolours,' said Walter, and then, 'I have three shillings.'

Mr Thoms was unperturbed. They embarked on a discussion.

Other customers came and went. The till rang. Another assistant came down. Walter and Mr Thoms pored over cakes and grades of colour.

'Of course the weaker pigment is generally for the amateur, but the student artist can generally make a great deal of it.'

They chose six half-pan cakes, set out in a sturdy little box. And then there were the brushes.

'You might like to consider opening an account.'

Was that possible? With references, it could be. On the whole they found students from the Slade satisfactory. Professor Tonks would never vouch for someone of whom he was not certain. Walter said he would think about it. He chose two squirrel-hair brushes. Sable, in due course, said Mr Thoms. There was plenty of time.

Walter, watching his small purchases being wrapped, could not recall when he had last felt so contented. The shop, the discussion, the transaction: it was all aesthetically pleasing, workmanlike and sound.

'Thank you.'

'A pleasure, sir. Look forward to seeing you again.'

Walter took his packets. He turned towards the door, just as it opened and rang. The shade beyond it was deep, and he at first didn't see who it was, coming in. Then –

'Walter,' said Sarah.

He waited for her outside, under the awning. Beyond it, the morning sun was dazzling. When she came out, he wheeled the bicycle beside her. They talked about the shop. Sarah often went there, even if only to look.

'What did you buy?' she asked him.

'Some watercolours. Steer seems to think it'll suit me.'

'Not quite the thing at the Slade.'

'So he said.' He moved the bicycle aside from a chap with a stick. They came into Long Acre, noisy and hot. 'Which way are you going?'

'Up to the School. I was going to get the bus.'

They stood amongst the passers-by. Traffic went past them, the sun beat down. He couldn't talk to her here, but –

'Did you get my letter?'

'Yes.'

'You haven't answered.'

'No. Sorry.'

'It doesn't matter. That is . . . Shall we go for a coffee, or something?' He looked about him. Where could they go?

'Monmouth Street,' said Sarah. 'I went there the other day with Henry.'

The coffee-house in Monmouth Street was cool and dark and almost empty. A fan whirred in a corner, newspapers hung on a rack, a waiter in a white apron was grinding beans. They found a little table at the back. Sarah set her hat down and they ordered coffee.

Distantly, St Martin-in-the-Fields struck ten.

'Sugar?'

'Thank you.'

Sugar had been rationed: the bowls on dark tables looked luxurious. How was he to pay for this? He thought about Sarah and Henry Marsh, coming here – when? Often? And then?

'How is your course?' he asked her. 'Your wood-engraving – have you enjoyed it?'

'Yes, very much. I have found my vocation: I knew straight away.'

'That's wonderful.'

'Yes. Yes, it is.'

There was a silence.

'Sarah.'

'Yes?'

How should he proceed?

'You remember the walk we took, that Sunday . . .'

Side by side on the path beneath the trees, a fresh spring wind blowing across the Common, a soaring kite, a declaration.

'I wanted to write to you, afterwards, but I didn't know what to say.'

'It doesn't matter.' She was turning a sugar lump over and over, on the table; white crumbs dropped on the polished wood.

'It does. You see, I – I had my head full of someone. I don't know why, it wasn't right between us, but it had such a hold on me. I thought about you when it all began, and I knew it wasn't right, but I still . . .' He felt himself fumble and stumble and blush. 'Anyway,' he said, 'it's over. It's been over for months.'

'Yes,' said Sarah. 'I know.' She dropped the sugar lump into her saucer.

He felt the blush grow deeper. 'Of course. You and Nina are friends.'

There was a pause.

'She says you treated her very badly.'

'What?'

'She says you dropped her like a stone. That you've never explained.'

'But she—'

What could he say?

'That isn't quite true. At least, it's true, but it doesn't make sense unless you know . . .'

'Know what?'

He'd managed to explain to Euan. This was different. He couldn't look at her.

'How she was with me.'

Sarah didn't answer. The silence between them grew. Within it, the fan whirred, coffee beans were poured into paper bags, the street door opened and closed. Walter thought of the contentment he'd felt, just half an hour ago, buying paints, looking forward to work; of the rush of pleasure at seeing Sarah, the chance to make things right.

He said slowly, 'I told you I didn't know much about these things – still don't. I suppose everyone must make mistakes.' He looked up. Sarah was watching him steadily. 'There's nothing else I can say about Nina, except that it wasn't right. I don't know what she wanted, but I don't think it was me. Please don't think too badly of me.'

Sarah sat listening, her chin on her folded hands.

'What about you?' asked Walter, feeling all hope drain away. 'Are you – are you and Henry – ?'

'No,' said Sarah.

'I often see you together. I thought—'

'No.'

They looked at one another. Walter looked away, and then he looked back. Their eyes met, and held. A different kind of silence grew. He sensed it contained something true and deep and lasting.

'Sarah.'

She gave him her hand. He took it in his, and he knew.

Neither of them could speak.

He climbed the stairs of 16 Shelton Street. Sarah, ahead of him, took out her key. The house was hot and close and narrow. Dusty geraniums stood on a windowsill, almost at the top; through the glass he saw a fire escape. The stairs wound on up. He stood below Sarah, watching her unlock the door, too shy to turn and look at him; he glimpsed a dark cramped hall, with a mirror. He followed her inside.

She led him into a small square kitchen. A table and painted chairs were pushed up beneath the window. She reached to open it and the wooden acorn of a rolled-up blind tapped against the pane in the sudden movement. The sun streamed in: on to cups and plates on a shelf, a book of engravings, fruit in a bowl. Still life. Something of Sarah's life. Walter stood taking it in. Beyond the window the rooftops and chimneys of Covent Garden were huddled up against each other. It looked as he had imagined Paris to be. A little engraving of the view hung on the wall.

'Where do you work?'

'In the bedroom – sometimes in here. It depends.' She turned towards a green-painted cupboard, took out glasses. 'Yes?'

'Please.'

Water gushed into the stone sink; he watched her hold her hand beneath it, until it was really cold. She gave him a dripping glass.

'Shall we sit down?'

They pulled out chairs: he beside the open window, she looking out. The sun was so bright that she had to shade her eyes. He reached up to the blind, tugged it down. It was heavy and dark – blackout from the war, said Sarah. She was going to make curtains, but she –

The room was shaded and still. Everything outside it felt so far away. She rested her hand on the table: he covered it. He thought, This is how our life will be. The sense of this moment, this hour in their lives, before everything opened up between them – it felt very precious, it filled every part of him.

Where should they begin?

Their eyes grew accustomed to the darkness; tiny holes in the fabric of the blind let in chinks of light. They entered once again on the long slow process of looking at one another: so deep, so serious and full.

'Well. Here we are.'

'We hardly know each other, not really.'

'Yes, we do.' He took her hand, and turned it over. He traced the lines, he opened out her fingers, he touched each one in turn. With each touch, he felt both of them enter undiscovered country: hill upon hill unfolding, the spread of the fields.

# III

## In Kent

# 1922

In the autumn of 1922, Euan went down to visit the Coxes. Their daughter Meredith was six months old; they had been living in Asham's Mill for only a few weeks.

It was early October, mid-afternoon. Beneath the wooden roof the platform at Denham was in shadow, but the yellowing trees across the track were lit by a deep autumnal sun. Euan was the only passenger to get off here: a branch line from Ashford, a Sunday afternoon. He stood watching the train puff away and sensed, when it had gone, the absolute quiet, the untouched, dreamlike quality of the place, the hour. He walked down the platform, left his ticket in a box on the bench and came out through an empty ticket hall on to the village street.

The silence was broken by birdsong, and from somewhere the throaty voices of hens. The only shop was shut, with the blinds down; a cat slept on the sill. There was a pub, the Hopsack; there was a row of cottages; there was an oak on the green, with a seat beneath it. He saw the locked gates of a school near the church, and knew that it must have been Walter's school. Outside one of the cottages stood a box of apples and a sign offering eggs and honey. He bought both, from a girl aged about nine or ten in a drooping skirt, who counted out change from a tin. She leaned on the gate in the shade and stillness, and watched him walk away.

He followed Walter's directions, making for the newly erected war memorial, just outside the village, stopping to look at it. The grass beneath the plinth was well kept; there were six names, men from the East Kent Regiment, The Buffs, living for evermore. John William Cox was the first.

*My brother was killed. It feels like half my body, still.*

Euan stood in the autumn sun. Birds sang; the wings of his own past beat about him. Beyond the little island of the memorial the road was bordered by a low hedgerow; through a gate he saw the stretch of fields, the ochres and russets of turning leaves on oak and elm and sycamore. A couple of bullocks came down to the gate and stood there, staring; when he went over, they shied away. He had another look at Walter's letter.

*Walk on from the memorial. After a good mile and a half there's a crossroads with signs to Parsonage Wood and Potman's Heath, but you carry straight on for another half-mile. We're right next to the church. The house is part of the Weston Park estate, like my parents' cottage: the vicar has moved into Denham, and this place got very run down in the war, when Charles and Richard Monkton, the sons, were away. Only Charles came back. He let the house, but the tenants didn't last the first winter. Perhaps we shan't, either, but for now it feels full of promise. We'd never have managed in Shelton Street with the baby.*

*I can't wait to see you. No bus on Sundays – are you sure you don't want us to meet the train?*

Euan slipped the letter back in his pocket. Then he stood again for a moment, taking everything in: the village behind him, the narrow road ahead, spattered with cowpats. A hoverfly darted, and was still. Then it was off again. The sun was very warm.

Standing there in the empty lane, by the tall pale stone to the memory of the fallen, Euan felt years of exhaustion well up within him. He listened to the birds in the woods, the buzz of flies, the slow progress of the bullocks, leaving the bare caked earth at the gate, walking back up the field. He put down the knapsack; he stretched out his arms; he lifted his face to the sun and stayed there, letting it all sink in.

Then he said aloud, 'Right. Carry on.'

He rubbed at his face, he picked up the knapsack, and walked on to Walter and Sarah.

They were out in the garden. He came past the wall and saw them, just as the church clock struck the hour: four slow clear notes in the silence. Sarah was sitting on a blanket on the grass beneath the apple trees, turning the page of her book. A pram stood beneath a ragged elder growing near the hedge on the far side. Walter, in shirt sleeves, was carrying a heap of vegetation over to a compost heap in the far corner, next to a clump of nettles. Euan could see where he'd cleared the ground. He stood on his side of the wall and coughed.

'Euan!'

Sarah looked up, Walter dropped his armful of weeds. He came across the rough grass, brushing leaves off his shirt. He looked fit: brown and no longer so slight, but sinewy. He also looked older – a young man with domestic responsibilities, like a nineteenth-century French domestic portrait: *Le jeune homme marié*. He pulled the gate open, as Sarah got up from the blanket.

'How good it is to see you.'

They shook hands, they embraced. An old boy went past on a bicycle, lifting his cap.

'Afternoon, Fred.' Walter turned to Sarah, who had come up beside them. 'My love, forgive me.'

Euan stepped forward.

'Sarah.'

She was brown and thin and happy, her springy hair escaping its knot at the back, the fullness of early motherhood pared away.

'Hello, Euan.' She gave him her hand; he kissed her cheek.

'Well, now.' Affection welled up in him. He looked from one to the other. 'Here we are again.' He thought of the wedding, last November, the downpour in Wimbledon, everyone leaving the house beneath umbrellas, the church large and cold and Sarah shivering. She was three months pregnant, pale and drawn. He stood beside Walter, and passed him the ring. They were barely in their twenties, they had barely graduated; neither of them looked ready for this.

And now . . .

'Come and see Meredith.'

Sarah led him across the grass to the pram; he glimpsed the fields of stubble beyond the hedge, then he bent and looked.

The baby had woken. She lay quite calm and still, looking up with clear eyes at the elder tree. A sparrow was hopping about in the leaves; one or two dark berries had fallen on to her white covers.

'Hello,' said Euan, crouching down beside her.

She might have seen a strange face and started to cry. She might have given a radiant, undiscriminating smile. She was just at the age to do either. Meredith did neither. She turned at the sound of a

127

different voice and gazed at him: composed and watchful.

A twig or an insect dropped to the grass. Euan and Meredith looked at one another for the first time. He felt himself observed by an equal, across a great divide.

They drank tea and ate cake sitting out on the blanket, watching the sun go down. Across the lane the fields stretched to a river, and willows: a mile or so to the west they rose to low hills, and woodland. If you went on for ever you came to the sea.

'We'll go for a walk tomorrow,' said Walter.

Euan gave them the eggs and the honey.

'I feel like a prophet in an ancient land.'

'You look like a man in need of a rest.' Walter closed the egg box. 'Let me show you your room. I want to show you everything.'

Early October, late afternoon: it was growing colder. Sarah picked up the baby and took her inside. They followed her, passing a water butt at the door. The house was of worn red brick; it was long and narrow.

'There's this door,' said Walter, standing aside, 'and one at the front which no one ever uses, and then another at the church end. After you. Mind your head.'

Euan bent at the lintel. Inside, he felt at once how cold and damp and unused the place was, but the kitchen, overlooking the back, was roomy, and warmed by a range.

'We burn wood,' said Sarah, sitting down in a wicker chair. 'There's plenty of it.' Meredith was growing fidgety now. 'I'll feed her, while you two look round.'

'I'll give you a light.' Walter took off the globe from an oil lamp on the table. 'There's no electricity,' he told Euan, lighting the wick. 'The land agent doesn't think there will be for years – all the money in the estate is going to keep up the Hall.' He put back the glass, and adjusted the wick. The darkening kitchen was lit by the pure white moon of the globe; Sarah was unbuttoning her dress. Euan looked across at her. Woman in a basket chair. Mother and child. He caught a glimpse of the full white curve of her breast; their eyes met for a fleeting moment: for a fleeting moment he felt as if they were entirely intimate with one another. Then the baby was squirming, and Sarah was bending her head, drawing her close.

'This way,' said Walter.

Euan followed him out to the passage. The floor was uneven; he saw, in the dim light, stairs leading up on the left, and the door at the far end, the church end, set with panes of glass. He glimpsed the dark shape of a yew.

'In here,' said Walter, pushing open a door on the right. 'This is the dining room – we've never used it. Mind your head.'

In the light from the sinking sun across the lane, Euan looked round: a long plain room with table and chairs on a square of carpet, an empty fireplace. An old piano stood against the far wall.

'Do you play?'

'No, although Sarah did as a child. This came with the house. It's in need of attention, like everything else.'

Euan paced round the room. There were no curtains, no pictures, though squares where pictures had once been hung marked yellowing papered walls. Rivers of damp ran down them.

'There's a lot that needs doing. We'll live in the kitchen,' said Walter, watching him. 'That's what we did at home. Sarah's the one who grew up in comfort and she says it was all too comfortable.'

Euan crossed to the window. The garden at the front was just a strip of grass before the low wall, and the gate to the lane. The sun was sinking low behind the willows and the river flamed. Cows were filing across to the gate.

'Milking's at four,' said Walter. 'They're late on Sundays. Come and see the rest of the house.'

They went out down the passage. A couple of smaller rooms, both empty, led off to left and right. Walter's bicycle leaned against the wall. He unbolted the door at the end. A blackbird flew up and away; they went out, down the path to the churchyard. The clock struck the half-hour.

'They'll be ringing for Evensong soon. That chap who went by on his bike when you got here, Fred Eaves – he's one of the ringers.'

They stood taking in the evening air. It smelled of grass and cows and stone and water. The chill was growing deeper; footsteps and a bicycle sounded from the lane, the lychgate clicked open.

'Here they are.'

'Evening, Mr Cox.'

'Good evening, Mr Burridge. Evening, Fred.' Walter turned to Euan. 'You don't want to go to the service, do you? They want us to get involved.'

'Another time, don't you think?'

They went back indoors; as they came down the passage again they could hear the baby making little sounds from the kitchen, and Sarah, murmuring to her. They climbed up the darkening stairs.

'I should have brought a lamp.' Walter showed him the bedrooms. 'This one is yours. Mind your head.'

Euan looked into the little bare room at the back. A bed by the wall faced the window; the window overlooked the cornfields, stretching away in the dusk.

Walter pointed to a row of cottages, far beyond the trees which bordered the fields. 'That's where my parents live, in Asham's Mill itself.'

They walked past a bathroom, two bedrooms. A door stood ajar: Euan glimpsed a high iron bed, a rug on bare boards, a cot. Then they came to a step, and the door at the end of the landing.

'Here.' Walter pushed it open. 'This is the studio.'

Euan stepped inside. The room ran the full depth of the house; it had three windows. He saw a canvas on an easel at one end, overlooking the cornfields, like his bedroom. A table stood in the middle; there were a lot of boxes. Dim square shapes, and the smell of dust and oil paint. He stood there and looked at it all.

'What do you think?'

'It's just right, isn't it?' He walked up and down on the uneven floorboards. He looked at the view from the back, on the dusky stretch of stubble; from the middle, out to the church, where a light had come on in the tower; from the front, to the pasture. The gate was open, the cows had come out: when he turned to the right he could see the last of them, swaying down the lane. A boy with a stick walked behind: he realised it could have been Walter, a long time ago. Pigeons were beating their way to the woods. Beyond the willows the last glint of sun lit the river.

'I'll take it.'

'I wish you could,' said Walter. 'I wish you'd come down here.'

'One day I might.' He leaned against a wall and thought about it; he felt for his pipe.

'There are a few places.' Walter pushed back a couple of boxes on the table, and sat on it, watching him. 'Here and there, you know, up for rent. Nothing's picked up since the war, in farming. It's like everything else – unemployment, and too few men here anyway. It's beautiful, but it's hard, especially in winter.'

The light had almost gone. Walter thought of the first winter after the war, and something he'd tried to forget, when he took up the lease, returned to him.

'Did I ever tell you about the woman up at Mill Farm? Who hanged herself after the war?'

Euan frowned. 'No.'

Walter told him, recalling the horror of it, the chair kicked away, and the blabbering brother. Then the bells began to ring for Evensong. They stood there and listened, as the dusk grew deeper.

They stayed up late talking. Walter pulled open the door of the range; they all sat round it, watching the crackle of wood, the sudden fall of ash within the flames.

'I want to buy a press,' said Sarah to Euan. 'An Albion. If you see one in London . . .'

'I'll keep a look out. And what about you?' he asked Walter, thinking of the easel, up in the dusky studio.

'I'm going to paint this place. It's what I came back for. I'm going to paint Sarah and Meredith. That's all I know for now.'

'And how will you live?' wondered Euan, lighting his pipe again.

'My parents have given me a small allowance.' In the light of the fire Sarah's cheeks were burning. 'I tried to refuse, but with the baby – it's only until we get started.'

'And I'll help out my father,' said Walter. 'It's just a few bob, but it's work I know. How would we have lived in London? Until a gallery takes you on – and even then, you know how hard it is. There are plenty of people from the Slade struggling. We had a letter from Henry Marsh – he's doing some framing for the Leicester Galleries. He's the only one making a bean.'

'And Nina?' asked Euan. 'Did she graduate? Do you know what happened to her?' He broke off. 'I'm sorry, that was tactless.'

Sarah leaned back in the creaking chair. 'I saw her before we left. She's working in the Chelsea Arts Club, two evenings a week, and hoping to be taken on at Liberty's. She seemed happy enough. But I haven't heard a word since we came down here.'

'She isn't painting?'

'I don't think so. Nina is so bright, but somehow she couldn't really focus herself. I never understood quite why.' Sarah reached for her cup. 'What about you, Euan? Where's this new address?'

He drew on his pipe and told them about the warehouse space he was renting, behind the King's Cross goods yard, on a cheap short lease.

'I can't afford that *and* the digs in Euston. I've been going to City & Guilds classes at the Westminster Technical Institute. Practical masonry – lettering and carving. One day it might earn me a living. In the mean time I'm working in the dark, as it were.'

'But where do you sleep?'

'On a mattress, at one end of the warehouse. I go to the Islington bath house.'

'We must be able to find you something better than that.' Walter got up and took down a map from the shelf above the range. Upstairs, Meredith woke, and began to cry.

'I'll go to her.' Sarah rose from the wicker chair.

Walter spread out the map on the table. Euan got up and joined him. In the light of the oil lamp they pored over woodland and farmland, the river, reservoirs, quarries and gravel pits, the marshes that led to the sea.

'Tomorrow we'll go for a walk and look around.' Walter was tracing the line of the lane past the house. His finger moved through Hawkhurst, Goudhurst, Parsonage Wood, Darwell, Hurst Green, and Bedgebury Common. The wood in the range fell low. He threw in a couple of logs from the box, and closed the door again.

'It's burning too fast.' He turned back to Euan. 'What do you think?'

'About moving down here? It's a possibility.' He thought of the endless clank of the trains, the smog of approaching winter. He thought of his freedom, his anonymity. He said, 'It isn't all bad, in London.'

'No.' Walter looked at him, and London days and London light came back to him: the smoke, the soot, the brick, the endless rain on brick. 'I'd never have met Sarah if I hadn't come up to the Slade. Nor you.'

Upstairs they could hear a floorboard creaking, then the gush of water.

Euan said, 'I'm very happy for you.' He gestured at the kitchen, at the calm white moon of the lamp, with its gentle glow. 'All this . . .'

He got up and stretched, looking like a tree in a field. 'I think I'll turn in, if that's all right.'

'Of course. Let me find you a lamp.'

In the night, he woke, and heard them: the creak of the bedsprings, the muffled cries. Then the baby, waking. Footsteps to the cot, the lifting out and taking back to bed. Then silence. He lay in the darkness, deeper and quieter than any darkness he could remember, spread over the house, the fields. He sank back into sleep, and dream and memory drifted into one another, like smoke, like trees dipping into water. He felt himself drop deep to another silence, tense in the first light, before the guns began. His body gave a violent spasm. He woke, he shouted out.

Footsteps along the landing, a knock at the door.

'Euan?'

'It's nothing – a nightmare. Sorry.'

'Can I get you anything?'

'No. Go back to bed.'

He lay on the narrow mattress, sweating.

Next day, they went walking. The morning was fine and clear; they had made a slow start, looking at the map again over breakfast, packing sandwiches and a flask. Then they set off, with the great big pram: past the church, past the fields on the other side, the grazing cows, and the water meadows beyond them, where the willows hung over the river.

Walter put his arm across Sarah's shoulders as they walked; briefly she leaned her head against him. Meredith, propped against pillows, rose and fell with the rise and fall of the squeaking springs. She patted the covers and watched them all.

'What a calm baby she is,' said Euan.

'She has a calm life. After a terrible birth.' Sarah moved away from Walter's embrace and gave the pram a little push, releasing it to roll free. Meredith laughed. In the clear morning air the sound was glorious. Sarah did it again: Meredith gave a little whoop. They came to the end of the long church wall and soon to a narrow lane running up to the left.

'That's Mill Lane,' said Walter. 'That's where my parents live. We'll take you up there tomorrow. They'll be glad to see you again, after the wedding.'

'And I them. Thank you.'

'And they love seeing Meredith,' said Sarah. 'Don't they, my baby?'

Euan watched them: a mother so constant in her gaze upon her daughter, so light in her touch, and so content.

'Was it really a terrible birth?' he asked.

'Yes,' said Sarah simply, both hands on the handle again.

'Do you mind my asking?'

'No.'

'*There's nothing you can do, Mr Cox. Do you smoke at all?*' Walter put a hand to her face. 'I could hear Sarah screaming. They wouldn't let me near her.'

'The next one's at home,' said Sarah. 'Anyway, it's over now. I try not to think of it. I think about you instead, don't I?' she said to Meredith. Meredith regarded her. She gave an enormous yawn, and laughed.

'How I love you,' said Sarah. 'How I love the world today, and all things in it.' She turned to kiss Walter again; she turned to Euan. 'It's so good to have you here.'

He gave a little bow and smiled at her. 'You're very kind.'

For a moment they looked at one another, clear and full; for a moment he felt again as if they were entirely intimate with one another. Then she gave the pram another little push, and they all watched it, rolling away from them, with Meredith utterly at her ease, as the carriage rocked on the squeaking springs and the fields sailed past her in a flash of green and gold.

There we all were, thought Walter, years later, up in the empty studio. There we all were, setting out.

Down in the churchyard Fred Eaves was cutting the grass; the spray flew up and the birds flew past, and he buried his head in his hands.

They were in soft, fertile country – cornfields and orchards, hop-fields and farmland.

'That's Hobbs Farm,' said Walter, pointing. 'My father and I've spent a lot of time working over there. And in summer it's full of pickers from London – even in the war they came.' He began to sing:

> '*If you go hopping,*
> *Hopping down in Kent*

*You'll see old Mother Riley*
*A-putting up her tent . . .'*

He had a good pure voice. It rang out clear in the lane, like Meredith's laughter. She was tiring now, lying back against the pillows, gazing up at the sky.

'I can remember hearing that every summer.' He sang it again.

*'. . . with an ee-aye-o, ee-aye-o,*
*Ee-aye, ee-aye-o . . .'*

Meredith turned towards him. The passing clouds were reflected in her dreamy gaze. Their shadows drifted over her; she slept.

Sarah reached over, and pulled up the covers. They all stood and looked at the hopfields, stripped and bare. The bines were still taut on the poles; here and there, in the paths between them, lay a scattering of uncollected hops, scraps of sacking, somebody's cap.

'He'll be wanting that,' said Euan. He moved across to the gate and leaned on it, taking in the hypnotic rows of the poles, the empty bines, the footpaths; row upon row to the horizon, where the sky was hazy and pale. To the left, the nun-like cowl of an oasthouse rose from farm buildings against a clump of trees.

'Have you painted this?' he asked Walter, who had come to stand beside him.

'Not yet.' He looked out at the grey of the ashpoles, the baked, worn-down, milky-brown earth on the paths, the bleached horizon. Everything muted, autumnal and still: the yellowing trees at the field's edge, the mellow red brick of the farm, the pure white cowls.

Sarah was walking on, away from them, pushing the pram. Her footsteps and the squeaking springs were the only sounds. Then a cockerel crowed. Loud and triumphant in the middle of the morning, his voice carried clear across the fields.

'He's late,' said Euan. He pulled out his pipe and lit up.

'They won't be told.'

The smell of tobacco mingled with the earth, the last of the hops, the silage from the farms. The smoke drifted up in the morning air: a blue-grey thread, a puff. Walter looked at Euan's tired face, the rough brown beard.

'Euan?'

'Yes?'

'Last night, do you mind my asking – the nightmare . . .'

'I'm sorry you were disturbed.' Euan tamped down the pipe. 'I don't know why it happened then. I thought it was getting better. It is, on the whole.' He looked around him. 'Where's Sarah?'

She had walked on a way, and had stopped to wait for them, one hand on the pram and one hand shading her face from the sun.

They came to the village of Darwell, and stopped for a rest, sitting on a bench outside the shop, drinking from the flask of water. Women coming in and out of the shop stopped to look at the baby; they cast curious glances at the adults, two men and a woman, out on a Monday morning, queerly dressed and sharing a cup of water.

'Are we queerly dressed?' asked Euan. 'Is that what it is?'

'We give off an air,' said Sarah, bending to button a boot beneath her dress. 'It's like being at the Slade, amongst all the University medics and lawyers. We don't look quite respectable. Well – who wants to be respectable?'

'I do,' said Walter. 'I belong here, remember.' Had he really changed so much that people would wonder about him?

'I do,' said Euan. 'Or rather, I don't want to draw attention to myself. I just want to work, and get on with my work. Nobody looks at me in London.'

'Well, then,' said Sarah, rising to look in the pram, where Meredith was stirring, 'it's left to the women to rebel. Isn't that so, Meredith? Are you hungry, my darling? Shall I feed you here in the sun?'

'No,' said Walter.

A card in the shop said a house was to let. Walter and Euan went inside to ask about it, while Sarah stood rocking the pram.

'It's on the other side of the village,' said the woman behind the counter, closing a tin of biscuits. She came round the counter and opened the door. Meredith, in the pram, was growing fretful.

'I must feed her somewhere,' said Sarah, rocking.

'Do you want to do that in the shop?' The woman looked at her. 'You can, if you want.' She gave Euan and Walter directions, and they left her ushering Sarah inside as they walked up the street, deep in shadow.

'You see?' said Walter. 'I told you there were places.'

But the house, when they reached it, wasn't right: they knew straight away. Timberframed, leaning out from its neighbours, it had tiny casement windows. They rubbed at the glass and saw poky dark rooms, glimpsed a square of garden.

'Couldn't swing a cat,' said Euan, thinking of his warehouse, the sixty feet of floor.

They went back and waited for Sarah, looking again at the map.

'Hurst Green,' said Walter, his finger upon the next hamlet. 'I've never been there.'

'Near Romney Marsh.' Euan looked at the clusters of grass, imagining the spears of reeds, waterbirds on mudflats, winter migrants, stones upon the shore.

In Hurst Green, tethered goats were grazing on a piece of common land. A few tile-hung cottages were set around it; an old man was working in a garden. On the far side stood a plain square house which had once been poorly whitewashed. A small overgrown walled garden overlooked the common; rooks cawed in the elms behind a barn. The tiled roof had half-caved in, revealing the rafters.

'Do you think that was a tithe barn?' asked Sarah, wheeling the pram over the bumpy grass.

Nobody knew. They walked up to the house. Torn curtains were drawn across the windows, thistles blew in the garden amongst fallen slates. The air felt cooler here. Though the common was sheltered by the ring of cottages, you sensed an openness which lay to the south; the stretch of the marsh, and the wind coming in from the sea. They went back to look for the old fellow in his garden, but he had gone inside.

'Let's have a look at the barn.'

The double door was padlocked, but there was a stable door at the far end, and though the lower half was bolted the upper half came open with a tug. Euan leaned over, and looked inside. Sun slanted in through the hole in the roof; he saw the packed earth floor, pools of rainwater, crumbling brick. Here and there bits of planking were propped against the wall; beyond a partition stood a haycart, its shafts at rest on the earthen floor.

'What's it like?'

'Like a barn.' Euan reached for the bolt inside the lower door. It was rusted and stiff but he managed to move it, twisting until it gave. He pushed at the door: it creaked and swung open. Walter and Sarah followed him inside.

A crossbeam had rusting nails and hooks banged into it; cobwebs laced the corners. Euan reached up and knocked on the timber.

'Feels pretty sound.' He looked up at the hole to the sky. 'What do you think of these rafters?'

Walter craned his neck. 'Rotten right through.'

Broken tiles lay everywhere. Sarah picked one up, and brushed the dirt off. Woodlice scurried away. They walked round the haycart, with its broken wheel and warped grey wood. The scent of distant summers, old hay and straw, was faint in the air. Walter lifted the shafts and set them down again. Light streamed in: from the gaping roof, and the open stable door, through the cracks in the locked double doors.

'You could do something with this,' said Euan.

Clouds sailed over the sun. The goats on the common were bleating. When they looked out they could see that the late morning sun was fitful now and a wind was beginning to rise. Sarah went across to the pram, where Meredith was sleeping; she pulled up the hood, and took out the sandwiches.

They ate leaning up against the haycart, looking out at the common, the cottages with their plumes of smoke, the goats and the rippling grass.

'Well,' said Walter, chucking a crust at a couple of sparrows. 'What do we do now?'

'Knock on a door,' said Sarah. She looked at Euan. 'Yes? Are you interested?'

'If it goes with the cottage, I am. Where is everyone?'

They shut up the doors again, wheeled the pram over the grass. The goats raised their heads: two nannies and an eager young billy, half-grown, tugging at the rope. His cries followed after them as they made their way towards the cottage where the old man had been digging. He'd left his spade in the turned earth; his boots stood at the door.

'I'll wait here,' said Sarah at the gate.

'No,' said Walter. 'You go and talk to him, he'll like that.'

'It's true,' said Euan. 'Two strange men who've been trespassing across the way – most unsettling.'

She left them with Meredith, and walked up the brick path. A proper cottage garden. She looked at the peasticks propped against the wall, the well-dug earth, the twigs marking rows already sown. A white handkerchief fluttered in the wind from a peastick left in the middle. She knocked on the door, and while she was waiting turned to look back: at Walter and Euan, the pram between them, at the windy common and the dull red brick and dark timber of the barn, the elms beyond it and the racing clouds.

How my life has changed, she thought, smelling the freshly dug earth, looking at the men, her daughter, this new place. Then the door of the cottage was opened, and she turned to make her enquiries.

The old man took a key from a tin and led them back across to the house. The goats belonged to his daughter-in-law. The cottage and barn had belonged to Edith Fletcher, who'd lived there since 1883 and died there in 1920. It had been on the market since then but no one had bought it, or wanted to rent it: too much needed doing.

'By the time she passed on, the mice thought they owned the place. Reckon they do, now.'

He kicked at the peeling green garden gate. Meredith had woken; Walter carried her in through the thistles and nettles and yellowing bindweed.

'Bain't nobody been in here for months,' said the old fellow, unlocking the front door. 'We did have a clear-out, with her niece, but there's still a tidy bit. Untidy bit, I should say.'

They entered the dark little hall. Meredith's eyes went wide; they heard her small intake of breath.

'She senses everything,' said Sarah.

'You look around, take your time. Bring the key back.'

'It's the barn?' said Euan, looking in through the door on the right. 'The barn, as well?'

'Barn's not going anywhere. It's only the roof needs doing. Been like that since before the war. Needs doing here, and all.' He left them to it, leaving the door wide open. 'You know where I am.'

They went from room to room. It was plain, it was dark and dirty. They drew back the curtains, and they almost came to bits. Dank carpet, rotting staircase, cracked stone floor in the little dark kitchen at the back, where a trickle of rusty water ran into the sink. Upstairs – 'mind that tread, be careful' – the plaster crumbled to the touch.

Euan forced open a window at the front. The sill had been gnawed at by rats or squirrels.

'Probably squirrels,' said Sarah, looking up at the hole in a corner of the ceiling.

'Probably rats,' said Walter, looking at the skirting.

'Don't put Meredith down.'

Euan leaned out of the open window. Sun and shade danced over the thistles and weeds, and over the common. He could hear the goats cropping the grass. Behind the sunken roof of the barn, through the turning leaves of the elms, he could see the old nests from the spring, and the spring before that. Below the sloping common, the road where they had come walking an hour or so ago was bordered on the far side by a long hawthorn hedge. Fields lay beyond it. Walking, they had not been able to see into them, had only heard the sheep, but sheep were everywhere. Now he could see that the land ran for a great, unbroken distance: that the fields became open and marshy. Though the eye could not reach as far as the sea, you could sense in the air that it lay there.

Shingle and shoreline and crash of the waves. Stone to pick up, and stone to work on.

Walter came to stand beside him, with Meredith in his arms.

'What do you think?'

Euan looked back at the barn: its length and breadth and peaceful position alongside the common, beneath the trees.

'How would I live?'

'Hand to mouth,' said Walter. 'That's the truth of it. How are you living in London?'

They closed the window, walked back over the uneven floor. Sarah appeared in the doorway, from the landing.

'Well?'

They took back the key, they wrote down the name and address of Miss Fletcher's niece, over in Wye.

'She won't believe her luck,' said Mr Baines, seeing them out to the gate.

They walked home slowly, talking it all over. The wind blew in from the marsh: it grew colder. Walter pushed the pram for a while, pulling the hood up.

'We'd love it if you were near us,' said Sarah, taking Euan's arm.

☆

On Tuesday afternoon they went to see Walter's parents. The lane up to Asham's Mill, a hamlet of half a dozen cottages, tied to the Weston Park estate, was bordered by beech and sycamore: a sheltered place, the cornfields stretching away to the left and on the other side orchards and gardens. Here and there a ladder rested beneath an apple tree; hens scratched about in the afternoon sun. A scattering of leaves and beech nuts lay on the verges. Euan, walking alongside Sarah and Meredith, bent to pick up one of the hard little husks. He broke it open, four stiff petals, and prised out the nut.

'Pigs eat a lot of those,' said Walter. 'Mast, the farmers call it. They shovel it down them in barrowloads.'

'Are there pigs kept here?'

'Up at Mill Farm they've a few.'

Euan turned the smooth triangular nut between his fingers, and slid it back into its case. Meredith, rested and wakeful, watched him drop it into his pocket. They walked on, past the tall grave beeches. A row of plain cottages, two up, two down, was partly shaded by the trees, with small front gardens on to the lane and fruit trees on larger plots behind.

'Here we are,' said Walter, as they approached the second. He opened the gate, Sarah pushed the pram through, and at these sounds there came a honking of geese from behind the cottage. Meredith was at once alert to this, patting her covers joyfully. 'They're as good as guard dogs,' Walter said, holding the gate for Euan. The little garden, with its cabbages and dahlias and rows of beansticks, was filled with them all: the big black pram, Euan so tall, himself and Sarah, tapping on the door.

What did his parents make of it all, these Londoners, this new family?

The door was opened.

'Mother.'

'Hello, Walter. Come along in.' Her eyes were upon the baby, whom Sarah was lifting from the pram.

'You remember Euan Harrison,' said Walter.

'From the wedding, of course I do. Come along in,' she said again. 'Do mind your head, Mr Harrison.'

Euan ducked through the dark doorway. Inside, the open back door let in the sun and the sound of the geese, waddling over the grass. Meredith's eyes were huge; she clapped her hands as they all went outside and then the gander stretched out his neck and hissed. She shrieked, and buried her face in Sarah's shoulder.

They sat on hard chairs beneath the apple trees. The last of the bees of the summer droned in and out of the hives at the far end; the grass, sprinkled with chickweed and dandelion clocks, was a dazzling green. Euan remarked on it, getting out his pipe.

'That's the geese,' said Mrs Cox, handing tea from a tray. 'They do it a power of good.'

The geese were making their way back to their corner in the hedge, settling down again, beady and watchful. Meredith, set down on the grass, began to cry again, turning to Sarah, holding out her arms.

'He gave you a fright, that gander, didn't he?' said Walter's mother, as Sarah picked her up. 'Wicked old bird.' She went across to the washing line hung between trees on the edge of the cornfield. 'Here, my duckling, you have a look at this.' She shook a cotton bag of clothes pegs as she came back over the grass: Meredith stopped crying.

Euan sat watching and smoking.

'This is your painting,' he said to Walter. 'The one of your mother.' He gestured with his pipe: at the orchard garden, with its brilliant grass, the bees, the geese, the hazy yellow stubble of the fields, the distant church.

'Yes.' Walter looked at it all, and at Euan, beside him, enormous on the wooden kitchen chair. 'Four years,' he said slowly. Blue-grey pipe smoke rose into the autumn air; he thought of the summer afternoons before the war had ended, home on leave, setting a borrowed easel on the grass, out here with the smells of oil and turpentine, lavender and corn, painting his mother at work upon her mending, heaps of blue and khaki cotton in the grass.

'It's hard to believe,' he said, watching her now absorbed with Meredith and Sarah, a trinity of women, underneath the trees. There was a painting: it could be something huge. 'Four years,' he said again. 'A vocation – a wife and baby – you.' He turned back to Euan, listening. He was filled with emotion. 'You meant a great deal to me, in London.'

'And you to me,' said Euan.

☆

Meredith was tiring of clothes pegs. She dropped one to the grass and looked about her. Euan got up from his chair.

'Here,' he said, picking a dandelion. 'What do you make of this?'

He knelt before her and blew at the soft crown of seeds: just a breath, very light. A cloud of tiny parasols floated towards her, brushing her face. She laughed and reached out towards him. He blew her some more, and the air was full of them, spinning out over the grass.

'The passing of the hours,' said Euan gently, watching her delight. 'The passing of the years – how fast they fly.'

But I shall remember this moment, thought Walter, watching, and painting it all in his mind's eye, as Euan blew the last of the dandelion hours away and the clock struck in the church tower, far across the fields.

Next day, Euan went back to London, to sort out his affairs. Sarah and Walter went to see him off at the station, and stood waving as the train pulled out between the banks and the steam puffed into the autumn afternoon. They bought tea and jam in the village and walked home again, pushing the pram in turns, watching Meredith look about at everything. It felt strange to both of them to be alone again.

'When Euan comes back, Meredith will have forgotten all about him.'

'You can't be sure.'

The hedges were full of hawthorn berries and the hips of dog rose. Sarah picked a bunch, getting scratches; she laid them on Meredith's covers, crimson against white blanket.

'Don't prick your finger, Snow White,' said Walter, as she reached for them.

'It was Snow White's mother who spilled her blood,' said Sarah. 'On a silver needle, sewing baby clothes. And then she died.'

Walter lifted her hand to his lips. 'Don't say that.' He ran his mouth over the scratches. 'You should put witch hazel on them, when we get home.'

When they got home, they made tea and took it up to the studio. Meredith lay on the floor on the rug, beneath the middle window. She turned towards the light, watching the clouds pass over the garden and churchyard, as Walter and Sarah unpacked boxes, and walked about.

'Are you happy for me to have this window?' he asked, moving the easel, looking out from the back on the cornfields of his childhood, stretched out between here and there. Now that the trees were losing their leaves he could see right across to Asham's Mill, and his parents' cottage.

'Perfectly,' said Sarah, looking out at the front across the lane. The gate was open: they had met the cows going for milking on their way home, pressing back on to the verge as they passed. Meredith's eyes were enormous, taking it all in. The clouds were gathering now; Sarah thought of the afternoon of Euan's arrival, the sun slipping down behind the willows, the river a path of flame. Now it held the reflections of the clouds, and the dying leaves of the willows, drifting downstream. Every day, every afternoon and evening there was something fresh, something different. Meredith will have all this, she thought, remembering the streets of her own childhood, the clop of the milkman's horse, tame little dogs out on Wimbledon Common, the lifted hats when she and her mother went out. Everything ordered and solid and safe. What would have become of her, if she had stayed? She leaned out of the window, thinking about it all. Pigeon and jackdaw beat over the field. This was the house she was born to live in: that's how it felt.

'Yes?' said Walter, coming up behind her, his footsteps loud on the dusty floorboards. 'Yes, my beloved? What thoughts do you have today?' He rested his arms on either side of her, leaning against the window frame, his face against hers.

'How fortunate I am,' said Sarah, listening to the birds. 'How fortunate we are to be together.'

'I think that all the time.' He turned to look at her, the thin brown face with her springy hair escaping from its knot. When she lay beneath him, it was spread upon the pillow. When she knelt above him, it was cloudy about her narrow shoulders. He could twist it in his fingers and it held the shape he made: then it sprang out again, glinting and free.

'And now we have Euan,' she said, leaning her cheek against him as his arms enfolded her. 'It feels as though we'll be complete.'

'Aren't we complete already?'

'Yes. If he didn't come, it wouldn't matter. But . . .'

He drew her close. Desire flooded through them, like a river, running into every empty place. Behind them, Meredith kicked and began to grow restless. They turned to look at her, called her name. Her eyes filled with tears as she searched for them.

'Baby.'

'She's hungry.'

'She's lonely.'

Sarah went over, she bent to lift her. 'Here we are, darling.' Meredith sought her breast, panting. Sarah unbuttoned her dress and sat down on the only chair, boxes all around her.

'Here we are, here we are.'

Walter stood watching them, mother and child in the fading light. He had brought up an oil lamp: he lit it. The studio was filled with a radiant contentment. I shall paint this, too, he thought. I must keep hold of this for ever. He took up his sketchbook and began to draw.

Sarah said, 'When Euan is here, you can be men together.' She lifted her head. 'Or Meredith and I will be too many females, won't we?'

'I don't think so. It doesn't feel at all like that.'

'Not yet.'

'Well . . .' He was looking up and down, from the page to the two of them, quick and intent. 'We might have a son, next.'

Sarah looked at him. 'If we do, you'll want to call him after your brother.'

'Yes. Yes, I suppose I will.' He hadn't thought about it.

She said, 'My father's so old. It would give him a future – a boy with his name.'

'Let's see how we feel when the time comes.' The lamp needed a new wick: it was smoking a little, the flame flickering. 'We might want to name him after Euan.'

'Euan will have his own children.'

That evening, to mark the occasion when Euan had visited them for the first time, and found his house and workshop, Walter sat down in the kitchen, drawing a map. He drew the railway, the branch line from Ashford to Denham; he marked the school in Denham, and the road leading out of the village; he marked the war memorial, for John William, and for Eddie Pierce, who used to come fishing with them, and for Richard Monkton, the younger of the two sons at Weston Park Hall. All the men from The Buffs, all the young men from round about. He drew the crossroads, he drew the lane which ran past their house, and he marked it: Church Field, next to a cross for the church, and on impulse a weather vane, pointing towards Asham's Mill, and his parents' cottage: 2 Mill Lane.

He marked the surrounding farms. Hobbs Farm, Mill Farm, up the lane from his parents, newly tenanted, the halfwit brother kept on as cowman because nobody knew what to do with him; Middle Yalding Farm, where the cows in the fields across the lane belonged. He marked Weston Park Hall, where Ellie had spent the war nursing, where Charles Monkton, the surviving son, lived with his mother, and managed the estate, and spoke only when he had to.

Sarah was putting Meredith to bed. He could hear her upstairs, moving between bathroom and bedroom, talking all the time. He got up to open the door to the range, and put on more wood, for when she came down. Then he went back to the map.

He marked out the hopfields on the way to Darwell, and the road to Hurst Green, where Euan had found the right place. He put in a goat, for Meredith. He drew in the grassy symbols for the marsh beyond; the curving shoreline, where he had spent the war as a young cadet; the estuary of the Stour. He went back over it all, to show the river, and then he sat back and had a look at it.

Sarah came down. She leaned over his shoulder in the lamplight. He put up a hand and drew her head down to his shoulder, feeling in the space between the dress and the back of her neck.

'Is she asleep?'

Her tongue was in his ear; he tipped the chair back and pulled her round on to his lap.

Next morning, looking at the map again, waiting for the kettle to boil, he saw that the most important places in his life made a rough triangle: Church Field to Hurst Green, and back to Asham's Mill. He picked up the pencil and drew dotted lines between them, joining the three points as if with connecting footpaths.

Later, seeing the whole thing about to be ruined, with cooking, and cups of tea, he took it up to the studio, and pinned it on the wall by his window. There.

'I want you to sit for me,' he said to Sarah at lunchtime. 'You and my mother and Meredith. A trinity of women. I want you all out in my mother's orchard. I want to paint something huge.'

He was possessed by the idea.

'It's getting too cold to sit out in the orchard. It's getting cold in the house.' Sarah was spooning milk pudding into Meredith's open mouth.

'We'll just make a start, with a sketch. Then you can sit in the studio. I might not finish for months, but I want something big and important, something human, to work on through the winter. I saw it all on Tuesday, when we were up there with Euan – I knew what I had to do next. Meredith's growing so quickly – I must make a start.'

Sarah looked at him. 'I can't remember you so excited.'

'It's what I came back for,' said Walter, pushing his chair back. 'Just this feeling.'

They walked up Mill Lane with the pram. It was cold but the afternoon light was what he wanted: steady enough to make a start.

'Sit out in the orchard?' said Walter's mother. 'I've work to do.'

'Leave it for once. Where's Dad?'

'He's up at Mill Farm today.'

'I might walk up there later.'

He left them all in the kitchen, and went out to the orchard with a couple of crusts. The geese came over towards him and he stood there amongst them, as he had done with different flocks throughout his boyhood, scattering crumbs. Then he shooed them away and walked about, looking for the right place. He went back for a chair; the women came out with him.

'Sit here,' he told them, and placed Sarah on the chair between two Bramleys. Meredith sat on her lap and played with clothes pegs. 'You here,' he said to his mother, and had her stand beside them, her arm on the chair back. 'Don't look at them, look at me,' he told her.

'I'll look where I like,' said his mother.

He opened his folding stool, he sat before them. He took out his sketchbook and turned it upright; he took out his pencils. He gazed at the three of them.

'Mother?'

She turned to face him.

He thought, I shall fill this with the deepest light in the world. He began to draw, filling the page with two monumental women: his mother with her strong plain face and her hair back, looking straight into him, knowing him always, right from the beginning; Sarah, her hair coming loose, her breasts full, her gaze steady and pure;

Meredith, sensing the calm, everyone settled and still, dedicated to this endeavour, now tranquil and steady herself, just being.

The afternoon sun lit the last of the leaves and the brilliant grass. He thought, But I could make this any colour I wanted, like Gauguin, like Matisse. He was filled with the power of this thought, and the intensity he could feel between them all, the gaze of the women upon him, his gaze upon them.

Then Meredith flung down a peg, and the gander noticed. He rose from his place by the beehive and came towards them, his neck stretched out for a morsel.

'Go away,' muttered Walter, but the gander came on, and as he reached them his mighty grey wings unfolded and he beat them through the air. And he belonged here, Walter knew at once, sketching quickly, as Meredith began to cry, and he marked in the place where the goose would stand in the painting, his wings outstretched beside the women, his dark eyes glinting, his beak agape.

'Walter,' said Sarah.

He hardly heard her.

Days passed. Up in the studio, Walter pinned a huge sheet of paper on to a board, and pinned up the drawing beside it. He began to square it up, enlarging a ten-by-eight page to the promise of a painting bigger than anything he had ever attempted, feeling the two women grow in stature and severity as he did so. Yes, he wanted something austere and magnificent, biblical, rural, with the great bird beating –

It took him days to do this. He brought his mother and Sarah up to the studio, and had them all sit there again, with the oil stoves lit to take the chill off. He wanted to make the sittings as important for them as they were for him, and he knew they were, and that he and Sarah, at night, were closer than they had ever been because of this, even though in the day he was preoccupied and distant, and she absorbed in Meredith but growing restless.

'It's time I did some work of my own.'

'I know.'

'When I stop breastfeeding . . .'

He looked at her. 'I love you feeding Meredith.'

When the huge squared-up drawing was finished, he took a break. He couldn't afford such a canvas, he couldn't afford all the paints. He went out with his father and worked on the farms. He cleaned out the pigs at Mill Farm and the strange, half-complete brother stood watching, and brought out a bucket of turnips. He did a week's milking on relief, at Middle Yalding. Then he went back to the studio.

He began to settle himself at his window, looking out over the garden, the long dark line of the ditch, and the harvested land. He put up shelves, made from planking his father had rubbed down in the woodshed; he unpacked the sketchbooks and notebooks from London, and put them up there, with his paints and brushes. He went into Denham and bought paraffin for the stoves; he went into Ashford on the bus and bought offcuts of plywood, and rolls of lining paper, from Merchants the ironmongers, to use instead of expensive paper and canvas. He met David Wicks for a drink.

'I'm getting married,' Wicks told him, as they sat in the snug at the Crown.

'That's a pity,' said Walter. 'I think my sister Annie had her eye on you.' He raised his glass. 'Congratulations. Who's the lucky girl?'

'She's someone from art school – Emily Feaver. She used to come and visit me in hospital, you know, when I came back with this.' He tapped his shoulder. 'Terribly kind. At first I thought it was just friendship, but it's grown into more than that.'

'You mean it's grown into love,' said Walter, filled with his own new happiness.

'Well. Yes.' Wicks gave a smile which lit up his face like sun on a field in winter, and Walter realised how tense and strained he had often looked in the past: something which had simply been a part of him, like his awkward walk, and the way he had brushed aside his ruined hopes of painting.

'I couldn't be more pleased for you,' he said. 'I owe you so much – I hope you'll be very happy.'

'Thanks. I'm sure we will be. We're going to settle in Canterbury, we've both found some teaching there.' David Wicks made a rueful little face. 'I'm sorry about your sister Annie. I'm sure she'll find the right man.'

'Not so many about now, that's the trouble. Well,' Walter raised his glass again, 'cheers. Here's to you and Emily.'

'And here's to you and Sarah. And the baby. May you all flourish.'

'I hope we don't starve. God knows how I'm to earn a living.'

'You could take my classes here, perhaps. How would you like that?'

They looked at one another. 'Now that's an idea,' said Walter.

They talked it over; David gave him the name of the principal. 'Mr Bury – he's a bit of an old stick, but write now,' he said, 'and give me as a referee. You could start after Christmas. Mind you, to be honest, it'll only keep you in packets of tea.'

'Never mind, it's a start,' said Walter, feeling hope rise.

Outside, they could feel the first real chill of the changing weather. Wind blew across the market square; they shook hands and turned up their collars.

'Good luck.'

'Thanks for everything.'

Walter climbed on to the bus with the bundle of plywood and paper, and stowed it beneath his seat. He wrote out his application to Mr Bury, all the way home, looking out at the last of autumn, blowing across the fields in red and gold.

October ended, and with it came the burning of the stubble. Low flames crackled along the furrows, smoke rose in dark clouds and the air was hazy for hours. Then everything was empty and charred. Walter made drawings, and quick watercolour sketches. The wash and the patches of white on the paper filled him: the clouds of smoke, dissolving into the cloudy sky, the struggling sun. He lay awake, thinking about it. Then the ploughing began. As a boy he had loved the chink of harness, the steady progress of the blinkered horse, the shriek of the following gulls. Now he stood and watched a tractor chug across the burned earth, the thin puff of blue from the chimney, the new man from Mill Farm at the wheel, wind flapping the celluloid window. The gulls flew in from the marshes shrieking; the blade of the plough flashed in a gleam of sun.

Walter painted a series of little oils on board – the empty expanse of furrow, bare trees, following the changing light and sky. A man with a gun and a dog came walking: the son from the Hall, Charles Monkton, back from France, and brotherless. He and Walter passed one another from time to time, out in the lanes, and Walter sensed, in the brief exchange of greetings, the acknowledgement of what they shared, but it was never spoken of. The gun cracked, there was the frantic beat of wings, the thud to the ground, the racing dog.

Gunfire in a field in Kent, echoes of guns in France: Walter could feel it, watching and painting. He took up his sketchbook, and drew the tall retreating figure, and the dog, lolloping over the earth, as he used to sketch out in Regent's Park, on burning summer days, as he had once sketched out on the coast, right at the end of the war.

But now he was trying to find himself as a painter, trying new things. The trinity of women waited. He turned his easel towards the line of cottages, over at Asham's Mill, visible beyond the bare trees, and the buildings of Mill Farm, far up the lane, everything dwarfed by the soaring sky. The sunlight this morning was fitful, the clouds piled deep. With a rising wind, they were blowing away, and light poured over the fields like water. Walter looked, he stood back, he saw it all framed by the window, and he went back and painted the half-open, white wooden casement enclosing the earth and sky. A Matisse, but here in Kent, in an English autumn. He stood back again, looking from the window on the easel to his window on the world, with a mixture of elation and contentment: this is where I belong. I shall make something of this.

Somewhere in the house Meredith was crying and crying.

'Didn't you hear her?' asked Sarah, bringing her in. 'I was hanging the washing out – poor baby.' She sat in the low chair, unbuttoning her dress. Meredith sucked and sucked.

'I'm sorry,' said Walter. 'I was so deep in this.'

Meredith grew drowsy. Sarah laid her on her rug, and wrapped it round her; she came to look.

'What do you think?'

She nodded, looking from the painting to the sunlit fields. 'I love it. We should go to France, we should go to all the galleries.'

He had propped up the smaller oils on the shelves by the churchyard window, so the light from his window washed over them. She walked up and down, looking at them all. Across the room, the great drawing stood upon its board, propped up against the wall. 'And this?' she said.

'I'm coming to that. That's next.'

'You're putting it off.'

'I know. I'm afraid.'

'It's going to be the best thing you've ever done.' Sarah stood back. 'And when it's finished, we should have an exhibition. *The Trinity of Women*, and recent landscapes, by Walter Cox.'

'And where would we have that?'

'Here.'

'Here? Aren't they good enough for a gallery?'

'Of course. But for now – we can invite people to the studio, can't we?'

'Like Sickert,' said Walter. 'Like Sickert in Fitzroy Street, on Saturday afternoons.'

She took his hand. 'Let's do it.'

'Who'd come?'

'Oh, Walter . . .'

He took his hand away. 'I can't think of all this yet,' he said, as the clouds blew in again. 'It's enough to be back here, to have you and Meredith. Isn't it enough for you? Are you missing London already?'

'No,' said Sarah, walking over to Meredith. 'I just want to help you, that's all.'

'Do you mean that?'

'Yes.'


November came. On Armistice Day they all walked the miles into Denham: Walter and Sarah and Meredith in her pram, his parents and the girls, everyone subdued and sombre, the scarlet wreath borne by Walter's father bright against his Sunday suit, and the greys and browns of lane and leafless hedgerows. Other families joined them. Ahead, after a while, they saw the car from Weston Park, the son at the wheel and his mother beside him, move at a snail's pace towards the church. Private grief in a public place. The greetings at the door were muted, as everyone filed in; Walter, next to his mother, thought of the first time, when no one had been able to face such a gathering and it had been just family, standing in the parlour, waiting for the chime of the clock, the tolling of the bell, the silence. And now – he was here with his wife and child. He looked at his mother; she did not turn her head. He looked at Sarah, with Meredith in her arms; she nodded: I am here, I am with you. He felt he had never loved her more.

After the service they all walked down to the memorial. It started to rain. White stone, black umbrellas, the laying of the wreaths. The men from The Buffs stood grave. Then came the Last Post, then came the patter of the rain, and the silence, broken by Meredith's cry.

☆

A letter arrived from Euan, towards the end of the month. He had been in touch with Miss Fletcher's niece in Wye, and was waiting for the lease. He had given his notice at the warehouse and raised a small loan at the bank: just enough for the first six months' rent and essential repairs. He hoped to be down by Christmas.

'He'll freeze,' said Sarah, feeding Meredith with little squares of toast.

'No more than we will.' Walter folded the letter. Euan's hand was pleasing, open and flowing in blue-black ink. 'His hands used to shake,' he said, propping the envelope against the milk jug.

'Remember the nightmare,' said Sarah.

Wind shook the windows. Draughts came in under the doors. The last leaves were blown across the garden and Walter made a bonfire; he stood looking out from his window at the plain and perfect furrows of the cornfields. Rain soaked into them, sleet blew over them, the country was frozen and still.

He was summoned to Ashford Technical Institute for interview, and sat in the college principal's office, a tiny upstairs room with just space for desk and chairs and filing cabinet. A wicker wastepaper basket overflowed; the windows rattled in a brisk morning flurry of rain.

'You have no teaching qualification,' said the principal, wiping his glasses.

'I'm afraid that's true,' said Walter. 'However,' he cleared his throat, 'I have been extremely well taught.'

The glasses were replaced. Mr Bury read through the papers before him. 'Mr Wicks has given an excellent reference, and I see you were at the Slade. A letter from Professor Tonks would be a great recommendation. But you decided not to remain in London. Are the opportunities there not greater?'

'Of course you are right,' Walter said carefully. 'All the galleries are there, and so on, but I had no connections, and I feel I have only just begun. I felt I had to come home, to give myself a chance to develop, and to paint what meant something to me. London is horribly expensive. We have a baby and we want her to grow up here, where she can have some freedom.'

'I understand.' Mr Bury put down the papers. 'But I'm sure you will feel it in your best interests to obtain a teaching diploma, Mr Cox. Without it –' He spread his hands. 'A young family . . . it will take you some time to become established.'

Listening, Walter was filled with anxiety. Was this what he should have done? Remained in London, taken a diploma, moved to be near Sarah's parents, as they had so wanted her to do, be guided by her father, and let him smooth the way? What would become of them here?

'But for now,' said Mr Bury, rising, 'I am sure we need not worry about the formalities. The spring term begins on January the tenth. We look forward to seeing you then, if that will suit you.'

'It will suit very well,' said Walter.

Outside the college, he went into Ashford's only art shop, and opened an account.

'I start teaching in January,' he told the girl at the counter, and came out with a roll of canvas and a box of six Winsor & Newton oils. He had just enough primer at home.

'I'm employed,' he told Sarah, back at the house. 'There is hope for us yet.'

'My printing,' said Sarah, pouring coffee. 'My box wood, my press.'

'You shall have it all.' He took his cup upstairs.

She wrapped herself up and went out with the pram. She walked down the lanes and picked up fallen beech wood, elm and sycamore, heaping it up in a box and resting it on the pram. Meredith stirred beneath the covers. 'Ssh,' said Sarah.

At home she examined all the different grains. It was true what they'd said at the Slade: most woods were too coarse for fine engraving. If you wanted to be Bewick, and show every vein on the oak leaf, each feather on the thrush, box wood was what you needed. But I am Sarah Cox, said Sarah. I can do woodcuts. I can try things out.

Meredith woke in the pram in the corner.

'Here I am,' said Sarah, throwing the wood on the range.

Up in the studio, Walter stretched the canvas across a frame made of beech wood, sawn and rubbed down by his father. It was still rough and heavy; he liked it like that – something different, and individual, not smoothed in a factory. He banged in the last of the tacks. The sky was clouding over with the end of the afternoon: he would have to use every daylight hour. Downstairs the door banged – Sarah's return with the baby. He lit a lamp, stirred a can of primer and knelt on the floorboards, brushing it on in quick, excited strokes. He left it to dry, and went down to the kitchen.

'I've started,' he said to Sarah, who was undressing Meredith before the range. She had filled the tin bath with warm water and the flickering firelight was reflected in it.

'I've started *The Trinity*. Well – I'm just about to.'

'I'm so pleased,' said Sarah, taking off Meredith's vest.

Upstairs again, he was filled with fear once more.

He picked up his pencil. He thought, There is always a gulf between the vision and the work. What will become of this, transferred to the canvas? It's weeks since I did the first drawings: have I lost it all now? He closed his eyes, then he looked again at the drawing, shadowy in the oil lamp's glow. Go on – go on into it – the gaze of the women, the beat of the wing.

He drew out the squares upon the canvas. The sky had gone dark at the windows, a winter wind raced through the orchards of Asham's Mill and across the cornfields. He made the first marks: the lines of his mother's head and shoulder, looking rapidly from squared-up paper to squared-up canvas, beginning to lose himself at last, feeling again the sun on the grass, the stirring of the last, yellow leaves on the Bramley apple trees, the stern dark eyes of the women.

Weeks passed. Euan came down from London with bags and boxes. Walter went to meet him; they piled all the luggage on to the bus outside Denham Station.

'Looks like snow,' said the driver, starting up.

Three o'clock on a December afternoon. They drove out of the village, leaving the lights behind. The wreaths on the war memorial were bright against the stone.

'Did you go?' asked Euan, feeling for his pipe. 'For the Armistice?'

'Yes. We all went, including Meredith. Did you go to the Cenotaph?'

'Yes. The crowds felt thinner. Even so, I found them oppressive.'
He lit up, and looked out of the window.

Walter watched him. He thought, That is the last exchange we will have about the war for a long time. He could feel it.

He said, 'I'm working on something important.'

Euan turned back from the window. 'Tell me.'

They settled to talk. Walter thought, This is how it will be, now he's here.

The first few flakes of snow, very fine, blew across the road.

'What did I say?' called the driver, switching the lights on.

# 1923

Euan moved into the house at Hurst Green and a long bitter winter began. Each morning, the weeds in the overgrown front garden were glittering and stiff with frost; inside, he lit fires in every room. He patched up the broken treads in the stairs, he threw out the torn damp curtains and rotten carpet, and down by the wall made a bonfire, which smoked for days. For the fires he was using the last of the woodpile, found in a lean-to behind the house, where the wind swept over the sloping fields. When it ran out, he brought in brush wood, and heaps of dead elm, gathered from the trees behind the barn.

'Takes an age to dry out and burn, that elm,' said Mr Baines's daughter-in-law, soon after his arrival. 'It's apple wood burns the best. Can't beat that.'

'Is that so?' Euan walked on with her, over the empty common. The goats had been taken into a shed behind the cottages, where every chimney was smoking.

Mrs Baines watched him lower the armful of wood to the top of the garden wall, to rest for a moment.

'What will you be using the barn for?' she asked.

'As a workshop – well, a studio.' He saw her curious glance. 'I'm a sculptor – I need the space.'

'Plenty of space in there, I should think. Mind, that roof's going to need a bit of work. Let us know if there's anything you need.'

He watched her trudge back over the common in her gumboots and headscarf. Then he carried the wood in, leaving it to dry on the bare floor of the sitting room. Mostly, he lived in here. Walter had said they would live in the kitchen, over at Church Field, but theirs was a light and roomy place, with windows to front and back and the range at the heart of it. Here, the kitchen was the one poky room in the house: a mean brick extension with a tin roof and single small window, overlooking the back, with its old privy, and tiny patch of garden before the fields. The range was an ancient, temperamental beast, within which the elm sat smoking. It didn't matter: he'd got used to roughing it on the King's Cross factory floor, sleeping on the mattress, washing in the bath house, eating with the men in the café down the road. And long before all that, the trenches were where he roughed it.

Euan made tea, and walked from room to room in his house on the common. He looked out on to the barn, with its gaping holes in the roof, and mighty door into the quiet interior.

He had not had a nightmare since he came here. Not that he could remember. He lit a fire in the freezing bedroom and fell asleep beneath a heap of coats and blankets, watching the flicker in the grate, hearing the wind in the elms, sleet at the window, the rattle of the barn door. In the mornings, he held out his hands and mostly they were steady. Steady enough.

The war was leaving him.

He went into Ashford on the bus which stopped by the common three times a week. Clouds of black smoke puffed from the exhaust; it rattled and shook as it waited.

It was early morning, and Euan the only passenger. He sat at the back and looked out over the fields, where the mist still hung low and the trees, rising like statues from clouds of drapery, were dark with moisture. He still had not been to the marshes beyond, but he held to the thought of them, squelching and treacherous in winter, geese honking over them, the grasses flattened by an icy wind, the shore-line forbidding and stony grey, beneath the wheeling gulls.

In the town, people were muffled up against the cold. He got off in the square and pulled up his collar. It started to rain. He made for the post office, where he looked in Kelly's Directory for coal merchants, timber and builders' merchants, stonemasons' yards. He wrote it all down and then stood in the doorway, watching the rain drive across the square, and people making a dash for it. Then, as it cleared, he set off.

He ordered coal; he ordered the timber for the roof, embarking on a long discussion about the barn, its age and state of dereliction, and who to get in to help with the tiling, a skilled job. He thought he could do that himself – perhaps Walter could help him, or young Mr Baines. The builder looked doubtful; he wrote out the bill for a gross of tiles. 'Some'll be new ones, I'll get what I can of the old. They'll all be local clay.' Euan asked him for directions to the stonemasons.

He walked down an alley off Ditchmarsh Street. Puddles lay on the ground and rain dripped from guttering; he passed a sign for a bookbinders and saw another: Challock & Sons, Monumental Masons. A black-painted door was set into the wall. He rang the bell and waited, listening to the drip of the rain. Footsteps approached across a yard.

'Yes, sir?' An elderly man in an apron held open the door.

'Good afternoon. I wonder if I might have a word?'

'Of course.' The door was opened wider; Euan stepped into a half-covered yard. The moment he did so, he felt at home. Slabs of stone were stacked beneath the roof on the far side; he could hear, from within the building, the sound of hammering. He was led across the yard to an office. A small stone madonna stood in the window, a hand holding lilies upon uncut stone. Inside, the elderly man introduced himself.

'Ernest Challock.'

'Euan Harrison.'

'Do take a seat.'

A fire burned in the grate, a ledger and diary lay on a modest desk, behind which Mr Challock sat down.

'Well, now. What can we do for you?'

'I've come to talk about stone,' said Euan. 'I'm a sculptor, I trained at the Slade.' He began to talk, to describe his background, his classes at the Slade and the Westminster Institute, his move out of London. 'I've found a tremendous place to work.' He took out his pipe and described the barn, and the house he had taken and hoped to settle in.

Mr Challock listened. From the workshops beyond a closed door came the sounds of hammer and chisel and running water.

'You won't find a local stone you can use for sculpting,' said Mr Challock, when he had finished. 'Even the Normans found it difficult: they built Canterbury and Rochester with stone from Caen. And now . . .' He got to his feet, and led Euan across the little room to where framed photographs hung on the wall. 'Otterpool Quarry,' he said. 'That's over by Sellindge, out on the road towards Hythe. One of the last of the Kentish ragstone quarries. You'll find that was used for a lot of local churches, but now, that's all gone.' Euan looked at the faded prints: quarrymen working the stone beds, a donkey hauling the slabs in a cart, cutting and washing in sheds. 'All overgrown,' said Ernest Challock, taking out his own pipe. 'What we use now is sandstone and limestone from the Weald, and you can't do much sculpting with that, not for anything that will last out of doors anyway. All the rest we get brought down from London. Still – no doubt you can arrange that.'

'It's expensive,' said Euan. 'I was wondering – I hope you don't mind my asking – I haven't yet had a commission. I wondered if you might ever need another man . . .'

Mr Challock went over to the fireside and put on a shovel of coals. 'I can't say we've room at the moment.'

'I don't care what I do.' Euan tamped his tobacco. It was starting to rain again: he watched it pattering on to the roof in the yard, where sandstone and limestone lay waiting. 'I'd like to go on with lettering. I don't even mind delivering, or carting stuff about, being a dogsbody. I just want to be in a place I understand.'

Mr Challock passed a pad across the desk. 'Leave your address. I'll see what I can do.'

Euan took out his pen, and wrote it.

'Hurst Green,' said Mr Challock. 'I know it. Out near Denham, isn't it?'

'And Asham's Mill,' said Euan, slipping his pen back into his jacket. 'My friend Walter Cox lives there – we met in London, at the Slade. It was his idea I should come down here.'

'Cox,' said Mr Challock. 'Cox,' he said again. 'That's a name I remember. Why's that, I wonder?' He stood thinking, as the rain fell faster, splashing on the paving in the yard. 'Usually only one reason, I'm afraid.' He and Euan looked at one another.

'The war memorial,' said Euan slowly. 'The memorial outside Denham. Did you do that?'

'We did,' said Mr Challock.

Up in the studio, Walter set to work. He stuffed newspaper in the gaps in the windows. Sarah tacked felt along the bottom of the door, to keep the draught out. There were two stoves. With all this, the room never lost its chill.

Walter moved the easel out to the middle of the room, pushing the table back. Even such a small thing, turning the easel to take all the light from two windows, made a difference: he felt he was working on a different painting. Then he realised that yes, he was, that it would always be changing, with every new day, each time he came up here. How could he hold fast to the vision in the orchard, the vision of these women, so stern and so important?

Hung on a nail on the wall was the little sunlit painting of his mother, sewing in the orchard in a wartime summer which felt distant as a dream. What he wanted now was something timeless, ageless, and yet entirely modern. He mixed a blue as radiant as the gown of a Raphael madonna, and set about the sky as if he were entering heaven. But the women's pencilled faces could not have come from Raphael. They made him think of days in the British Museum, with Euan, a cold spring rain sweeping across the forecourt and the two of them inside in dim-lit galleries, walking up and down past Aztec deities. At the time, the carvings had left him untouched: it was Euan who filled sketchbooks, while Walter had gone off to draw flints and coins. Now he found himself thinking of ancient goddesses: huge with child, guarding the entrances to tombs.

'How are you getting on?'

Sarah, late at night, with tea. He looked at her as if from another country. She set down the tray; she came to look, said nothing. He could not have answered her, whatever she had said. She sat quietly by the stove, drinking tea from a blue china cup. He glanced at it, and back to the blue of heaven.

He worked all through the winter, in every hour he was not on the farms with his father. His hands were calloused again, as they had not been since he left for London. He was sawing and milking and carrying buckets, out in all weathers, cutting swedes, chopping wood for the fires. He came in and fell asleep by the range the moment he sat down. Then he went back upstairs, taking lamps at evening. He rubbed oil into the calluses, and flexed his fingers. He picked up his brush, and felt new energy creep back.

All through the winter afternoons, the light pale and steady over the empty fields, he lived within scarlet and crimson and gold; he lived in the orchard of his childhood set aflame. The hair of the women was dark as a starless sky. Their eyes burned into him, their lips were African. Before them the baby stretched out great limbs, as powerful as they were; beside them the goose reared up, with his wings spread wide and his beak gaping.

When he felt he had finished, Walter walked up and down on the bare dusty floorboards and wept. The last time he had done so was when Meredith was born. Then he signed the canvas, and hammered a nail in the wall and left it to hang there and dry there: his first major painting, he knew it. It was 3rd February, 1923.

His mother and Sarah came upstairs with Meredith. They all stood before the painting, the trinity of women in his life. He kissed them all.

'That'll do now,' said his mother, turning to the window.

Euan came over, and stamped off the first snow on the kitchen step.

'Quick, close the door,' said Sarah.

He thawed out by the open range. Then he climbed the stairs, following Walter. The falling snow lit up the studio; the morning was soundless and white. Against all this, the painting blazed on the distempered wall.

Euan stepped forward. He stepped back again. He stood for a long time, taking in its magnificence.

Later that year, Walter submitted *The Trinity of Women* for the winter exhibition at the Royal Academy. On a morning in September, the first with a chill in the air, he wrapped the canvas in brown paper and string, put sandwiches and an apple in his bag and kissed Sarah and Meredith goodbye. It was still very early, a mist above the river across the lane and the verges wet with dew. He left them in the warmth of the kitchen and set off for the bus with the painting bumping against him. He stopped and turned it on its head, but nothing was comfortable: it was too big to carry, and that was that. He stood at the corner of the lane and waited, propping the canvas on his feet lest it get wet from the dew. At last the bus appeared.

'Whatever have you there?' asked the driver.

'A painting.' He struggled down the aisle, past schoolchildren and women with shopping baskets, and propped up the canvas on the only empty seat. He sat down, his arm across it, and looked out at the misty fields, listening to the babble of the children as the bus went on to Denham. When he was a boy, he and John William and the girls had walked all the way to school, only ever missing if it snowed. He watched the boys ragging about, and the girls' disdain of them: one day Meredith would make this journey, and he or Sarah with her.

In Denham they all poured off and went racing in through the school gates as the bell clanged; Walter carried the painting awkwardly in through the entrance to the station, holding it before him.

'Look where you're going, young man!'

He mumbled his apologies. What a business this was. He bought his ticket, heard the train puffing in and made his way through the clouds of steam to the guard's van.

'I'll take that, sir,' said the guard, reaching out for the parcel.

'I'd rather stay with it, if you don't mind. I'm changing at Ashford.'

'As you wish.' The guard looked down the platform and blew his whistle. Walter stood all the way, and all the way from Ashford to London, too, leaning against the side of the guard's van with the painting behind him, amongst boxes and bicycles and a basket of carrier pigeons, poking their heads out.

Pigeons from Kent, going up to London; how strange it felt to him now, to be going back there, and how his work was changing, from the little wartime portrait of his mother, to this huge endeavour. Mother and daughter-in-law and grandchild had entered the realm of myth, and he himself did not quite understand how this had happened, nor the full significance of the great bird who spread out his wings beside them, except that the bird, like his mother, went back and back, had always been a part of him, and had had to find a place.

From Charing Cross he weaved with difficulty in and out of the crowds, holding the painting this way and that, stopping to rest in Trafalgar Square. He took out a sandwich and ate it on a bench beneath the lions, scattering crumbs to the pigeons like everyone else, watching the children race about, the office workers hurrying across the square and people climbing the steps of the National Gallery, as he had used to do.

Long afternoons, when he first came to London, walking through rooms newly reopened after the war, copying Constable, Turner, the little Vermeers, standing in awe before Raphael and Rembrandt. He remembered it all, the footsteps coming and going past him as he drew and turned the pages, the smell of dust, the cough of the attendant. How young and how ignorant he had felt; even worse on the rare visits to Cork Street, Bond Street and Grafton Street, to sleek small galleries displaying oils in windows draped with velvet. How had he ever thought he might find a place there?

Well. Here he was with his work. Here he was, beating upon a door. He brushed off the crumbs from his lap and stood up. As he turned to pick up the painting, a slender young woman walked towards him, a bag tucked neatly beneath her arm and her bob of fair hair bright in the midday sun.

Nina.

Walter felt his stomach turn over. Then he looked quickly and saw that it was not her, of course it was not her. Whyever should she have happened to be in Trafalgar Square on the one day that he came up to Town? But he found that his fingers were shaking, and sat down again, astonished by the power with which memory now assailed him: of those months spent walking at night between Fitzroy Square and Camden, the misery and turmoil. It was gone, it was forgotten, he scarcely thought of her, and then with indifference: but it still lay there, buried deep, and a glimpse of fair hair was enough to turn his guts to water.

He sat in the sun in the heart of London. Pigeons flew over the fountains, omnibuses roared towards the Mall. The girl had disappeared into the crowd: he knew that he would not catch sight of her again, and gradually his heartbeat slowed. He thought, Less than fifty miles from here Sarah and Meredith are out in the garden, or walking the lanes before lunch. This afternoon they will sleep in our whitewashed bedroom and the curtains will blow in and out at the open window. This evening I shall be back there, holding them close.

The frame of the painting lay in its brown paper wrapping beneath his hand. He breathed more steadily. He leaned back on the bench, and before him the fountains rose and fell – like love, which came and went and came again; like reawakened memory.

Walter carried the painting down Piccadilly, and up to the entrance to Burlington House. Flags fluttered in the first light wind of autumn. Over the road in Green Park, a few leaves were blowing across the grass. He stood at the open gates to the courtyard. A window was open; a typewriter clattered.

A porter in a long brown coat came out across the courtyard, wheeling a trolley stacked with paintings. Walter hurried up to him.

'Excuse me . . .'

He was given directions to another door, and stairs down into the basement. He heaved the painting down there, and along a dim-lit corridor. An office door stood open, a telephone was ringing. He knocked and stood there, waiting to be noticed.

*The Trinity of Women* was received at last, with the business of forms and labels. Walter was instructed to remove the wrapping paper.

'If you would put it up there,' said the secretary, nodding towards a trolley.

He put it up there, holding it face towards her, waiting for an intake of breath, a murmur. None came. He struggled with the size and weight once more, laying the picture on its side, stuffing his copy of the form into his pocket and retreating as the door swung open.

Well. That was that. He made his way out into the corridor, climbed the stairs up to the courtyard door and stood there, beneath the fluttering flags and passing clouds, feeling entirely deflated. All that energy, up in the studio, into the night, Sarah drinking tea from a blue china cup and he working on and on.

'If you would put it up there . . .'

Well, what had he expected? And this was only the first stage.

One or two people were crossing the courtyard; he watched them, and thought of the last time he was here, in the winter of 1919, the courtyard filling with the queue for the War Artists show and he, with David Wicks, coming to join it, noticing ahead of him a girl with a little velour hat upon springy hair, her arm in her father's, as he read the *Morning Post*. She had turned, he had caught her eye, her gaze was clear and serious.

*But that was you*, they said to one another, not so many years later, lying in bed in the cramped little flat in Shelton Street: new lovers, looking and looking. *That was you . . .*

Now, in the autumn of 1923, in the quiet courtyard, Walter allowed himself to feel a sense of destiny. He walked up and down, as the traffic rumbled up and down Piccadilly, looking for the place where he thought that he had stood, and she had stood, recalling the cold, the glance, the sudden swift sense of belonging, before she turned away.

And now she was waiting for him, at home with Meredith, resting in their whitewashed bedroom, rising to work in the studio before the baby woke.

He looked at his watch. Two o'clock. An hour in the National Gallery, then home. He walked out of the gates and back to Trafalgar Square, climbing the steps of the Gallery as he had done that day with David Wicks, drinking in Constable and Vermeer to push away images of war. Now he walked through to the Constable rooms once again, and stood looking at sky after changing sky, at windswept clouds above the Heath, sun streaming on to mills and water meadows. Walter thought now, as he had thought then, and often during his years in London, This is what I understand, this is where my roots as a painter lie. But then what of the towering *The Trinity of Women*? Goddesses in the British Museum; colours from Gauguin. He would never have painted like this if he had not come to London, but he had had to go home to do so.

The morning's mist and the chill in the air had long since vanished. London in mid-afternoon was warm and close when he left it. By the time he got off the bus from Denham the day was fading but it was still warm, and he walked down the lane from the turning with his jacket slung over his shoulder, hearing the cows, back from milking, moving over the dusky fields. The sky was streaked with purple; rooks beat their way to the deep and distant woods. He came to the gate to the garden, and saw Sarah, waiting for him, sitting beneath the apple trees in the basket chair from the kitchen. Beside her, Meredith lay on the rug, gazing up at the darkening sky through the leaves; on the other side of the chair stood a jam jar with a lighted candle. Moths whirred about it; Sarah was watching them. She heard his footsteps, the click of the latch, and turned towards him.

He pushed the gate open. He said, walking over the grass towards her, 'If you knew how it feels to come home and see you like this.'

'How does it feel?' She was wearing one of his shirts, white and collarless; a scarf was trailing; her sandalled feet were bare. Beside her the candle burned, and the glass of the jar was smoky. The moths whirred away, and whirred back again.

He was filled with emotion; he could not answer her. She held out her hand as he sank before her, and he took it, and placed it upon his chest, his heart.

The letter from the Royal Academy came six weeks later. The letterbox banged and Meredith, walking quite steadily now, followed

Walter out of the kitchen, down the dark passage at the bottom of the stairs. She ran to the doormat in the hall, and picked up the post.

'Thank you, darling.' He took the square white envelope and she watched him open it, unable to wait for a moment, hearing the postboy click the gate and ride off down the lane.

*Dear Mr Cox, The Selection Committee of the Royal Academy of Arts regrets to inform you . . .*

He stood stock still, as Meredith pattered back to the warmth of the kitchen. There were details of arrangements for collection: they swam before him.

'Walter?' called Sarah.

He turned his face to the passage wall and leaned against it, crumpling the letter. He heard the scrape of her chair, her footsteps, coming to comfort him.

'Oh, Walter.' She touched his arm. 'They must be mad.'

He shook his head. 'Don't. Don't.' He climbed the stairs, as slowly as his father climbed them. He went into the studio, looking at empty easel and unswept floor.

Well. So this was what it felt like.


Over the years, the map which Walter had drawn in 1922 grew weathered from the damp in the brickwork, from the wind and sun and rain at the open window, if he were careless enough to leave the window open, when it was raining. That happened. In the early days, with a growing, inquisitive baby and a house much in need of attention, there were moments of carelessness in many things.

Then the new baby came, in the summer of 1924: born at home, with Meredith staying at his parents' and the midwife bicycling over from Denham. The sun was high and the corn was endless; the trees rustled all afternoon, in a summery wind. Sarah gasped and panted; Walter never left her.

When the midwife had gone, ringing her bell at the corner, he knelt beside the bed, encircling Sarah and the baby on the soaking pillow.

She rested against him. The summery wind blew in the curtains and cooled her face; she slept. Walter went on kneeling, stroking the scrunched-up little face with the tip of his finger. The baby opened his eyes.

'What can you see?'

They gazed at one another, Walter intent and the baby dreaming. Who did he look like? Meredith looked like herself. This one – was he Cox or Lewis?

Hard to think of anyone else with John William's name.

Meredith had been christened in London. Geoffrey was christened here, in Asham's Mill, in the church of Walter's childhood. He was six weeks old; it was nearing the end of summer, the trees dense and dry, the harvest and hop-picking in full swing. All through the long hot days you could hear the sounds of scythe and thresher, smell the bittersweet hops being stripped from the bines.

Sarah carried the baby down the path to the church on a blue and gold morning, his long cotton robe in a fall of white against her. Beside her, holding Walter's hand, Meredith was filled with the sense of occasion: new baby, new dress, all the grandparents gathered, Euan come over from Hurst Green, her aunts all dressed up . . . All this, just for a baby.

The vicar was waiting at the open door: he greeted them all except her. Inside, the smell of wax and stone and flowers made her head swim but nobody noticed. They all stood round the font. Then Sarah gave the baby to the vicar and the christening began. Meredith tugged at her father's hand. He picked her up and she looked down into the water, so dark and still in the deep stone bowl, as if it had been there for ever.

Then the vicar's hand entered the water and broke it: he lifted a shining stream of drops and made the sign of the cross on the baby's head. 'In the name of the Father, and of the Son, I baptise thee Geoffrey William . . .' The baby began to cry. She turned to her father, who was watching it all so intently, and put her face against his. He held her close, but did not turn to her. But on the other side of the font she saw Euan watching them, and as she looked back at him he gave her a smile which filled her with sudden happiness, as if everything was now in the right place. She turned to her father again, but he was looking at the water in the deep solemn bowl of the font and she knew he was miles and miles away and had forgotten all about her.

*All that water, all that light –*

Walter stood with his arms around his daughter. He watched the water settle from its disturbance, as he had watched the shining fall of drops from hand to baby forehead. Sun came in from plain high windows. As the water grew still, but not quite still yet, a gleam of reflected light danced up and down on the stone: a pulse, a quickening, a tiny life.

Then the service was over, and they all came out into the sun.

With the new baby, carelessness was sometimes chaos. Up in the studio, the map became one more thing on the wall, with the shelves Walter had put up there for brushes and paints, amongst postcards and sketches and notes and shopping lists. But he liked its weathering, and the memory of the evening he had drawn it: Sarah upstairs with Meredith, the range burning, the knowledge that Euan would be leaving London, coming down to join them. Then Sarah descending the stairs, coming into the kitchen, lying across his lap . . .

One afternoon, when Meredith was playing on the studio floor, he picked her up and showed it to her. She was three, and serious about things. Sarah and Geoffrey were resting: the night had been broken and long. He and Meredith were talking over their shoulders to one another, about nothing very much – the brush he couldn't find, the house she was building with bricks. The weather was cloudy and threatening rain. The trees which bordered the cornfield were blowing about. Tomorrow was Sunday, and they were going to visit his parents. His eyes caught the map as he rummaged about on the shelves.

'Have I shown you this?'

'What?'

'Come over here.' He picked her up. 'What a big girl. I drew this when you were a baby.' She followed his finger, moving from place to place, along the dotted paths, and then he pointed out across the fields.

'See?' He shifted her weight in his arms. 'There's Asham's Mill through the trees, and here's where it is on the map.'

She nodded. 'Point to where Euan lives.'

'Here.' He showed her the goat on the map; she smiled. He realised what a grave child she was generally becoming. 'And here.' He carried her over to the middle window, overlooking the churchyard. 'Right over there, far beyond the church.' They went to Sarah's window, past the press on the table, the box of prints. They looked out on to the lane. 'We walk down there, remember, on past the hopfields.'

'Sometimes we get the bus.'
'Sometimes we get the bus.'
'How far is it?'
'To Euan's house? Three or four miles as the crow flies. Longer by bus.'

Meredith frowned. 'What crow?'
'It's an expression.' He tried to explain.

The baby woke up, and began to cry. He put her down. 'Let's go and see Geoffrey.'

He went out, down the step and along the landing. Meredith didn't follow him. She wanted to look at the map again, but couldn't see it properly. She pulled a stool across, and clambered up on it. She looked at the capital letters she knew, and the three connecting paths. It started to rain.

She thought of the crow, taking off from his tree on his big black wings, beating his way through the rain across the fields, over the farms and the dripping strings of hops, growing hoarse and wet, flying over the common and landing on another tree, cawing and cawing until Euan came out of the barn and looked up.

# 1926

Daybreak, the first liquid light. It seeped through the gaps in the curtains on to Sarah and the children, asleep in iron bedsteads; it played on whitewashed walls. Downstairs, Walter laced up his boots, took down his canvas bag from the coat rack.

Daybreak. Spiders' webs beaded with dew on the garden hedge, the yews in the churchyard dark in unfurling mist beyond the wall. Walter clicked open the gate to the lane. A wren darted into the hedge; a ewe asleep in the churchyard raised her head. He came out of the garden; the ewe got to her feet. He walked across to the gate to the field, his footsteps distinct in the quietness. Not a soul was about.

A single note rang from the church clock: half-past six. The sun was rising, over farm and field and hedgerow. As he jumped down from the gate he saw flat white mushrooms in the grass. They'd come up since Sunday, then, the last time they were all out here. That was yesterday's rain, that was summer ending. He'd stop for them on the way back.

He walked over the wet field and the cattle stared at him. This was the day's perfection: the earth made new while the earth slept, the sun diffuse and melting, thin as a wash on paper. And he abroad to see it, the bag on his shoulder, with brushes and paints and folding stool and screw-top jar of water.

Cows tore at the grass. Sheep moved over the hillside. Walter came to the far gate, and a jackdaw on the post flew off it, making for the trees. He climbed over, into the water meadows, where the willows hung deep in the river. The sun was rising behind him now, the mist in the meadow dispersing like a dream. The sound of the river was everywhere.

Walter stood still. Had a morning ever been more beautiful? Far across the field came the cock crow: four hoarse notes.

He thought of a summer dawn in childhood, waking as early as this, everyone else still asleep. His mother came quietly into the room. She stood pouring water from a white china jug into a white china bowl.

*All that water, all that light.*

The mist in the fields was rising, the cockerel crowed. He lay there watching the dance of reflected light on the wall: leaping, alive.

So many years ago.

Everything was certain, then, and everything had meaning: all through his childhood. Then John William was killed, and nothing meant a thing.

And now? Walter walked over the meadow, his bag and the folded stool within it bumping against his side. The woods on the hill were dark and full, lit by the rising sun. They stood on the skyline and received the dawn.

*We are making a new world.*

When he came back, they were all getting up. Water gushed into the drain by the back door; he could hear the children running about upstairs. He went to the kitchen to rinse out the screw-top jar, and leave the mushrooms; he went up to the studio, stepping over a trail of clothes on the landing, and spread out the paintings to dry on the table.

'Walter?'

'Coming.'

He opened the studio windows, went back along the landing, opened the bathroom door.

'Hello.'

Geoffrey was standing up in the bath, his flannel in his mouth. Meredith, in her nightgown, was brushing her teeth; Sarah sat on the bathroom chair, her dressing gown loose, her hair a cloud about her. The room was full of steam and sunlight.

Moments of vision, like beads of glass.

At breakfast, Meredith sat watching the sand stream through the egg-timer.

'We're not having eggs,' said Sarah, watching her. 'We're having the mushrooms.'

'I know.' They were sizzling on the range. She turned the timer over. The sand was an endless fall of silver, like rain, but soundless; on and on and on. It took exactly three minutes, never more, never less, but when it began it felt as though it would last for ever.

Geoffrey reached out, and tried to grab it. She pushed him away. He started to fuss and she took no notice, waiting for the very last grain to fall. There. She turned it all over and it began again. Each time she thought it would be a little different, and every time it was – not the time it took, but the way the grains landed, countless thousands of them. Nothing could stop it and no one could save them, falling through glass to their deaths.

After breakfast they went to play in the dining room. No one ever dined in it, it felt cold and ashy. Geoffrey went over to the piano, with its long yellow teeth, and started to bang about. Plink plonk plink. Plink plonk plink. 'Stop it,' said Meredith. In the wallpaper opposite the windows, the damp made a map of many countries: she journeyed across seas to reach them, travelling alone. No one knew where she had gone.

Outside the garden door stood a sage bush: leggy and thin in the winter, dense and full in the summer, blue-green against the brick, the step, the painted door. Coming in, going out, Meredith stopped now and then to rub a leaf between her fingers and sniff. All summer and early autumn, the smells of mown grass, cut hops, cut corn, were borne over fields and garden, but this was different: rich and strong and savoury. She crushed it, she breathed it in and in.

Walter came upon her, as he went in or came out.

'What were you thinking about?'

'Nothing.'

She dropped the broken leaf, she went off to do something else. The smell clung to her fingers and then it faded. She forgot about it, until another time.

On the other side of the garden door stood a water butt, like the one at the grandparents' house, but even taller. It towered above them. She and Geoffrey had to be lifted up, to see how deep and full the rain had fallen.

She looked down over the rim. The water which lay there was dark and still, with a skin of light. If she kicked the side, there was a low dull sound; the circle tilted, the light broke in pieces. She was lifted down again. She turned on the tap at the bottom, to mix things: earth and stones and bits of twig and grass, leaves from the sage bush, lavender. She stirred and stirred with the stick and bucket. The water poured and splashed. Sarah came out and turned it off.

'What are you making?'

Lunch. Supper. A land after an earthquake.

How far away other places were. She stood in the dining room and imagined them, all through the maps of damp. River and mountain and sea and storm and earthquake. Everything tipping up, slipping down, falling into a chasm . . .

'Meredith?'

A long way away, all these huge things happened.

And she knew only here.

Sarah was up in the studio. It was late September, a Saturday afternoon. Walter had taken the children into Denham. The sun streamed in through the open windows; down in the churchyard she could hear Fred Eaves, hauling the mower through the gate. This must be almost the last cut of summer.

Sarah stood at her table. Woodblocks and her box of tools lay waiting. She looked through a pile of prints. The paper was rough: held up to the light, you could see the fibres. Each print was set deep in a wide, untrimmed border. She went through a sequence, thinking. Harvest moon, hanging full above the corn; winter moon, glinting on frozen fields; moon on the churchyard – the yew, the stones, the sleeping sheep; moon above leafless winter willows, the rippling river.

She would sell them as prints, nine by six; she would print them on cards for the Christmas Fair at Denham. She laid them out on the table, pinned the one of the willows up by the window overlooking the lane. Her window. She thought, I should have a studio mark. A trademark, a stamp – something. She walked up and down.

The mower had come to a halt. She went to have a look. Fred was lifting the box off; she watched him carry it over to the heap of cuttings in the far corner, beneath the wall to the fields, and the corner yew, whose bark glowed reddish brown in the sun. People threw dead flowers here, from the vases and jam jars set beneath the gravestones. Now and then there were bunches or wreaths from a funeral, but not often, though people still spoke in the winters of the influenza of 1919. Last winter it was Mrs Eaves, Fred's old mother, taken off with bronchitis, as she'd always said she would be. She lay amongst other Eaves; now Fred was on his own. He shook out the box of cuttings, and the air was full of the scent of cut grass. She waved to him as he came back, leaning out of the window.

'Hello, Fred.'

'Afternoon.' He lifted his funny old hat then got back behind the machine. Sarah went back to the table and doodled on a pad. Her initials. Her initials and Walter's, set in a square together. That looked all right: what more did she want? Something else, something more. She looked at the row of prints; winter from three windows.

She picked up her pen, pulled the chair up.

When Fred had put away the mower, she could hear him with the clippers, snipping the long grass all around each grave. Just giving Mother a trim, as he'd said once to Sarah, in the spring. Snip snip, clip clip, all through the end of the Saturday afternoon, the sun slipping down into the river, the light in the studio mellow and deep.

I am happy, said a part of Sarah, drawing in pen and ink. Another part did not notice. The clock in the tower struck half-past four. Soon they'd all be back.

Fred was raking now. He gathered the last of the long grass, and carried it over the churchyard, to the heap. Then he came back, and lit a cigarette, leaning against the wall.

'Afternoon, Fred.'

That was the verger, opening up.

Sarah blew on her pen-and-ink drawing, and left it to dry. She went across to the churchyard window. Mr Byatt's Springer was sniffing over the grass.

'How're you, then, girl?' said Fred.

'Hello,' Sarah called down.

Mr Byatt looked up from unlocking the door. 'Mrs Cox. Good afternoon.' He slipped the key back in his pocket and came across to the wall, where Fred was patting the dog. 'Forgive me for troubling you.'

'You're not. I called you.'

They smiled at one another.

'I was going to call on your husband – well, on all of you, of course.'

'Everyone's gone into Denham,' said Sarah. 'I'm working.' She felt the difficulty of conducting this conversation across the garden and the churchyard wall. 'Shall I come down?'

'No, no, I don't want to disturb you. But could you ask Mr Cox, when he comes back; we wondered if he might consider ringing. Isn't that so, Fred?'

'That's right.'

'One of our ringers is retiring – Mr Temple. He hasn't been well and it's getting rather too much for him, I'm afraid. It's not too easy to find people these days. We wondered if your husband . . .'

'I'll ask him. He shouldn't be long.'

'Thanks so much. I'll be here for a while.' He walked back to the open door of the church. 'Stay, girl,' he said, and the spaniel flopped down on the flags.

After a few moments the first strains came from the organ. 'Je-su, Joy of Man's Des-ir-ing.'

'That's the one,' said Fred, listening.


The bus drew up in the lane. Walter came in with the children and the shopping.

'How have you been getting on?'

'Rather well. I've got something to show you later. Mr Byatt wants a word.'

'Why?'

'Go and see – he's still practising.'

Sarah unpacked the groceries, took tea out into the garden. The children drank milk on the rug, and lay about. Geoffrey kicked at the plate of bread and jam.

'Stop it,' said Meredith. 'Stop it!'

A beetle walked over the rug: they all watched it. Walter came back.

'What do you think?' asked Sarah, passing him tea. 'Would you like to ring?'

'I've said I'll have a go.' He flopped down beside her, yawning. 'Please don't speak to me for an hour.'

'Why?' asked Meredith.

The cows were coming back from the milking. Sarah and the

children went to watch them; Walter slept. Dusk fell.

'What were you going to show me?' he asked after supper.

'Stay there.'

She went upstairs, past the sleeping children. She brought down the drawing and showed him.

Walter looked at the open casement, the frame, the sill, the trees beyond. *Three Windows* written beneath. Their initials in a small square box in the right-hand corner.

'But think of it reversed,' said Sarah. 'White on black.'

'Yes, of course.' He held it up to the oil lamp. 'This is us,' he said.

'This is us,' said Sarah. 'Our mark.'

'Very good.' He handed it back. 'We must show it to Euan.'

Later, in bed, he drew her close. The moon was high and came in at the gap in the curtains. It was so quiet they could hear the cows, moving across the field towards the river. There was the faintest breeze.

'Not just three windows,' said Walter.

'What?' She lay full-length against him. Their breathing slowed as they settled to one another again, feeling the dreamy ebb and flow of sleep and desire.

'Four elements,' he said slowly, drawing her closer still. 'The earth – the land all around us. The air – the spirit – the church beside us. Earth and heaven.'

'And you'll be a ringer.'

'Perhaps.'

'Go on.'

The cattle were drinking in the moonlight; they could hear them step into the shallows.

'There's the water,' he murmured.

'And fire?' She moved to lie over him, spread herself over him, the long stretch of sunlit afternoon still held within her, sun sinking into the river.

'Here,' he said, his hands moving over her, into her. 'Here, and here.'

Rustle of the sheets, movement of the curtains in the moonlight, blowing in, blowing out, between here and there.

Mid-October. Euan was waiting to take delivery of stone from London: he walked down to the barn to open up. The afternoon sky was overcast, with a fitful sun. He pulled back the door and the goats, as always, looked up at the sound of it, dragging across the ground. Over the years, it had worn an arc: grassed over when he had first come here, in 1922, now re-opening along the line made by generations of local farmers pulling it back to bring in corn or haybales.

He set the brick by the bottom and the goats began to graze again, white beneath the heavy sky, their ropes brushing the grass.

Inside, it was cold and shadowy. The intermittent sun lit the shelves on the far wall, the table of tools, the heads of figures modelled in clay or plaster, mostly, because when he'd come down here that was all he could afford. More recently, he'd begun to carve again, using offcuts from Challocks' yard. Now, with money scrimped and saved from working at the stonemasons, he had put down the deposit on a half-ton piece of Hopton stone.

He had cleared a good space to receive it, shifting stuff back to the walls. Waiting, he moved about a bit, his footsteps heavy and quiet on the earthen floor, hearing through the open door the sounds he was used to now: the creak of the wind in the elms, comings and goings in the cottages over the common, the bleat of the goats. He walked past the table and went over to the shelves.

Stones and bones and branches lay there, things found, things made. Pieces of chalk, and chalky snail shells, from walks with Walter and the family over the North Downs; driftwood and shells and pebbles from the shore; stones and bark from the fields behind the house, the woods. There were figures and models – small-scale essays, or pieces complete in themselves – little clay heads, or figures; figures in groups. Some went back a long way, like the fallen men he'd made in London, soon after the war; some were from long before the war, before the Slade – animals he'd carved as a boy from long walks out on the Cornish moors: foxes and rabbits and birds. A boy without a father, spending much time alone.

Euan drew on his pipe. The wind whistled in the elms and through gaps in the timbers; chalk dust blew over the floor. He heard the sound of a lorry, rumbling down the lane.

He went outside, heard its sides brush the hedgerows, and he strode down over the common, waving as it came round the bend and drew up. A huge, canvas-covered mass stood in the back, secured with ropes. Cottage doors opened. The driver and his mate waited as Euan approached, the engine idling.

He reached the cab. 'You found it – well done. Can you back up to the barn? The ground's pretty dry at the moment.'

'Right-oh. Got anyone to help you, sir?'

'I'm afraid not.' He thought, I should have had the Coxes over. The children would have enjoyed all this. Well, another time. 'You've brought a platform?'

'Oh, yes. We'll manage.'

'Good man.'

The driver looked in his mirror and began to reverse slowly over the bumpy ground. Euan walked alongside. The goats bleated, then stood and watched as the lorry pulled up at the barn door. The men jumped down.

'Right, then. In here, is it?'

It took the three of them the best part of half an hour to get the stone inside, lowering it with ropes through the dropped flap on to the platform, wheeling it over the ground and in, inching it on to the floor.

'Steady, steady.' They were streaming with sweat.

'There.'

They all wiped their faces.

The monumental piece stood wrapped and tied, five feet high by three. The delivery men moved forward, making to untie the ropes.

'Wait,' said Euan.

'Sir?'

He felt there should be a pause, an acknowledgement of the moment: the unwrapping, unveiling and revealing. There was something both holy and erotic in what they were about to do.

Then he became a workman again, a craftsman, plain and practical, taking delivery of his material – that was all.

'Nothing,' he said. 'Let's have a look.'

They untied the ropes and pulled aside the canvas. The stone stood there: grey-green, massive, impenetrable. Then a gleam of sun broke through the cloud, glanced in at the open door, and the solid stone became, for an illuminated moment, something more than that.

Euan nodded.

He took the men up to the house for a cup of tea. They hung up their caps and jackets and talked about London – the weather, the General

Strike in May, when public transport had come to a standstill. The miners were still out. They looked over the peaceful common.

'Must seem like another world, I should think, sir.'

When they had gone, Euan went back to the barn. The afternoon was drawing in, the smoke from cottage chimneys rising towards a cloudy sky. He walked through the great open door and beheld in the shadows his mighty piece of uncut stone, there in the middle of a new space, resting. He walked round and round it, leaning his weight against it, ran his hands over its height and breadth and roughness.

What lay within? What would he make of this?

The light was going. He locked up the barn and went back to the house, lit a fire and his pipe and sat smoking. He fell asleep in the chair and as he did so found himself thinking not of the stone as it now was, out there in the darkening barn, but of how it had been before the men unwrapped it: blind and bound and shrouded.

When he awoke, the fire had sunk to its last embers, and he could hear rain at the window. He sat for a while, coming to, overpowered by a receding dream. He couldn't recall the detail, only felt now its sensations of sorrow. He thought, I was elated this afternoon. I saw that gleam of light on the stone and I was filled with hope. Why have I dreamed of something – what? – something hidden, and filled with sadness and longing?

He threw another log on, kicked the fire into life again, then lit lamps and went into the little kitchen to cook. I am alone too much, he told himself. As in my boyhood, I'm too much alone. When I get to grips with that stone – then nothing else will matter.

Years later, his life in hidden turmoil, Euan recalled this night: waking from a dream suffused with melancholy, brooding by the fire.

He was up in a London gallery, with Walter and Sarah and Meredith. Around them people came and went. He walked away from all of them, seeing on a far wall a sombre painting. Two lovers kissed, with their faces shrouded. He stood before the canvas and his heart turned over, seeing two figures kiss through thick soft cloth with blind and hopeless passion, as lost and pale as ghosts.

Late October, and an early frost. Frost on the windows first thing in the morning. Sarah, in two cardigans over her nightgown, sat in the studio before breakfast, drawing the ferny flowers direct on to scraper board, paring away black to white.

'I want to do that,' said Meredith, watching.

'It's very sharp, this little knife.' She kept all her tools out of reach on the shelves, flooded now and then with the hideous visions of motherhood: a game, an experiment, a sudden flare of temper. A spurt of blood, scarlet from baby-white skin . . .

She ran the thin pointed blade through a stem, a thorn, a blade of grass; tiny black parings fell to the floor.

'Let me –'

'No. Where's Geoffrey?'

'*I* don't know.'

Late October. Frost on the flags and the graves in the churchyard, thawing as the sun broke through, leaving the stone glistening. Walter walked through the gate from the garden at ten o'clock. A little knot of ringers was gathering at the door to the tower.

'Morning.'

'Good morning.' He walked down the path towards them. Fred Eaves in his gloves and muffler, stamping about, Elsie and Florrie Peake, from Middle Yalding, Mr and Mrs Burridge from Hobbs Farm.

'Nice to have you with us,' said Mr Burridge. 'Mr Byatt will have told you I'm your captain? Tower captain, that is.'

'Yes, yes, indeed.'

'He'll show you the ropes all right,' said Fred, and they all had a little laugh.

Walter looked at them with affection: people he'd known all his life. He followed them, filing in through the door, ascending the winding flight of stairs. They rounded the first bend.

'All right?' asked Mr Burridge below him.

'I – yes, thanks.'

Above him the tower staircase wound up and up. He heard the footsteps of the others, striking the stone, the brush of their coats against the wall, their breathing, growing laboured. How narrow and high were the winding stairs, how faintly lit on the turns from slender windows.

'Mr Cox?'

He swallowed. People above and a man below. If they fell, or he fell . . . He heard his breath coming in short shallow gasps. The tower was so tight, so echoing and enclosed and endless.

His head was swimming. If they fell, or he fell –

Then they came to the top.

The ringing chamber he entered was about ten feet square. He stood there breathing deeply, as the others took their things off, and draped them on the chairs round the walls. On the floor was a piece of red patterned carpet, put down about 1900, corrupted by moths. He focused his gaze upon it.

'All right, Mr Cox?'

He nodded. 'Just getting my breath.'

'Young man like you?' Fred unwound his muffler. 'Come and have a look at these.'

On the walls were framed notices of great occasions, with the names of all the ringers: the Diamond Jubilee in 1897, the Relief of Mafeking in 1900, the Armistice. They all remembered that.

'Took a bit of getting used to, didn't it, after four years silent?'

'What a sound, though. That was a day. Rang a full quarter-peal.'

'Well, now,' said Mr Burridge. 'Shall we make a start?' He stepped forward. 'A ring of bells is what we have in Asham's Mill,' he told Walter, bringing down six looped ropes. 'That's six bells.' Walter was handed the soft red-and-blue striped tail of rope. The others were taking their places; they stood with their feet planted squarely.

'Now you bring that tenor down, Mr Cox, on a good strong handstroke, and just let the rope slip through your fingers on the backstroke, but mind you don't let it slip right through: if that bell goes up to the belfry someone will have to go up there and bring it down again.'

'And that's dangerous, of course,' put in Mrs Burridge. 'With a loose swinging bell.'

'Never mind about filthy,' said Elsie Peake. 'Not that I've been up there, mind.'

'Come along, Mr Cox.'

Walter pulled, and was astonished by the weight of it, as far above a deep note sounded.

'That's it, keep a hold, that's it. Now what I'm going to suggest, Mr Cox, is that you take the tenor today, then you've just the one note to ring in a touch of grandsire doubles.'

Walter looked at him. His hands were sweating on the rope.

'A very nice sound it is. The tenor strikes the sixth note every time, so you watch me and you'll do very well, Mr Cox.'

He watched, as each of the ringers pulled on a rope and the first chimes sounded. In moments, he was lost and absorbed, waiting for the nod, the call, learning how to pull and release, pull and release, the handstroke, the backstroke – his arms were aching.

'Look to! Look to!'

'Trebles gone!'

High above them, swinging and ringing, out across the fields where the frost was melting. He realised he knew some of the rings already, had been listening to them since childhood.

'Look to the fall'.

That was the ring down.

'That is all.'

Then it was over. The last echo died away from the tower.

They paused for a moment. 'All right, Mr Cox? You did well.' Then they looped up the ropes, the six in a single loose knot in the middle, meeting above the square of red patterned carpet. Dust danced in the sun through the plain glass windows, narrow and high. They picked up their hats and coats from the wooden chairs.

Then they began to climb down.

'You all right there?'

He inched down the winding steps, his head swimming.

Daylight. The sweetness of the open air. They all stood about in the churchyard.

'You'll come again?'

'Oh, yes.'

His feet on firm, ordinary ground. The chaffinches, hopping about in the yew.

'I have vertigo,' he said to Sarah, when he got home. I never knew.


Winter. They were pollarding the willows. From her window in the studio, Sarah and the children, kneeling up on chairs, watched the three men tramp out over the fields: Mr Burridge from Hobbs Farm, Walter's father, so lean and wiry beside him, and Walter, his collar turned up against the cold. The cattle had been taken in. Here and there in the empty fields a fieldfare or starling pecked at tussocks of grass. The men were carrying a ladder, and saws in a leather bag. They went through the open gate to the second field, walking more slowly now, over the ground churned up for months by the cattle, setting their things down on the muddy bank. After last week's rain, the river was full and slow. The men rubbed their hands, stood looking up at the cloudy morning sky, moved along the riverbank amongst the trees, taking a look at it all. Then they propped up the ladder, and got out their saws.

A painting by Clausen, thought Sarah, remembering New English Art Club exhibitions, from long before the war, taken there by her parents, as they had taken her to everything: agricultural labourers, the peasants of Courbet and Bastien-Lépage transplanted from France to English farmland, lifting potatoes, slicing rock-hard swedes, out in the open in all weathers, pinched and ragged and whipped by the wind. And this is Walter's heritage, she thought, watching him steady the ladder as his father climbed: in life, in art. The English landscape – and who, as the war approached, had much cared for that? The machine, the metropolis, that was all anyone talked about, in the London studios, in cafés, in the Cave of the Golden Calf in Percy Street. It was when they got to France that they cared; it was after the war that painting came back to the land.

So perhaps Walter's moment would come.

'Grandad's going up and up,' said Meredith, leaning against the glass.

'Up and up,' said Geoffrey, beside her.

'Don't copy!'

'Sssh.' Sarah drew Meredith away from the window. 'Your hand could go through the glass – be careful. Look, he's going to start cutting now.'

Walter's father was barely visible at first amongst the dense crown of branches: a slight figure high on the ladder, watched by the men below. Then from far across the fields they heard the faint sound of the sawing, awkward and slow at first, finding a strong steady rhythm. In a few moments the first long withy dropped to the ground. Then it all began again, beneath the winter sky.

After a while, Geoffrey clambered down from the chair, but Meredith stayed there, watching it all, the grey-green fields, the grey-white clouds, the men: her grandfather sawing, high on the gnarled old willow, Mr Burridge and her father below, gathering up the falling branches. Behind her, Geoffrey had gone to the toybox. Her mother was over by the press. Her grandfather went on sawing and sawing, still on the first tree.

She turned to her mother. The air above the oil stoves was shimmering.

'Is Euan coming to help?'

'Not today, I don't think.' Sarah was inking a woodcut. 'How are they getting on?'

Meredith looked back to the window. The last of the slender withies had dropped to the ground, and her grandfather was coming down the ladder. In summer the willows wept into the water. But now – now the tree was naked, all cut up and cut off and horrible, bits poking out from great big knobbly lumps – ruined. Wounded and ruined.

'What?' asked Sarah, hearing her sigh.

'I don't like it.'

Sarah came to look. 'You're right. But it will all grow back, even stronger.' She rested her hand on Meredith's shoulder. Then she went back to the press.

Meredith stayed by the window. They were moving the ladder. Who was going to climb up now, and ruin another tree? Serve them all right if they fell. Serve them all right if they fell to the ground from that great tall ladder and never got up again.

When I was a child, said Meredith slowly, years later, naked in her lover's arms – when I was very young, I had violent fantasies.

– Tell me.

– I can't.

– Yes, you can.

– No.

He turned her face to his.

– Meredith?

Her eyes were filling with tears.

– What, darling? You can tell me.

She began to sob.

– I can't. I can't tell anyone.

☆

185

Sarah pulled over the arm of the press, and held on. She moved it back slowly, one hand on the edge of the print. There: the impress of the ink, night-black and clear as starlight. She lifted the paper and set it aside to dry; took another sheet. Down came the press, over and over: willows on the curve of the river, winding deep into the page. Gull and plough. Frozen furrows. The fall of snow in the churchyard, on yew and stone; sheep at a farm gate. Black and white, black and white. Night and day – here was the turn of the earth. And here in the corner of every print, their square, their mark: Three Windows.

Behind her the children were playing on the floor. The oil stoves had been lit since seven, and the studio was warm now, so long as the door was kept closed. Sarah rolled ink on the last of the wood blocks. A good morning's work, the children settled and peaceable, going to the window now and then, to watch the men. She set down the roller. This last engraving came from a drawing done at Hurst Green, in late autumn: bare elms, dark rooks, white goats before the barn. The best print would be Euan's, for Christmas. She lowered the paper upon the block. Across came the arm of the press, over and over again.

Sarah peeled off the last of the prints and numbered it; she held it up to the light. It was smoky and subtle, the birds a soft grey on misty branches, the textures of the goats and the grass and the brick of the barn blending into one another, as if they were all seen from a long way away, hazy as memory, receding over distant decades. Well, that was how it would be, one day. That was how they would all be: part of a pattern of things, that was all.

The men were coming back from the fields. Sarah and the children stood at the window and watched them, tramping back with the saws and leaving the ladder propped up. Behind them, the pollarded willows were dark beneath the sky, the graceful fall of branches gone, the crowns shorn and naked. Meredith had been right: it looked brutal.

Geoffrey banged on the glass.

'Careful,' said Sarah. 'You'll break it.' She prised his hands away, picked him up, held him close.

Meredith was waving to the men, and as they drew close they looked up, and began to wave back. Wintry gleams of sun lay on fence and hedgerow. They parted with a nod, Mr Burridge and Walter's father turning off to Hobbs Farm and Mill Lane, Walter crossing to unlatch the garden gate.

'Lunchtime,' said Sarah, setting Geoffrey down. The flames from the oil stove flickered as she opened the studio door; out on the landing it was draughty and cold. They raced to the freezing bathroom.

Walter went back to work after hot soup and bread and cheese. Sarah put the children down for their rest and drew the curtains. Geoffrey, in his cot, lay sucking his thumb, one arm round a bear from Walter's childhood.

– Or was it John William's?

– No, said his mother to Walter. It was yours. John William's things I keep in the cupboard. She turned away, brushing invisible dust from worn fur.

'All right?' said Sarah to the children now, standing at the door.

'I'm much too big for a rest,' said Meredith.

'Soon you'll be at school. You won't have rests then.'

'After Easter,' said Meredith, as she had said many times.

'After Easter. Go to sleep now.'

She went out, leaving a shoe in the door. Meredith lay gazing across the shadowy room. Geoffrey rattled the bars of his cot. He hauled himself to his feet and threw the bear out.

'Geoffrey!'

She clambered out of her bed and went to fetch him. He was all bashed about and old. She put him back into the cot, very carefully. Geoffrey threw him out again. She picked up the bear and stuffed him back in through the bars, hard. It hurt him, she knew. He was coming to bits.

'Now keep him,' she said to Geoffrey. 'Keep him. Go to sleep. Otherwise something horrible will happen.'

He wavered and trembled and dropped to the mattress. He sank into sleep like a stone in a well, dark and endless.

Sarah looked through the piles of prints and stacked them. She put all her tools up high on the shelf with the inks and roller, and sat in her chair at the window; she pushed back her hair and looked out over the fields. The gleam of winter sun had gone: how bitterly cold it looked. Now it was Walter, up on the ladder, sawing at the withies, dropping them to the ground.

– I have vertigo, he'd said, coming in from the morning with the ringers. I never knew.

– Tell me.

He told her, describing the long claustrophobic climb, the terror of the descent. He held her hand. How good it felt to be back here again, in the ticking kitchen.

– Will it stop you going?

– No. I must overcome it. It's joyful, the ringing, it's heavenly. I wish I'd begun years ago.

Now he was up at the top of a willow, but he was used to that, had been climbing up and down ladders all his life, lifting bales into haylofts, patching up roofs. He and Euan had spent hours on the top of the barn, doing such a good job, and he'd never spoken of vertigo then. It was the closeness of the walls, the fact that you couldn't see round the turn, it was people ahead and behind you – that's what he'd said. Not out in the open, with the wind in your face and the land all around you.

A heron flapped slowly over the field. She saw them all stop to look at it, following its progress into the distance, making for the woods.

'What do you think?' she asked Meredith the next morning, boxing up the prints for the Christmas Fair. 'Which one of these shall I give to Euan?'

She laid out three for her to choose from, while Geoffrey was banging about in the toybox. The first was so dark it was brooding; the second was crisp and clear; the third was the last in the run, smoky and hazy and fading like a dream. Meredith looked at them all.

'This one.' She pointed to the middle.

'Why?'

'It's the best.' She slid off the chair and went back to the window. Everything was cold and grey. She could see how cold they all were out there, cutting and bundling up the branches, sawing away up the ladder. You could see much more of the river now, so rainy and full. And there was the heron!

Meredith pressed her face to the glass. The heron wasn't bothering at all about the men, he was quite a long way downstream. He stood on the bank, still and fierce, watching the water. But the fish were asleep at the bottom, deep in the winter mud: he might have to wait there for ever.

# 1927

Spring rain, and the biblical broadcast of seed. Courbet and Clausen and Van Gogh – figures tramping over the ploughed fields, muddy boots, sacking, the grip of cold and poverty all winter. Winter ending, a thin sharp green.

Spring rain, and overnight the tight buds in the orchards were open, the apple trees white as clouds, white as snow, blackbird and thrush in the branches, songs like a bubbling stream. Watching, working, after months of sombre weather, Walter felt as if he had never been more alive, the wash of water on paper the unlooked-for flood of the Holy Spirit.

Meredith and Geoffrey stood beneath an apple tree, looking up, up. Whiteness was everywhere, water was everywhere, drop upon clinging drop. Meredith reached for a low-hanging branch and shook it. Showers of fallen rain and petals fell all over them: their faces and hair were full of it. Geoffrey spread his arms out wide.

'This is our wedding,' she told him. 'We're married now.'

'What do we do?' He brushed wet blossom from his jumper.

'Now we have a baby.'

He looked around him.

'It's in my *tummy*,' said Meredith.

His eyes widened.

'Feel it. It's going to be a girl.'

'I want a boy,' said Geoffrey.

'Well, you can't have one.'

'I want—'

'Feel it.'

He put out a finger.

'Stay there,' said Meredith. She ducked down under the snowy branches. Petals lay all over the grass. She ran to the house.

'You look busy,' said Sarah, coming along the passage. The door at the far end was open; the house felt fresh and alive again.

'I'm having a baby,' said Meredith, climbing the stairs. She raced along the landing. The studio door was open and light came streaming through. In the bedroom her baby lay waiting. She picked her up and carried her carefully, all along the sunlit landing.

'I've had a baby,' she told her father.

He turned from the easel. Her face was radiant.

'May I see?'

She showed him the sleeping face in the shawl.

'Beautiful. What a beautiful baby. And who's the father?'

'Geoffrey. We've just got married.'

'Ah.' He picked up his brush again, turning away.

Meredith carried the baby downstairs, and out into the garden. The birds were singing and singing. 'Here's the baby now,' she said, ducking back down beneath the apple tree.

Geoffrey had gone. She looked around her. 'Geoffrey?' No answer came. She looked out. He was right across the garden, poking about in the ditch.

'Never mind,' she said to the baby, rocking her close. 'This is our snowy white house. It doesn't matter.'

Spring rain, the river rising. The cows returned from their long confinement to fields full of young wet grass, the hedges alive with darting wren and bluetit. Sun shone in puddles at the gate, the verges sparkled. It was almost Easter.

Walter blew eggs at the kitchen sink.

'How do you *do* that?' asked Sarah. The children were awestruck.

'My father taught me.' He set down an empty shell and began another, pricking each end as deftly as his mother sewed. He lifted the egg to his lips and blew: a stream of viscous yellow poured into a bowl.

'*I* want to do it.'

'Let *me*.'

They all had a try. The sink was full of broken shells. Drops of egg yolk clung to their hair, and their cheeks were scarlet.

Next morning, they all sat round the kitchen table, painting. Rain was trickling down the windows, the sun was coming out again, prisms of light shone on the glass. Meredith decorated her eggshell with careful flowers, Walter in cloudy washes of colour, Sarah in geometric patterns. Geoffrey held his egg with enormous care and bent low over it, breathing deeply. He dabbed on splodges of green.

'Very good,' said Meredith kindly. '*Very* good.'

Euan was coming on Easter Day: one of her eggs was for him. She covered it with daffodils.

'It makes you very tired,' she said. 'All this delicate work.'

'Doesn't it?' Sarah dipped her brush in a jar of water. Meredith did the same. It made a satisfying little clink, every time you did it. She did it again.

'It makes me think of my first painting classes,' said Walter, watching her.

'The trouble *is*,' said Geoffrey, turning his splodgy wet egg, 'the trouble is I've had enough of this.' He slid off his chair and the jars of water rocked.

'Careful.'

He left them all being careful and went off down the passage. Quick past the shadowy stairs. The playroom was empty and light and nobody cared what he did here. He stood at the piano and banged about. A huge watery storm filled the room. Thunder rolled over the fields. There, that was better. He did it again, much louder. The sky was tearing open, the wind and the rain were roaring –

'Geoff-*rey*!'

'Leave him, Meredith. It doesn't matter.'

'It's *awful*!'

Everything in the world was shaking. He could feel the storm coming all the way through him –

There. That was enough.

Here was the rain, going drip drip drip.

He picked out a yellow old key in the middle, and played it twice. No, still too stormy. He tried higher up. That was better. Now something else. Back to the note in the middle. That was all right. He did it again. And much softer.

Plink.

The very last drop.

Geoffrey stood back and looked at it all. Every key was different – different notes, different faces. Some of them looked like goats. Some were old witches, with peeling skin. Some were still snowy and young. Every single one felt different – he knew it, he could tell as soon as he touched them. Some of them hated each other – these two, he could feel them tremble with how wrong they were together. But this, and this, and this one – they were just right.

And they all had their secret lives.

He clambered up on to the stool. People kept leaving things on the top. He took them down again, books and dolls and teacups. Now then.

He lifted the lid, and peered down deep.

There they all were, in the dark.

He would make them all do what he wanted.

Easter morning. Dew and birdsong, the children up at sunrise, the sun glancing off willow and water. The willows beginning to shoot again, moorhen scudding towards the banks.

Walter walked down to the churchyard gate through a garden dense with daffodils. This was his first Easter as a ringer, and he felt the joy of it, the morning so clear and alive, the thin trembling bleat of the lambs sounding right across the fields, right up the lane at Mill Farm and over at Hobbs Farm. From Hobbs, on Good Friday, Mr Burridge had come over to toll the single bell: a measured, sombre hour till three o'clock, then silence.

*And darkness fell over the land.*

Geoffrey had sat listening to that note, marking it out on the table, as they all sat making the Easter garden, until he grew tired of it and went outside. Sarah and Walter watched him, his hand beating in slow time, his intent face. When he'd gone out, they looked at one another, as they had done a few days before, hearing the crashing about in the playroom turn into something quite distinct: a tune.

'Is it in your family?'

'A little,' said Sarah, helping Meredith. She pushed in a catkin tree amongst moss. 'Perhaps my grandmother, now I come to think of it. I never heard her, but my father always said. And my mother played, when I was little, but more to encourage me, I think.'

'What are you talking about?' asked Meredith, sticking in primroses.

'Music,' said Walter, reaching across with another. 'We think Geoffrey is musical.'

Meredith gave him a look.

'But we must develop it,' said Sarah. 'He should have lessons.'

'It's early days. We can't afford it. Let's wait and see.'

'*I'm* the one who's going to school,' said Meredith.

Walter clicked open the churchyard gate. He had left them all getting dressed, before coming over for the service. His parents and sisters would be there, coming back to the house for the hunt in the garden; Euan was joining them all for lunch.

'Morning, Mr Cox.'

'Good morning, Fred. Good morning, Miss Platt.'

There they all were, walking up to the door to the tower. He followed them, drawing a breath. It was getting better. He was making it get better. But still, every time . . . up went the winding stair, so dark and close.

And then the blessed square of light from the chamber, the entry through the open door, the worn red carpet, the graceful loops of the ropes.

– Good morning, good morning.

– Nice morning for it.

– Beautiful, isn't it?

– How are the children, Walter? All excited?

He took his place as the ropes swung down. The chamber was bathed in the light of spring. A touch of plain bob and a touch of grandsire doubles, and a touch of April Days, which they had been practising for weeks. He was getting the hang of it. More than that: he was becoming a ringer.

Mr Burridge gave them the nod.

'Look to!'

Down came the trebles, down came all the rest.

He watched them all, pulling the ropes as for years they had swung haybales up in a barn, baled up the straw and stacked it up for the winter, as he had done for years with his father. Rhythmical, graceful, the handstroke and backstroke, and the bells alive and pealing, calling, out through the churchyard, out across the fields, ringing through Kent, through earth and heaven.

After church, and all the standing about and talking, they raced back into the garden. Where should they start?

'In the ditch! In the ditch!'

'They wouldn't put eggs in the *ditch*.'

Sarah gave them each a paper bag. Walter poured glasses of his father's elderflower wine.

'Cheers.'

'Cheers. A happy Easter.'

They all stood drinking amongst the blossoming apple trees, watching the children run about.

'I've found one!'

'Where? Where was it?'

'Don't they grow up fast?' said Annie. 'Hard to believe it.' She and Ellie were wearing smart little cloche hats for church, Annie's in grey, with a grosgrain ribbon, and Ellie's in green, with a bunch of violets pinned to the side. Rather loud, said Annie to Sarah, as they'd walked up the path. Hats were coming down, you could hardly see a single hair, and hems were rising, even in Kent. Walter's mother cast a glance at skirts above mid-calf.

'You'll get a reputation, if you're not careful.'

'Wouldn't want that,' said Ellie.

Their father gave her a look.

Sarah passed round a tray of little canapés, sent down by her mother from London.

'I won't, thank you very much,' said her father-in-law, watching the children again. 'Don't want to spoil my dinner.'

'I've found one!' called Meredith, emerging from beneath the elder.

'Clever girl. How are you getting on, Geoffrey?'

'I'll go and help him,' said Annie.

As Walter refilled the glasses, Euan came walking up the lane. At the front gate, he stood there, taking it all in: the bridal fall of blossom, the darting children, Walter and Sarah, their arms round one another, he so dark and wiry, she so vital, all the family there.

'Euan! Euan!'

Meredith had seen him. She came running down through the garden, waving a bulging paper bag and panting.

He pushed the gate open, and scooped her up into his arms.

The table was laid with a snowy cloth, the Easter garden and painted eggs in the centre.

'That one is for you,' said Meredith, pointing out all the daffodils on it, as everyone sat down. 'But you can't have it until after lunch.'

'Very well.' Euan sat down beside her. 'And you shall have your present then, too.'

'What is it? What is it?'

'Sssh.'

Lunch was a happy affair: more elderflower wine, much talk and laughter. Looking back, years later, Walter recalled it as a flawless day. Or perhaps it just seemed so, now, after all that had happened since.

Afterwards, out in the garden again, Annie and Ellie gone up with their parents to Asham's Mill, Euan unstrapped his knapsack and withdrew three small packages. He gave one to Walter and Sarah. One to Geoffrey. One to Meredith.

'Be very careful,' he told her. 'Hold out both hands, this is rather heavy.'

She cupped them, she almost dropped it.

He heard her small intake of breath.

'Sit down,' he said gently, taking back the package. 'Then it will be safe.'

She sat at his feet on the grass with her legs crossed. He gave her the present again. She felt in the paper. Several things! Slowly she unwrapped them.

White and smooth and cool in her hot hands. Three snowy marble eggs. A snow-white nest. She placed it on the grass, amongst the fallen petals, and put in the eggs, one by one. They were just new-laid and they fitted perfectly.

'What do you think?' he asked her gravely, squatting down before her.

She touched them, one by one. She nodded. 'Just right. Thank you.'

He ran a hand over her hair and got to his feet again. Walter and Sarah had watched Geoffrey tear off the wrapping from his package: an egg in a cup. Larger, for smaller hands. He took it out. He put it back. He did it again.

'These are so lovely,' said Sarah, watching him, coming over to see Meredith's gift. 'Oh, darling.' She looked at Euan, taking out his pipe. 'How exquisite. How entirely beautiful.'

'And look at this,' said Walter, taking off layers of paper. Marble cut to the shape and size of a goose-egg, buffed to the patina of a shell. He turned it in his hands. 'Is all this stone from Challocks?'

Euan nodded, puffing on his pipe. 'Offcuts – they let me have it for a song.'

'And look what you've made of it,' said Sarah. She knelt down by Meredith's eggs.

'You must be very careful,' said Meredith. 'They have to last for ever.'

Euan set off after tea, for the long walk home on a cool spring evening, before the light had gone.

'I'd walk with you,' said Walter at the gate, 'but I have to ring for Evensong.'

'I'll walk with you,' said Meredith.

'Then I'd have to bring you back again.' Euan was swinging his empty knapsack on to his shoulder.

'Then I'd walk back with you.'

'And then – and then – it could go on for ever.'

Geoffrey was swinging on Walter's arm, looking down the lane for the farmer's boy. The cows were gathering at the gate across the lane. Here he came, with his stick.

'Evening.' He unlatched the gate. The cows came lumbering through. Some were the size of houses.

'Soon there'll be calves,' said Meredith.

'You'll like that,' said Euan. 'Well, now – I must be off.' He moved towards Sarah. Meredith watched them kiss.

'Your egg!' she said suddenly. 'Wait! Wait!'

She raced round the side of the house. The kitchen was terrible, all that clearing up. She reached up to the table, and picked out the daffodil egg; she carried it out again, slower than slow. The cows were swishing past the wall, enormous in the fading light.

'G'arn!' the boy shouted, as one of them stopped at the house. 'G'arn!'

'Here,' she said to Euan, waiting for her. 'This is for you.'

He took it very carefully, and held it in his palm.

'Well, now – isn't this a lovely thing?'

'Will you put it with all your other things?'

'Would you like me to?'

'Yes.'

'Then I will. You can see it next time you come over. Thank you.'

And then he was gone, walking away down the lane by himself, and she leaned on the gate and watched him, as the cows all went lumbering down the other way and Geoffrey ran after them, shouting.

☆

In the middle of the night she woke, chilled and afraid.

– Mummy.

She heard herself whisper, she felt a bad dream wrap round her, she fought it off. The blankets were all in a terrible tangle; she must have been fighting for hours.

– Go away, go away!

She kicked off all the bedclothes. There.

The room was quite light, bathed in silver. A clear spring moon shone through the curtains and on to the hills and valleys of her eiderdown, all in a heap on the floor; on to Geoffrey's hand, flung out through the bars of the cot as pale and still as marble. Something on the chest of drawers was white as the moon.

The dream was in pieces, flapping away like dark birds in the distance.

There was her nest.

She slid out of bed and stepped over all the blankets. She stood at the chest of drawers beneath the window and looked at the three smooth eggs, cupped in the hollow, tip to tip. Three was her number: she knew it, it lay in her blood. She touched each egg in turn, she lifted one out and held it in the palm of her hand, heavy and cool. The others lay waiting for its return. She lifted it to her lips and put it back. How well they fitted, how deeply they belonged together.

The moon shone on to them. The moon belonged to them, white on white, snow on snow. They would always be like this, perfect and unbroken.

Meredith moved to draw aside the curtain. Outside, in the world of the night, dark tree and hedge and empty field were touched by silver. On this side of the house there was no cow, no glinting river, only the long dark line of the ditch, the endless furrows. The massive shapes of the yew in the churchyard loomed by the mighty tower, with its weathervane, turning this way and that in the cold night air. The world of daylight lay asleep.

But she was awake.

Far across the fields, the geese in her grandparents' garden slept, head beneath the great smooth curve of wing; in the cottage, her grandparents sighed in their huge brass bed, as the clock ticked away beside them. Three miles from here, as the dark crow flew, Euan was sleeping, too, the goats on the common resting on moonlit grass, the

199

barn locked up and full of shadows. Pieces of stone and white marble lay within, waiting for him to make them into something.

How quiet and still and cold it was at night. In the silence she could hear the church clock draw its breath, before it began to strike.

Three solemn notes, chiming through the dark.

Then they were over, not even an echo left behind. Where did all the time go to, when it was past? What happened to all those hours? They flew away, like the hoarse dark crow, growing smaller and smaller, until everything that had happened was just a speck, tiny and unimportant, blown away.

Spring rain. Meredith started school. Each morning she set out with Sarah, walking up the lane, satchel bumping on her back, umbrella up, umbrella down again, sun and showers and gusts of wind, the last of the blossom borne away, everything green and bright. At the turning to Parsonage Wood, a jackdaw flew up from the signpost. There was the bus!

'I can go by myself.'

'One day.'

'I can go by myself *now*.'

It drew up beside them. She clambered on.

'Morning, young lady. How are you today?'

'Quite well, thank you.' She took the ticket and went to sit by the window. Sarah sat beside her, the bus started off again, she gazed out at the sparkling fields. Beyond them wound the river, splashed by rain or shining. When it rained she watched the wipers sweep across the glass before the driver, up and down, back and forth. At rest, they lay together, one upon the other, quite content. When they were moving, it felt always as if one was trying to reach the other, this way and that way, always out of reach.

'What are you thinking about?'

Everything, nothing, the way the world began. Once two is two, twice two is four, three twos are six, a hundred twos are . . . The numbers wound up and away into somewhere impossible. Here was the war memorial, with Uncle John William's name. Here was the turning, there was the village, the oak, the shop, the bus pulling up and everyone getting off, everyone rushing about at the school gates.

She tugged at Sarah's hand. The sun was out, the bell was ringing, up and down, up and down, all through the playground, all through the day. It sat on the table outside Mr Hawthorn's office, heavy and shiny and bold as brass. When you were in the top class, you took turns to ring it. On the wall above was the map of the world, enormous. She stood beneath it, crossing seas.

'Meredith? What are you doing here?'

She jumped. 'Nothing, Mr Hawthorn.'

'You should be out in the playground.'

'I was just passing.'

He stood beside her, looking up at distant places. Where should they go?

'How are you getting on?' he asked her. 'Are you enjoying school?'

'Oh, *yes*.'

He smiled. 'It's very nice to have you here. You know I taught your father. And your uncle.'

'Yes, sir.' He had told her this before, when they all came to meet him in the autumn, sitting in his office with the shelves of maths books. He must be getting old and forgetful.

'I'm getting old and forgetful,' he said. 'Of course you know all that.'

'I expect it's because you were in the war,' said Meredith.

He shook his head, looking down at her, at the secondhand frock and darned cardigan. 'Yes,' he said slowly. 'I expect you're right.' He held the door to the playground open. She should have gone out at the side. Well, you couldn't always do what you were supposed to. The sun was dazzling, everyone dashing and shouting. 'I expect you sometimes find it all a bit too noisy,' said Mr Hawthorn.

'Sometimes I do,' said Meredith, 'but it was time I came. I've been wanting to come for ages.'

'Run along, then.'

She ran along, out to the skipping game.

*'Up and down in every weather*
*Over the stream and jump together –'*

Someone was pushing her: she ran into the ring and jumped over the beating rope. Up, down, up, down, up and down in every weather. Here was the rushing stream – she leapt, holding hands and shouting.

'How was it?' Sarah and Walter asked her, every afternoon. 'Have you had a good day?'

'Very good.'

The bus rumbled home just in time for the milking. She often fell asleep on the way. After tea, she tried to teach Geoffrey to read. A lot of other thoughts she used to have were crowded out, now; sometimes she could hardly remember who she used to be.

The corn was ripening, the trees were full, the hops had begun their elaborate climb.

'We have no money,' said Sarah.

Walter was packing his bag for Ashford. She followed him out of the studio.

'My parents could help us more. They'd love to help us.'

'No.'

'Meredith needs school dresses.'

'My mother can make them.'

'She needs new shoes. So does Geoffrey.'

'He's just had some.'

'He's growing. That's what children do.'

In the kitchen, Meredith was packing her satchel.

'Where's Geoffrey?'

'In the garden.'

'He and I could come with you,' said Sarah, brushing Meredith's hair. 'I'll look for cheap sandals.'

He felt in his pockets. 'I'm not sure if I've got two train fares. I could look for the sandals at lunch-time.'

'How can you buy sandals if you haven't enough for two fares?'

'I'll see if I can open an account at Knight's.' He looked at his watch. 'Meredith?'

She followed him out to the gate.

When they had gone, Sarah cleared away breakfast. The kitchen window was open; she could see Geoffrey's dark head moving along through the huge spread of hogweed in the ditch, and hear him mutter to himself as he poked about with his stick.

'None here – none here.'

Long days without a sister. The ditch and the compost heap and water butt had claimed him: creatures in jam jars clambered and glared on the sill.

'I'm going upstairs,' called Sarah.

Sweeping and dusting and making of beds. The sheets had been turned and re-turned by Walter's mother. Sarah picked up books and toys and scattered clothes. She went to the window of the children's room and looked out. No dark head amongst the green.

'Geoffrey?'

'Yes?'

'Where are you?'

'Here.'

She craned across the chest of drawers to see. He was right at the far end of the garden, heaving up stones. 'I'm going into the studio,' she called, and as she withdrew from the window, she brushed against the snow-white eggs in their nest, cool and smooth against her skin. She took one out and held it. From far up Mill Lane she could hear through the open window the sounds of the hens in cottage gardens, and the geese in the orchard. She stood and listened, and the church clock struck the half-hour. Half-past nine on a summer morning. Euan would be working with the barn doors open wide, the sun growing stronger and warmer, falling on wood and stone. They had not been over there since Easter. What was he working on now? She lifted the heavy white egg to her lips. Sculpture invited touch, was a physical experience for the beholder as well as the artist. She put the egg carefully back with the others, snug in the cup of the nest. She thought, I never knew anyone working like this in London. Euan is different, he's doing something different – not Epstein or Gill, but himself.

And what will become of him? she asked herself, walking along the sunlit landing to the studio. She stood there, looking at unsold canvases stacked against the wall, at the monumental *The Trinity of Women*, at the press on the table she hardly had time to use and the boxes of prints which, with Walter's teaching, were almost their only income. What would become of them all? After last year's Depression and General Strike, people were struggling to find jobs, not buy pictures.

'This is no good,' she said aloud.

Downstairs the kitchen door banged open. She could hear Geoffrey struggle with his boots on the doorstep and then the sound of the tap. More jam jars. She looked through Walter's paintings, the landscapes and interiors and still lifes which had grown stronger and more assured with every year and still found scarcely a buyer. Last year he'd sold at the New English Art Club where her father had shown all his life – this year he'd had nothing accepted.

Sarah went to her table. Drawings lay beneath a woodblock. She lifted it off and the breeze stirred the paper. River and fish and bank and willow spilled out of a frame. As she reached for tracing paper she heard Geoffrey coming along the kitchen passage.

'I'm here,' she called, but he went on past to the playroom. After a moment she heard him on the piano, two or three notes tried over and over again. Then silence.

'I'll come down in a minute,' she called, and he began again.

*Lon-don-Bridge . . . Lon-don-Bridge . . .*

That's what it was. Meredith had come home singing it yesterday.

*Lon-don-Bridge-is-fall-ing-down, fall-ing-down, fall-ing-down . . .*

Note by slow note it sounded through the quietness of the house.

High summer. Thick hedges brushed against the sides of the bus as it drove through the lanes into Ashford. Getting off in the square, Euan felt the morning sun beat down and he took off his jacket and hung it over his shoulder as he walked through the town towards Challocks. The alley off Ditchmarsh Street was shady and cool. He wiped his face and pushed open the door to the yard, already thirsty. Inside, sparrows were noisy on the tiled roof over the lean-to; beneath, the uncut blocks and slabs of stone rested against the wall. In summer Euan and the others sometimes worked out here on headstones, plaques, sundials, angels – commissions for public and domestic places: parks and gardens, churchyards. There was always a demand.

He greeted Mrs Challock in the office, then walked through the door to the workshop. High summer. High windows open at the top, the big plain room splashed with shadow and the early morning light. On a corner of a table a little sheaf of papers, weighted by a stone, stirred in the rush of air as the door swung open and shut. In the centre stood an angel, towering over smaller casts and models: carved by Tom Challock in Sussex marble, waiting for polishing, and a place above a grave.

Euan hung up his jacket. He took down his apron, washed at the sink and dried himself on the roller towel. Then he went to his bench between the windows. Stone stood before him; tools lay beside him. The headstone he was working on bore the heavy pencil outlines of Gill's *Perpetua* traced and enlarged and now half-cut: his choice, selected from pages in the catalogue of The Golden Cockerel Press.

Euan picked up his hammer and chisel. The door swung open; he greeted Tom Challock. He set to work.

When he had first come here it felt as if he were back at the Slade: working alongside other men, each intent upon his task, each understanding, more or less, what the other was about. But he knew, after a time, that this was different. What he had brought from the Slade had been taken into the rented factory space in King's Cross, and then into the barn at Hurst Green: something individual, and driven, which belonged only to him, and represented some kind of break with the past. Here, unquestionably, he was part of a tradition, and if the place, and his place in it, resembled anything from earlier days, it was the City & Guilds classes at the Westminster Technical Institute, where he had been learning a craft.

Artist and artisan. As Euan lifted his chisel and began to tap away at the smooth clean lines of the T in REST IN PEACE, centuries of stonemasons stood behind him, before him. Unknown, anonymous; cutters and carvers who left no signature. Sometimes a mason or his workers made a mark, an indication of the part played in a great house or cathedral, but generally the gargoyle and madonna, the gravestone and plaque in the wall stood for themselves, without introduction or attribution. The cutter, the craftsman: a day's work for a day's pay, and home at the end of it, without fame or glory.

Euan, glad to be earning his keep, was also glad to be anonymous. In the barn, his work and his name were everything. This is who I am, he thought, polishing eggs in a nest for Meredith, carving out elmwood into the body of a man, hammering stone to look as if it had grown that way. This is how I shall make my mark in the world. Here, his name meant nothing, would never mean anything. And perhaps that meant it was closer to art than anything else: the creator subsumed to the work. Not I, but the work. Not I, but something greater.

He tapped out the cross of the T, leaned forward to blow out the crumbs of stone.

'Coming on all right,' remarked Tom Challock, walking over to stand beside him at the end of the afternoon. 'How long do you think you'll be on that?'

Euan leaned back. 'Another couple of days should do it.' He looked up at Tom, a steady, contented chap, like his father. 'Why? What's next?'

'Something a bit different. Would you be interested in a memorial? It's to go in St Mark's, out at Asham's Mill.'

'How extraordinary.' Euan put down his tools. 'That's where my friends the Coxes live.'

'Yes – we remembered that. It's one reason why we thought of you. But we also thought you might be just the right man for the job.'

'Which is?'

'It's a commemorative plaque for Richard Monkton, the son at Weston Park. I don't know if your friend has mentioned him. There were two brothers . . .'

'Officers in The Buffs. And only one came back. Yes,' said Euan. 'I've seen his name on the memorial in Denham. And Walter has talked about them. The Monktons are his landlords.'

'Is that so? Well, the son that's left, Mr Charles, he wants something more than the name on the village memorial. Evidently he doesn't feel he can rest until there's something in the local church. And he wants something special – maybe a carving, a relief. How would you feel about that?'

'I've put the war behind me,' Euan said slowly.

'Think it over,' said Tom Challock. 'Take a couple of days. Even then, it's best to meet up with Mr Monkton before you decide. We'll see you tomorrow.'

He went out, leaving the door to swing to.

Euan got up. In the late afternoon, the workshop was filled with a deepening yellow light. He lit his pipe, and tobacco smoke drifted into the air, blue-grey becoming nothingness, amongst the dancing dust. He thought of a new commission, tugging him back to lost lives.

He remembered a painting, a little square oil on board which Walter had done years ago: bare trees, ploughed land, a man with a gun, tall and solitary, walking away with his dog.

Not I, but the work. Not I, but something greater.

I'll meet him, thought Euan, pacing about in the empty workshop.

'Euan has a commission,' said Walter. 'Or the chance of one.'

They were out in the garden, the children playing about after school, he and Sarah drinking tea, watching the sun sink low towards the river. He told her about it, what little he knew. 'He'll be coming over soon, to meet up and discuss it. I don't know whether it will work out.'

'A memorial to Charles Monkton's brother,' said Sarah, thinking. 'They might have asked you for a painting.'

'They might have, but they haven't. It doesn't matter.'

June green and gold, the cuckoo calling, the larks at a dizzying height in the burning afternoons, nightingales in the woods at evening. All these invisible things. Geoffrey stood listening in the middle of the garden. *Cuckoo. Cuckoo.* Two soft notes, hollow and throaty and far away.

Sound of a bicycle, out in the lane. He went to see.

Squeak of brakes, scrape of a foot on the ground. Euan came to a halt.

'Hello, Geoffrey. What are you up to this morning?'

'Nothing much.'

Euan propped the bicycle against the garden wall. Sarah leaned out of the studio window. Across the lane, cows had ambled up to the gate. They flicked away flies and stood staring.

'Walter said you were coming. You know he's teaching today?'

'Yes, it's a pity. But this was the day Monkton suggested.' He took out his handkerchief and wiped away sweat. 'We're meeting in the church at twelve.'

'Well, Walter will be back with Meredith later. He's ringing tonight. Will you stay for lunch? Or have you been invited up to the Hall?'

'I haven't.'

The clock struck the three-quarter hour. Geoffrey kept time on his fingers. Euan noticed.

'I'm coming down,' said Sarah, from the window. 'You must have a drink.'

He and Geoffrey walked round the house to the kitchen. 'Do you always do that?' he asked him.

'Do what?'

'Keep time to the clock.'

'What do you mean?'

Sarah came out through the kitchen door, bearing a tall glass of water. He drank and drank. Geoffrey watched him.

'Another one?' asked Sarah, as a car drew up in the lane.

'Please. That must be Monkton now.'

She walked with him round the house again, down the path to the churchyard gate. Geoffrey trailed after them. The air smelled of ripening corn. Outside the church, a tall figure was closing the door of the car. He raised his hand.

'Good luck,' said Sarah, unlatching the gate. 'See you for lunch.'

He walked through the cool of the churchyard.

'Mr Harrison?' The man at the door of the church came forward. 'Charles Monkton. Good of you to come.'

'Not at all. It was good of you to ask me.'

They shook hands. Monkton's grip was firm, but his smile was fleeting. He was dark and spare, wearing a light summer jacket; his features were thin and intense. He gestured to the porch. 'Shall we go in?'

The clock was striking the noonday hour. They walked through the door to the church of Walter's childhood. Euan remarked on this, smelling polish, old hymn books, roses.

'And my childhood too,' said Monkton, leaving the door wide open. They walked down the nave. The gold cross gleamed on a snowy altar. 'I remember the family very well from those days. I'm pleased to have Cox as a tenant. And then his brother was in The Buffs, of course, as we were.' Monkton spoke these words lightly, as if merely noting any shared time from the past. There was a pause. 'And you? What was your regiment?'

'The Artists' Rifles.'

'Very good. And you and Cox met in London, I understand – at the Slade.'

'We did.' Euan was looking round him, at the simple marble plaques, an urn in a niche. No room in here for tombs or effigies. They came to the altar steps, and Monkton made a gesture, at the transept wall.

'I've had a word with Grant – Michael Grant, that's our padre. Parson, I should say. Of course he has three parishes now, lives over in Denham, as you know. Anyway, he's quite happy to have something here.'

They stood looking up at a space on the whitewashed wall. Light poured on to it from the window opposite, plain leaded glass in the southern wall, where the trees in the lane cast leafy shadows.

Euan considered it. A good, well-lit, generous space in a small country church: he could settle to this.

'And what do you have in mind?' he asked Monkton.

There was no answer.

Euan turned to him. Through the open door the sounds of the summer morning washed into the cool interior: the distant cuckoo, the drone of a bee, sheep from the farms, everything full and alive and endless.

Beside him, Monkton was silent, looking at the empty space where the memorial was to be.

'Forgive me,' he said at last. 'It cast a long shadow, the war.'

'All through the rest of our life,' said Euan. 'I know.'

As he walked back to the house, he could hear running water. He came round the side and saw Geoffrey, crouched beneath the water butt, the tap full on and the ground awash. The children were always playing here.

'What are you making?'

'A mess.'

'So you are. Well done.' He walked up the path to the open kitchen door. 'Sarah?' He knocked and waited, fingering the sage bush which grew beside the step, crushing a leaf. The scent was rich and heady: he remembered seeing Meredith doing just this, stopping to sniff at it, as she ran in and out.

Sarah came down the stairs with a bowl of apples. 'I was up in the attic,' she said, seeing Euan framed in the doorway against the sun. 'How did you get on?'

They sat on the rug beneath the apple trees, with a cloth spread out, a loaf of bread and hard-boiled eggs and salad. 'All this is from the Coxes' garden,' said Sarah, passing a bowl of lettuce. 'And the eggs are from Hobbs Farm.' She unpicked a shell with strong brown fingers. 'What happened?' she asked him. 'What are you going to do?'

Geoffrey lay on the rug and the sun played over him. Behind them, in the cornfields, a lark made miraculous song.

'What I wanted to do by the end,' said Euan slowly, breaking a piece of bread, 'was to carve an avenging angel.'

She waited, watching him brush away crumbs.

'Because Monkton is broken,' he said. 'He's reined in like a thoroughbred horse, but he's broken.'

'I know,' said Sarah, 'I know. We've always sensed it.' She reached out to Geoffrey, growing drowsy in the heat, and stroked his head.

'But then, so was Walter. That's what he told me.'

Long nights in London came back to her: the hot little flat in Shelton Street, the windows wide open on to the baking city.

*'Nothing felt right for years – not until now – not until this.'*

'We all were,' said Euan. 'You know that. Well, I think you must know that.'

She nodded, feeling an intimacy between them she had never felt before, through all their shared encounters. Except – the first time he had come down here: in the happiness of early motherhood, she had felt open to everything.

'You suffered more, perhaps,' she said carefully. 'I mean, Walter lost his brother, but he never went to France. He never saw what I imagine you saw.'

'No one could imagine it.'

And then there was a silence, as she tried to do so, while the bees hummed all around them, and Geoffrey fell asleep.

'Such a beautiful child,' said Euan, at last. 'They both are.'

'Thank you. We're so lucky. Of course,' she said, and then – how thoughtless, how foolish, what made her say that? 'Of course, Charles Monkton has never married. Perhaps that's why . . .'

Euan looked down at the grass, where ants were scurrying. She felt a deep blush spread over her.

'And neither have I,' he said, raising his head and feeling for his pipe, as she realised he always did when anything close or important was touched on. She did not respond, fearful of saying the wrong thing, of hurting or offending or asking too much. 'And why is that, I wonder?' he asked her, lighting up and casting the match aside.

She swallowed. The sweet strong scent of tobacco drifted over the rug; blue-grey smoke spiralled up, up.

'Don't look so frightened,' said Euan.

Her face was burning. He touched her cheek – just a brush, so light, so warm. Then he leaned back on the rug, long legs stretched before him, looking up into the leaves, where hard green fruit was ripening.

'I just cannot find the right person,' he said. 'Or, if I think I have found her, the idea is entirely improper.' He looked at her, grave and direct. 'How fortunate Walter has been to find you.'

☆

Walter and Meredith got off the bus at the turning to Parsonage Wood. They stepped back on to the verge as it rounded the corner, waving away exhaust fumes, holding hands. The late afternoon was hot and dusty: it had not rained for days. Meredith took her hand away and they ambled home, keeping to the shade of the trees. The church clock struck the quarter-hour, a tractor droned in the distance. I shall lie on the rug, thought Walter. I shall lie beneath the apple trees and sleep before the ringing. Meredith was trailing her satchel. Her sandals were scuffed and her dress looked skimpy. He had opened an account at Knight's for ten pounds a quarter, and it would have to be enough. He heard her sigh, the satchel bumping behind her.

'Nearly home.'

'All this school,' said Meredith. 'On and on and on.'

They came to the long low wall of the garden. He saw Geoffrey sitting on the kitchen step, running a battered black engine up and down; he saw Euan and Sarah, sitting on the rug beneath the apple trees, drinking tea and deep in conversation. For a moment this gave him pause. Then they came to the gate and Meredith saw them, and pushed the gate open, suddenly alert, and went running over the grass.

'Euan!' She fell into his lap; his arms went round her.

Walter clicked shut the gate. He leaned against the wall and observed his family, as he might have framed a painting, deep in the garden, deep in the summer afternoon. His wife in her faded summer dress, her hair coming loose from its knot, turned towards their daughter; their daughter looking up at his closest friend, her face full of life and enquiry; his friend bent towards her, as if she were his; the little son on a worn brick step, absorbed in a game – the day like any other day, one in an endless childhood, stretching away like the fields, like memory, like the river, so dark and full.

'Hello.' He walked towards them, dropping his bag on the grass. 'You're still here,' he said to Euan. 'This is a nice surprise.'

'I'm trying to tear myself away.'

'Oh, please don't go,' said Meredith.

'No, stay.' Sarah looked up at Walter, shading her eyes. 'You'd like to have supper with Euan?'

'Remember I'm ringing,' said Walter, kneeling down on the grass beside her.

☆

He climbed up the tower, counting every step. The stone was mellow in the evening sun, streaming in through narrow windows; the ringing chamber was bathed in glory. He stood at the window which overlooked the churchyard side of the house and the garden behind it, waiting for the others to arrive. He could only see the back of the garden, bordering the cornfields, gathering shadows as the sun went down. Geoffrey was standing there, talking to himself, fiddling with a stick. Walter had left Euan listening to Meredith read, her clear high voice sounding through the liquid song of thrush and blackbird, the sounds of the cows filing out down the lane to milking. A day like any other day, Sarah gathering things from the rug, shaking the crumbs off, moving the life of the family towards the evening. A day like any other, but something had changed: he could feel it.

'Evening, Walter.'

'Evening, Fred.'

He turned from the window. There were more footsteps on the stair, everyone arriving, wiping their faces, fanning themselves with hymn books. 'I've never known it so hot.' Far below, Geoffrey's shadow lay dark upon the grass. When the bells began, he would stay there, listening: Sarah had told him about it. 'Not every time, but often enough.' It touched Walter to think of this, but he had never seen it, could only imagine his little son out there on a summer evening, as he hauled down the rope and released it, just as he could only imagine the bells, far above them, swinging so high, and falling back again.

'Ready now?' asked Mr Burridge, unfastening the loop. 'Shall we make a start?'

They took up their places, the ropes came swinging down, he reached for his own.

'A touch of bob minor, then Steadman doubles. One-two-three – look to!'

And they began it, the bells swinging slowly at first, then pealing out through the summer air, far across orchard and cornfield and hopfield, coming towards a crescendo, ringing down carefully, bell by bell.

'Look to! Look to the fall!'

The last notes chiming, one by one, then silence.

A ringing like any other ringing, everyone off home in their ones and twos. Walter descended the winding stair, his hand on the mellow stone wall, wondering at his earlier disquiet.

All through the summer, Euan worked on his commission. The barn doors were open wide; beyond them the sun was dazzling. Inside, it was as cool as a cathedral. His stone was before him, a great slab of Portland, the colour of bleached sand. He was carving a relief, after some consultation and a number of drawings, bicycling up to the Hall on long evenings, spreading them out on the gleaming mahogany dining table, Charles Monkton smoking, leaning over beside him, tense slender fingers moving over the unrolled sheets of paper.

'I don't want a fallen soldier. I'm not sure that I want a soldier at all – there are any number of bloody military memorials. I want something specific to him, to our home.'

'But he was a soldier,' said Euan. 'We all were.'

Monkton raised an eyebrow. 'Even in the Artists' Rifles?'

'Even there.'

Chink of the decanter. 'Stay and have a drink.'

He felt the current of liking flow towards him; he knew it was more than that; he would not be drawn.

'You'll stay for supper?'

'Another time, if I may.'

He bicycled back to the Coxes', between hedgerows heavy with dog roses. From far across the hopfields to the east he could hear the clank of buckets, smell cooking on primus stoves, hear the pickers' children calling. He propped up his bicycle against the garden wall.

'Euan!'

Meredith came racing down the garden in her nightgown. He swung her up high, set her down again. 'Come and look at this,' he said to Walter. They climbed up to the studio with his drawings. Meredith followed. She sat by the window, and listened to them talk and talk.

In the end he drew something simple and pure: he thought perhaps Gill might have liked it. A soldier in profile, drawn from photographs, a lamb at his feet, a stylised border of hops.

Beneath it the lettering, stern and deep. *Richard Monkton 1893– 1917*. No need for more.

And it was all agreed, decided, the stone delivered and his task just beginning. He spent hour after hour upon it.

☆

School had ended, the harvest had begun. Meredith hung on the garden gate and waited for something to happen. The trees were mighty above her; behind and before her the lane stretched away. Euan came over, and went into the church, making notes, taking measurements. She followed; she sat in the airy quietness, swinging her legs in a pew, watching him. Outside the harvester roared.

Right at the end of the summer he finished. Then he came over in the Challocks van, and brought two men with him. She followed them into the church, and watched all the ladders and planking and ropes put about. Everyone crowded in behind her: she willed them all away. Then the men climbed up the ladders and hauled the great slab of stone up, up. They were quiet but straining every inch, she could see it. If somebody made a mistake, or wasn't strong enough: how far it was to the cold stone floor. How it would shatter, and bring them all down with it –

She covered her face with her hands, filled with a terrible excitement.

Footsteps behind her: she dared to look. Her father walked past her, right up to the front. He sat there and drew it all, looking up, looking down, as the men heaved and panted. Then Euan made a great triumphant gesture, the stone slipped into place; they started hammering.

There was a service, there was a dedication. Hops hung everywhere, the church was full of them. She stood with all the others, singing hymns about the war.

# 1929

## 1

'We have no money,' said Sarah. 'We have no money. What are we going to do?'

It was March, cold and rainy. It felt as if spring would never come. They were up in the studio, the children asleep, a single oil stove burning. Sarah wore gloves, and was wrapped in a shawl which had once belonged to her grandmother. She sat in the basket chair, holding her hands above the cut-out flowers on the top of the stove. When she took them away, the petals cast a gentle radiance on to the ceiling. It felt like small comfort.

Walter walked up and down. After all these years the windows were still uncurtained; whichever way he looked, he saw rain and darkness.

'Oh dear. Oh dear, oh dear.'

He walked past boxes of unsold prints on the table. He walked past unsold landscapes, still lifes, interiors, drawings of farms. Up on the wall, *The Trinity of Women* was bathed in shadow. He had had it turned down by the Royal Academy, he had had it turned down by the New English Art Club and a group called the Seven & Five. He had shown it in a group show in Canterbury. People had laughed.

'If I had the money, I'd buy it,' said David Wicks, there with Emily and their new baby.

'Have it,' said Walter. 'You can have it for ten pounds.'

'You'll regret that,' said David. 'One day its time will come.'

At home again, Walter had turned it to the wall. Then he hung it up again. If he was not loyal to his work, who would be?

'We should go down to the kitchen,' he said now. 'We should go down to the warm and do our accounts.'

'I've done them,' said Sarah. 'And I'm too cold to move. I spend half my life in the kitchen. I'd rather be up here.'

He looked at her. 'What do they show, the figures?'

'In the last twelve months you've sold three little oils and five watercolours.'

'As many as that?'

'Stop it. I've sold ten prints and six sets of book plates.'

'We're doing quite well.'

'Stop it.'

He knelt before her. 'What do you want to do?'

'Oh, Walter.' She gave him her hands in their woollen gloves. He kissed them and sat down before her, watching the little blue flame in the oil stove sputtering, turning to gold. Not enough oil. The wick was smoking. They needed so many things.

'Euan has managed so well,' he said, thinking. 'One thing leads to another. You only need one or two good commissions.'

'He doesn't have a family,' she said. 'It's completely different.'

'Why doesn't he?'

'I don't know.'

'Isn't it strange?'

The rain blew against the windows.

'Sarah?'

'What?'

'Euan. Don't you think it's strange?'

'He can't find the right person.'

'Is that what he says?'

'Yes.' She felt herself blushing.

'When did he say that?'

'Ages ago. What does he say to you?'

'Nothing. We never talk about it.'

'Well. Men are strange creatures.' She hesitated. 'You realise – you realise Charles Monkton fell for him?'

'What?'

'Oh, Walter.'

He was astonished at how much this troubled him. 'How do you know?'

'It was obvious. You only had to look at them together. In the church, when the stone was set. At the dedication. Monkton was watching his every move.'

'Well,' said Walter, and was silent. She had taken his hands again. 'What were we talking about?' he asked her.

'Money. Our livelihood.'

'Yes.' He stroked her fingers. 'What do you want to do?'

'I should be working,' said Sarah. After Easter I must find a job. Don't you think I could teach at the college? Printmaking, woodcuts and engravings – I'd love it.'

'You'd be so good at it,' said Walter. 'But even so, one or two classes a week wouldn't bring in much. What else can we do?'

'Teach in London? Do you think you could do that?'

'But where? Who would have me? I haven't a gallery, I haven't any kind of name.'

'At the Slade? Steer always had a soft spot for you.'

'Do you think he's even there, now? He must be so old. And he only came in once a week. It's Tonks I'd need to talk to.'

'He's old, too. He must be close to retiring. But it's worth trying, isn't it? And if not, there's always Westminster, Chelsea, the Royal College . . .'

'They all want names.'

'My father could put in a word.'

It was true.

'Let him,' said Sarah, 'please. He's so old, it would make him so happy to do something useful.'

'I feel that I've failed you.'

'Of course you haven't. You've worked so hard, you've worked on your painting, the teaching, the farms . . .'

'But we have no money.'

'Not enough.'

He got up from the floor, stiff with cold, and walked up and down, moving landscapes and still lifes and pictures of the children on to the easel, taking them down again.

'Oh, Sarah.' What should he do?

She came across the floor and held him.


Now she was older, Meredith could go out. They let her cross into the field for primroses, they let her walk up Mill Lane to her grandparents and back. She wasn't allowed to go beyond there. Once she did. The spring term had ended, the grass was wet and bright and the ditches gurgled.

'Play with me,' said Geoffrey.

'I will in a minute.'

She stood at the gate to the lane. Warblers sang in the reeds by the river, and the hedges were alive with wren and bluetit.

'What shall we play?'

'I'm thinking about it.' She swung on the gate. Across in the field, the cows were staring at them. 'Where's Mummy?'

'I don't know.'

'Go and have a look for her.'

'Why?'

'Because I say so.'

When he had gone inside, she slipped through the gate.

'Meredith?' Sarah was at the studio window.

'I'm going to see Grandma.'

'Take Geoffrey with you.'

'I'm only going for a minute.'

She ran to the turning and set off. The beech trees were endless above her; beyond them the rows of young corn went on for ever. As she approached the line of cottages the geese began honking from the orchard. They were like guard dogs, her father said.

'Hello, Meredith.' Her grandmother was at the front door, wiping floury hands. 'I was wondering if I'd see you this morning. Where's Geoffrey?'

'He's coming next time. What are you making?'

'Just a pie. You can come and help me trim it, if you like.'

She sat at the table with the cutter and the wavy lines of trimming fell away. Through the open window she could hear the geese, settling down again, the clack of their beaks on the old tin dish. She could hear a tractor come rattling down from Mill Farm and the grunting of the pigs as they were fed mid-morning slops. She laid the pastry trimmings all across the pie.

'That's it.' Her grandmother opened the oven door and the little kitchen was filled with a gust of heat. 'In you go.' She slid in the pie dish, and turned to Meredith. 'Well, now.'

'Well, now,' said Meredith, thinking of her plan.

They went out into the orchard and took down all the washing. She folded up tea towels and aprons and shirts; she put all the clothes pegs back in their bag.

'It's time I went home,' she said. The kitchen was full of the smell of baking; her grandmother saw her off at the gate. When she had gone inside again, Meredith turned back, her heart beating, and walked as quiet as anything. But the geese heard at once, and began their racket; she ducked down and ran past the wall.

'Hello, Meredith.'

She leapt. Her grandfather was coming down the lane towards her, back from Mill Farm for his dinner. She hadn't thought of that.

'What are you doing out here?'

'I came to meet you.'

'Did your grandmother send you?'

'No. I mean yes.' Her mouth was dry with lying.

He gave her a look. She took his hand. 'Can I come back with you, after? Can I come up to the farm?'

'What do you want to do that for?'

'I want to see the pigs.'

'You've seen them often enough.'

'I like them. Please.'

'Very well.' They had come back to the cottage gate: the smell of the pie wafted out of the window. Young spring cabbages, munched by snails, grew next to the onion bed. Redcurrant flamed by the wall. 'Best be off home for your dinner,' her grandfather said. 'You can come back with me for the milking.'

She ran all the way home.

'Where have you been all this time?' asked Sarah at the back door. Geoffrey came running up.

'Talking to Grandad.' She was panting too much to speak. 'I'm going up for the milking later.' She flung herself down on the path.

'Take Geoffrey with you. He can't always play by himself.'

'He doesn't.'

'Yes, I do.'

In the late afternoon they went up Mill Lane together. Sun slanted down through the beeches; a pheasant croaked far across the fields.

'I wanted to be by myself,' said Meredith. 'That was the whole point.'

'Well, I'm here,' said Geoffrey, picking up a stick. 'You can't just make me vanish.'

'When you start school—'

'That's not for ages.'

'Don't interrupt. When you start school, you mustn't always follow me.'

219

'I won't.'

'I bet you will.'

He marched off ahead with his stick.

'Hello, you two.' Her grandfather was leaning on the garden wall, puffing on his pipe. She could smell Euan in that blue-grey smoke.

'We've come for the milking,' said Geoffrey.

'He *knows*.'

'Speak nicely, Meredith.' The pipe was tapped out on the wall, the sweet smell drifted away. 'Off we go, then.' Click of the gate, a hand held out to each. They walked up the lane all together.

Soon they could smell the pigs. Then, as they rounded the corner, and came to the farmyard, they saw the cows, filing towards the gate, making splats everywhere. The cows in the field across the lane from their house were from Middle Yalding, a mixture of Guernsey and Friesian, patterned in red and white and black and white, like toy cows. The Mill Farm herd were great big Shorthorns, huge.

'Mind out of the way,' said their grandfather, as one of them came away from the rest.

'Get in 'ere!' called the cowman, running after her. He was toothless and strange and his voice was like nobody else's. Meredith watched him. He was kept on at the farm when the new tenants came because nobody knew what to do with him: that was what her father said. He rounded up the straying cow and she followed the others, but angrily, you could see. In the yard she stood bellowing. The cowman clanged the gate shut, and called to them.

'What did he say?'

'She's had her calf taken,' said her grandfather. 'Better wait here.'

They hung on the gate and watched all the cows filing into the parlour. Swallows skimmed over the yard. She could hear the pigs snorting about in their sties.

'Can we go and see them while you do the milking?'

'Just let me get settled, Meredith.'

She and Geoffrey stood in the doorway and watched it all get started: the cows in their stalls, the feed rattled into the metal bowls, the fetching of buckets and stools. Her grandfather hung up his cap on the hook. Her father had drawn that once, she'd seen it, pinned up on the studio wall: 'That was before I went up to London.' Then the milking began, thin streams in the buckets, her grandfather at one end, the cowman at the other, leaning against the great flanks, his horrible toothless mouth open, grinning at them. Haydust danced in the gleams of sun, huge tongues scraped out the bowls. She'd seen it a hundred times, at Hobbs Farm, at Middle Yalding, here – wherever they needed helping out. But only Mill Farm had the pigs.

'Can we go now?'

'Go on, then. Keep right away from the slurry pit.'

'We will.'

They walked down the yard, where the shade was deepening, and in through the gap by the barn. Hens scratched about by a clump of nettles. There were the pigsties, all warm red brick in the last of the sun. There was the boar! He was right up on his back legs, leaning over the gate, pink as anything. Enormous. They burst out laughing.

'Come on.'

Nettles brushed their bare legs and the stings came up at once, but they were used to them. They stumbled towards him and stood beneath him, gazing at his slobbery snout and stiff white bristles, the wicked little eyes. Geoffrey raised his stick.

'Don't.'

'He likes it.' He reached up and scratched him, just where he could reach. The boar grunted; up came the sows from the next sty.

'Look at them all!'

They stayed there for ages, scratching and talking to each one in turn. A couple of pallets were poking out by the nettles, left there ages ago. They dragged them over the ground, and stood on them, so they could see right in over the walls. The muck was inches deep.

'Lift me up,' said Geoffrey. 'Lift me up on the wall.'

'No.'

'Go on.'

'No. If you fell in there you'd be trampled to death.'

She closed her eyes, trying not to think of it, wanting to think of it: the shout, the fall, the sudden snorts and grunts and nosing, the weight of them, clambering over him. If it was the boar . . .

She put her hands over her mouth. He made to lean over. She grabbed him.

'Stop it! Stop it!'

'Meredith! Geoffrey!'

The voice of their grandfather echoed out through the yard.

'Come on.'

They jumped down from the pallets, and ran back through the gap by the barn.

'Look at you both.'

They looked down at scratches and stings.

'He was up on his legs,' said Geoffrey. 'The boar. He was taller than you.'

'Was he, now? You stay and wait till I've finished.'

They waited for ages, running about in the yard. Their shadows grew longer and longer.

'Stand back! Out of the way now!'

They pressed against the wall, as the herd came out one by one.

'Where's the bad one?' asked Geoffrey.

'She isn't bad, she's lonely. How would you like it if your calf was taken away?'

'I haven't got a calf.'

She looked at him pityingly. Out came the sad lonely cow, last of all. She stood in the yard as the rest of them went through the gate, and she bellowed and bellowed. Streams of drool swung from her open mouth. From up in the calf pens came a thin little answering moo. The cow swung round towards it. It was awful. How could anyone bear it?

Then the cowman came out with his stick and shouted. The great grieving animal lowered her head and swayed out of the yard, off up the splattered lane, following the others, stopping and roaring again.

Agony. Agony –

'What's up, my lass?' Her grandfather was beside her, his hand on her shoulder.

'I hate it. I hate it!' She burst into tears.

'What's that? That old cow? She'll soon be over it, don't you worry.'

She wouldn't, she wouldn't, how could she ever be?

He carried her out to the gate. Geoffrey dawdled. He didn't care. Well then, she didn't care about him.

'Come on, now.'

By the time they came out to the lane the cowman was returning from the fields. He stopped when he saw them, and pushed his cap up, scratching his forehead. He looked down at her, hung on her

222

grandfather's shoulder, and he grinned, and put out a hand black with dirt. His eyes were black, too, and glittering in the dusk. She shrank away.

'Goodnight, Eddie,' said her grandfather firmly, and took Geoffrey's hand. They all walked away towards home.

'Grandad? Will she really get over it quickly?'

'Who's that, then?'

'The *cow*.'

For once he didn't answer straight away. Then he said, 'Yes. I reckon. Animals do.'

Then he stopped in the lane and set her down and squatted down to both of them, holding their hands. 'I want you to promise me something.' She knew it was serious. What? What?

'Both of you, do you hear me? Don't you ever go up there alone, is that clear? Don't you ever go up there without one of us, is that clear?'

'Because of that cow,' said Geoffrey.

'No,' said their grandfather. 'Because I say so. Promise me?'

They nodded. How dusky and cold it was now.

'I want to go home,' said Meredith.

'Off we go, then.' He took a hand each. They swung arms up and down but she didn't feel better.

All the things I feared, she said, years later, naked in her lover's arms. All the things I feared and yet wanted to happen, all at the same time. Horrible, horrible. And then, when it happened . . .

She started to howl.

The summer term began; Meredith went back to school. Sometimes, now she was seven, they let her make the journey by herself. Next term, Geoffrey would be going with her. Walter wrote a long letter to Steer, at the Slade. Doing so brought back a flood of memories. He waited and waited: no reply came. Sarah wrote to the principal of the college in Ashford and was summoned for interview. She set off with Meredith and a box of her work on a wet April morning, leaving Geoffrey with Walter.

'What shall we do?'

They cleared up the kitchen then went into the dining room, long the playroom. Sarah had distempered the walls but the damp still came through, in flaky patches. Geoffrey had picked at them, Meredith had drawn pencilled outlines. Walter noticed this properly for the first time: the map they made, vast continents, great oceans, intricate clusters of islands. It made him think of the map he had drawn years ago, soon after Euan's first visit, small and full of detail: paths marking connections between here and Asham's Mill, here and Denham, here and Hurst Green, where Euan was to settle. He remembered showing it to Meredith one windy afternoon, soon after Geoffrey was born. It was still pinned up by his studio window. Was that what had given her the idea?

Geoffrey was picking things out of the toybox in half-hearted fashion. The rain poured down in the lane. Walter saw the postboy come cycling along through it all, slowing down, getting off at the gate. He came up the path, his cap dripping. Walter went to the front door, and took in the letter from London, smudged with wet.

'Thanks very much,' said the postboy.

'Thank you,' said Walter. He left Geoffrey looking for his engine and took the letter into the kitchen, holding it over the range to dry out. Then he opened it carefully, with a knife.

The letter was in an unfirm hand. Steer thought he could recall him, but was not at his best these days, though he shouldn't complain: he'd had a retrospective at the Tate in April. *First time they've shown a living artist, quite an honour. Took up a lot of time, of course – I made the selection myself. People seemed to like it, but I'm getting too old for much fuss.* He had had an operation and was still not quite right; his sight was fading, and that was very trying. His housekeeper, Mrs Raynes, was old and frail. *She is now ninety-one: I have been blessed to have her with me all my life.* He did not like to leave her, but still went into the Slade once a week; he would retire when Tonks retired, next summer. As for teaching, as for Walter, he was unable to offer suggestions, had nothing to do with that side of things. *But do come and call if you will.*

Walter read the letter again, sitting at the table. He felt as if a door had swung shut, and realised how, once the idea had taken hold of him, he had pinned many hopes on this prospect. Well. Now what?

Geoffrey came back into the kitchen. 'What can I do?'

'I don't know.' He read the letter again, then folded it quickly and slipped it back inside the smudged envelope.

'When's Mummy coming home?'

'Later. With Meredith.'

'Please come and be with me.'

'Soon you'll be at school,' said Walter, pushing his chair back.

'I like it here.'

They went back into the dining room. Walter sat on the piano stool and Geoffrey sat on his lap. He picked out notes at random.

'When you go to school,' said Walter, his arms round Geoffrey's middle, 'perhaps you can have music lessons. Would you like that?'

'I don't know.' He started a tune.

'That's "Jack and Jill".'

'I know.'

'Did Meredith sing it to you?'

'I can't remember.'

Walter listened: such a few notes, climbing high, coming down again. He sang as Geoffrey played them, one by one, and the rain splashed into the garden.

'– *to fetch a pail of* wa-*ter.*
*Jack fell down and broke his crown*
*And Jill came tum-bling* af-*ter* . . .'

After a while, Geoffrey sang it with him, in his thin high voice. The rain fell on and on. When Walter turned to the window, he saw it pelting down into the fields, over the fresh young green of the willows. The river would be rising. He should teach both the children to fish.

'To fetch a pail of *wa*-ter,' Geoffrey sang.

They were the only two people in the world.


Sarah came home in the afternoon, bringing Meredith.

'How did you get on?'

'He's given me a class, to start next month.' She was almost dancing.

He kissed her; she hung the wet coats in the passage.

'I'm starving,' said Meredith.

They sat round the table drinking tea, eating toast and dripping.

'What about you?' asked Sarah.

'We had a good day, didn't we, Geoffrey?'

He showed her two drawings of Geoffrey, at the piano; he also showed her the letter from Steer.

'Poor old boy.' She slipped it back in the envelope. She looked at Walter. 'You're disappointed.'

'Yes. But it doesn't matter.'

'It does.' She turned to Geoffrey, who was digging about in the bowl of dripping. 'Leave it.' She moved it away. 'Write to my father,' she said to Walter. 'Please?'

He wrote that evening, after the children had gone to bed. The rain had stopped; he could hear it dripping through gutters that needed mending. He must get up there and do something. He sat at the table in the lamplight, while Sarah did the mending.

*Dear Geoffrey –*

Dear Geoffrey. What a good day they had had. It had soothed the disappointment. When he went off to school, the house would be empty for the first time ever. How strange that would feel.

*Dear Geoffrey,*
*I wonder if, after all this time of trying to make a go of things, I might now ask your advice . . .*

When he had finished, he saw that Sarah had fallen asleep. He reached for Steer's letter and drew her, quickly, on the back of the envelope, her head to one side, her hair loose, half-darned socks in her lap. The fire had gone down. It was getting cold. He got up and kissed her awake.

'What's the time?'

'Time for bed.'

'Have you written?'

'Yes.'

Upstairs, as they were undressing, he said, 'No more children.'

'What?'

'When Geoffrey goes to school, there'll be nobody here. Today I thought about it and didn't like it.'

'The days will go so fast,' she said, slipping her nightgown over her head. 'You wait and see.'

A long letter came from Sarah's father, almost by return. He would be happy to do what he could, he was making enquiries. It was possible there might be something at Westminster where, as Walter knew, Sickert had once held memorable classes. He and Sarah's mother had been last month to the new show of the Seven & Five, at Tooth's, in Cork Street. They'd started showing pots and fabrics. He wasn't sure this was a good idea, but there was some very good work on the walls, some good people: Hitchens, Jessica Dismorr, Ben and Winifred Nicholson. He was sure that Walter should have another go – and Sarah, too. The gallery had been full of young things, and there were certainly plenty of landscapes. Some of it was getting too modern for him, particularly Nicholson, but – anyway, if Walter were teaching in London, he'd be able to visit the galleries again, take his work along. '*I know a chap at the Central School, come to think of it . . .*'

Walter turned the page, feeling dazed.

In the meantime, Geoffrey Lewis continued, would he not like to bring the family out to France this summer? They had taken a house in Brittany, where of course Matisse had made such discoveries in the 1890s, his whole palette transformed by sun and sea.

'*The children would love it – it would do you all so much good. As for expenses, I know you won't take it amiss if I say we'd be only too happy . . .*'

Walter folded the letter. 'Would you like to go?' he asked Sarah that evening. They were walking with the children down the lanes, now that the days were longer. After last week's torrential rain the grass was lush and the ditches deep with water. Meredith and Geoffrey were running ahead. Sarah took his arm.

'I would if you would,' she said. 'They've been asking for years and now that the children are old enough to travel . . .'

Somewhere a blackbird was singing his heart out. The sky was streaked with gold.

Walter said, 'Everything I've ever wanted is in this place.'

'Anyone would think we were going for ever,' said Sarah. 'No wonder you couldn't paint in London.' She put her head on his shoulder. 'You decide.'

'We'll go,' said Walter. 'Of course we must go.'

They walked on down the lane. The children were peering into a hedge.

'There's a nest! There's a nest!'

'Sssh! Come away!'

Sarah walked quickly ahead. Walter followed. He thought about France, and a flood of light, pouring through shutters, soaking sleepy little towns. He thought about Manet and Monet and the dazzling palette of the Impressionists, which Steer had made his own. He thought about a telegram, brought by a boy on a squeaking bicycle, thirteen years ago this autumn, carried out to the field where he and his father were sawing.

That was France. That was what France had always been.

'Walter?' Sarah had turned. She and the children were waiting for him; endless shadows stretched out on the lane.

Sarah began her teaching on Tuesday mornings, coming back via Denham so she could pick up Meredith at the end of the afternoon. Tuesday was not one of Walter's teaching days, so he looked after Geoffrey. They got into their own routine. In the mornings Walter worked in his studio, and Geoffrey played or drew on the floor, or messed about outside in the ditch, where Walter could keep an eye from the window. After lunch they did things together: they played about on the piano, the windows wide open on to the summery grass. They walked up the lane to his parents, or gardened, or made things. Walter got out the ladder from the privy, long used as a tool shed, and wiped away cobwebs. He went up to the gutter over the kitchen to see what was what, stepping over the wobbly rungs, and cleared leaves, and patched up the holes. His head was steady while he did all this, out in the warm afternoons. He never had a moment's vertigo: it was all right, here in the open. When he turned, he could see far over the ripening corn to the cottages of Asham's Mill, and his mother, mowing the grass.

He came down and did their own grass: Geoffrey carried the box of cuttings over to the heap by the nettle bed, where Cabbage White butterflies danced. On the other side of the house they could hear Fred Eaves mowing the churchyard, and smell the petrol fumes. 'Everyone's busy,' said Geoffrey, coming back with the empty box. Walter climbed the ladder into the apple trees, and let Geoffrey go up there while he stood at the bottom, watching him search for old nests amongst the Bramleys.

'Mind those rungs. I must mend them.'

Full high summer: May slipped into June. In the privy he found his old fishing rod, and brought it out, and cast it across the garden, the little wheel ticking, the line like a living thing, swooping out over the grass and gleaming. 'Let me,' said Geoffrey, but the rod was too big and heavy and the line just trailed. 'I'll make you your own,' said Walter, and went to the tool shed to look for a cane.

They sat in the sun and carved it with notches, using Walter's penknife. They threaded a long piece of Walter's line, and found a thin bit of wire on a shelf which would do for a hook. 'I'll get the bait from the ditch,' Geoffrey said, going in for a jam jar. Then they set off with a jar of worms and the canvas bag for the catch, walking out over the fields towards the river. The cows turned and watched their approach.

'Garn!' shouted Geoffrey, waving his rod.

One or two moved away; mostly they stood there, chewing and chewing, swishing at the flies. Walter and Geoffrey walked on downstream beneath the willows, full-grown again and trailing into the water. Dragonflies darted, coots brought out their young, the heron flapped away. Geoffrey sat on the bank with Walter and watched them, his line next to Walter's line, flicking it back and forth.

'You have to keep still,' said Walter. 'Really still.'

Long peaceful hours. He tried to remember when he had last felt such contentment: the air full of warblers, the leap of the line, Geoffrey intent upon it all. When they'd used all the worms in the jam jar they dipped it for tiddlers and tadpoles. Once they came back with a gudgeon. They carried it in the bag across the fields, reaching the gate just as Sarah and Meredith came down the lane from the bus.

'What sort of a day?' Walter asked them.

'Very good,' said Sarah. 'I like it. We're having a class exhibition at the end of term.' She opened the gate to the garden. 'I had lunch with Euan,' she said, going in.

'Did you? Where?'

'Just in the Crown.' She turned to Meredith, looking at the bag on Walter's shoulder.

'What have you got?'

'Supper.'

'Let me see.' She peered into a glassy eye.

'We caught it,' said Geoffrey. 'I caught it.'

They fried it and ate it with lettuce and bread, sitting out in the garden. Nightingales sang in the woods on the hill, swallows flew low.

'There's a bat!'

The trees in the lane were full of them. They sat watching the frantic little beat of wings, then another and another, as the dusk grew deeper and the moon began to rise above the willows.

Next morning, a letter came from the Central School of Arts and Crafts. Walter was invited for interview at the end of the following week, for a post in the autumn. He should bring a portfolio. He spent two days putting one together, up in the studio, the windows wide open, Sarah beside him, Geoffrey mucking about in the garden. Soon it would be his birthday.

'I've never felt so close to him,' said Walter, leafing through drawings. 'We've really got to know each other.'

'Because I'm away,' said Sarah, holding up a pencil still life, the preparatory drawing for a little oil which now hung in the kitchen: a corner of the table, a crumpled cloth, a jug, a bowl of eggs. 'You should take this,' she said, setting it aside. 'Take it with the painting.' She felt busy and purposeful. Four weeks to France. Everything was opening up. A bee sailed in at the window and sailed out again; she moved to a new pile of drawings.

'It's gone very quiet,' said Walter suddenly.

'What?'

'It's gone very quiet. Outside.'

She went to his window, overlooking the back. 'Geoffrey?' No answer. She looked up and down. His engine lay before the ditch; there were always toys on the grass. 'Geoffrey?'

Walter had gone to her window, looking out on to the lane. The front garden was empty, the gate was shut. 'Geoffrey?' The trees were rustling, like the day in high summer, when he had been born. 'Geoffrey?'

The church clock was striking the quarter-hour, four slow notes in the heat. The silence from the garden was deep and endless. They looked at one another. Then they ran.

White shirt on dazzling green. The ladder was still propped up beneath the apple tree. It was still propped up, but a rung near the top was broken: rotten and ugly and snapped in two. Beneath it, he lay on the grass. No little living boy could ever lie so still.

'How did he die? How? How?'

'He fell,' said Sarah, and began to sob again, the tears pouring out like a river, endless, unstoppable, on and on, her head on her arms on the table.

Meredith stood in the summery kitchen, the breeze blowing in from farm and hopfield, across the beautiful yellow cornfields, in through the window, in through the open door. She looked out to the garden. Everything looked as it had always looked: the path, the towering water butt, the apple trees, the ditch and nettlebed, the long stretch of grass.

But he had fallen –

She heard herself say, 'Geoffrey,' in a strange, strange voice.

A single bell. Four single notes, deep and slow in the still summer air. Each interval was filled with him alive: poking about in the ditch, watching the water splash on the path from the butt by the kitchen door, keeping time to the church clock, as it chimed the quarter-hours. He ran his engine up and down along the path, he cast out a line across the river, tranquil and shady on endless afternoons. Shimmering dragonflies darted and were still; little fish flickered in the shallows. He trudged across the fields with his catch in a jar; he sat by himself at the piano, working out a tune. On long summer evenings he stood in the garden, listening to the bells. One afternoon he climbed up a ladder, into the leafy boughs of an apple tree.

Now they were tolling his life.

One year. Two years. Three. Four.

Never had a silence in the church felt so full, so empty.

Then the vicar who had baptised him began the service, his words falling into the hush like stones, and when it was over, he came down into the aisle and waited, and after a moment Walter and his father stepped out of the pew and raised Geoffrey in his coffin on to their shoulders and bore him out of the churchyard, as they had borne him in.

White surplice brushing the stone. Slow slow footsteps, up to the covered font, and the open door, with everything so full and alive beyond it: sheep cropping the grass between the gravestones, birds flitting in and out of the trees, a cuckoo calling from the distant woods.

They buried him in a little plot by the wall which ran between field and churchyard, overhung by yew. On the far side they could hear the slow walk of the cows. Beyond, from the great yellow stretch of the cornfields, a lark was rising, rising, into the morning blue. The coffin descended. They scattered their dust to dust: William Cox and Geoffrey Lewis, his grandfathers; Alice Cox and Jane Lewis, his grandmothers; Annie and Ellie Cox, his aunts; Euan Harrison, his godfather; Meredith, his sister.

They had not wanted to let her come, but she had made them.

The earth pattered down upon him. No one spoke. Then they moved away and left him there, walking slowly through the church-yard towards the garden gate: two by two; one by one; three: Walter and Sarah and Meredith. We are a different family now, thought Meredith, as they followed the path to the house. Completely different. She could feel the darkness within her grow and grow, filling every part.

A hand touched her shoulder. She turned and looked up: there was Euan, steady and serious, so far above her. They stood there and looked at one another, then she dropped her gaze. The path was full of the silvery trails left by the snails in their long night feed; ants were scurrying into the borders. All these things went on happening.

'Meredith?' Sarah had stopped on the path.

'I'm here,' said Meredith, knowing she was always going to have to say this, all through her life.

Euan's arm was around her shoulders, drawing her close. They walked to where Sarah was waiting, white as snow, white as marble. Then they all followed Walter, opening the side door to the passage which ran through the house, with its coconut matting and coat hooks, where Geoffrey's coat and scarf were still hanging, his boots beneath them, next to his father's, next to hers.

She stopped, as they all walked through, so slow and silent, and looked back at the summery garden, the church beyond.

There was everything which she had always known: the path to the churchyard gate, the wall by the lane. There were the massive yews, the clock in the tower, the weather vane turning, this way and that. There across the lane were the fields, the cows, the river, running on and on. Up in the woods on the hills the cuckoo was calling again: two soft hollow notes, like an echo, calling from somewhere so far away, while the clouds slept in the sun.

# 2

Guard your child. Watch your children. What is a painting, a book, a song, beside the one life of a child? My child. Geoffrey. My baby, baby, baby –

The clock in the tower struck one, two: unchanging notes in the long dark hours, lit by the clear summer moon. Every quarter-hour, every half-hour – the sweet progression that he had listened to so intently:

One two three four –

One two three four.

Then the hour, the small small hours in the dead of the night, so deep and sombre.

People slipped away in the small hours. It often happened, she'd heard it said when her grandmother died, years and years ago, in her solid square bedroom in Wimbledon. End of a life, a last breath, sighed out into the dark.

But he had died on a summer's day.

He was so young, so small and purposeful.

Up in the bedroom, Sarah paced the floor and wept.

One. Two. Three. All through the darkness, all across the fields. Every relentless ticking minute, on and on, into the future, leaving him behind.

Come back, come back, my baby baby baby –

Turn back the hands, the hours, turn back my life.

Give me his life, his life, my little one, my Geoffrey, Geoffrey.

Sarah bent double, and howled.

Night after night after night.

Sarah, Sarah, Sarah.

– Leave me alone.

– Come here, let me hold you.

– No, please leave me. Please, please go away . . . go away.

☆

Night after night, Walter sat down by the range in the kitchen. Above him the floorboards of the bedroom creaked and creaked. Wood ash sank low: he could hear the branches falling. He sat in the darkness, hearing other small sounds, within the great cavern of grief that the house and his soul had become: a rattling window, a mouse in the skirting, the tick of the clock. Things in the world.

He was hollow and hoarse with weeping; his clothes hung off him. When Sarah let him hold her, she felt weightless, like a sick animal, flesh falling away in a fever, bones like the bones of birds.

He sat in the kitchen, the heart of their life with the children, where the range crackled and clothes were hung to dry. They sat round the table, the four of them, over and over again, an ordinary family, passing things, making things, spilling and dropping things, getting on with the morning, the evening, with the next thing and the next.

Ordinary days. Precious ordinary days. They flowed into one another like streams into a river, full and deep, and within them were transfigured moments, touched by light like the light in Vermeer, the domestic made radiant, eternal: milk poured from a jug, eggs in a bowl, silver grains of sand in an hour-glass, running on and on.

Now a great emptiness lay at the heart of the house.

Dawn broke, just a thin pale crack in the dark.

Walter sat motionless at the kitchen table. A long time ago, he had sat here and drawn a map, of every place dear to him, connecting it all through rail and lane and footpath, soon after Meredith was born. No one had dreamt about Geoffrey then, of his small, individual presence, the place he had taken and filled.

He was here, he was gone.

Walter, flooded over and over with memories of their days in the sun, hearing the birds sing in another day, laid his head on the table and wept anew.

Upstairs, Meredith lay listening.

Sometimes she woke in the dark and heard her mother sobbing, behind the closed door of their bedroom, trying to cry quietly, she could tell, but she could still hear it. Sometimes she woke at the sound of a creak on the landing, as footsteps went quietly past her door and down the stairs, or past her door and along to the studio.

The house was filled with sounds she had never heard before. She was filled with feelings she had never had before. She didn't know what to do.

This isn't really happening, she said to herself, as the dull dawn light touched the gap in the curtains. This isn't real.

Across the room the empty bed was like something in a painting. The covers were drawn up and the bear still sat there with his old worn patches and glassy eyes. They were just objects: a bed, a bear. That was what they had to be now. If you thought of them as they used to be, warm and alive, you wouldn't be able to stand it. So. There they were, two shapes in the dull grey light. She turned away from them.

The light at the curtains grew stronger; they stirred in a little gust of air. The three white eggs in their marble nest were cold and ghostly. Had he known, when he made them, that this would become the number in their family? Once there were four of them, a mother and a father and a girl and a boy: tick tick, tick tick, everything even. Now they were all lopsided, and she was in the middle. The eggs in the nest looked so perfect and pure, but three was a terrible number now.

She drew it all out on the covers.

A square, with all the corners, just right. Her fingers went tapping and tapping, making it all. One two three four: here they all were, and none of this had ever happened.

Footsteps came creaking up the stairs, past her door, and along to their bedroom. She heard the door open and close. One, two, in their big high bed.

And here she was. This was where she deserved to be.

One two three –

A corner had broken off, had snapped and fallen. Now there wasn't a square any more but a horrible gaping torn-out piece. Her fingers were scrunching the sheet so tight that it hurt her. Good.

Far across the fields came the sound of the cockerel, tearing the sky apart. He shrieked, he crowed, he was huge and uncaring, he knew that this house was all ruined and broken, and he crowed and crowed and crowed.

Help me, whispered Meredith, tightening the sheet around her fingers.

☆

235

The work of the summer began: the hops, the harvest. Walter and Sarah and Meredith, a different family now, woke from the anguish of the night to the sound of threshing as the tall yellow corn fell away. Meredith stood in her nightgown at her window and watched it, the men from the farms in shirt-sleeves, stooping and tying and setting up the stooks. The big blue tractor from up at Mill Farm throbbed along the rows. Larks flew up, panicking; a hare went racing away, zig-zagging madly towards the distant hedge.

'There's the hare!' she said to Geoffrey, and then remembered.

'I can see Grandad,' she said, and stopped herself.

Their grandfather – her grandfather – had pushed open the gate from Mill Lane and was joining the others, arriving late, walking slowly, wearing his hat against the sun. He looked different. Everything looked different, but especially him. He walked like a stiff old dog across the stubble. The sun was rising and rising: the men wiped their faces.

Behind her the door was opened.

'Meredith?'

Sarah, still in her nightclothes, her hair unbrushed, her face so awful.

Meredith turned, and looked back at the falling corn.

'Hello, darling.' Here she came, over the rugs. 'Did you sleep all right?'

'Yes. Did you?'

'Yes.'

Everyone pretending, now it was day. Throb of the tractor, swish of the corn, all those blades spinning so fast. Her mother stood beside her, drawing her close.

Walter came in. 'I've made tea. I'll make breakfast.' He walked past the bed and the bear. He came up, put his arms round both of them.

'How are you this morning, my darling?'

'All right,' said Meredith, standing between them, feeling how thin they were.

They stood looking out at the swishing corn, the whirring blades, the bending and tying. Two rabbits came bolting out, making for the garden. They swerved at the ditch, as if they knew.

It was late to have breakfast, but nobody cared. Nobody ate very much, but they had to try. The door to the garden stood open, as it always did in the summer, and all the sounds of the world came through: the threshing, the shouts of the men, the distant hens, the bees, the liquid birds. From where she was sitting, she could see the apple trees. That tree. She looked away. On the window ledge overlooking the garden, his creatures swam about in weed-filled jars. The sun glanced off them, they were shady and mysterious and glinting. Sarah had her back to them: she sat clasping her blue china cup, looking through Meredith, miles away.

Walter set down the hour-glass. 'Meredith? You time the eggs.'

They bubbled away in the pan and she watched the glittering sand stream through and through. She always saw it; she always had – the millions and millions of people in the world, going down and down and down. It had always felt dreadful and she always had to look.

But now –

Her fingers tightened round the fragile frame. It snapped, there was a crunch of glass, then blood and splinters and the white sand reddening, her mother's sudden gasp.

They cleared it all up, and her hand was bathed and bandaged.

'How did that happen? Darling, be careful, careful, please.'

'Don't be afraid,' said Meredith.


Between here and Hurst Green lay the hopfields. By late August, all the pickers were long down. The day they set out to visit Euan, the first time since it happened, the air was full of the heady, bittersweet smell of the flowers, as they rounded the bend past the church and saw it all ahead: the women with sacking tied round their middles to keep off the worst of the dirt, standing over the huge bushel baskets, stripping the vines; the men up on ladders and boxes, cutting down more with a knife; the children running up and down between the slanting poles.

It was early afternoon, the sun high, the festoons of tassels green as grasshoppers against the dark leaves. Meredith had seen it all many times, seen the gypsies arriving and setting up camp at the start of the season, and the trainloads of pickers from London pouring out of Denham Station, weighed down with baggage and bundles, looking for the bus, laughing and shouting how quiet it all was, down here. For weeks it stopped being quiet: for weeks every summer you could hear all the calling and laughing and singing as the bines were stripped and the baskets weighed, all day until Mr Burridge called out, 'Strip no more bines!' and the water carrier rumbled along from Hobbs Farm up the track to the huts at the end. Every evening you could smell the camp fires and the sizzling supper, hear all the clanking and pouring and banging about of pails and pots and pans, the children sloshing about in tin baths. Sometimes you heard people singing round the fires.

'*We are the Deptford girls,*
*We are some of the lads,*
*We know all our manners, spend all our tanners,*
*We are the Deptford girls . . .*'

'I want to be a Deptford girl,' Meredith told Sarah, the first time she heard it, on a walk one summer evening last year.

They swung arms as they walked down the lane, singing their hearts out:

'We are the Deptford girls . . .'

Behind them, Geoffrey stopped to climb a gate; they reached home without him, and had to go back.

'What are you *doing*?' said Meredith, as he climbed down.

'Nothing.'

'It's always nothing, and then we have to come and look for you.'

'Don't be so sharp with him,' said Walter. 'He's only small.'

Now they walked down the lane just the three of them, she in the middle. They walked past all the pickers, all the hops on their bines, being cut down in great rustling heaps, lifted and stripped with bare fingers.

'Afternoon.'

'Lovely day.'

The pickers were friendly, but they didn't know. The smell of hops roasting in the oasthouse kilns came drifting over the fields, mingling with the heaps of flowers, and baking earth. She knew it was a beautiful afternoon, as she knew that the sun rose in the east and that seven eights were fifty-six. None of it mattered.

No one was talking: they walked on and on in the heat. They were going to see Euan because they had to do something. She thought of all the things they used to do, all the time in the holidays, all that running about.

Now Walter and Sarah went into the studio and came out again, almost at once. They looked inside the empty playroom and shut the door. She never went in there either.

People came to pay their respects: the vicar, Father Grant, coming over from Denham; Mr Monkton, leaving his dog at the gate, coughing awkwardly as he came up the path; Mr and Mrs Burridge, all the ringers, one by one. Would Walter ever be thinking of coming back? It was early days, of course, they knew, but they wanted him to know he was missed.

Meredith watched her parents usher in their visitors, and listened to their conversations. Nobody really spoke to her: she felt them shy away from it. Sometimes they spoke about her, as they drank their tea. She heard them, as she came in from the garden. Sometimes she stood in the passage, leaning up against the coats, listening. 'Poor little mite, she won't know what to make of it.' 'She does look so peaky, poor child.'

Sometimes they brought her things. Miss Platt brought a little rag doll, with button eyes and a pink stitched mouth. Meredith thanked her, and put the doll in a drawer. It wasn't her birthday. She didn't deserve it. She watched the visitors go to the front door, and Sarah or Walter say goodbye, and close it. Then, from her place amongst the coats, she saw them lean against it, exhausted and pale.

'Where's Meredith?'

'Somewhere about.'

'Don't say that! Meredith?' Sarah's voice rose like a panicking bird.

'I'm here,' said Meredith, coming out of the coats, or down the stairs, or in from the garden. 'I'm here.'

They went into the kitchen. Sarah cleared things away. She sat at the table, gazing out of the window. Meredith drew things – the kettle, the milk jug, all his watery creatures in their murky jars. It was the only time she forgot about it all: she drew and drew. Walter put the pictures up on the wall.

Now they walked past the hopfields and a song floated out behind them, clear in the still summer heat.

'If you go hopping, hopping down in Kent . . .'

'It's years since I heard that,' said Walter.

'You used to sing it to Meredith,' said Sarah, taking her cut and bandaged hand. 'When she was a baby. Don't you remember?'

'That was another lifetime.'

Meredith flexed her sore fingers within her mother's grasp. She thought, When I grow up, I shall have another lifetime, and none of this will have happened.

Long before you turned the corner, you could smell the sea. Especially in summer, the salt breeze blowing over the marshes, everything borne within it: ships and shingle and surf and sand, the cry of the gulls, the smoke of distant tankers. All this came in, blowing over the sheep cropping pale scrubby grass near the shore, over the waterlogged reedbeds, and stunted trees.

Meredith smelled it all, and began to quicken her pace, as she always did. They rounded the corner, high hedges on either side of them, came to the gate on the right where you could look down towards the marshland, came up to the common. Chisel and hammer sounded from the barn, just as always. There were the goats! She and Geoffrey ran towards them.

No. She walked towards them. They were grazing steadily, just as usual, their ropes stretched out and the grass just beyond them thick and bright. Each day they were moved, and how well they kept it down, like the geese in Asham's Mill. This year's kids were both white; they looked up at her with their clear yellow eyes and strained towards her, bleating.

'You're getting big,' she told them, and sank down on the grass. When Geoffrey was here, they had one each. Now the kids both butted and nuzzled her everywhere, nibbling her cotton dress, nosing at her bare arms. 'It tickles! Stop it!' Their coats were so snowy and soft: she held her face against them, warm from the sun and smelling all grassy and goaty. Rooks were calling in the elms behind the barn; her parents were walking up to its open doors. Euan was coming out to greet them, his sleeves rolled up and his blue apron covered in dust.

She sat with her arms round the snow-white kids and looked across at him. She saw him raise his hand to her parents, and walk towards them – slowly, as everyone did things now. She saw him stop, and look round, and knew he was looking for her.

'I'm here,' she said, to the goats and the hot summer grass and the clouds sailing over the elms. 'I'm here,' she said to Euan, and waited for him to see her, a different person now.

☆

She was there on the thick summer turf, stick-thin in her old cotton dress and sandals, a sunburned arm round each of the two white kids, her eyes dark hollows beneath the unkempt fringe. She was gazing across at him, and he looked back, feeling the deep connection that had always run between them stretch out like a rope across the common: You are there, I am here. This is how things are.

Walter and Sarah were walking up towards him. He turned, and waited. They made him think of a field of wheat, which once had stood strong in the sun. Wind had flattened it, a shadow had passed over it, a great mass of cloud blowing over the hills. Now they were gaunt, they were slow, they were broken.

Euan thought of his men, felled like trees, blown asunder, all those years ago. He thought of the first conversation he'd had with Walter, drinking in a London pub on a sharp spring evening, in 1920.

*I lost my brother. It feels like half my body, still.*

He thought of Geoffrey, running down the garden, swinging on a gate, counting the musical hours. Did one little life and death make others pale beside it?

He waited; he held out his arms.


The garden in front of the cottage was a different place from when he had first moved here, burning rotting carpets, clearing out nettles and choking bindweed, digging up stones. Now within its walls were two small patches of lawn, a lilac; the old brick path was uncovered, clumps of geraniums planted on either side. The sea breeze blew in, but the place was sheltered, things grew.

They sat in the shade of the lilac.

What did they talk about now?

'I don't want to talk,' said Sarah. She sat on the blanket and cushions which Euan had laid on the grass, her arms round her knees. Sparrows were hopping about on the wall; gulls drifted in from the sea. 'I just want to be here,' she said. 'I just want to rest.'

'Rest,' said Euan. 'Rest for as long as you like.'

She yawned in the heat and stretched and lay down, her head on a cushion, settling. Ants scurried over the blanket; he brushed them away.

Walter sat on the edge of the blanket, drinking strong tea. He looked at Sarah, curling up, drawing the cushion beneath her cheek, Euan's hand close to her, smoothing it all.

'Meredith?' He turned to her.

She was drinking lemonade on the step at the front door, propped open with a stone.

'Yes?'

'Are you all right there?' He put out a hand. 'Come and join us.'

She shook her head. 'It's cool here. I like it.'

She was framed by the doorway, an oblong of darkness behind her. The two plain square windows on either side showed nothing of the rooms beyond, only things left on the sills: a couple of books, a jug, geraniums in a pot. Now and then reflections of the clouds, full and high, passing slowly, shone on the glass.

Child on a summer afternoon.

For the first time since Geoffrey's death Walter was seeing a painting, and it made him think of another afternoon: coming home with Meredith from school, finding Geoffrey running his engine up and down on the path in the heat, and Sarah and Euan beyond him beneath the apple trees, deep in conversation, close and quiet.

He turned away from Meredith and glanced at the two of them now.

Sarah had fallen asleep. Euan was watching her, smoking his pipe. She was pale and drawn as an invalid; his face was filled with tenderness.

'Euan?'

'Walter.' He looked up; their eyes met. For a moment the passing clouds were reflected in his gaze, too.

They left Sarah sleeping in the shade and walked down to the barn, past the goats, who were resting now, yellow eyes half-closed in the sun. Meredith stayed on the step and watched her father and Euan, their voices borne in on the breeze.

'How are you getting on?'

'Come and see what you think.' A pause. 'Are you managing to work?'

Her father shook his head; Euan's arm went briefly across his shoulders. Then they went into the barn.

Meredith felt the silence vast around her. Her mother slept, her father and Euan looked at carvings, the goats were quiet and still. One or two people were doing their gardens, in the cottages over the common, just as if nothing had happened.

She thought, This is what it's going to be like. There will always be a silence, and I shall always have to fill it.

The little walled garden led out to the common. The common led down to the lane. Beyond it were the fields of sheep, the marshes, the shingle, the limitless sea.

'Geoffrey?' said Meredith.

The summer was fading. Autumn blew scarlet and ochre and russet over the fields. Meredith got ready to go back to school. The mornings held the first chill, the first mist. She was to wear new long stockings and a new green cardigan her grandmother had knitted for her all through the end of August. Sarah took her up to Asham's Mill to have it properly fitted and sewn along the seams, just before term began.

It was early evening, the beech trees turning coppery above them, the grave grey trunks lit by shafts of sun. Beyond them, rabbits ran over the stubble in the empty cornfields. There was the hare! He stood on his great haunches, his paws up, his ears up, watching them pass.

Meredith tugged at Sarah's arm.

'What?'

'The hare. Look.'

They stood there and watched him, but as soon as he sensed this he ran, streaking away to the hedgerow, raising tiny clouds of earth. He had been saved from the whirring blades; he was strong and free.

Footsteps round the bend. A man came down the lane towards them, a dog nosing along in the verge beside him. He slowed as he saw them, and called her to heel.

'Mrs Cox.' He touched his cap. 'Good evening.'

'Hello, Mr Monkton.'

He would have walked by – Sarah knew that he wanted to. What did you say to a grieving mother, once you had paid your respects? She knew that he did not know.

'It's a beautiful evening,' she said, for it was, though a hollow of darkness lay at its heart. She must manage the pleasantries, once in a while: she must make the world normal for Meredith.

'Yes, yes it is,' said Charles Monkton, and then, with such diffidence, 'How are you? How are you all?'

'We're managing,' said Sarah, who woke at four every morning. 'Thank you.'

'My very best to your husband.' And then the dog smelled the rabbits, and shot away after them, and he had a reason to turn, and go after her, his empty bag ready. 'Excuse me.' The moment had gone.

They walked on, round the bend to the cottages. Meredith thought, I am invisible. Mr Monkton did not even notice me. Smoke was rising from her grandparents' chimney; bonfire smoke, too, from a neighbour's garden. Blue, grey and gold on a summer evening, and she was disappearing. Soon, like the rising threads of blue, she would be gone. Nobody knew this.

They came to the gate, saw the door standing open. Her grandmother heard them, came out down the path.

'Hello, my dears.' She was so old now, her hair all streaked with white.

They clicked open the gate, and the geese began their racket. 'I've everything ready for you,' she said to Meredith. 'Should fit a treat, unless you've grown.' She stood for Sarah's London kiss, as always.

– I've shrunk, said Meredith. Can't you see?

They walked up the path. Clumps of Chinese lanterns stood in a corner against the wall, orange flaming on deep green leaves.

'Where's Grandad?'

'Still at the milking. He'll be back soon, he's wanting to see you.'

Inside the dark little cottage they went. The geese settled down, the clock ticked away in the parlour.

'Everything's upstairs,' said her grandmother. 'I've laid it all out in Walter's room.' They climbed the narrow stairs. The room where her father had spent his boyhood was still, he had often told her, much as it was when he had left it, to go up to London and learn to be an artist. This was where he used to sleep, sharing a bed with her Uncle John William, years and years ago, before he went off to the war and got killed.

'Here we are, then. You come and try this.'

Pieces of dark green knitting lay on the bed, curling at the edges, next to a box of pins. Her mother went to the open window, and stood looking out at the lane. The smell of the bonfire drifted in; a sleepy Red Admiral stirred on the sill. Meredith stood in the middle of the room and held her arms out, in turn, as her grandmother pinned the sleeves on.

'She's a thin little lass,' she said to Sarah.

'I know. We've all lost so much weight.'

Her grandmother held pins in her mouth, closing the curling seams. Footsteps went past and the geese started honking.

'Who's that?'

'Charles Monkton. We saw him on the way up.'

Meredith held the other arm out, flexing the one which ached.

'What a good girl. What's your dad doing while you're up here?'

'He's in the studio,' said Sarah. 'He can't paint – he just wants to be in there.'

Agnes didn't answer, she just went on with the pinning.

Meredith thought of the studio, and of her father in it, looking at all his pictures. Her grandmother did the buttons up, and turned her to face the window, tugging the cardigan down all round her.

Sarah, at the window, said, 'Every time I come up here I try to imagine it all – Walter's childhood.'

'Ordinary enough,' said her grandmother, turning Meredith round again.

'That's not what Walter says. He says it made him a painter.' Shadows were deepening in the lane; someone was sawing in another garden. She turned back to the room. 'How are you getting on?'

'Reckon it'll do.' Her grandmother turned Meredith round again. 'What do you think?'

'Lovely. Thank you. Do you like it, Meredith?'

She looked at herself in the glass on the chest, almost giddy with all the turning. Behind her, her mother and grandmother were framed like a painting, three heads close, all looking, no one talking about what had happened.

'*The Trinity of Women*,' she said, as the last rays of sun touched the glass, thinking of her father up in the empty studio, wondering how to go on.

'Fancy you thinking of that.'

'Why is it strange?' asked Sarah. 'She's looked at it all her life.'

From far up the lane came the sound of the herd at Mill Farm, going back to the fields: slow footsteps, the shout of the cowman, splattering cowpats. Then above this rose another sound, the great grieving bellow of a cow without her calf, a roar through the summer evening, on and on and on.

Nobody spoke. Meredith moved, and the pins dug into her.

☆

Next week, she went back to school. They all walked down to the corner at quarter-past eight, just as usual. Dew lay on the verges, mist hung over the river. Meredith said, as she had said at breakfast, 'You don't have to come with me. I was used to going by myself.'

'Just the first morning,' said Walter and Sarah again, and shepherded her on to the bus. The boys from Parsonage Wood were fooling about already.

'Their parents will be glad to see the back of them,' said the driver, punching the three tickets. Then he realised who he was talking to, you could see it all over his face. So everyone all around must have heard about it, and have to think twice before they spoke.

Meredith sat by the window, with Sarah beside her, and Walter across the aisle. The bus moved off, and as they rumbled between the yellowing hedgerows her stomach was suddenly churning with nerves. It was always like this at the start of the term, but today was different. What would she say to them all?

– There's Meredith Cox.
– Sssh, there's Meredith Cox.
– Why, what's happened?
– Haven't you heard?

Whispers, shocked faces, nobody knowing what to say.

'I don't want to go,' she said to Sarah. 'I don't want to go.'

'We're coming in with you,' said Sarah, taking her hand. 'We'll help you.'

They pulled up in the village: she saw everyone going along towards the gates. Here we are, she said to Geoffrey. I'll show you everything. You can follow me if you want.

She shut her eyes, hearing the boys come shoving each other along the aisle, getting off laughing.

'Come on,' said Walter, and the three of them got up, and got off the bus. A train had pulled in at the station, the 8.45 to London, she knew, it was there every weekday. Clouds of steam hissed up over the tiled roof; people hurried into the booking office.

They walked hand in hand up the street to the school gates, following other families. Maureen Parker was there with her mother; Emily Walker came up with hers.

'Hello, Meredith,' said Mrs Walker, in a kind strained voice, and she greeted Walter and Sarah. 'My dears, I'm so sorry.'

She listened to her parents thanking everyone for being sorry, their faces white and smiling. She could feel them both trying to be brave, and she stood there like a statue in the hot green cardigan, her stomach like water, her knees like water, willing it all to be over, be gone, like the summer, like the cuckoo, flown back to Africa, leaving the woods deep and quiet.

The bell rang out through the playground, clanging and bright. Mr Hawthorn was coming towards them, beckoning to her parents.

'Hello, Meredith.' He was huge and kindly. She couldn't speak. Then Emily Walker took her hand. 'We'll be here this afternoon,' said Sarah, kissing her. 'We'll think of you all day,' said Walter.

Meredith nodded. They followed Mr Hawthorn into his office, the bell died away, and the train puffed out of the station. She lined up with all the others, facing the side door. The school day began.

Walter and Sarah came out of Mr Hawthorn's office, with its desk and its glass-fronted bookcase and black and white Constable print. He saw them to the front door, propped open to let in the sun. Behind, from the two classrooms, they could hear children chanting their tables. Mr Hawthorn looked at his watch.

'We'll be going in for assembly in a moment.'

'We've kept you,' said Walter.

'Not in the least. Not in the very least.' He shook their hands. 'She's a bright little girl,' he said again, so sadly. 'We'll do our very best.'

They thanked him, hearing the chanting stop, and the scrape of chairs.

'We must let you get on,' said Walter, and he took Sarah's elbow and guided her out of the tall iron gates, where he and John William had used to run in.

'What shall we do now?' he asked her.

'I don't know.'

They walked down the street to the green, where the oak's first leaves had begun to fall. Now that the train had gone, and the school day had started, Denham was quiet, the bus driver reading the paper in his cab, a few mothers talking outside the post office, where the cat was washing.

'Let's sit down.'

They sat on the seat beneath the tree. Above them a squirrel scampered about in the branches, and more leaves fell. Then an acorn fell, bouncing off the wooden arm of the seat, and falling on to the grass before them. Neither of them bent to pick it up.

'This is the first time we've been alone,' said Walter.

'Yes,' said Sarah, looking at the scattering of leaves.

'What are we going to do?' he said. 'What are we going to do?'

'I don't know,' said Sarah again. She didn't know anything. The day stretched ahead, and the empty house lay waiting. How were they to return?

They went on sitting in silence. Then on to the quiet street came the sound of children singing, as the hymn at assembly floated out of the open schoolroom windows.

> *'All things bright and beautiful,*
> *All creatures great and small . . .'*

'Oh, Walter!' Sarah felt herself crumple; she covered her face. 'Meredith will be . . .' She thought of her standing there, trying to sing with all the others.

> *'All things wise and wonderful,*
> *The Lord God made them all . . .'*

Walter's arm went round her; they held one another, as the squirrel above them leapt from branch to branch, and acorns came pattering down.

'Let's walk back,' said Walter at last. 'We'll take our time.'

She nodded, feeling in her pocket for a handkerchief, wiping her eyes. Outside the station the bus started up, and the driver hooted. Walter turned, and made a gesture. It pulled away, puffing its clouds of exhaust.

'We need some things,' said Sarah, trying to collect herself. 'We need to do some shopping.'

'I'll do it. What do we need?'

She couldn't remember. 'Bread. Milk. Butter? Anything you can see.' She watched him walk slowly across to the post office shop, with its enamel plaques nailed into the brick, for Brooke Bond and Senior Service. She watched him stop to stroke the cat on the sill, and stand aside for an old boy coming out with a full string bag, and greet him, as if this were any ordinary day, any ordinary time. She thought of herself greeting Charles Monkton, a few days ago, out in Mill Lane.

Civilities, pleasantries, getting them through.

We should be raging, she thought now. I am drained, I am bitter, I am someone I do not recognise.

She sat there and waited, hearing the squirrel dance above her, amongst the rustling leaves. Walter came back, his canvas bag filled with provisions. 'Shall we go?'

They made their slow way down the street.

The early morning mist had quite gone. They walked past cottages where late geraniums bloomed on the sill, as if it were summer; the air was warming. A young woman came up the pavement with a small fair-headed boy on a small wooden tricycle, puffing his way up the slope.

'Lovely day,' said his mother, as they stepped out of his way. 'Mind now, Eric.'

Walter took Sarah's hand in silence; the little boy pedalled past them, ringing his bell on the flat.

They left the outskirts of the village and came to the war memorial, tall and pale on its patch of grass. They stood before it, as they had done many times, coming down here every Armistice since Meredith was a baby, bringing both children, the service a part of their lives. The roll of the six familiar names was beginning to weather: there were streaks of rain, bird droppings, small patches of lichen.

'It isn't fair,' said Sarah, her hand in Walter's. 'It isn't right.'

Walter nodded. 'I do keep thinking,' he said.

He looked just like his father as he said this: he sounded just like him. Sarah in these words heard generations – people to whom terrible things happened, who got on with their lives and rarely spoke of what meant most to them, as Walter's father had never spoken to her of John William. He hardly spoke of Geoffrey now, but his whole appearance had altered. He was stiff, he was shrunken, his face beneath his old felt hat was pinched. And Agnes had gone white.

As for her own parents, they had gone back to London ten years older.

'Come and stay with us – please. Bring Meredith. Let us look after you.'

'I will,' Sarah told them. 'I will in a while. I can't leave this house yet. I have to be where . . .'

They nodded: they knew. They got into their car in the lane, and drove away, slow as a hearse.

A sparrow flew on to the war memorial, then it flew off. Somewhere a tractor started up.

'Let's go,' said Walter.

They started the long walk home.

Sarah said, 'I was thinking about our parents. I told my mother I had to stay in the house. I said that I couldn't leave it. Now I don't want to go back.'

He looked at her. 'Do you want to go up to London, then?'

She shook her head. 'I don't know what I want. Nowhere is right.'

Bullocks came slowly down the field, making for the trough by the gate, where water beetles darted. The last of the dog roses rambled over the hedgerows.

'Do you remember,' said Walter, looking at the papery pink flowers, with their thorny stems, 'do you remember walking back here when Meredith was a baby, after we'd said goodbye to Euan? The first time he came down here?'

'Yes. Yes, I do. We were so happy then, weren't we? Everything was so new. Meredith was so beautiful.'

'She's beautiful still.'

'She's changed. She's a different child.'

'She almost pricked her finger that day – you said it was Snow White's mother who died. I thought that if anything happened to you –'

They stopped in the lane. He drew her to him; Sarah sank her head on his shoulder. He stroked her mass of knotted-back hair, feeling the springiness and life gone out of it. Flies buzzed here and there in the stillness. Neither of them spoke. After a while, he said slowly, 'I want to ask you something.'

Her arms were round him. How slight and thin he was now, no longer wiry but bony and frail. 'Go on.'

'About Euan.' He swallowed; he felt her tense against him. 'Sometimes I – once or twice I've wondered if he – if you and he . . .'

She drew away from him, flushing. 'I don't know how you can ask that. I don't know how you can even think of it now.'

'I'm sorry,' he said, feeling the moment's closeness slip away, running out of his hands like sand, like water. 'Forgive me. I'm overwrought. I don't know what I'm saying.'

They walked on down the lane, winding away from them, on to the crossroads, on and on to the house, which had once held everything.

# 3

In the late 1920s, monumental pieces of sculpture were commissioned for public buildings in London. They included Epstein's *Night* and *Day*, Eric Gill's *East Wind* and Henry Moore's *West Wind*, all set in the façade of the London Underground headquarters on Broadway, near St James's Park.

The Epstein caused an uproar. Two vast seated figures, which could have guarded an Abyssinian palace, were set prominently above the entrance. Within the giant knees of *Day*, a slender naked boy stood with upraised arms before him: new life brought forth, or youth awakening night's long sleep. The tabloids found it obscene. Moore's relief, in three great slabs of Portland stone, attracted less attention. Solid, earthy, simple and strong, the huge plain limbs and mask-like features might have come from ancient statues in the Cyclades, gazing out over the surf of the Aegean. Gill's *East Wind* had none of these massive qualities. The young naked male in relief was graceful, lyrical, long fingers plucking the currents of air like harp strings, eyes half-closed in a dreamy, ecstatic smile.

Three monumental works in stone, three mighty figures in English modernist sculpture. The carvings stood high above the rush of London traffic: above the commuters, pouring out of the Underground to shops and offices; across from the lakes and trees of St James's Park where, on a winter afternoon in 1910, Sarah had stopped to look at the waterbirds, on her way with her parents to the Grafton Galleries. Cold rainy London, with its coal fires and foggy skies, lit up by Gauguin, Van Gogh, Matisse.

Three monumental works in stone. By the end of 1929 they were all in place.

In the late autumn of 1929, a stone was set in place in a small Kent churchyard, carved by the sculptor Euan Harrison.

The morning was overcast and threatening rain; the last leaves blew down the lane and over the garden. Fred Eaves was out, sweeping them off the paths between the graves. They could hear the steady swish of the broom as they gathered in the dining room, which had become the playroom, which had become, without anyone acknowledging it, Geoffrey's music room.

'We can't keep it all shut up,' said Sarah, the morning before, when Meredith had left for school.

'I can't go in there,' said Walter, going upstairs.

But Sarah laid a fire, and swept the carpet. She opened the windows, letting in fresh cold air. She polished the table, and laid it with a heavy cloth, which had belonged to her grandmother; she polished the piano, and dusted the yellowing keys. When she had done this, she wept. Then she went out to the garden, and cut a small bunch of holly, and a spray of ivy, shivering in the wind. Indoors, in the kitchen, she set them in one of his jam jars, its creatures put back in the ditch weeks ago. She carried it back along the passage. Walter was leaning against the playroom door, looking in, very pale.

'Walter?' She showed him the jar of glossy green.

He nodded, and watched her put it on top of the piano.

'I'm sure that it's right that we gather in here,' she said, made calmer by the activity, cleansed by the cold. 'It's in his memory, tomorrow. We must keep the room alive for him.'

He nodded again.

'Walter?'

'Yes. Yes, I know.'

The sound of a van was approaching from beyond the church: she went to the window. 'That's the Challocks van,' she said unsteadily. 'That's the stone.' They heard it pull up at the churchyard gate. 'Shall we go and—'

'No,' said Walter. 'The men will do it.'

'Euan's come with them,' said Sarah, as the van doors opened.

'Has he?' Walter watched her leave, going to open the front door. Then he made himself enter the room. It smelled of polish and firewood; the open sash windows rattled. He walked up and down past Meredith's pencilled maps of damp; he looked at the clean glass jam jar, with its spiky leaves, a berry here and there amongst the green, the cream-streaked ivy trailing over the shining lid of the piano. He heard a high clear little voice, he saw himself sitting there on the stool, Geoffrey's warm body against him, on his lap, the summer rain soaking the garden, the fields, the weeping willows.

'*To fetch a pail of wa-ter . . .*'

He covered his face.

Somewhere in another country the front door opened and closed. Euan's voice. Sarah's voice.

'Walter?'

He made himself look at them. Euan's face was full of sorrow.

'Forgive me,' he said. 'I'm intruding. I didn't want the stone to travel without me.'

'You were right,' said Walter, when he could speak.

'I'll go back with the van, once we've unloaded.'

'No, don't do that,' said Sarah carefully. 'Meredith will be home soon – I know she'd love to see you.' She looked at her watch. 'I'll walk up to the corner, the bus will be here at any minute.'

She went to get her coat. 'I'll go and unload,' said Euan. He looked at Walter. 'You don't want to come with me?'

'No.' He stood in the big cold room, listening to their voices, their footsteps, going in different directions. He went to the window, saw the doors of the van unlocked, and the little square stone lifted out, wrapped in canvas, tied with a slender rope.

'That's better,' said Meredith, coming in from the cold, still in her school coat and knitted hat. She looked round the darkening playroom, where she and Geoffrey had done things. What had they done? All that playing about. She sniffed. 'It smells nice.' She walked around, fingering the tablecloth, looking at the jar of holly, with candles set in saucers on either side. The piano case was gleaming. 'Much better,' she said to Sarah, putting out glasses and plates. 'He'll like it.'

'Who will?'

'Geoffrey. If he ever comes back, he'll think it's nice.'

Sarah stopped still, with a glass in her hand. 'What did you say?'

'Nothing,' said Meredith, wandering out to the coat rack.

Next morning, they all walked down the path to the churchyard gate. It was still cloudy, with rain in the air. Fred Eaves had swept up the last of the leaves and put them on the pile. He stood by the gate to the lane, and lifted his hat as they came into the churchyard: Walter and Sarah, William and Agnes Cox, Euan and Meredith.

'Are you sure she should come?'

'It might make it real for her.'

She had heard them, down in the kitchen, while she lay awake in the dark.

'Euan? What do you think?'

A silence. Then, 'Yes. Yes, I think she should come.'

Two by two up the path, past the church, beneath the yew, over to the wall which divided the churchyard from farmland. The cows had gone in for the winter, the cornfields were endless bare furrows. There was the place where he lay, and there was a digger, and the vicar, and the stone, wrapped in canvas, leaning against the wall, where ivy clambered.

Walter and Sarah turned to her. She went to stand between them, giving them a hand each. The place where he lay was still just bare earth – not a blade of grass had crept towards it. She stood there and looked at it, and looked at Euan, moving to the wall, taking the canvas off, lifting the stone. Then he and the digger set to work, placing it, firming it, stamping down the earth till the stone was in place, secure. It stood there, so small and plain.

*In loving memory of*
*Geoffrey William Cox*
*10th June 1924–22nd May 1929*

'Well. There we are,' said Euan quietly, and he stood to one side, across from them all, as the vicar stepped forward and began to say a prayer.

'Geoffrey?' said Meredith, deep inside where no one could ever hear her.

The prayer blew about in the autumn wind. Across on the other side of the grave Euan had bowed his head. Then the words had vanished, all blown away, and there was a silence, and everyone looked up. A pheasant croaked out in the empty fields, a few dry leaves danced up from the pile in the corner. Meredith looked at Euan, so serious and sad for them all, and at the lettering, so small but so deep and strong.

'You've done it beautifully,' she said.

He looked across at her. He gave her a smile which went through her entirely, as if everything else had fallen away and nothing else was ever going to happen again: there was only this strange, long-lasting feeling. She tried to smile back but she couldn't do it properly, there was only a flicker, and a huge great lump in her throat, so she had to look down at the flattened grass, and swallow down everything, everything, till it had gone.

# 1930

## 1

Early in the year, a letter came from London, addressed to Walter at Asham's Mill. Since the post never came till mid-morning, his father dropped it in on his way to Hobbs Farm the next day. It was still dark and early, and threatening rain, the trees tossing in the February winds. Meredith heard the letterbox bang on her way downstairs, and went to the mat. She opened the door and waved to her grandfather, already closing the garden gate.

'Thank you!'

He turned and nodded, all muffled up in his scarf and gumboots. 'You off to school?'

'In a little while. I'll give this to Father.'

'Good lass.' Off he went, old and slow in the wind.

She carried the letter into the kitchen, looking at the postmark.

'What's that?' Walter was frying eggs.

'It's from W. C.' She propped it against the teapot and pulled her chair up. Now term was in full swing she was always busy; she reached for her book and began to read, waiting for breakfast.

Walter put down the egg slice and came over. He looked at the smudged Remington typeface and opened the envelope with a knife. All her life Meredith remembered the way he did things: neat, careful, unhurried. Even now, when he was not himself. None of them were themselves any more.

'Well, well.'

She turned the page. 'Who's it from?'

'It's from the Slade. It's about my old professor.'

'Terrible Tonks.'

'Fancy you remembering that.'

'I remember everything,' said Meredith, and then, in the pause, 'Those eggs are burning.'

Walter went to the range and took off the frying pan. He scraped the eggs on to the plates, with fried bread, and poured more tea. Wind shook the black glass in the windows.

'Well?' asked Meredith, eating little bits.

'"*Dear Mr Cox,*"' read Walter aloud, '"*As a former student of the Slade I am sure you will wish to know that Professor Henry Tonks will be retiring this summer, after almost forty years of distinguished teaching. He has, as you know, been with us since 1893, and Professor of Painting since 1918, and the School has benefited immeasurably from his long career here. As a token of the esteem in which he is held by the Governors, a party is to be held in his honour, and we are also offering former students the opportunity of contributing to a retirement gift. Please find enclosed details . . .*" And so on . . . Oh. "*You may also wish to know that Mr Philip Wilson Steer will also be retiring this summer, after a long and happy association with the School. Again, the opportunity is offered . . .*"'

Walter put down the letter. 'The end of an era.'

'Why haven't they written to Mummy?'

'I expect there's a letter for her in Wimbledon, with Granny and Grandpa.'

'Didn't you tell them you got married?'

'Perhaps we didn't. Perhaps we did, and they forgot. We were ordinary students, you know, not dazzling people.'

'Who were the dazzling people?'

'Before the war, there were lots. Augustus John, Mark Gertler, Stanley Spencer . . .'

The church clock struck the half-hour. It had started to rain. 'How are you getting on?' he asked Meredith, looking at her plate, with most of her breakfast still upon it, yolk running everywhere.

'I've had enough.'

'No, you haven't.'

'Yes, I have.' She finished her beaker of milk. 'I'll go and say goodbye to Mummy.'

'She's still fast asleep,' said Walter, slipping the letter back. 'She didn't go to bed until very late. I should leave it this morning. Go and get your things.'

Meredith went out to the passage, dark and cold. She knew why

Sarah hadn't gone to bed till late: she'd woken and heard her, pacing about. 'Goodbye, Mummy,' she said to the coat rack, and took down her own coat, found her gumboots and slipped her shoes into the satchel. She put on her scarf and gloves and knitted beret and then she was ready, meeting Walter at the door with the umbrella, opening it out in the dark garden where it almost blew away. It was pouring, now.

'Are you painting or teaching today?' she asked him, as they made their way down the lane. There were the lights of the bus.

'Teaching. It's Tuesday, remember.'

'You never paint now.'

A gust of wind blew the umbrella high above them, but she knew that wasn't why he didn't answer.


It rained and it rained and it rained. Sarah woke to the sound of it, lashing the windows, and lay there feeling the damp and the darkness of the house all around her, not a sound anywhere except for pouring water, rushing down the pipes, soaking the garden, splashing out in the lane. They must have left. She pulled herself up and peered at the clock on her table. Almost ten. Almost ten on a weekday and she just waking, her head heavy, everything cold and empty. She lay back on lumpy pillows, pulled up the slippery quilt, closed her eyes.

I will lie here all day and rot. I will lie here all day and it will not matter. No one will know, and when they come back I shall be up and about, with everything warm and clean again.

If I can manage that. Perhaps I can't.

I was getting better. Now I'm getting worse.

Dreadful to lie in a cold bedroom.

Dreadful to lie in a cold grave.

Sarah reached for one of Walter's pillows and held it to her, sobbing.

It rained and it rained. She got up finally, her head hammering, drew back the curtains and saw that the river had flooded the field, a great lake of water with more water falling, the trunks of the willows half-hidden, the pollarded withies and stumps grotesque – that was what Meredith had thought, one winter, when they were all up in the studio, watching Walter and his father set out with their ladder and saws. A mutilation. And now the sky had opened, and was swallowing the world. Sarah pictured herself as a piece of flotsam, floating away downriver, out to the sea, bobbing out for ever over the waves. Then she need never do anything again.

The room was so cold: she was shivering. She reached for a jersey, one of Walter's, knitted by his mother, lying on the blanket chest. It was old and dark blue and had holes in the elbows: the one he had worn on a wet winter day at the Slade, years ago, coming into the Antique Room, where she had unbuttoned her boots and laid them to dry on the great iron radiator. He came in, in this jersey, so awkward and shy. There they both were, amongst the potted palms and plaster casts, the drawings pinned up all along the walls. I knew that I loved you then, she thought, pulling the jersey over her head, fingering the places where the wool had unravelled, not just on the elbows but all along the ribbing. Things in need of mending: a jersey, a hole in the gutter where the rain came pouring through, a rung on a ladder, left where a child could climb it.

Sarah turned away from the view of the fields. She left the room with the tumbled bed and cold grate, where soot was falling, and she walked through the empty house with its streaming windows, from room to empty room.

All thoughts of love were gone.


They came back at the end of the afternoon and found the lamps lit, the range smoking because all the wood was damp, but the kitchen warm and swept, all the breakfast cleared away and the kettle singing. Wood was drying at the back of the range for the bedroom fires and the beds were made smooth, with clean pillowcases. They hung up their coats and left the umbrella to drip in the bath.

'You've been busy,' said Walter, standing with his back to the range.

'I haven't cooked,' said Sarah, taking off Meredith's sodden clothes, holding out a towel. 'You must have a hot bath,' she told her. 'You must have a hot drink.'

'Yes,' said Meredith, seeing her mother's ashen face and swollen eyes.

'Did you see the letter?' asked Walter.

'What letter?'

'There's one from the Slade. I left it on the table – look.'

'I didn't take it in.' Sarah was rubbing at Meredith's soaking hair.

'Tonks and Steer are retiring.'

'Oh.'

'Sarah?'

'What?'

Meredith looked from her father to her mother, chilled to the bone.

Within twenty-four hours, the rain had been swept away, blowing out to the marshes, the coast, the sea. It took until the weekend for the floods in the fields to go down. For days the water lay there, shining, inching down the trunks of the willows. 'Monet,' said Walter to Sarah, looking at it all from their bedroom window, early one morning.

'What?'

'Monet painted this once – rain and a river and pollarded trees.'

'Did he?'

'We saw it in Zwemmer's, on a postcard. Don't you remember?'

'No.'

That evening, Walter sat in the kitchen, writing a letter.

> *Church Field*
> *Asham's Mill*
> *Near Denham*
> *Kent*
>
> *19th February, 1930*
>
> *Dear Professor Tonks,*
> *You will not, I am sure, remember me, but I studied at the Slade between 1920 and 1922. I have last week received news of your retirement, and should like to offer you most sincere good wishes for happiness and fulfilment in the years ahead. I am writing separately to Mr Steer, and should like to express my gratitude to you both . . .*

He dipped his pen in the inkpot and wiped it, thinking of the two of them: a long-legged waterbird, with a clipped sharp beak, stalking about the studios, making young women cry; a comfortable dormouse, snoring away in a teapot, waking with a start.

'*Carry on. Carry on.*'

He sat there in the warmth of the kitchen, the winter wind shaking the windows, blowing through the bare trees in lane and garden: not more than fifty miles from London, but a world, a world away, and it all came back, in scenes he had not thought about for years. He could smell the dust and plaster in the Antique Room, the pencil and charcoal, hear the scrape of the donkey-stools, feel the shiver of anxiety amongst them all as the door opened quietly and Tonks came to look at their work.

*'And what have we here, I wonder . . . I have to impress upon each of my students the necessity of drawing. Until you can draw, you cannot paint, and you cannot paint without observation . . .'*

Long surgeon's fingers moved over the paper, his eyes upon cast or model were sharp and intense.

*'At medical school I was continually learning out of a book – in the hospital I began at once to observe . . . The study of nature, Mr Cox! The study of nature is all.'*

Walter wiped the nib of his pen, hearing another voice, light and scathing, across a linen tablecloth, amongst the clatter of forks and glasses.

*' "All this talk of Cubism is killing me! I shall resign!" Does he want us to go on painting girls in hats for ever?'*

Nina. Someone else he hardly ever thought of.

Upstairs he could hear Sarah moving about in Meredith's bedroom, putting clothes away, the creak of the boards as she went to sit down on the bed, and kiss her goodnight, passing the other, empty bed, and the worn, glass-eyed bear propped up against the wall.

He wrote:

> *My wife and I met at the Slade. Perhaps you remember her – Sarah Lewis, as she was then. In her last term she was taken up with wood-engraving, in which she has been quite successful.*
>
> *But at the moment I fear that neither of us is able to pursue our art. We have suffered a terrible loss.*

Ash fell in the range and the oil lamp flickered. Walter stopped writing once more. Why was he saying all this to Tonks? Or thinking of pouring it all out to Steer? Two old bachelors, who had painted pretty girls. Girls in hat shops. Girls resting after the ball, in full-skirted gowns. Girls on a pier on a bright summer morning, the sea breeze playing with blue and white dresses. What could they know about losing a child?

None the less, he told them, not quite knowing why, except that it was the only thing that mattered, and they were painters, and had taught him, and he could no longer pick up a brush.

He posted the letters next morning, in Denham, after seeing Meredith in through the school gates. The first tight buds of spring were visible, just, on the oak tree over the green. He caught the connecting train to Ashford, and taught other people, as he had been taught, by David Wicks, and Henry Tonks, and Philip Wilson Steer, a sleepless night behind him and no mention made, these days, of his own recent work, for there was none.

He might, after the class, have gone to see Euan, in the Challocks yard. Sometimes he did so. Often he did not.

He felt himself shrinking: from friendship, from marriage, from all the bright world.

It was March, and the morning was gusty, full high clouds sailing over river and farm and hopfield, lambs calling everywhere, reedy and high in the wind. Walter was working out in the garden when the postboy came whistling by on his bike; he took the letter from over the wall, wiping the earth from his hands on his trousers, looking at the postmark, the sepia ink, knowing at once who had written.

'Sarah?'

But Sarah, upstairs in the bath after waking late, did not hear him. He took the letter into the kitchen, opened it with the butter-knife, smudging it with earth.

> *The Vale*
> *London SW*
>
> *12th March, 1930*
>
> *My dear Cox,*
> *It was most kind of you to write. I do indeed remember you: there are few of my students I forget, and Miss Lewis, too, as she was then – I remember her a little. I would offer you my sincere congratulations on your marriage, but how sorry I am to learn of the grievous blow you*

*have both suffered. To lose your little son – my heart goes out to you, and I offer my deepest sympathy, although I am sure that nothing I can say will assuage your grief.*

*How strange and terrible life can be. What meaning can there be in such a tragedy? I sense only that there is a curtain that blows between here and there, though none of us can know what lies beyond it.*

*How sorry I am to hear that you are not painting. Painting is a blessed thing – it quiets the mind. I am sure you will find the strength to rediscover this. For myself – painting is my life . . .*

Walter, turning the pages, found he was crying.

*You must not expect to hear from Steer – he is frail, following an operation, and grieving himself for the loss of his old nurse, who died last summer after a lifetime of devoted service. And his sight is not good – a sad business. Still, he has done some fine watercolours, and we intend to paint in our retirement, we shall not be idle.*

*I hope that if ever you and your wife are in Town you will come to visit, although I would ask you to make an appointment through my housekeeper, since I fear that I am not one for interruptions.*

*In the meantime, may I thank you once again for your kind good wishes. I pray that in time you will indeed recover.*

*Yours ever,*
*Henry Tonks*

Walter, with trembling fingers, put down the letter on the kitchen table. Beyond the open door the gusts of March wind blew through the garden, carrying the first sharp scents of spring: tilled earth, young wet grass.

*I pray that in time you will indeed recover.*

'Sarah?'

She was letting the water out of the bath, and did not hear him. It came down the pipes in a rush.

He went outside, past the water butt by the door where the children had always been messing about, walking blindly through the garden.

He was always awake before dawn. Ever since childhood, he'd stirred before first light, hearing his parents rising, the bang of the kettle downstairs on the range, his father's stockinged footsteps creak along the landing, his boots tugged on at the back door, the click of the latch as he went off to work down the lane. When Walter came back here with Sarah, when the children were babies, and the world was a radiant place, he was fulfilling the rhythm of his lifetime in rising early, going out with paints and sketchbook in spring and summer, drinking in the daybreak, watching the mist rise, climbing the hills to see dawn spread over the fields, the farms, the river.

This was different. This waking early was sudden and cruel, like the bang of a door, or a gunshot. He opened his eyes in the darkness; he lay in the high iron bed as still as stone, feeling the weight of the waking hours ahead.

Sarah lay beside him, her hair spread over the pillows, breathing quietly. He wanted to wake her, but knew he must let her rest. Their patterns of sleeping, once so close, had broken apart: it was becoming a deep disjunction between them. And they had not made love since Geoffrey's death. This was something they could not speak of.

He woke, and he lay there, dreading the day. The church clock struck the half-hour: which hour? The first faint light was seeping in through the curtains. He turned to his watch on the table beside him, made out the hand inching past four. From up at Hobbs Farm came the cock crow, vivid and fierce and unrelenting: I am awake, this is the day, be up with you. Once, he had loved to hear it. It came again, as the light grew stronger. An early April morning, full of blossom and buds and moisture. Dew on the rim of the world, the moorhen scudding from bank to bank. A morning for painting.

The cock crowed the night away, and Walter pushed back the bedclothes. He pulled on his dressing gown, moved the shoe in the door which they always left there, in case Meredith woke and called them. He walked in bare feet along the landing; he opened the studio door.

Dawn at three windows. A couple of papers lifting in the draught at his entry, a movement of dust on the floor. He closed the door behind him; he opened the windows, one by one. Spears of green on the furrows in the cornfields pierced the milky light; from the window overlooking the lane and the river he could see the dark shapes of the cattle, getting to their feet as the sun rose over the hills, and the river glinted. He went to the churchyard window, eased the casement catch and pushed it open. Beyond the garden gate a sheep raised her head; the scents of the yew and the earth were full and strong. If he looked out a little to the left, he could see beyond the first tree to the line of the wall, the heap of leaves and grass cuttings in the corner and then, beneath the further yew, the little mound and headstone, where the grass was beginning to grow.

The sun's first rays touched grass and stone and the dew sparkled. The chorus of birds was as musical as he could ever remember. He leaned on the sill and let the beauty of the morning enter him, although he knew that nothing would ever quite fully enter and possess him again: not love, not a painting, not the dawn. He closed his eyes, listening to thrush and blackbird, finch and wren and warbler, the single songs, the fullness of it all: something which had always been a part of his life and which now was somewhere distant – as beautiful as ever, but no longer truly touching him, as for a long time after John William's death nothing could touch him.

Birds sang. A day began. This was the way of the world.

At length, he drew in from the window. He leaned back against it, and looked round the studio. If the kitchen had been the heart of the house, this had been its spirit. Was that true? No, this was where he and Sarah had found fulfilment, but the spirit of the house, of their lives together, had been everywhere, all around them, in every cup and plate and billowing white sheet, in the children calling and racing about in the garden, in Geoffrey's music.

Where was it now? Where was the pulse, the living breath, the gleam of light on water?

The studio had become a place which neither he nor Sarah could work in. They could go into Ashford and take their classes, watch other people put paint on canvas, paint on paper; they could guide the brush, the burin on box wood, the blade through scraperboard. Walter could work on the farms with his father, milking and sawing and cleaning out byres. Without all this they would have had no income or occupation. But to paint, to work at the press again, to stamp their mark, Three Windows – this should have been their salvation, as Tonks had been trying to tell him, but they could not find it. To work in here together, as they had done on the day he died –

No.

So then what is to become of us? thought Walter, looking at small still lifes, at landscapes of oil on board, and glimpses of the world through open windows. By the window on to the cornfields hung the little wartime oil of his mother, sewing out in the garden with the hives and geese. On the wall by the door, lit by the churchyard window, *The Trinity of Women* was huge and blazing, even in the dawn. Beside it was Sarah, feeding Meredith, the rocking chair set in the midst of the studio, mother and child in their own space, the blue china cup on the floor. There were the children, Geoffrey by the open toybox, Meredith at the window overlooking the lane, the fields, the distant willows. There were drawings of Geoffrey at the piano, drawings of Meredith drawing: she was the only one who still drew now, sitting at the kitchen table, doing simple, domestic pictures, a loaf, a jug, a bowl of apples. Little still lifes, like his.

Behind him, behind the church tower, where he no longer rang the bells, the sun was climbing, and it lit the wall of paintings, touching crimson and cobalt blue and gold, the muted winter greys and sombre earthen colours, the brushmarks and the grain of canvas. Everything that had given his life depth and purpose.

The clock struck the hour: six o'clock. Warbler and finch and blackbird sang.

Walter went out of the studio. He went softly along the landing, back to their bedroom. Sarah was fast asleep, pale cheek on white pillow, beneath the mass of hair, dark circles beneath her eyes. He did not bend to kiss her, fearful of waking her, but more, perhaps, than that. Which one had first turned away from the other? Sarah, in anguished summer nights. Then he, exhausted.

Well – what did it matter now?

Out on the landing, he walked in stockinged feet, as his father had used to do, past the children's room. Meredith's room, it was now, the door propped open, in case she called them. She never called. Down the winding dark stair, along past the playroom, which Sarah had tried to keep fresh and alive but which nobody went in. He took down his jacket and hat from the coat rack; he unlocked the door to the garden, and walked down the path to the churchyard. Dew on the spider webs, soaking grass, click of the gate and the sheep trotting quickly away. All these familiar things.

He walked up the path between the graves.

The stones were old and worn and leaning; he'd known them all, all his life, as he had known the church, and the font where he and his brother and sisters and son had been christened, and each leaded window, each place in the pews.

And where was the spirit of it all, the Holy Spirit within it all to help him now, when he most craved it? Did old polished oak and mottled prayerbooks have meaning because they had always been with him, or because he believed? Who, after the war, had gone on believing? Who, when he had lost a brother and a son, might even think of it?

His footsteps were soft on the path. The air was fresh and sweet. He came to the little grave beneath the wall, with its pure and simple stone.

'Hello, darling.'

Breath of the cattle, streaming into the misty dawn, on the other side of the wall. Flit of a finch in the yew. His own voice – had he spoken aloud? Had anyone heard him?

Clumps of primroses grew amongst moss against the wall and the faintest early morning scent drifted towards him. There was a stirring of air, tender as the opening notes of a sonata.

*Here I am.*

Had somebody spoken?

Walter groaned. He looked round, at the quiet churchyard, the leaning, lichen-covered stones, the clambering ivy and ancient yew beneath the tower.

Geoffrey?

Only the lightest breath of air, as the mist drifted away. Only the rustle of a blackbird, hopping about by the compost of autumn leaves. The last of the night's cloud was on the horizon, rolling back further and further away.

Where was he? Where had he gone?

Walter thought, I'll go mad. I'll go mad.

He lifted a hand at the graveside – a kiss, a farewell, a hopeless gesture: he didn't know what it was. Then he turned and walked back down the path to the house. He thought, Tonks was right. There is only one thing to be done with all this. Where else does meaning lie?

He hung up his jacket and hat, with shaking fingers. He climbed the stairs and walked along the landing. The studio door was open, and Meredith was sitting on the step in her nightgown, framed by the streaming light of dawn from the churchyard window.

She said, 'I've been watching you, out there.'

He gathered her up in his arms. Little bird, little thin bony bird. Inside the studio, he set her down by the empty easel, overlooking the cornfields, with their viridian shoots; by the notebooks and sketchbooks and map of their world he had drawn one night, when she was still a baby, and Euan had come to stay. Footpaths criss-crossed it, linking everyone. Brushes and bottles of linseed and poppy oil, turpentine and dried-up tubes of paint lay on the shelves.

*Painting is my life.*

'It's time you got back to your work,' said Meredith.

I was a studio child, she said to her lover, years later, lying in his arms. Like Matisse's daughter – like the children of artists all down the ages, playing about, lying on the floor and drawing, mixing paints and cleaning brushes. Sitting for portraits – all that sitting. We both were like that: we were in there all the time when we were little.

– Then it was only me.

Walter painted his family at evening.

It was April, the days still drawing in early, dusky cloud drifting through a sky rinsed with showers. Walter took his easel out of the studio, into the big cold bedroom. He laid a fire. Meredith came home from school with Sarah and saw it, on her way to the bathroom.

'What are you doing?' she asked, as he pinned paper on to a board.

'I want you both to sit for me,' said Walter. 'When you're ready.'

'Why in here?'

'Because I've never painted in here.'

Because it is not the studio. Because this room has become a despairing sleepless cold empty place and I want to give life to it again. Because – I don't know why, I just have a feeling, that's all.

'Walter?' asked Sarah, coming upstairs.

'I want you to sit for me.'

The fire was lit – it just took the chill off. The dusk was deeper; he lit the lamps.

'Stand here,' he said to Sarah, his hands on her thin shoulders, guiding her between the high iron bed and the window, darkening. 'Look at me from there.'

'I will sit here,' said Meredith, perching on the blanket chest at the foot of the bed. She was still in her school clothes, the cardigan knitted by her grandmother still too big, long woollen stockings beneath her pinafore.

He stood back and looked at them, looking at him: his family, two, where there should have been three. He went to the board on the easel, with its sheet of plain white paper, waiting. He picked up his pencil; he started to draw.

He drew the high iron bed, with its slippery mounds of quilt and eiderdown, and Sarah, the window behind her framing her knotted-up hair, her thin white face, her eyes, which looked beyond him. He drew, in the foreground, Meredith, sitting on the chest, so tense and still, and beyond her the open door to the shadowy landing.

The firelight flickered. The first faint stars appeared. The room was slowly filled with concentration.

Then something creaked on the landing, like a footstep, and they turned towards it. Meredith shrank, her face illumined.

This was the painting's defining heart: he knew it.

'What was that?'

'Nothing. The house is full of noises. But stay there – stay like that. Don't move.'

And he drew them, looking at the gap to the landing, as if something immense, and cold and mighty, were about to enter their lives and change them utterly.

And in the painting the presence became an angel, walking along the creaking landing, colder than the air of winter, which was when he finished it, up in the studio, up until midnight, as the stars hung bright over the fields. The angel brushed the torn patch of paper above the dado, and stood outside the plain square bedroom, wings folded, waiting, full of severity and power.

Like *The Light of the World*, said Meredith's lover, years later, up in the studio, standing back from the huge, unframed canvas.

No, said Meredith. Like the angel of death.

# 2

December, 1930. Walter stood there, taking it all in, everything he had done: a painting as huge and sombre as a Rembrandt. The lamps and the oil stove shimmered in the empty studio, the last of the natural light was going fast. His hands were trembling, as Euan's hands had trembled, for a long time after the war. He signed the canvas, he set the brush in the easel's ledge and he stepped back, standing a good way away from it all, taking in its fullness, and strangeness, and completion.

He rubbed his mouth, smelling the paint on his fingers.

For months he had been possessed by this: a shadowy bedroom, a mother and daughter, an angel approaching the open door, colder than ice. Light from the oil lamps, the flickering fire, the stars, touched here and there the brass on the bedstead, the satin quilt, the window's dark glass and Sarah's hands. It illumined Meredith's face, full of awe and apprehension, and it touched the whiteness of the angel's robes, the feathers on the mighty curve of wings, and the half-seen features, cold and implacable as marble.

A presence, a visitation. An Annunciation – but this was not a tender Fra Angelico, golden-haired, kneeling before a virgin in a courtyard.

*Behold I stand at the door and knock* – but this was not a Pre-Raphaelite Christ, with a lamp and a crown of thorns, announcing:

*I am the Light of the World* . . .

No. There were echoes, but this was entirely of itself: this draughty bedroom, on a cold spring night; this mother and daughter; this moment of fear and awe. This, in the shivery air of a cold damp house, was the Angel of Death, come to take away a child, as he had come on a rustling summer afternoon.

So I might have treated it all entirely differently, thought Walter, standing back further, walking about. I might have painted the garden, the sun and shade, the nettlebed and water butt, the long dark line of the ditch. I might have painted the apple trees, with the first small hard fruit just forming, and a ladder propped up against the tallest tree, a child in a white shirt climbing, up through the leafy boughs, and something approaching, a presence as cold as water, a huge and terrible shadow falling over the brilliant grass.

But that I could not bear to do. Not now. Not yet.

And he felt all at once the entirely dispassionate way in which he had been considering this – a theme, a composition – and a chill ran through him. Was this what it meant, to rediscover painting?

Downstairs, the kitchen door banged: Sarah and Meredith, home from school on a winter evening. He went out on to the landing, calling. How strained his own voice sounded after a day without them, without speaking to anyone. There had been many days like this, while he painted.

'Hello?' He hung over the banister on the corner of the winding stair. They were taking their hats off, hanging their coats on the rack. Geoffrey's boots still stood beneath it, next to his.

'I've finished,' he said. 'Do you want to come up?'

They climbed the stairs, they stood before the painting.

I was a studio child, Meredith said to her lover, years later, held in his arms. Always being asked to sit, to look, to give an opinion.

– Did you mind?

– No. No, not at all. I loved it.

– But what did you think of this?

She stood between her parents, and gazed at the new picture. Walter's arm was round her shoulders; she leaned against his old blue jersey. How strange it was, to look at herself like this – a girl in a green school cardigan and pinafore, shrinking as a cold light fell from the open door. It was her and it was not her, just as the baby in *The Trinity of Women* was her and not her. What a peculiar feeling it was.

– But I know who you are, said the angel.

She shrank against her father.

Sarah was looking and looking. She had hardly been in here for weeks; when she came up he had turned the easel to the wall. He had wanted to finish it alone, unseen.

She said slowly, 'I can hardly bear it. For myself I can hardly bear it.' And then, 'But it's magnificent. You must show it – next year you must send it to London.'

'No,' said Walter.

'What?'

'I don't want to send it anywhere. It's for us, it's only for us. I don't want other people to see it.'

'But Walter –'

Meredith stood between her parents.

'Meredith?' her father asked her. 'Do you think this should go in an exhibition?'

She thought of it, always being here in the house, a part of them all, as Geoffrey had been a part of them all. A part of me, she said inside herself. She moved away, thinking of the angel, always in here, waiting.

'I don't know,' she said. 'I've just come home from school.'

'Of course,' said Walter. 'Of course you have. Forgive me.'

'There's nothing to forgive. Can I go now?' She went to the studio door. The landing stretched before her, dark and shadowy.

'Sarah?' said Walter. 'Please understand. Look what happened with *The Trinity*. I couldn't endure that again, not with this. And I could never sell it.'

'No, of course not. But not even to send it . . .'

There was a silence.

Then, 'Well. Perhaps you're right.'

'Thank you.'

Meredith turned on the step. She saw her parents, standing before the painting side by side, and her father's arms go round her mother, who had grown so quiet and cold. Her head sank upon his shoulder. You see, said Meredith to the angel, with the long cold stretch of the landing behind her. You can't destroy us all.

– But I can see you, he told her. I can see right into you.

That painting was like a phoenix, rising from the ashes, she said to her lover, folded within his arms. It was great, and important. It probably saved my father.

– But for you? Meredith?

# 1933

In April 1933 a London gallery opened new premises in Cork Street, with a show attended by all the press. *Recent Paintings by English, French and German Artists*: the invitations were in black and ochre. On the cool spring evening, smart young men in suede shoes and unusual ties crowded with smart young women through a doorway freshly painted in vermilion and white. Inside, the Mayor Gallery was light and airy, offering an entirely modish 1930s interior of painted plywood walls, steel tube furniture, and concealed lighting. Down in the basement, reached by an iron spiral staircase, slender abstract sculptures rested in niches on underlit, opaque glass. A huge square armchair sat in a corner.

The critics took their glasses of champagne and made their way through the crush. On the pale blue walls hung Cubist still lifes by Braque, a drawing by Picasso of a girl in profile, a white white *Composition* by Ben Nicholson. Paul Nash showed a *Kinetic Feature*, and Francis Bacon *Woman in the Sunlight*. Max Ernst's *Dove* had a small wire birdcage set neatly into its painted breast, which one of the reviewers, Gwen Raverat, found agreeably silly. Henry Moore showed sculptures in wood and stone. These, thought Raverat, were the real thing.

Walter and Sarah heard about all this from Sarah's father, who read the coverage and sent them cuttings from *The Times*.

'We have not seen in London before an exhibition that is so frankly and consistently of the moment.' In the margin, Geoffrey Lewis had pencilled, '*What about Fry, at the Grafton, in 1910? The Post-Impressionists. Does no one remember anything these days?*'

'I remember it,' said Sarah, when she had deciphered her father's shaky hand.

'You were so young,' said Walter, who had been listening to her read it all out. It was lunchtime, a Saturday, soon Meredith would be back at school after the Easter holidays. Soon it would be her birthday.

'I was eight,' said Sarah.

'And you can remember?'

'Gauguin in the rain. The women of Tahiti. The Manet – *The Bar at the Folie Bergères* – everyone remembers that. But yes, quite a lot sank in.'

'I can remember when I was eight,' said Meredith, leaning back in her chair. 'And long before that, as well. I can remember everything.'

'And now you are almost eleven, please don't lean back in your chair,' said Sarah, reaching out a hand.

'Why?'

'It's dangerous. You know it is.'

Meredith leaned forward again, reaching for an apple, one of last autumn's, brought down from the store in the attic.

Sarah turned back to the cuttings. 'They're reviewing another exhibition with this, at Tooth's. *Thirty-eight Important Landscapes*. Oh, Steer's in it. Steer and Sickert and another Camden Towner. All sorts of people – Duncan Grant, Matthew Smith . . .'

Walter began to peel an apple with his penknife, something else which Meredith noticed, and remembered all her life. She saw his little frown.

'What are you thinking about?' she asked.

'Nothing.' He turned the apple, trying to peel it all in one go, she could see. 'Just wondering where we are in all this.'

'What do you mean?'

'He means,' said Sarah, 'in relation to galleries, and openings, and London.'

Walter let the spiral of peel fall on to the plate, unbroken. 'I suppose so.'

'The avant-garde, modern thinking . . .'

'Perhaps.' He began to cut the apple into quarters. Through the open windows came the eternal sounds of spring: new lambs, calling from the farms; full-throated birds. A starling flew past with his beak stuffed with hay.

'You wanted to come back here,' said Sarah quietly. 'You never wanted to live in Town.'

Walter did not answer.

'You stopped submitting work.'

Meredith stopped eating. Last year's apples were soft and tasteless: they just had to be finished up. Well. She wasn't going to. She looked at the quarters on her father's plate: one two three four. Everything even and right.

'May I get down?'

Sarah looked at her. 'What are you going to do?'

She was calm, but there was an edge: Meredith could feel it. It came now and then and quite often at mealtimes, suddenly, out of the blue, as just now. And it cut through her skin like a knife.

'My homework.'

'Do you need to do it now?' asked Walter. He was nicking the pips out of each quarter in a neat triangle. Now they were like little ships, ready to set sail. Where would they go?

Meredith stood up. 'Just my maths. If I'm going to go to the High in September, Mr Hawthorn says extra maths, remember.'

'Yes, of course. Let me know if you want a hand.'

'I will.' She went out of the kitchen, and up the winding stairs.

Sarah put the letter and cuttings back in the envelope. Walter got up, and began to clear the table, sweeping uneaten apples into the bucket under the sink.

'I'm going to write a letter,' he said. 'I'll talk to you about it later.'

'All right.' Sarah pushed her chair back. She opened the door to the garden. 'I'll do some weeding, I think.'

'Good idea.'

They all went their separate ways.


Walter went into the dining room. The playroom – 'We can't call it that now,' said Meredith, some weeks ago. 'I don't exactly play any more.' They had never called it Geoffrey's music room, except inside themselves. It went back to being the dining room, and although they rarely ate in there they tried, after the setting of the gravestone in 1929, and the little gathering in here afterwards, to go on using it. Sarah and Walter hung prints and drawings, or spread them out on the table to consider. Sometimes Sarah sewed at the table, pinning paper patterns, cutting out Meredith's school clothes, and skirts and dresses for both of them. Sometimes Meredith did her homework here: it was peaceful, with a change of view from the cornfields seen from her desk upstairs, and she could still talk to Geoffrey as she worked. Nobody knew she did this. She hardly knew it herself: it was just something she did, and caught herself doing, and stopped, and then went on. Sometimes her parents came in to write letters, and heard her.

'What did you say?'

'Nothing.' She turned the page of her exercise book.

– She talks to herself. I've heard her.

– She's an only child, now. Perhaps she needs to.

She heard them discussing her, when they thought she'd gone to sleep.

Walter went into the dining room, in the spring of 1933, and wrote a letter, to the Principal of the Central School of Arts and Crafts, where in the summer of 1929 he had been invited for interview, and had spent a sunlit afternoon sorting out a portfolio with Sarah, while Geoffrey played down in the garden.

Had he ever written to explain why he hadn't gone? He couldn't remember. There were lots of things he couldn't remember about that year: whether or not he had written a letter; the days of the stockmarket crash, in the autumn, which shook England and America, and passed him by. Sarah's parents had lost a great deal, and never mentioned it, not for a long time, sending a cheque at New Year just as usual. He couldn't remember what any of them had done with themselves for months. He remembered sleepless nights, and teaching, and farmwork, all in a blur; he remembered, in 1930, coming in from the dew-soaked churchyard just after daybreak, feeling again the stirring of desire: to pick up his brush, to paint again.

*Preparing for Bed*: a turning point – in grief, in work.

And what have I done since then? he asked himself, pulling his chair up at the table, unscrewing his fountain pen. Not enough, not nearly enough. He wrote his address on the paper before him, he wrote the date. Soon it would be Meredith's birthday. He sat looking out of the window at the willows across the fields, the spring clouds sailing above them; the slender withies, just in leaf, rose from the crowns and fell into the river, drifting this way and that in the current.

This was the course of grief. A river which ran on and on, taking things with it, moving them this way and that. It ran through your bloodstream, like love, and it never ended: not with a painting, not with a tender dawn, not with the spring.

He knew that now, as he had known it in the winter of 1931, the freezing months of January, February, the wind whistling all down the lanes, the sleet driving over the fields. The painting hung on the studio wall, huge and sombre beside the blazing *Trinity*. The two took up all the wall space now, between the door and the window to the lane.

Nothing since had matched it.

A great creative rush of energy, and then – Geoffrey still wasn't there.

He drew, he painted: he was working, as Sarah, also, had begun to work again. They shared the studio once more: he at his easel, she at the table and press. Three Windows: she stamped it on everything that went out – on all her correspondence with printers and galleries, on dust-jackets and posters. It was her emblem, their mark: Walter and Sarah Cox.

It wasn't the same. The absence of a child ran on and on, and the more they moved forward, the more he was left behind.

Walter sat in the dining room, in the spring of 1933, looking out over the fields across the lane. Cows suckled calves in the sun. Blackbird and bluetit flew in and out of the hedge, building nests, bringing food to their young.

*Dear Sir*, he wrote to the Principal of the Central School of Art, whose name he could not remember. *Some years ago, you were kind enough to offer me an interview for a teaching post. Unfortunately, I was on that occasion unable to attend, but I wonder now if I might ask you to consider once again . . .*

The pen moved slowly over the page.

I hate Saturdays, Meredith said to Geoffrey, up in her bedroom. She sat at her desk beneath the window, her maths books open before her, swinging her feet back and forth. The trees bordering the ditch were just in bud: through the branches she could still see the group of cottages that made up Asham's Mill, and her grandparents, out in their garden. Her grandmother was pegging up the washing: sheets and shirts and pinafores blew back and forth in the light spring wind. Her grandfather was down by the hives, taking the lid off, taking a look. The geese had followed him, curious and always hopeful: she saw him shoo them away. He was wearing his gloves and his hat, and

a handkerchief was tied across his mouth, just in case the bees
swarmed. He should have been wearing a proper great hat with a net,
like Mrs Monkton, up at the Hall, but that was the kind of thing he
could never afford, and anyway, he was careful, he knew about bees.
She saw him peer, and replace the lid; she saw him slide out a tray. All
that swarming buzz, inside there. All that secret life.

He slid back the tray. Her grandmother pegged up the dusters.
They passed one another in the garden. The geese settled down.
Then he went out to the front, to plant spring cabbages grown from
seed. That was the sort of thing he did on Saturdays. Her grandmother went inside again. Then she came out, with her knitting. She
sat on her little hard chair beneath the damson tree and knitted and
knitted. Something grey.

– Probably socks, Meredith said to Geoffrey.

– Probably, he said. Grandpa goes through socks like anything.
And Father.

– And me at school, said Meredith, swinging her legs back and
forth. In September I'm going to the High, in Ashford.

– Ashford is where Mother and Father go to do their teaching.

– Yes, I know.

– And it's where Euan works.

– Yes. In the stonemasons' yard.

And there the conversation ended, because she couldn't tell Geoffrey about his own gravestone. He knew all about that.

Meredith looked at her maths book, and out of the window again.
She sharpened her pencil. Her grandmother knitted, her grandfather
dug. When did they ever talk to one another? What did they talk
about? Not very much, that she could remember. This and that. Jobs
to be done. The weather. Family doings. Some things were never
spoken of. But they got on, you could feel it. They knew one another,
they knew how the days should run.

The days ran here, on and on. They all kept going. Sarah and
Walter were back in the studio. They kept on with their teaching –
Sarah had more, now. They talked about things, like the garden, and
shopping, and big things like exhibitions.

Did they get on any more?

– What do you think? she asked Geoffrey.

– I think they do.

– I don't.

The breeze at the open window ruffled the pages of her textbook. Six fractions to go. Then the decimals, with their moving points. Why couldn't they stay where they were? – I'm hopeless at maths, she told Geoffrey. You probably would have been good. Musical people often are. Everyone said you were musical.

She picked up her pencil again, and gazed at the exercise book. All those squares: like her father, squaring up a drawing, before he painted it. She felt like drawing now, right there, in the corner: the endless furrows of the cornfields with the new spring shoots, and her tiny grandparents, knitting and digging, on a Saturday afternoon.

Why were Saturdays so awful?

– I should be doing something else, she said to Geoffrey, not just boring homework.

But she didn't know what.

– Soon it will be my birthday.

– Yes, I know. The twenty-ninth of April. And then it will be mine. Soon after the day when I died.

Meredith put her hand to her mouth.

Out in the garden, Sarah, kneeling on a piece of sacking, pulled up the last of the weeds. She was working on the long bed that ran beneath the wall to the lane. Over the years, with help from Walter's mother, she had made this into something flourishing, a border full of geraniums, lupins, delphiniums and foxgloves. There were bulbs here, too, as there were all through the garden, daffodil and narcissi spread everywhere – clumps beneath the apple trees, drifts along the ditch. They were just going over now, and everything else pushing up. She tugged at the seedlings of chickweed, which got everywhere, and threw them on to the pile. She wasn't a gardener, not really, but Agnes had taught her, given her seeds and cuttings of this and that, when the children were small and always with her. And now it helped, being out here and working, and watching things grow. At first she had thought she would never be able to come out here again: not in the summer, not by that tree.

'You want me to take it down?' asked Walter's father, soon after the funeral, seeing her crying one morning as he went past, coming back from the milking at Middle Yalding. He stopped by the wall. 'I'll take it down, if you like.'

She shook her head, trying to control herself. She didn't want him to see her crying. It wasn't the kind of thing he was used to. She felt for a handkerchief.

'Here.' He passed her one out of his pocket, clean that morning. No doubt he had a clean one every day.

'Thank you.' She blew her nose.

'Not very good for you, being reminded all the time,' he said, looking across at the tree where the Bramleys were ripening. 'I could take it down with Walter.'

She shook her head again. 'It's part of him. It's where he died. It would be like banishing him,' she said, and began to cry again. 'I can't explain.'

'No need,' he said slowly. 'No need to explain.' And he went off home, his boots creaking all along the lane to the corner.

Now, as she straightened up, and saw the clumps of daffodils sprinkled with blossom beneath the boughs where Geoffrey had fallen, she knew she had been right: the tree had had to stay there. Walter thought so, too. It had been something they agreed on, in those early, dreadful days.

But he had sawn up the ladder, all one afternoon. She saw his white face as he and his father carried it out of the garden, up to Asham's Mill, where his father had the sawhorse. She had not gone with him. He could saw it and saw it – she heard him, all through the August afternoon. An act of contrition, of penance, of raging grief. Back and forth, back and forth, every last rotten rung.

Nothing could ever put it right.

Sarah carried the heap of weeds to the compost heap, over by the ditch where Geoffrey used to poke about and find things. She dropped them on the top. A job accomplished. Something small achieved. Walter, from his grief, had painted the best work of his life. Then he had stopped again; then he had come to a halt. No one in London knew anything about him.

And she?

Cabbage White butterflies danced above the nettlebed. Sarah walked back across the garden, up the brick path to the house, where lavender and sage would grow all summer. Inside, she made tea, and took a cup to Walter, writing in the dining room, where the children used to play. He had fallen asleep, his head upon the letter. She touched him, she kissed him, though she could never feel the same, and she left the tea beside him, walking with her own blue cup up the winding stair.

Meredith's door was ajar: she heard her murmuring. Sarah stopped: she listened. On it went, this solitary conversation, but they could never make out what she said. She put her head round the door.

'Hello?'

Immediate silence; she could feel how Meredith jumped.

'How are you getting on?'

'All right.'

'Sure?'

'Yes.'

She did not turn her head, and Sarah left her, walking on past their bedroom to the studio, where she was working again. After a fashion. She set down her teacup, she went to the table. Behind her the two great paintings loomed.

Meredith finished the last sum as the church clock struck half-past four. The afternoon almost over: now what should she do? She shut up the exercise book; she opened her rough book. You weren't supposed to doodle or draw in here, just show your workings, if you knew how things worked. Never mind, it was right at the back, she could tear the page out. You weren't supposed to do that, either. She gazed out of the window. Her grandparents had gone inside. Now what should she draw?

Meredith drew the things on her desk, the inkpot, the pile of schoolbooks, the ruler and compass, making a little group of them. She drew the white marble eggs in their nest, that Euan had given her for Easter, a long long time ago.

– When I was alive, said Geoffrey.

– Yes.

The wind at the open window stirred the pages; pencil shavings blew across the desk. She brushed them away. She looked at her drawing.

– What do you think?

– It's not one of your best.

It was true. She got up. How quiet everything was. She went to the door and stood on the landing, with its long worn runner, where they used to race through the open studio door. Sarah was in there, looking through her toolbox. She had a new book to do; she was pleased, she'd said so.

'Meredith? Have you finished?'

'Yes.'

'Do you want to come and talk to me?'

'In a minute. I'm going out into the garden.' She went to the top of the stairs.

'Meredith?'

'Yes?'

'You won't go out, will you? Not by yourself.'

'You know I won't.' She went down the winding stair.

– It's because of what happened to me. That's why they worry.

– I know. Of course I know.

She went round the bend in the stair. Downstairs, she looked into the dining room. Her father had fallen asleep, with his head on a letter. A cold cup of tea stood beside him. How beautiful the fields and water meadows looked across the lane, the young spring willows waving in the breeze.

– You can't go to the river by yourself.

– I know. I know.

– We used to go there and fish. Just him and me.

Meredith turned, and went out of the house by the kitchen door, the usual door, where they always used to be running in and out. She reached for the sage bush, to rub a leaf between her fingers, as she always did, but it was still spring, the shoots just showing in the bed by the long brick path. She tapped the water butt, and heard its hollow boom, deep in the heart. Then she walked through the garden, and over to the ditch.

The trees were only just in bud, but the elder bush was in full leaf already, the great big bunches of tiny blossom flowers creamy and dense. Sarah used to put her pram beneath it, she'd told her, so she could lie and gaze up at the patterns of sunlight, moving here and there amongst the leaves. Then she'd put Geoffrey here, all through the summer afternoons.

Meredith walked along the ditch, where he always used to be. The church clock was striking the hour, five clear notes through the cool spring breeze. Across on the other side of the ditch the furrows of the cornfields stretched away, like the sea, like the sky. Somewhere beyond them, right round the bend in the lane, was Mill Farm, where she must never go by herself: her grandfather had told them, years ago.

So many places she couldn't go now. Not even allowed to cross the ditch.

Meredith stood on her side of it, with all the world beyond. She felt herself facing a great divide: almost eleven, almost into her teens. But it wasn't just that, it was much more than that; she could feel it, the wind of April cool on her face, blowing across the cornfields, between earth and heaven, here and there.

What shall I do with myself? asked Meredith. What shall I ever do?

A couple of crows were walking up and down the furrows, stepping over the stones, amongst the new young corn, looking about them everywhere with their bright fierce eyes. They stopped, they tugged at things, then they moved on. Meredith watched them. Then a gun went off, suddenly, from somewhere way up at the Hall, and they flew up in an instant, were up and flapping away towards the beech trees, and beyond. Soon they were only specks in the sky.

Three miles away as the crow flies.

Where had they gone? Three miles away as the crow flew was Hurst Green: the goats on the common, the wind from the sea, the barn doors open and Euan working, the smell of his pipe drifting out over the grass. The crows were beating through the sky towards him.

When I am older, thought Meredith, walking up and down, when I am older, I shall walk over and see you often. I'll just open the gate and go.

– Can I come with you?

– Yes.


Sarah looked through her toolbox, she pulled out her chair. She picked up the square of scraperboard, traced out yesterday, just begun: a fox, trotting away through moonlit woods. She had work, she was fortunate. Sometimes she had a commission from London, from the Golden Cockerel Press. But this was a book by a local naturalist, Lawrence Hill, the husband of one of her students, who had seen her poster for the class and liked the look of it. He was retired, he was writing the journal of a year in Kent, the kind of thing that Walter loved, but Hill was looking for an illustrator, not a painter. He couldn't pay much, but he offered a fee for twenty illustrations and the capital letters which began each month of the year. He didn't know if it would sell.

'I think it will,' said Sarah, when she had read the manuscript. 'It has the makings of a classic.'

'Ah, but classics take a long time to get going,' said Mr Hill, 'and these are difficult times. But thank you. I'm so pleased you're going to do it.'

And so am I, thought Sarah, running the blade through the silvered trunks of trees. If I didn't have this . . .

Outside, she could hear footsteps approaching the churchyard. The ringers, come for practice before the Sunday service. Would Walter never ring again? Was this how their life was always going to be, now – just holding on?

She heard their voices, she heard the door of the tower being unlocked and opened, and them all filing in, one by one. Then, after some minutes, the bells began.

Sarah stopped work, and sat listening. Across from the table, by the open churchyard window, hung the prints she had made years ago, when everything was full of life and purpose. Now she just did things, that was all. She looked at the print of Euan's barn: the goats, the misty bare elms, the rooks. She remembered choosing one for him, with Meredith, one Christmas. At the time, she had likened that to fading memories; she had thought of herself, of all of them, as part of a pattern, a cycle, human life coming and going in some great eternal rhythm of which she, and those she loved, were just a part.

Now, hearing the bells ring out through the cool spring air, she thought, I was young, I was philosophical – everything lay ahead. And then –

And then it happened, a great dark drop through everything, and the only thing that mattered was him, his individuality, everything that made him who he was: his endless collecting of creatures, his engine running up and down on the path, his wanting to be with Meredith, his music, his listening to the bells.

I don't care about the pattern, the rhythm, the being part of things. It was him, so small and individual –

The bells rang over the churchyard, the furrowed fields, the ditch and garden. Sarah bent to the fox, with his ears pricked up, and his long brush low, trotting away on a summer night through the dark and silent woods.

☆

Walter, invited to interview, took the train to London. It was early May, the blossom all blown over and the trees unfurled and bright. He went into Denham with Meredith, on the school bus. 'If I get this position,' he told her, 'I'll be going up to London quite often. You could come with me, perhaps. I could take you to the galleries.'

'And Mother.'

'Yes, of course, if she wants to come.'

'She hasn't come today.'

'No. Well, it's hardly worth it. I'll be back by teatime.'

The bus slowed down at the war memorial, letting an oncoming tractor pass. Then they were into the village. There was Maureen Parker, going up the street with her mother. Meredith dug out her satchel from the seat beside her. 'If we go up to London,' she said, 'I'd have to miss school.'

'I only mean sometimes. And we could stay with Granny and Grandpa. In Wimbledon.'

'They're getting so old,' she said, as the bus drew up by the green. 'Like Grandma and Grandad Cox.'

'Older,' said Walter. 'Much older. Grandpa Lewis must be almost eighty.' He got up, standing aside for her. 'What about you? How does it feel, to be eleven?'

'I haven't got used to it yet.' She made her way down the aisle, and off the bus.

He kissed her goodbye at the school gates. 'Good luck,' said Meredith, and went in with Maureen and the others, without a backward glance. Walter stood and watched her for a moment, crossing the playground as the bell rang. She was getting taller, something from Sarah's side of the family; still thin – so dark and thin. Something in the way she turned her head, and swung her satchel, put him in mind of someone. Who? He watched, and he knew: she took after John William. That was it. He used to cock his head just like that.

For a moment the years fell away and he and his brother were crossing the playground, long before the war – except that they had always been ragging about, in a group. That's how boys were. If Geoffrey were here, he'd be doing the same.

Next month he would have been nine.

The bell stopped ringing, and Meredith, just about to go in the side door, turned and waved.

287

'You'll miss the train,' she called out, and Walter heard it puffing into the station, and waved back and walked quickly across the street, all those childhood days before the war going up like clouds of steam in the morning sky.

He bought *The Times* from the boy outside the ticket office – an extravagance, on their income – and sat in the third-class carriage to make up for it, his portfolio tucked beneath the seat.

They chugged away from the platform. He scanned the headlines. Germany's new Chancellor had ordered the boycott of Jewish businesses, and the burning of 'unGerman books' at the University of Berlin. Walter frowned. Burning books – would they burn paintings, too? He turned the pages, glimpsed a familiar name amongst the *Letters to the Editor*. Professor Henry Tonks was writing from retirement in Chelsea, about the new show at the Mayor Gallery, with its modernist abstract sculpture and white on white painting and Cubist still lifes.

*The ship of art is far from the shore of Nature . . . As a one-time medical man I consider it my duty to warn the young enthusiast that there is some danger in thinking too much of Nothing . . . I have tried sometimes to do so, but found I had rather quickly to give it up, as it seemed to make my head reel; in fact, I feared madness . . .*

Walter put down the paper. What an old curmudgeon Tonks sounded still: how he could get people's backs up. But he wouldn't care.

*I had rather be damned with Steer, Turner and Ford Maddox Brown than go to heaven with Fry, Matisse and Picasso.*

The train pulled into Ashford. He got off, and headed for the London platform. Tonks *was* an old curmudgeon, but he had been so kind.

*To lose your little son – my heart goes out to you . . . I pray that in time you will recover, and rediscover painting . . .*

The London train came puffing in and hissed to a halt. Carriage doors slammed, the guard blew his whistle. Walter settled down in a corner seat. Shall I go and see him? he wondered. Shall I take Sarah, and Meredith, and tell him how much those words meant to me? Perhaps Steer might come up from Cheyne Walk, and join us. Or we could walk down and see him.

*You must not expect to hear from Steer. He is old, and his eyesight is fading . . .*

Poor old boy.

*Do come and call – but make an appointment with my housekeeper. I keep to a strict routine, and am not one for interruptions.*

Walter leaned back in his seat. Perhaps not. Perhaps it would be better to leave things as they were, and two old artists in peace. Not that Tonks sounded peaceful on the *Letters* page.

He looked at his watch. Almost ten. His interview was at eleven-thirty. Why am I doing this? he asked himself, as the train puffed past new suburban estates, bordering farms and hopfields. Do I really want to come up to London each week, and be in the swim again? If I was ever in it. He wasn't sure. He thought of Sarah, the edge of her voice that came and went, as the years went by, and he sold so little. Not just because they were poor, and even with her parents' allow-ance, and her own work, struggled to make ends meet, but because she had had such faith in him, and felt such disappointment.

'*It's magnificent – you should send it to London.*'

Well. That painting he could never part with. She knew that.

We'll see, he thought, opening the paper again. And I might not get the position. Jobs are scarce everywhere now. If I do, I'll call in on Euan, when I come back, and buy him a drink. It feels like such a long time since I did that.

'Ah, Mr Cox. You had a satisfactory journey? You found us all right? And I see you have brought some work for us to look at.'

He spread it all out before them, in the hot, partitioned room. The window was open, for the morning had grown warm: dust from roadworks in Kingsway blew here and there from the sill, and the Principal apologised, as Walter made to cover his papers, and drew down the window.

'Now, then – let's take a look.'

Walter watched them, the Principal and the Head of Fine Art, sifting through his drawings and watercolours, propping up little oils. There was Meredith, eating her breakfast; there she was sitting for him in the studio, in Sarah's basket chair, framed by the window overlooking the lane, and the distant willows. There was Sarah, working at her woodblocks, and there was Geoffrey, at the piano, drawn from behind, his head and shoulders and narrow little back, his hands spread wide over the keys.

The Principal smiled. 'Your family, Mr Cox?'

'Yes,' began Walter, and started to explain, then said simply, 'Yes.'

They looked through watercolour landscapes: field and farm and oasthouse, ploughed furrows, orchards, mist rising from the river in early morning, the woods on the hills.

'I like these.'

'Thank you.'

They stood back and looked at the oils, some old, some more recent: eggs in a bowl, a corner of the winding stair, the portrait of Sarah, leaning on the kitchen table, clasping the blue china cup, her hair tied back and her eyes with great hollows beneath them, looking at him, beyond him, so far away. He'd done that two winters ago. He tried to see it all as they might see it, but he could only see his broken family, and the places he loved, exposed to the gaze of strangers.

The Principal picked up a couple of drawings again. 'You trained at the Slade . . . this is evident. And where have you shown?'

Walter cleared his throat. He said, 'I have shown very little – only locally. I've done a good deal of teaching, though, over the years.'

'Yes, indeed, we have the reference from Ashford. But have you not shown in London?'

'No,' said Walter, and began to stumble. He said, 'You see, for a long time when I went back to my home from the Slade, I didn't feel ready to. I was too diffident, perhaps, but I felt I must develop more. I did a painting I'm proud of, but it was turned down all over the place – and then – and then something happened.'

He stopped, he made a gesture towards the drawing of Geoffrey, and withdrew his hand. Outside the window, still open at the top, the traffic was roaring down towards Holborn. He felt his head begin to pound. He thought, I shouldn't be here. I'm not fit for this, I'm not ready. I'm really only half a man now.

There was a silence. Then the Principal said quietly, 'Mr Cox, your work is very fine. We should be so pleased if you would join us.'

They had lunch in the canteen. London students milled about them. How different they were from his students in Ashford: so sharp and fashionable, the young women smoking, the men without ties. They sat in the corner, discussing the terms and conditions.

'I fear it is only one day a week, at present.'

'One day will suit very well,' said Walter, leaving a stale ham sandwich.

'To begin in the autumn, of course.'

'Yes, yes, indeed.'

They shook hands out in the hall.

'You should try to catch the show at the Mayor – stirring up a bit of dust, I'm pleased to say. Of course, you're a Slade man, you may feel as old Tonks does about the moderns. We're trying to move things along a bit here. Anyway,' the Principal looked at his watch, 'time I was in a meeting, I'm afraid. Goodbye, Mr Cox. We shall look forward to seeing you in September.'

He hurried away through the swing doors and Walter walked out on to the street. He was pouring with sweat.

But I did it, he thought, getting out his handkerchief, wiping his face and his hands, so slippery they had stained the handle on the portfolio. I've made a move.

A clock was striking two. He stepped back as a student came running up to the door, a young man with floppy hair and a flashing smile. Walter smiled back, watching him dash to his class. Something about him put him in mind of Henry Marsh: whatever had happened to him? Last heard of framing at the Leicester Galleries.

He could take a bus down there now – 'slip down there', as Henry used to say. He could go to the smart new Mayor and visit *Recent Paintings by English, French and German Artists*, or *Thirty-eight Important Landscapes*, round the corner at Tooth's.

Or he could go home.

Walter walked slowly along the street, moving the portfolio from hand to wet hand, his family all within it, Geoffrey too.

He sat outside the Crown with Euan, talking it all over. The sun was slipping down behind the buildings across the square; it had been market day, and they could hear the men clanging shut the empty pens, swilling down the gulleys with brush and bucket. Walter drained his glass; Euan puffed on his pipe. The rush and press and nerves of London were left behind.

'But it will be good for you,' said Euan. 'I think it's right.'

'I expect so.' Walter sat watching the quiet world go by: the lads on the corner, smoking, eyeing the girls going past arm in arm, pretending not to notice. Soon Meredith would be coming here every day to school – in the autumn, when he began teaching in Town. Then Sarah would be on her own, except for her classes. On the days when he was at the Central, she could – what could she do?

He said, 'I didn't tell them, at the interview. I didn't say anything about our lives. About Geoffrey. I nearly did. I'm glad I managed not to.' Euan sat listening, his long legs stretched before him on the cobbles, the smell of the pipe smoke mingling with the market smells of slurry and straw. Walter said, 'But it's the only thing that matters, still. I think of him almost every moment. I don't think I'll ever stop.'

'No,' said Euan, turning to look at him. 'You probably never will. That's the truth, isn't it? For all of you.'

Walter looked back at him. There was a pause. He said slowly, 'I seem to have spent half my life in mourning, and you've always been there.'

Euan didn't answer. He made a gesture which said simply: Yes, this is how it's been – and went on smoking.

And what about you? Walter wondered as they sat quietly together, watching the sun go down. Euan was strong, he was gifted and generous, he drew people to him. But what, in his heart, did he want of his own life? After all these years, he still lived alone. And when did he ever talk about himself?

Behind them, in the market, the men were emptying buckets, brushing wet stone. Everyday, workmanlike activity. The moment, for Walter now, did not feel ordinary.

He said, 'I've lost Geoffrey. You're right – I shall never recover, not fully. But I still have Sarah and Meredith. We're still a family, even if it will never be the same.'

Euan was looking out over the square, tamping down his tobacco, listening.

Walter thought, I must clear my own mind. I *must* be at peace about this. He wanted to make a great leap of courage, to say, Euan, forgive me – there have been times when I've wondered if Sarah – if you and Sarah . . .

'Euan?' He swallowed, feeling himself, after all these years, intrude on such a quiet, such a private man, and fearful of his answer. 'What about you? Have you never been in love?'

The question hung between them. The air was full of the smell of tobacco smoke, rising into the evening sky. There was a silence. Then, 'I can't answer that,' said Euan.

Walter felt a deep unease steal through him. 'Why?'

Another silence. 'I simply can't.'

'Is it—'

'Please.' The bus was starting up in the square; Euan got to his feet. 'One day perhaps I'll try to tell you,' he said. 'Not now. Let's go.'

It was growing dark. Sarah and Meredith, long home from school, moved about the house, lighting lamps, drawing curtains.

'He's late,' said Sarah, putting plates to warm.

– He's late, said Meredith to Geoffrey, going into the dining room. He said he'd be home by teatime. She stood by the window, looking out over the lane. The wind was rising, the branches of oak and elm had begun to toss. It was going to rain, he'd be soaked if he missed the bus. She pulled the curtains, and went out into the passage. The house felt huge without him: spreading out all round them, as night approached. If her father went up to London in the autumn, there'd be lots of times like this – just she and her mother, rattling about. And the days would be shorter, too.

It started to rain, pattering everywhere.

'Here you are,' said Sarah, coming out from the kitchen. 'I think I've left a window open in the studio. Will you run up and check?'

The rain was coming down faster; they could hear a window upstairs swing back and forth. It was so dark up there.

'My things will get soaked.'

Meredith made a dash for it. Up the winding stair, and all along the landing. The studio door was open and the rain was pouring now, she could hear it, driving through the churchyard window on to Sarah's prints and papers. She ran in, she pulled it to, she picked up a soaking wet print from the floor.

'Meredith?'

'It's all right – everything's all right.'

She carried the print to the door. Beside it, the mighty wings of the angel shone from the huge dark canvas. His hand was upraised and he looked right into her: as she was then, as she was now.

– I'm not the same person now. I've changed. I'm kinder, now.

But he looked deep into her, cold and knowing and unrelenting. What could one ever do, to be forgiven?

'Meredith?' Sarah was coming down the long dark landing.

She came out, shaking.

'What is it?' asked Sarah. 'Come here, let me hold you. What's wrong?'

'Nothing,' said Meredith, handing her the sodden print. 'I just got cold, that's all.'

I could never tell them, she said to her lover, lying beneath him, feeling his weight upon her, his naked heavy belly covering hers. He pushed right into her, deep and slow. He cradled her head; they gazed at one another.

– Because? Why couldn't you tell them?

– Because they had suffered so much. I used to hear them, crying in separate rooms. For years. They tried to hide it. I tried to hide from them.

– Hide what? My love, my darling.

– Everything, sobbed Meredith. Everything, everything.

# 1935

How long is childhood; how fast flies all the rest. Their lives were changing, and the world was changing, too: in art, in politics. The swastika blew on scarlet flags above rallies in Nuremburg. Artists were fleeing Germany: Wassily Kandinsky, Klee. Klee and Max Ernst had shows in London, at the Mayor Gallery. In London, in a house in Soho Square, the Artists International Association held an exhibition: *Against War and Fascism*. That was in November. Walter went to it on a dusky afternoon after his class, before catching the train back to Ashford. The last leaves were falling in the square; the day was drawing in. He walked on polished floors from room to high-ceilinged room, looking at work by Duncan Grant, John Piper, Ben Nicholson, Henry Moore. He told Sarah and Meredith about it that evening, over supper, which they always ate late on the days he was teaching in London.

'You could stay overnight,' said Sarah, gathering up the plates. 'You could stay with my parents, and come back next day.'

'Wouldn't you mind that? Don't you want me to come home?'

'Of course I do. It just seems so tiring for you.'

'I want you to come home,' said Meredith, getting her books out. She did her homework down here when the weather got colder. 'I need a hand with this.' She turned the pages of algebra.

'I'm not sure I can help you much here,' said Walter, looking at it all. He drew his chair up.

'It's hard, at the High.'

'All right. I'll have a go.'

Sarah fetched sewing. The range crackled. Anyone coming in then, walking down the lane on an autumn evening, knocking at the kitchen door and entering, would have thought them a wholly united family: pages turned in the lamplight, a thread drawn through a button, the room so warm.

– In some ways we were united, said Meredith, a long time later, remembering evenings like that, the three of them together, the darkness of the big cold house all round them. We tried. But it wasn't right. Nothing was right for years.

– Because of Geoffrey.

– Not only because of him.

– Because of me.

– Perhaps. For them. But you made everything right for me – at last, in the end.

– And you for me.

Looking back, years later, she thought, Everything was in turmoil – me, the world. I was going mad, and nobody saw it. The world was about to go up in smoke: again.

She was in London when she thought this, coming out of an exhibition, feeling the press of people all round her, finding that difficult, as her father used to find it. She walked away from them all, and crossed through the traffic into the park, smelling the grass as light rain began to fall on the lake and waterbirds, and London pigeons huddled within the trees. She closed her eyes, looking back: saw hopfields and cornfields and a river, winding away through the willows. Beloved, peaceful places, shot through with such intense emotion. The death of a little boy. The growth of love. The approach of war.

# 1936

## 1

It was March. Sometimes it felt like spring, and much of the time it felt like winter. There was a sudden, unexpected snowfall, and lambs were lost. The cows, just let out, stood close to the haystacks, on frozen mud. Then it thawed, and the air was full of moisture, the sky high and vaporous, the fields squelching with every step. The house had been shut up for weeks: every nook and cranny stuffed with rags and paper, oil stoves everywhere. Still, when they opened the door they closed it quickly: the cold damp air caught at your throat. Wear your gloves, said Sarah to Meredith, every schoolday morning. Wear your scarf. It's almost spring, I'm almost fourteen, said Meredith. Please don't fuss. Do as you're told, said Sarah. Please. You never know. Meredith did as she was told. On days when her parents were teaching in Ashford, they came in with her on the train, and met her after school. It felt as if she was always with them. On Tuesdays, she said goodbye to Walter on the platform, and then he crossed for the London train, to go up to his classes at the Central School.

'You must come up to town with me,' he said as he kissed her one morning. 'I want to show you the galleries.'

'I'd like to do that,' she said.

'There's a show on next month, at the Lefèvre. *Abstract and Concrete*. People say it's important.'

'I'll come.'

Then his train pulled in, and she saw him off, and came out through the station forecourt, hearing the newsboys call through the grey damp air.

'Hitler marches into the Rhineland! Hitler marches in . . .'

It was a ten-minute walk to the High School. Most of her friends had come on with her from the top class at Denham; most of them made the journey by themselves. She caught up with Maureen, and Edith Stacey.

'You look hot.'

'I am.' She unwound her scarf, and pulled her gloves off.

They came into the square. There was Euan, just getting off the bus. She moved away from the others, and crossed the cobbles.

'Hello.'

'Meredith.' He smiled down at her, he kissed her cheek. 'How nice to see you. Just off to school?'

She nodded. 'Yes.'

'And what do you have today?'

She tried to remember, suddenly shy. 'Maths. Double History.'

'Which do you like best?'

'Not maths, I'm hopeless.'

'I'm sure you're not.'

The bus had emptied; the driver switched the engine off, and jumped down from the cab.

'What about you?' she asked Euan. 'Are you going to Challocks now?'

'I am.'

'What are you working on?'

'Oh –' He made a gesture. 'Something for the Town Hall. A plaque. Not very exciting, I'm afraid.' There was a little pause. 'And how are your parents?'

'They're very well. I've just seen Dad off to London.' She hesitated. 'He was talking about taking me up for an exhibition.'

'Oh? And what was that?'

She couldn't remember.

'Never mind.' He looked at his watch. 'Time I was off. Perhaps we could all go up one day.'

'That would be nice,' she said.

He kissed her again, brushing the brim of her school hat. 'Good luck with the maths.'

'Thank you.'

And then she heard the school bell, ringing all the way down Marsh Street, and she raced to join the others, holding on to her hat.

'Who was that, then?'

'Just an old friend of my father's. Well, he's a friend of all of us. He's a sculptor.'

'Fancy.'

In the end, Walter and Euan went to the *Abstract and Concrete* show together, and Meredith lay in bed with a streaming cold and sore throat.

'I wish you could come,' said Walter, coming in to see her before he left.

'So do I.' She reached for her handkerchief.

'You look wretched.'

'I'm all right.' She coughed, and winced. 'It's ages since I've been ill.'

'The show ends on Saturday, or we could wait till next week. I feel I should go on a teaching day, though.'

'Save the train fare.'

'Yes.' He made a little face. The church clock struck the quarter-hour. 'I'd better go. See you tonight.'

'Bye.'

She lay there, feeling horrible. Sarah brought breakfast, which she couldn't eat.

'Darling, I told you to wrap up.'

'It's spring,' croaked Meredith, hearing the lambs.

'It's changeable.' She picked up the tray. 'Shall I come and work in here? Or read to you?'

'I think I'll go back to sleep.' She turned the pillow over, feeling her temperature rise, and her head start swimming. 'Perhaps I should have an aspirin.' How it hurt to talk.

Sarah brought aspirin and water. Meredith swallowed, and winced again.

'I hope this is nothing serious,' said Sarah.

'It's just a cold.' She lay back, closing her eyes, listening to Sarah go quietly out of the room. From far across the fields she could just hear the puff of the train, leaving Denham. Walter and Euan were meeting in Ashford, travelling up to London together. They were going to see work by Kandinsky and Giacometti. Such beautiful names. She said them in her head. Kandinsky and Giacometti. And Henry Moore, she had heard of him, and Barbara Hepworth. A woman sculptor.

– I'd like to carve things, she said to Geoffrey, but he didn't answer.

– Geoffrey?

No answer. Perhaps it was because she was ill. Perhaps it was because she was getting older.

– You're leaving me behind.

She shivered – Don't say that.

– But you are. You're growing up.

– That doesn't mean –

– It does. Of course it does.

– Geoffrey, said Meredith, the temperature coursing through her. You'll always be part of me. Always.

He didn't answer.


Walter came back late; she heard the door bang. Her temperature had gone down. Now it was up again: temperatures were like that. Her throat was raging. He came up the stairs to see her, creaking along the landing, putting his head round the door.

'Hello, darling.'

She couldn't speak.

He came over. The lamp was on the floor, to rest her eyes; enormous shadows were thrown upon the wall.

'How are you?' He knelt down beside her.

She shook her head. He felt her forehead, frowning.

'I just need more aspirin.' She could hear herself trying to say it. 'How was the exhibition?'

'Wonderful. Very modern. I'll tell you about it when you're better. I've brought the catalogue home.' She nodded. 'I'll bring you some water,' he said, getting to his feet, and then, 'Euan's here.'

'Is he? Where?' She listened, hearing the low murmur of voices.

'Downstairs, talking to Mummy. He's staying the night, it's so late. We missed the last bus, we had to walk from Denham.' He got to his feet. He did look tired. 'Would you like to see him?'

She nodded. How that hurt. 'But don't I look awful?'

'Oh, darling. He's known you all your life.'

So he had. All her life.

– And mine, said Geoffrey.

She put her hand to her mouth.

'I'll send him up with the aspirin,' said Walter. 'I'll come and say goodnight after supper.'

She lay there and waited. Euan came, creaking up the stairs. He knocked at the door.

'Hello, Meredith.' He put his head round the door.

'Hello.'

He came across the room, his shadow huge on the wall in the glow of the lamp.

'You're not well, I'm so sorry.'

He gave her a cold glass of water, held out an aspirin. It looked so small and felt so choking. She made herself swallow it down.

'Poor Meredith.'

'You mustn't catch it.'

'What?'

'I said you mustn't catch it.'

'No.' He straightened up from the bedside, took back the glass, stood looking down at her. He was so tall, he went on for ever.

'Father said – ' She croaked, and tried again. 'Father said the show was wonderful.'

'It was. You'd have liked it. Kandinsky especially.'

She smiled. It hurt. 'What about Henry Moore?'

'You go to sleep,' he said. 'The Moores were very fine. We'll take you to something else, when you're better.' He stretched out his hand, made a gesture towards her. 'Goodnight. Get well soon.'

'Goodnight.'

She lay there, watching him walk across the room. His shadow was so big when he passed the lamp: for a moment it almost filled the ceiling.

For a moment it made her think –

'Euan?'

'Yes?' He turned at the door, he looked across at her. Beyond him the long dark landing stretched.

No, thought Meredith, feeling her head begin to swim horribly. You're not the same – you're not, you're not.

'What?' he asked her, steady and warm.

She shook her head, feeling everything tilt inside it. 'Nothing. Goodnight.'

He went downstairs; she heard them all talking, the chink of plates.

It's all right, she told herself, smoothing the pillow. Everyone's here. The house is full. She lay down again. Everything spun, and her limbs were aching. She lay listening to every sound.

Next morning, when she woke up, he had gone.

Now Walter went up to London regularly, he knew about all the exhibitions. He went to the galleries, he used the library at the Central School, and brought home copies of *Studio* and *Connoisseur*. He read Herbert Read and Paul Nash on the train, writing in the *Listener* and *Weekend Review*. Nash had long recovered from his post-war breakdown, and now he was at the heart of things. In 1933, when Tonks was writing sarcastic letters to *The Times* about the new show at the Mayor, Nash took up arms, and wrote back. He was forming a new group of artists, Unit One, painters and sculptors who stood for 'the expression of a truly contemporary spirit . . .'

European modernism was making an impact again, as it had done before the war – and besides, thought Meredith, looking through *Connoisseur* in the studio, keeping her parents company, everyone was talking about Europe now. Hitler was on all the front pages: she saw his name everywhere on the train, as people read their papers. Hitler and Mussolini and Franco: names she had never heard in her life. Now it felt as if she had always known them.

She got up and went to the window overlooking the lane. A perfect summer evening, the sun melting into the dusky clouds, the river a path of gold. Her parents were working quietly behind her: he at his easel, she at the press. She wanted to ask them, Do you think there's going to be a war? But the anniversary of Geoffrey's death was approaching, and she didn't want them to have to think about dark things, especially not on an evening like this. The church clock was striking eight. Fred Eaves had been mowing in the churchyard this afternoon. She leaned out of the window, listening to the bell, smelling the cut grass, watching the cows plash into the water meadows, the swallows swoop low along the lane. How beautiful everything was. How could there possibly be another war?

She thought of her Uncle John William, marching down to Dover in 1916 with The Buffs, taking the troopship to France, killed with his friend Eddie Pierce, in the Battle of Flers-Courcelette. All these things she'd heard about, all through her childhood; seeing his photograph in uniform in the corner of her grandparents' parlour, going down to the memorial every Armistice, watching Euan set the stone memorial to Charles Monkton's brother high in the wall of the church: the soldier, the lamb at his feet, the hops, the deep stern lettering.

– Like mine.

– No, yours was different, yours was smaller.

She'd sat in the pew and watched him, the men on the scaffold, his arms upraised, a great triumphant gesture as his work was set in place.

– You thought about it falling, that stone.

– I didn't.

– You did. You know you did. You thought about it falling and it gave you a kind of thrill.

– Don't, don't.

She swallowed. She tried to drink in the cool of the evening once more.

What was Euan working on now? What was he doing this very evening, as the sun went down over the marshes, and the rooks flew home into the elms?

She turned back to the studio. The evening sun was streaming in, on to the floorboards, over the pictures, all along the wall: the prints, the drawings, the portraits, the little landscapes in oil and water-colour. It lit the blazing *Trinity*, with its great gaping goose, and it lit the huge angel, white in the darkness, his hand upraised, about to enter the room, their lives.

She looked away from it.

'Father?'

'Mmm?'

'You said you were going to take me to another exhibition when I got better. And Euan – he said so, too.'

'We could all go,' said Sarah, laying out prints one by one.

'And I know what we should see,' said Walter, wiping his brush.

The International Surrealists Exhibition opened at the New Burlington Galleries on 11 June 1936. They went the following week, on Walter's teaching day, Meredith having a day off school.

'I haven't been up to London for years.'

She could hardly remember the last time. They came up to see the London grandparents for their birthdays, but for most of her life the grandparents had come down to them. Most of her life had been spent within a radius of just a few miles. How strange that was, in the modern thirties: she knew it. Her schoolfriends had cars, and went all over the place. She didn't. That's how it was.

She sat in a corner seat and the train puffed through the countryside.

'It's getting so built up,' said Sarah, looking out at the neat estates. Roses, bay windows, mock-Tudor beams. Children in little fenced gardens looked up and waved. Sarah waved back. You look happy, Meredith thought, seeing her and Euan smile at one another. Her father pulled out his notebook and pencil and turned towards her, making a quick little sketch. He looked up and down, as if he were in the studio, or out painting in the fields.

'Can I see?'

He leaned across and showed her: girl in a railway carriage. She nodded, seeing herself as he saw her – print dress, long socks, felt hat. A serious person. She wished she'd brought her own sketchbook, as they all started talking.

They pulled into Victoria, took the bus down to Piccadilly, getting off near the Royal Academy, where her parents had met: so many times, she had heard that story. Then they were entering a sleek arcade, and she caught sight of her reflection in the window of a shop full of elegant little hats. She didn't look like a London person at all.

'I feel like a country bumpkin,' she said to Euan, behind her.

'You don't look like one in the least.'

They glanced at one another in the glass. Then he walked on, and looked in the window of a pipe shop. She followed. Rows and rows of pipes, all laid out in a fan on a heap of satin. None of them looked like his.

They came out into the sun. The gallery was just a short way away: couples were walking through plate-glass doors, the women in suits, and high heels, and little hats such as nobody wore in Ashford. They all went inside to the foyer. There was quite a buzz. Then Walter said suddenly, 'Henry! Henry Marsh –'

'I don't believe it,' said Sarah.

'Who?' asked Meredith, looking around.

'An old friend from the Slade,' said Euan, watching her parents greet him. 'Come and say hello.'

'Is he nice?'

'Very.'

They crossed to where the others were kissing and shaking hands. 'After all this time . . .'

Henry Marsh wore a pale linen jacket and a yellow rose in his buttonhole. He did look nice, shaking hands with Euan, smiling at everyone.

Walter put out his hand to her, and drew her into the circle. 'And this is our daughter, Meredith.'

'Meredith. How enchanting. How do you do?' He took her hand and gave a little bow. No one in the entire world had ever done anything like it. She felt herself blushing like mad. He stepped back and looked at her; he looked from her to Sarah. 'Are you alike? Just a little. More like Papa, perhaps?'

'She does favour my side of the family,' said Walter.

' "Favour my side of the family." ' Henry shook his head. 'God, Cox, it's good to see you again.' He looked back at her, and his smile was like champagne. 'And are you the only one?'

It was as if a shadow passed over the sun: a cloud, or a huge dark bird. She saw Henry Marsh give a little, embarrassed, enquiring frown in the silence.

'Yes,' she said, and the word filled the whole of her, and she couldn't move. She heard her father say something, and sensed how quiet her mother had gone, and she looked down at the polished floor. I hate this, she thought. I hate it and hate it.

Then Euan was beside her, and his arm went round her, guiding her away. 'Shall we go and look at the pictures?'

She nodded blindly.

'We'll let them explain,' he said gently. 'I think that's better, don't you?'

She knew he was right, but she couldn't answer.

They entered the gallery rooms.


The paintings were like dreams.

Brooding stones stood in a monochrome landscape. Shadows fell on to an empty street. It felt as though time had stopped for ever.

Everything was solid and real: a fireplace, a papered wall, a broken column, trees on a distant hill. But the way in which they were placed together, the way in which the world had been cut up, and reassembled . . .

Salvador Dali, de Chirico, Max Ernst, Paul Nash, Magritte.

Meredith walked from painting to painting. She thought, I understand some of this. I don't know why, but I do.

Water lapped into a room where the wall was missing. Cubes and cylinders lay stranded in a grassy field. A train puffed into an empty drawing room.

*Harbour and Room. Equivalents for the Megaliths. Landscape in a Dream. Place d'Italie. Time Transfixed.*

The human body had been dismembered: fists grasped naked limbs and a tortured visage wept over stony land. *Premonition of Civil War*.

Behind her the adults were talking quietly. Meredith walked away.

Moonlight fell on a pillared courtyard: a girl on a couch lay naked, sleeping. *Venus Asleep*. Around her women clothed and naked stepped in the silence across the chequered floor. Mountains rose into the distance.

Mysterious. Timeless and mysterious and profound.

Meredith thought, The only painting I have seen like this, at all like any of this, is in my parents' studio. *Preparing for Bed*: me, and my mother, and the angel. One world entering another.

Around her people came and went. She moved to sit down, on a leather couch. It was tiring, looking at all these paintings. Soon they'd be having lunch, perhaps with handsome Henry Marsh. Or perhaps, now he knew what had happened to them, he'd be too embarrassed to join them. Then her father was teaching. She and her mother were meeting her grandparents, Euan was going to –

What was he going to do? Go to another exhibition? Go home on the train by himself?

She looked across the room.

Euan was standing with his back to her, looking at a painting which she couldn't see properly from here: quite a few people were milling about by that wall. He was standing so still, so tall beside most of the others, looking and looking. People around him were talking, opening handbags, getting out diaries from inside pockets, all that sort of thing. Within all this fuss he was still and quiet. She remembered the stones in a dreamlike landscape, there as if they had always been there, looking just right. I know one of the things that I like about you, she thought. I like the way you occupy space. Just that. There isn't a single thing that's busy, or awkward, or distracting: you have presence. Whatever you do, you just look right.

He must have felt her looking at him: he turned, he glanced across the room. Their eyes met. She thought, This often happens, with us. Then he raised his hand, in that way he had, and moved a couple of fingers: a strange little gesture – Hello? Goodbye? – and he looked back at the painting for a long long moment, and then moved on, and left her.

Meredith sat by herself on the red leather couch and loneliness washed through her, quite unexpected: like water, flooding into a room where a wall was missing.

Sarah came in from the next room and saw her, fiddling with a button, her eyes beneath the brim of her hat cast down. She saw herself, more than twenty-five years ago: an only child, taken to a gallery by her parents, on a winter afternoon. She had stood before those bright, bright colours, London transformed by Derain, on a visit: the racing yellow Thames, the sweep of pink pavement, pink trees, clouds of white train smoke billowing over blue Hungerford Bridge. She thought of Gauguin's women, half-naked, wrapped in bright cotton, their fall of dark hair and their watchful, watchful eyes, and herself before them, a child before the war, waiting for everything in her life to happen. She had wandered away from the grown-ups, she had stood beneath a big domed skylight, listening to the London rain trickle and patter over the glass, all by herself.

Just like Meredith.

I didn't mean you to be an only child, she thought, filled with such sadness, watching her daughter fiddle with a button, then look round the crowded room. I do remember what it was like.

But for Meredith it was different.

I was the daughter of middle-aged parents, thought Sarah, walking across to her. That's how it had to be. That's why I wanted more for you, and I never knew how death could happen – just like that, on a summer's day.

She came to the couch, she sat down beside her daughter.

'Darling. Are you all right?'

Meredith looked at her.

'Yes,' she said.

Walter, in the foyer, had made an arrangement with Henry Marsh, who was already lunching with friends, to meet for a drink, next week, just like the old days.

'And I'm so sorry,' said Henry, putting a hand on his arm. 'What a dreadful thing.'

Walter shook his head. 'Never mind,' he said, hearing two words stand for the whole of his son's small life. What could he say? 'Thank you. I'll see you next week.'

'Very good.'

'By the way,' said Walter, 'I don't suppose you know what became of Nina Frith.'

'Nina? Not any more. We kept up for a time, then she got married. A rather ghastly chap, quite honestly. Then she got divorced – quite quickly. After that, she dropped from view.' He looked at his watch. 'I must be off. So good to see you again.'

Walter went into the gallery, and leafed through the catalogue. Where should he start?

Salvador Dali, Paul Klee, Henry Moore, Paul Nash.

Where was the Nash?

He walked round until he found him.

Years ago, just after the war, before the Slade, he'd come up to London with David Wicks, who'd changed his life, he knew that: seeing what he might do, and setting him off on the path. They'd walked into the Royal Academy, queuing in the courtyard with Sarah and her father, all unknowing, and climbed the stairs to see the War Artists. He'd walked through the rooms, his first time in a London gallery, shocked by the paintings of the wounded, the screaming and dying, the rain-sodden trenches and uprooted trees. He'd thought about John William, hardly able to bear it; and he'd found the little Nash: churned-up mud, the same skeletal trees, and the sun, rising behind blood-red hills, its rays touching mud and branch and water.

*We are making a new world.*

And I felt I was making one myself, he thought now, recalling the visionary intensity of the early days of his marriage, them both so in love, and the children so vivid and free. All those walks in the early morning, painting the sun coming over the hills, glinting off the river, suffusing the rising mist and the soaking willows, coming home to the family, getting up, washing, the bathroom filled with clouds of sun and steam.

He shook his head; he came back to this room, this year, this exhibition. Here was the Nash.

*Equivalents for the Megaliths*. Watercolour and chalk. Monumental cylinders, on grass beneath the hills. Upright, fallen; mysterious and monumental.

*Harbour and Room* – a modest-sized oil, which felt enormous: a high-ceilinged room, with Regency wallpaper, gilt mirror, marble fireplace. And a wall cut away, and the dark sea entering, flooding in from the moonlit harbour, with its hulk of a barge, and silent buildings.

It was still, it was timeless: like the megaliths in their field, like Magritte's train transfixed in a fireplace, Moore's vast stone amongst empty hills, the naked girl dreaming on a couch on a chequered floor.

The world was changing, the world was being cut up and reassembled, as it had been by the war. But all the frenzy and fury of the machine, which had pounded through painting in the years before the war – the Futurists, the Vorticists, the violent colour – all this was gone. Here, in these brooding paintings, was time transfixed in a fireplace, the frozen moment.

Except for the Dali, which presaged something hideous. *Premonition of Civil War*.

Walter looked around him. Where were all the others?

He saw Sarah and Meredith, rising from the couch and coming towards him. It was time to go. And Euan?

'Where's Euan?'

They didn't know.

'He was looking at a painting over there,' said Meredith, nodding towards the far wall. The knots of visitors were thinning now, people going off to have lunch.

Walter looked at his watch. He was teaching at two. 'We'd better be going.'

'Wait just a moment,' said Meredith. And she walked across the room to the painting which Euan had gazed at, for such a long time, while her parents talked about where to have lunch, and Wimbledon, and train times.

She stood before the canvas and her heart turned over. She'd never known what that meant before.

Two people were kissing, but their heads were shrouded, so you couldn't see their faces. A thick heavy cloth was covering them entirely. They had to kiss through it, and their mouths could never meet – they just went on and on, seeking and seeking one another, in a blind and hopeless passion.

'Meredith?'

She turned away, walked back to join them. They all went out into the foyer and saw Euan outside on the steps, walking up and down with his pipe. He turned, he saw them. For a moment their eyes met again, and then he was looking at Sarah, and shading his face from the sun.

High summer, the cuckoo calling. The trees full and the grass lush, and the hop-pickers working from morning to sunset amongst the dappled bines, picking and cutting and weighing in bushels and moving on to the next. The corn was harvested: great swishing falls, and larks rising into the blue. Kingfishers flashed down the river. All along the lanes the ditches were thick with hogweed, willowherb and burdock; nightingales sang in the distant woods and moths were everywhere.

Long afternoons. Long lines of cows in calf, ambling heavily home to the fields, flicking away the flies.

Walter cut down the nettles, and mowed the grass. Sarah worked in the flowerbeds, hoeing and weeding and heaping up weeds. Meredith stood by the water butt, watching them, rubbing a sage leaf between her fingers, sniffing it. The church clock struck half-past four. Pigeons were murmuring, up on the tower. Sarah carried the heap of groundsel and couch grass and dandelions over to the compost heap, right on the far side of the garden at the end of the ditch, where Walter was shaking out the box of cuttings. He put his hand to her face, and brushed it, where grass had landed. They stood there, talking to one another in the sun.

Meredith looked at the stretch of cut grass beneath the apple trees. Euan was coming over for supper. Thinking about it gave her a queer little twist. She tugged at the sage bush, sniffed again, walked down the brick path and through the garden.

– This is the tree where we got married, Geoffrey said, all of a sudden. Do you remember? You had a baby, and I ran away. Blossom was everywhere, the birds were like a symphony. If I'd grown up, I'd have written that.

Meredith heard him, all through the garden, everywhere she went.

– That's the tree. That's the tree where it happened, on an afternoon just like this. You were at school, and I went climbing –

– Please, Geoffrey, please.

'Meredith?' Sarah had seen her, muttering away.

She covered her mouth. I want to cover the world, she thought then. Let me pull down a great cloth over me, let it swirl over and cover me for ever, so I need never see any of this again, never hear his voice.

'Meredith?' Sarah was coming towards her.

'I'm going out,' said Meredith.

'Where?'

Anywhere, anywhere, the other side of the world. With my map and my staff and a star to guide me –

– Can I come with you?

– No. Yes. You know I will never be able to leave you.

She could hear the geese, honking away in her grandparents' orchard. Evening corn, rattling into their dish.

'Just up to see Grandma,' she said.

'You don't look well,' said Sarah.

'I'm all right.'

'You look pale.'

'I expect it's the heat.'

'You won't go further than Grandma's, will you?'

'Mother,' said Meredith. 'I'm fourteen. I'm going to see Grandma. Let me be.'

She turned and walked out of the gate. She walked down to the corner to Mill Lane and turned it, never once looking back.

– You shouldn't speak to her like that. It's only because –

– I know why it is, I know, I know.

Swallows were swooping low before her. The beech trunks were lit by the afternoon sun, so tall and smooth. Beyond, in the harvested cornfields, stooks stood drying, row upon row.

There was the hare! All of a sudden, still as anything, up on his big back legs with his ears right up, just waiting there, watching her walk up the lane. She stood and watched back and the swallows swooped past her; then – had she moved? Had she twitched a muscle? – he was suddenly tearing across the stubble, and had vanished.

Oh, I wish, said Meredith, I wish, I wish . . .

– What? What do you wish?

– I don't know, I don't know.

She walked on, round the corner, seeing the row of cottages, all the runner beans clambering up the poles, scarlet flowers everywhere.

There was her grandmother, out with her watering can. Cool spray pattered all over the leaves.

'Hello, my duckling.'

'Hello.' Meredith leaned on the garden wall and watched her. Water dripped from the runner beans; her grandmother shook out the can.

'What I need out here is a tap.'

'Or another water butt.'

'That's a good idea. Not much room, that's the trouble.'

'Shall I come and help?'

'There's a good girl.'

Meredith clicked open the wicket gate and closed it behind her. She followed her grandmother in through the open front door, seeing the back door open too, and a path of sun fall through the dark little cottage. Here came the geese up the garden. Honk honk honk.

'Come to see you,' said her grandmother, standing the watering can in the sink, turning the tap on. The evening sun sparkled on the running water. 'If you get a bucket,' she said, 'that would be a help. There's one just out the back there.'

Meredith went out to the step and looked for it. The gander came hissing up, ahead of all the others. His neck stretched low towards her, and his orange beak was gaping. How he hissed.

'Used to frighten you to death when you were little,' said her grandmother, turning the tap off.

'Not the same bird,' said Meredith, seeing the bucket, there by the water butt.

'Not the same bird, but they're all the same, ganders. Mind you, that's not what Grandad would say. He says each one has a different character.'

Meredith picked up the bucket, and turned on the water-butt tap. Water poured through, and a great big spider. She picked it out, and threw it on to the grass. The gander had it at once.

'Where is Grandad?' she asked, turning the tap off.

'Over at Middle Yalding this afternoon. Nice for me to have you help out with the watering.'

Meredith carried the bucket through. Out in the front garden she tipped it up carefully, carrying it all down the row of cabbages. Snails had been at them, and a thrush had been at the snails: little bits of shell lay here and there on the earth.

'Expect you're glad it's the holidays now,' said her grandmother, watering the carrots.

'Sort of.'

'Sort of? By the time I was your age, I was at work.'

'Up at the Hall.'

'Up at the Hall, with old Mrs Monkton. I mean old, old Mrs Monkton. That was a long time ago.'

'Before the Flood.'

'That's enough cheek from you, young lady.'

The water sank into the earth, pearly drops lay amongst the cabbage leaves shining in the sun.

'I saw the hare on the way up here.'

'He's out most evenings.'

'Is he?'

They went back and forth through the cottage, carrying bucket and can, leaving damp footprints.

'Oh, I feel so much better,' said Meredith, when they had finished.

They stood in the doorway, the garden all wet and fresh.

Her grandmother looked at her. 'You're a bit peaky.'

'Yes.'

'You're at the age.'

'What age?'

'That age. When nothing feels right.'

It was true.

'It's true,' she said. And then, 'But it's not just that.'

'No.' There was a little silence. Then her grandmother said, 'I know. I know. Poor Meredith.'

'Poor Geoffrey.' How rarely she spoke his name to anyone.

'Yes. Yes, indeed. Poor lamb.'

There was another silence, deep and close. The sun was sinking, the air was cooler.

'Well,' said her grandmother, giving her a little pat. 'Better be getting on. Your grandad will be home before I know it. You going to stay and have some supper with us?'

Meredith shook her head. 'Euan's coming over.'

'Is he now? He's a good man.'

'Yes. Yes, he is.'

'Your grandad thinks well of him.'

'Does he?'

The swallows were swooping, the swifts were high, the air was full of life. She turned to her grandmother and kissed her.

'That's a good girl.' Her grandmother's hand was tight on her arm. 'Off you go now, my duckling.'

'See you soon.'

'See you soon. Straight home, now.'

'Yes.'

But when her grandmother had gone back inside, leaving the door wide, opening the kitchen cupboard, Meredith clicked shut the gate and thought, I don't want to go home, not yet. Now I feel better, I'll go for a walk, not far. Just for once.

The shadows were lengthening, long lines from the beech trunks falling right across the lane. Meredith didn't turn back, to walk past the beech trees, and down to the house. She turned left, and walked up towards Mill Farm, smelling caked earth in the fields, hearing the pigs. They'd always kept pigs up here.

– We used to come and watch them, snorting about in the sties. The boar was enormous. I used to tickle him, with a stick.

Meredith walked on, growing hot again.

It was different up here. She had always sensed it, and she sensed it now, turning the corner, seeing the old iron gate to the field on the right stand open, waiting for the cows' return from milking. Why was it different? Right away from all the other farms, for one thing, up here by itself in a deep quiet place, when Hobbs Farm and Middle Yalding were down on the flat, and always busy, with the hops, and families, and Mr Burridge and her father and grandfather all knowing each other. Mr Burridge was the tower captain, when her father used to ring. But here . . .

Meredith, walking in the heat, swallows swooping low on the verges, the ditches dank and full, remembered something she had forgotten, a story from her childhood only heard once, in her grandparents' kitchen: told by her father, and quickly interrupted.

'Don't let the child have her head filled with things like that.'

A long time ago, in the war, the woman who ran Mill Farm had hanged herself. Her husband hadn't come back, and she'd hanged herself, one dark winter night: coming out to the barn, getting up on a chair, slinging a rope up over the beam.

When Mrs Skinner did it, she'd been found by her halfwit brother, who'd stayed on the farm through the war, for The Buffs wouldn't have him, nobody would: he wasn't fit to go fighting in France. He'd come out to the barn in the early morning, looking for her, and his breakfast. He'd found her, he'd looked up and found her, come panting and blubbering all down the lane to her grandparents' cottage. At first, they couldn't make out what he was on about.

When the new tenants came, nobody knew what to do with him, so they kept him on as the cowman. Sometimes her grandfather came to help out.

Meredith turned the second corner. Milk churns stood on a platform in the long grass. The hedges were overgrown, untrimmed up here. They made the narrow lane feel even narrower, and you couldn't see over the top. It felt as if it had been like this for ever, and always would be: lonely, unvisited, remote. She heard the pigs, she could hear the clank of the cows in their stalls in the milking parlour, great heads leaning into the bowls, great tongues licking the feed.

– Grandad said we should never come up here without him. Never, never.

Meredith stopped.

Midges were dancing in clouds before her. Everything else was absolutely still. She saw the peeling green doors of the farm buildings, she saw the gate to the yard wide open, and bits of machinery lying about. Even with new tenants, the place was run down and neglected. A fork stood in a pile of dung by the wall, a couple of hens scratched about. The sun was slanting across it all, barring the crumbling plaster which patched the brick of the house, barring the big empty yard. The door to the milking parlour was slid half back, on its metal runner, letting the air in: she could hear the hiss of the milk in the pails, she could see the huge hindquarters of the cows, the tails swishing, back and forth, back and forth.

It was just an ordinary farm. She'd been coming up here on and off all her life.

– Not by yourself.

– I'm much older now.

– I don't think that makes any difference. Not here.

– Of course it does.

Meredith took a few steps into the yard. From a long way away, right across the fields at the Hall, she heard a gun go off. It was early for shooting. She thought, One of these days, Charles Monkton will take that rifle out to the fields and push it right into the back of his throat and blow his brains out. I know it. Somehow I've always known that.

She stood in the empty farmyard, shocked. What a terrible thought.

– That time we were up here, with Grandad, when he said not to come up by ourselves, one of the cows was bellowing. She'd lost her calf, had it taken away: she roared and roared and it made you cry.

– Yes.

– We didn't know then, what would happen to me.

– Oh, Geoffrey.

Meredith stood in the silent farmyard, and tears pricked the back of her eyes. She swallowed, and once again a great wave of loneliness washed right through her, as if water were flooding an empty room, long locked up, with the curtains drawn.

I can't go on like this, she thought. How am I going to go on?

Then the door of the milking parlour was slid right back, with a bang. Meredith almost jumped out of her skin.

Out came the cows, one by one, their great heads swaying.

Out came the cowman, following.

At first he didn't see her. Then he did.

'Hello, my girlie.'

Is that what he said? His speech was so strange, and his mouth half-toothless. His cap and his hands were filthy.

'Hello.' Meredith heard her own voice sound strained and high. She backed away. One of the cows, enormous, with a calf about to drop, turned her head towards her. Her horns were uncut and her eyes great dark dangerous pools.

'What are you doing here, then?'

Was that what he said?

'Nothing.'

The huge cow was moving towards her.

'Come to see me?'

He grinned, coming right up behind the animal, slapping her massive rump, where flies buzzed round a sore. 'G'arn! G'arn!' She lifted her tail and the stream of muck poured out of her, splashing the ground, his boots, Meredith's sandals. Then she turned towards the others, following them out to the open gate.

'I said, Come to see me?'

He grinned again, and his mouth was horrible, all blackened teeth, and holes. His face was unshaven, a crust of dried snot on his upper lip. Meredith backed up against the stone wall, where the hens were scratching about by the dung heap, and he came closer still. She turned her head aside, saw how the yard was filled with shadow, heard right in the distance, far down the winding lane, the geese in her grandparents' orchard, honking as someone went past.

'Come on, my girlie, don't be afraid.'

He was coming right up to her, and his eyes in the shadows were glittering. She pressed back against the wall, tried to slide along it, but she couldn't move.

He stepped towards her, feeling his trousers, his head outstretched, his filthy other hand upraised.

He made a sound, at the back of his throat, like a hiss.

Meredith's hands flew up to her face: she could feel them hit her lip against her teeth.

He moved towards her, hissing, his arms outstretched.

Goose wings flapping up, beating the air – the long, long neck stretched out towards her, the beak agape, the hiss, the hiss, and the grey tongue taut, so deep inside –

Wings of the angel, huge and mighty and cold as death, white in the darkness, opening out –

Meredith screamed.

He lunged towards her.

She screamed again, and she kicked him, she pushed him away. He staggered, then made for her once more.

Somehow she ducked, and she ran – across the yard, slippery with cowpats, out to the open gate, pushing between the cows, then into the lane and pelting down it, running and gasping between the towering hedgerows.

Someone was running up towards her.

'Meredith! Meredith! I'm here, I'm coming!'

She stopped dead and stood there, shaking and shaking, sobs rising through her like burning coals.

He was there, panting; his arms went round her.

'Meredith.' He drew her close and she sank against him. 'I'm here, I'm here.'

'Euan –'

'I came up to look for you. We were worried – thank God you're safe.' He was stroking the top of her head, his hands so warm and

317

comforting. Her arms were round him, her wet face against his shirt. It smelled of plaster, tobacco and sweat.

At last she stopped crying.

He knelt down before her and looked at her, smoothing wet hair from her face, wiping her cheeks.

'Are you all right? Has he hurt you? Did he try to –'

She shook her head.

Behind them she could hear the last cows step across the lane, and the iron gate clang shut. Then the footsteps of the cowman, walking back to the yard.

'Do you want to tell me about it?'

Glittering eyes – wings of the goose, and wings of the terrible angel of death.

Not just the cowman, but everything, everything.

Including you, Euan. Including you.

'Meredith?'

She shook her head. 'I'm all right.'

'When you're ready,' he said, and kissed her fringe. 'Tell me one day, when you're ready.'

'Yes.'

He stood up, touched her shoulder. 'Shall we go?'

They walked down the lane. The sun had sunk low and the light was so rich and deep, streaming between the tall grave trunks of the beech.

'Euan,' said Meredith.

'Yes?'

'Nothing.'

His arm went round her, he drew her close again, just for a moment. Then he released her. They walked on.

Her grandparents were out at the gate, her parents coming quickly up the lane towards them.

'Meredith, we were so worried. Darling, what's happened?' Sarah saw her tear-stained face, and came running up.

'I'm all right,' said Meredith. 'Really.'

'But what – ' She looked up at Euan.

'In her own time,' he said gently to Sarah. 'Don't you think?'

Meredith leaned on the garden gate and watched him walk away down the lane. The clouds were massing, pricked here and there by

318

summer stars. They had all had supper, out in the garden, watching the bats flit from the trees, and the moths hover over Sarah's flowerbeds. The air was sweet and cool; she had told them as much as she wanted. Not very much. 'Stay the night,' said Sarah to Euan, lighting a candle in a jar, but he said that he had to get back. Work tomorrow, the long walk home.

Meredith watched him approaching the corner: his easy stride, the whole set of him. He turned and saw her, raised his hand and made that strange little gesture again – two fingers in the slightest movement. What did it mean? Hello? Goodbye? I am leaving? I am coming back? Then he had rounded the bend and was gone.

I love you, said Meredith, deep inside herself, and wondered if there had ever been a time in her life when this had not been true. I really love you. She felt the words fill her entirely, as if they had always been meant to do so.

# 2

Smoke and steam and autumn passing. Leaves blew along the lanes through Asham's Mill; they blew through London parks, and along the Embankment, where the Tate was about to open a retrospective exhibition of the work of Henry Tonks, retired Professor of Painting at the Slade. In Walter's classes at the Central School the talk was less of this event than of Spain, where the fighting had started. The Artists International Association held its meetings at the Central: there was talk of an International Brigade. One or two students had already left.

'Will you go, do you think?' Walter asked Euan, meeting in the Crown one evening.

'I'm thinking about it. I'm not sure if I'd be much use, it's young men they need.'

'Don't be absurd.'

'I'm thirty-nine,' said Euan. He drew on his pipe. 'Sometimes I feel much older. What about you? Might you go?'

'No,' said Walter. 'I'll only fight if I have to. I couldn't leave Sarah and Meredith.'

'No, of course you couldn't.' Euan felt for his matches. 'How are they?'

'They're both well.' He rubbed at his face, thinking. 'Meredith's recovered, at least I hope she has. She still seems unsettled. You were very good with her, that day. Sarah often says so.'

'I didn't do anything. I'm just glad I was there.'

'So were we. My father wanted to go up and shoot old Eddie.'

'Perhaps he should.'

Walter looked at him.

'He's a menace,' said Euan. 'He's dangerous. He ought to be locked up.'

'Well . . .' Walter sat in his corner, wondering when he had last heard Euan sound so vehement. 'I think that to do that we'd have to put Meredith through more than she'd want to go through, don't you?'

'Probably.' Euan drained his glass. 'Anyway, I hope she's all right.'

'It's a restless age.' said Walter. 'That's what my mother says.' He looked at his watch. 'I must get back. Come over again soon, won't you?'

'I will. And give them both my love.'

They walked across the square to the bus, just starting up.

'I don't suppose you want to come up to the Tonks?' asked Walter, as they settled into their seats. 'Henry Marsh thinks he can get us into the private view.'

'I might. Tonks means more to you, though, doesn't he?'

'Yes. Yes, he does.'

The bus rumbled out of the town. Soon they were on the unlit country roads, the headlamps catching a rabbit or owl in the beam. Euan got up, and nodded to the driver in the mirror as they approached Hurst Green; they pulled up by the common and he climbed off. Walter watched him walk over the darkened grass, raising his hand in farewell. One or two lights were shining in the cottages on the far side; the goats had been taken in. He saw Euan feel for his keys, approaching his own, unlit cottage, then the bus pulled away, and he settled back into his seat again, looking out across high hedges. Here and there a white cowl shone beneath the stars; they drove past the empty hopfields, the long stripped bines like ghosts in the darkness. How lonely was Euan? Walter wondered, thinking of his own house waiting, the range warming the kitchen, Meredith's face lighting up as he came through the door.

'Supper's ready.' Sarah, who never taught now on days that he taught, so there was always someone at home, got up each evening to receive his kiss. She was busy, working on two books at once. She dealt with correspondence from publishers, the Society of Wood Engravers, the Golden Cockerel Press, talking of exhibitions and prizes. Despite the Depression, the marches from Jarrow, the strikes and unemployment, and amongst all the artists scrimping amidst heaps of unsold canvases, Sarah was making a modest mark.

She was steadier, calmer, the edge gone out of her voice. They made love again.

'Do you really want to?'

'Yes, yes.'

She spread herself over him, raised herself above him, hair unknotted and loose about her naked shoulders. He reached up, and wound streaks of grey around his fingers.

'I love you,' he said, closing his eyes as she eased herself on to him. 'I shall always love you.'

But this she rarely answered.

He asked her afterwards, more than once, 'Sarah, do you want another baby? Shall we have another child?' He held her in the high iron bed, the box and the tube of cream from her cap beside the pile of books – *To the Lighthouse*, with its dust-jacket of swirling waves and stippled rays of light; *The Weather in the Streets*. 'Beloved? Shall we try?'

'For you or for me?'

'For all of us.'

A long silence.

'No. I'm too old. And we are as we are, now.'

'But for Meredith?'

'She's growing up. This is how it is, that's all.'

The church clock struck the night hour; from a long way away came the soft hollow hoot of an owl. 'Besides,' said Sarah quietly, 'I don't think I could bear it. Especially if it were a boy.' She shut her eyes. 'No.'

He kissed her, and drew her towards him; they slept once again in each other's arms.

And yet – and yet.

Something was always held in reserve. A light had gone out with Geoffrey's death and it had never been rekindled. The flame was gone. And still, he sometimes wondered, seeing her greeting Euan when he came over, seeing them talk to one another – about her work, his work, about Gill, and Ravilious, carving and lettering and book design, seeing her face as Euan spoke gently to her, returning her daughter from the brink of mortal danger – yes, especially then – Walter wondered, Do I dream that look? Is there something between them? And if not, who is it that Euan cares for?

*I can't answer that. One day, perhaps. Not yet.*

The bus had pulled up by the churchyard; the headlamps lit gate and yew. A sheep sleeping next to a gravestone looked up, startled, her yellow eyes caught in the beam. The driver looked back, and called to him, 'Don't you get off here?'

Walter picked up his bag and hurried down the aisle.

'You were a long way away.'

'I was.'

☆

Smoke and steam and autumn passing. Riverboats chugged down the Thames. Dark clouds billowed from Battersea Power Station. On the steps of the Tate Gallery, his collar turned up against the October wind, Professor Henry Tonks was greeting old friends. So tall, so frail, so white – like fading smoke, thought Walter a few days later, watching the activity above him, suddenly filled with emotion. A gust of the wind sent everyone inside; the glass doors took with them the reflection of the clouds.

Walter stood at the gate, waiting for Henry, who'd wangled an invitation via Tooth's in Bond Street, where he was working now. 'Buying good contemporary work,' he'd told Walter, over their drink. 'Spencer is our star. Some of our artists have been living on crusts. Literally. So I'd better have a look at yours.'

'I've certainly found it hard,' said Walter. And then, 'You're not painting yourself?'

'Dear boy, did you ever really think I would?'

Walter smiled. 'And you – may I ask if you've married?'

'You may, and I have. The sweetest girl, much too good for me. Little house in Chelsea – I'm a lucky dog. You and Sarah must come and have dinner one day. Bring Meredith. The girls would love her.'

'The girls?'

'Two. Pretty enough for Sargent, if one could ever have afforded him. Perhaps you could paint them.'

'You could certainly afford me,' said Walter.

Henry laughed. Then he was serious. 'I really am so sorry,' he said, reaching out a hand. 'You know – about your little boy.'

'Thank you.'

'I bet he was a grand little chap.'

'Thank you. He was. One day I'll tell you –'

'Quite. Quite. Plenty of time. Now, then: Tonks. Could you make it?'

'I'm sure I could.'

And here was Henry, climbing out of a cab. He waved as he paid the fare. 'Sorry I'm late.'

'You're not, I haven't been here long. I've caught a glimpse.'

'Have you, now?' They climbed the steps. 'And how does he look?'

'Getting old.'

Inside, they crossed the foyer and followed the signs to the Tonks rooms. Henry showed the invitation: they signed their names.

'Makes me think of signing in at the Slade,' said Henry.

'Me too.' Walter put back the top of his fountain pen. 'Do you know my father gave me this, when I first came up?'

'And it's lasted all these years? Dear Cox, what a wonder you are. Now, then, what time are you teaching?'

'I've got a couple of hours.'

A buzz of conversation and the chink of glasses came from the doorway. 'Come on. I wonder who we'll see.'

'I'd love to see Steer,' said Walter.

Tonks was standing in the midst of a knot of people in the middle of the first room. Loud laughter floated across. A bearded man in a velvet jacket was holding forth. 'Augustus John,' said Henry, taking a glass from a tray. 'Couldn't be anyone else, could it? Shall we go and mingle?'

'Not yet.' Walter took a glass himself. 'I don't know if I'm quite up to all this.'

'Of course you are. Cheers.'

They moved through the crush to the first wall. *Lady in a Garden*, *Nymphs Surprised*, *Mrs St John Hutchinson*.

'There's nothing from the war,' said Walter, leafing through the catalogue. 'But he did a lot, I remember. He went to France with Sargent – when Sargent made studies for *Gassed*.'

'I'd forgotten that.' Henry moved on, caught sight of someone he knew. 'There's Richard Webb – remember him?'

'No,' said Walter, glancing across the room.

'Mind if I –'

'No, no, of course not. I'll catch up with you later.'

He moved to the opposite wall. And there was Steer, ponderous as a walrus, small head on huge shoulders, leaning upon a stick. He was peering at a group portrait, as he had used to peer at work in the studios, all those years ago. Walter looked over, checked the catalogue: *Steer at Home on Christmas Day with Nurse*. He felt a smile spread through him, drew a breath, and went up.

'Mr Steer?'

'Hello?' Steer turned, and dim eyes blinked. 'Is this someone I know?'

Walter introduced himself. 'I'm sure you won't remember me.'

'I'm afraid that's true. Cox, you say. Nineteen-twenty-one.' He shook his head. 'But still, good to see you, my boy. How are you getting on these days? Enjoying the show?'

'Very much, so far – I've only just arrived. And you, sir?'

'Not enjoying the crush very much. Still, mustn't be a wet blanket.' He turned as a tall thin man touched his arm. 'MacColl? Ah, MacColl. How are we getting on? Do you know Mr – Mr –'

'Cox,' said Walter, holding out his hand.

'Dugald MacColl. How do you do.' Sharp eyes flashed round the room.

'I must be going,' said Walter. He wanted to shake Steer's hand, but the hands were clasping the stick. He nodded to both of them.

'Good man,' said Steer. 'Good to see you.'

Walter knew he would be saying this all morning. He slipped away, hearing another roar of laughter from the circle gathered round Tonks. The room was filling up with new arrivals. 'Ah, Carline, how good of you to come. Is Spencer with you?' Walter saw Tonks shaking hands, loosening his tie. He saw Steer lumbering over towards him, and Tonks put out an arm and say to a pretty girl, asking about retirement, 'Like a couple of old barges, are we not, Steer? A couple of old barges resting side by side in the Thames, and quite content to be so. Isn't that right?'

'I wouldn't say I'm finding this restful,' said Steer, mopping his brow.

Walter left them all to it. Perhaps he would never manage, here, to thank Tonks for his letter, the turning point. Perhaps it wasn't, anyway, the place. I'll write, he thought, going into the next room. I should have written years ago. Why am I so diffident?

He looked around in a room full of oils and drawings. Nothing here from the war: only girls in ballgowns and hat shops, a number of nudes, and half-nudes. Where was Henry? He saw him caught up in a knot of people, recognised faces from the Life Class, fifteen years older: the smooth public schoolboys so like, and so unlike Henry, who was clearly enjoying himself, catching up.

I should have brought Euan, Walter thought, going to look at the drawings. I should have made him come. He stood before the drawing of a male nude, done in the studio: very Tonks, very Slade, finely worked and shaded.

*'Drawings must be stern and unbending . . . Human beings, though lovely, must still have backbones secreted under their clothes . . .'*

He could hear it now, could remember coming out of the Life Class for the break, into the corridor, hearing Nina's quick little step, filled with embarrassment and longing, in the days before their – their what? Courtship? Never. Love affair? A kind of love affair. He could remember only torment, and his relief at ending it.

What had happened to Nina?

Even as he wondered this, he knew, all at once, that she was here, that she was in the room, and he turned from the drawing and saw her, making her way across the floor towards him. Neat little suit and heels, silky pale hair brushed with grey, a Liberty scarf.

'Walter!' She held out her hand, with a dazzling smile. 'Dear Walter. I thought it was you.'

Six o'clock, cold and dusky, the last light going, lamps from the riverboats winking in the Thames. Walter walked over Chelsea Bridge and through the streets of Battersea. He looked again at the small page, torn from a notebook, where Nina had written her address; he stopped to ask directions; he found himself outside a mansion block. He stepped back, and looked up. Lights shone through gaps in the curtains; the curtains were undrawn. He saw a middle-aged man pour a drink, and take it to the window, loosening his tie; he saw a young woman with a telephone, crooked in her shoulder, laughing and powdering her nose; he saw a couple kiss, and the man cross to the window and pull the curtains to. Life in London. Something of Nina's life.

He looked at the nameplates, as years ago he had looked at the nameplates on the door of a lodging house in Fitzroy Square, his heart pounding, the music of the twenties floating out from other windows, tinny and bright.

He found her name: Mrs Peter Beard. 'Of course, I could have gone back to Frith,' Nina had said in the Tate, scribbling in her notebook. 'But I thought I might as well hang on to something. A shred of respectability, even if I am divorced.' She tore out the page, and handed it to Walter. 'Being divorced is ghastly. Better, of course, than being married.' She gave a little laugh. 'Do come and see me, Walter. Please say you will. Come and have a drink, just for old times' sake.'

He rang the bell. He waited.

From not far away came the sound of a local train. He looked at his watch. He'd have to get the train from Clapham, and change. The train hooted, puffing away from the river.

'Look at it one way, and it's near the railway line. Look at it the other, and it's really quite close to the park. It's a nice little flat: holding on to it was about the one clever thing I've done in my life.' In the island they made in the crush of the private view, Nina leaned forward and kissed his cheek. He felt the soft smudge of lipstick, and lifted his hand. 'Tut, tut,' she said, laughing. 'Oh do come, Walter, you needn't stay long.'

Why hadn't he said they could meet in a public place? A pub or a nice little restaurant, after his class, and then home. You always did what she wanted, he thought, swallowing, feeling himself no older than twenty again.

And then he heard the clank of a lift in the hall, the gate pushed back and footsteps hurrying towards the door. Little light footsteps. He swallowed again. The door was pulled open.

'Walter. How lovely. You're here.'

Outside the lift, on the fifth floor, he followed her down a silent corridor. 'Here we are,' said Nina. The door to her flat was ajar; it had an iron doorstep, and a shaft of light fell on to the hall carpet. 'Come in, come in.'

A little hall, with a coat rack, lamp and mirror. He gave her his hat, put down his bag. A pretty sitting room, furnished with bright geometric fabrics, a few antiques. A gas fire flickered, books lay on a polished table, prints hung on the walls.

'That little desk is from my mother,' said Nina, following his gaze. 'The table belonged to my father. Now, then, what will you have to drink?' Decanters stood on a lacquered tray. 'There's whisky, gin, soda.'

'I'll have a whisky and soda,' said Walter, who hardly drank, and never spirits. The decanters chinked, a syphon hissed into two tumblers.

'Cheers.' Their glasses chinked. 'Do sit down.' She gestured to the armchair by the fire, curled herself up on the sofa, reached for a cigarette box. 'I don't suppose you smoke?'

'No, but please –'

'Oh, I will, I'm afraid, I will.' She tapped a cigarette on the box lid, flicked open a slender silver lighter. 'Peter gave me this. A wedding present.' She inhaled and coughed, just a little. 'That's better.' She looked across at him. 'Well now, dear Walter, where shall we begin?'

The whisky burned his throat. He turned the tumbler in his hands, hearing the faint putter of the fire, and a door bang, down in the street.

'You start,' he said slowly, and looked round the room again. 'It's very nice here – your parents' things, all these books and pictures. And your parents are . . .'

'Dead,' said Nina, drawing on her cigarette. 'Dead and gone, I'm afraid. My mother in nineteen-twenty-nine, my father last year.'

'I'm so sorry.'

'It happens.' She reached for an ashtray. 'Happens to us all, doesn't it? I do miss them, actually – well, my father. We were quite close in the end. Until he went ga-ga.' She looked across at Walter. 'What about yours? Still here?'

'Yes. Yes, they are.'

He thought of the autumn wind, blowing down Mill Lane, his parents shutting up for the night, climbing the narrow stairs. Geese sleeping out in the orchard, the chime of the clock in the tower. Everything that had nourished him since childhood. He turned the tumbler. Nina watched him.

'You always were so serious.'

'Was I?' He smiled. 'Sorry.' He had another sip, looked round the room again. 'And all these nice fabrics and things?' He could hear his attempt to sound light.

'Liberty's. I get a discount.'

'A discount – are you still working there? What happened to your painting?'

'Oh, I was never very good. I was dabbling, really and Tonks knew it – he wanted me out. I should have gone into design, but what with one thing and another . . . Liberty's was just for fun, at first. Now I really enjoy it. I'll probably last till I drop.' She drained her tumbler, gave a little frown. 'How did you know I was working there?'

He tried to remember. 'I think Euan told us.'

'Euan?'

'Euan Harrison. Do you remember him? He was in the sculpture school – not very many of them in those days. He'd been in the Artists' Rifles.'

Nina was trying to think.

'He had a bicycle,' said Walter. 'We used to go around together a lot.'

'Oh! Him. Very tall. Yes, I do remember him, as it happens. I thought he was rather nice, not that we ever had two words to say to each other. Isn't it funny, looking back on those days? I knew I had to come today – invitation or no. I had to get a glimpse of old Tonks, and I wondered who would be there.'

'How did you get in?'

'Oh, fluttered my eyelashes, said I was somebody else. Usual sort of thing.' Walter laughed. 'That's better. Isn't it nice seeing Henry again? I was sorry when we lost touch.'

'He said you dropped from view.'

'Did he? Oh, well – sometimes you feel you have to make a fresh start. Don't know why, it's bloody difficult.' She stubbed out her cigarette, swung her legs on to the floor. 'Now, have another.'

'I won't, thanks. I really mustn't stay too long.'

'Oh, Walter.' She unstoppered the decanter, then the syphon hissed. 'I do wish you'd relax. It's years since we've seen each other. I haven't heard a word about *you*.' She brushed his shoulder, went back to the sofa, lit up again. Such a bright little flame in that slender silver case. 'You do realise who I really hoped to see today, don't you?'

'Who?'

'Who do you think?' There was a little silence. 'You,' said Nina. 'Of course it was you.'

'Well,' said Walter, turning his glass round and round, like a boy. 'Thank you.'

'Didn't you hope to see me?'

Walter looked up. Pale silky hair with a strand of grey, lipstick and scent and a cloud of smoke.

'Yes and no,' he said slowly. 'If I'm to be honest.'

Nina drew deeply upon her cigarette. 'Oh, dear. Haven't you thought about me, just now and then? In all these years?'

'Now and then.' He drank down the whisky. 'Not often.'

'I expect you've been very busy. Families take up so much time. So – tell me. You married Sarah – I know that, she sent me a card. Lucky girl. And then . . .'

'We moved out of London, back to be near my parents. Not just for that, for the whole place. And then . . .' He drew a deep breath. 'I don't really want to talk about this.'

'Why? Because you and Sarah aren't happy?'

'No. Nothing like that.' Down in the street a taxi drew up and stood ticking. Someone came hurrying out of the mansion block, calling to somebody else. 'Come *on*! It starts in twenty *minutes*!' Life in London. How could he even begin to convey what his and Sarah's life had been like? And, at this moment, how far away it all felt.

'What, then?' asked Nina. 'Do you have children?'

He looked down, turning the empty glass again. There was only one way to say it.

'We have a daughter. We did have a son, but he died.'

'Oh, Walter . . .'

'It's a long time ago, and I should be used to saying it. Somehow I'm still not. Sorry.'

'Oh, Walter,' said Nina again. 'How terrible.'

All the flirtation and teasing had gone.

'Thank you. It's all right. It is getting better, in a way. Only . . .' He was just beginning to see this. 'When it gets better, you feel worse. As if you were betraying . . .' He looked around the pretty little room, with its books and pictures and Liberty cushions. What was he doing here? 'Perhaps I will have another drink,' he said. 'And then I really must go.'

'Of course.' She got up, took his glass, returned it. The soda fizzed. She sat down again, picked up her cigarette. 'Walter, shall I tell you something? May I tell you something?'

'Yes.' He was watching the gas fire: little blue jets popped and hissed.

'Look at me,' said Nina.

He looked up and saw her, serious and still. For the first time ever, it felt, they were looking at each other as equals.

'Shall I tell you why I was such a bitch to you?'

'Yes,' said Walter.

Outside, the taxi had driven away. The street was quiet, the room was warm and smoky.

'Have you heard of a novel called *The Weather in the Streets*?'

He frowned, trying to think. 'I'm not sure. I think perhaps Sarah has a copy. I don't read a great many novels.'

'No, men don't, on the whole. It came out this year – it's by

Rosamund Lehmann. She wrote *Invitation to the Waltz*. Never mind, you won't have heard of that, either.' Nina nodded towards the polished table, with its pile of books. 'It's over there. The story of my life, I discovered. Well, some of it.' She had stubbed out her cigarette, was lighting another.

'You smoke too much.'

'I know, I don't care.'

'Go on.'

'Well. Girl falls in love with a married man. Rollo, in the novel. Mine was called – oh, never mind. But this was in the war – near the end of the war. He was on leave, and I was very young. We met at a party – I absolutely fell. And we had an affair, very short, very passionate. I was mad about him. I didn't, actually, know he was married, not at first. By the time he told me, I didn't care. And then – I got pregnant. Like Olivia, in the novel.'

Now it was she who was looking into the fire. Walter watched, listening. It felt as if all of him was contracted into this moment, this revelation. He waited. Nina was running a hand through her hair.

'He went back to France. He didn't get killed, but he didn't write, so as far as I knew he might have been. And anyway, what the hell could I do? I did what Olivia did. I had an abortion, a horrible, botched abortion. Actually, I nearly died. Truly.'

'Oh, Nina.'

Little light footsteps, tripping up the stairs at the Slade, the day of his arrival.

*'I've been ill.'*

*'I'm sorry to hear that.'*

*'Oh, it was nothing serious.'*

'But I didn't,' said Nina, with a swift little smile. 'As you see. Here I am. It just meant no more babies. Ever. And that . . . did something to me.'

She drew on her cigarette, picked up her drink. 'Shall I go on?'

'Only if you want to.'

'Well. He came back from France, and he went back to his wife. As men always, always do. Except my husband, of course. Peter. He didn't last long. He didn't mind about the babies – well, he said that he didn't. He minded about the sex. Lack of it, I should say. He said I was frigid. He said it rather a lot. In the end, I bloody hated the sight of him.' She stopped. 'Sorry, I'm getting carried away.'

'Go on,' he said. 'You can tell me now.'

She gave him a funny look. 'Oh, Walter.' There was a long sigh. Then she got up, and went to the tray of drinks. 'My gynaecologist – I don't suppose you thought I was going to talk about my gynaecologist when you came here this evening, did you? Neither did I, to be honest.' She was pouring another glass. 'But he says there's no such thing as a frigid woman, only an inexperienced man. I think he's rather advanced. And nice. Married, of course – nice gynaecologists always are. Anyway, I've never found anyone who –' The stopper went back with a chink.

She returned to the sofa, sinking on to it. 'So: now do you see?' She looked at him. 'About us?'

He nodded, slowly, rubbing his mouth. 'Yes.'

'Not just you,' said Nina. 'Every single man I met for years. Revenge? Misery. Anyway, the whole idea of sex made me feel ill, for ages. Perhaps I was frigid then. And underneath all that Bright Young Thing-ness I was as miserable as sin. You were so nice, I did know that, but frankly I just didn't care.'

'No.'

'Was it horrible?'

'Yes.'

The clock on the mantelpiece was ticking and ticking, fast and bright. She held out her hand. 'I'm sorry.'

'It's all right.' Walter sat thinking, no longer feeling like a boy. Nina drew her hand away. 'Of course it's all right,' he said. 'And I'm so sorry. Poor Nina.'

'Poor Nina, poor Nina. I can't bear being poor Nina. Anyway – now you know.'

'Yes.'

'One more drink.'

'No, really.'

There was another little silence. 'Just a soda? Or a tonic?'

'A tonic,' he said, and got up and went to the window, drawing the curtain aside. He stood looking down on the lamplit street, hearing a distant train, a distant riverboat. He shook his head, filled with sadness.

Nina was opening a bottle of tonic. 'These are my father's decanters,' she said, standing by the tray. 'I'm so fond of them. I was fond of Peter, too, at first. I thought it was going to be all right.'

'How did you meet?'

'He was at Liberty's. Now he's at Peter Jones.' She looked at him; they both began to laugh. 'That's better.' She came over, gave him his glass, stood next to him. He let the curtain drop; he turned to her –

'Cheers,' said Nina again, and her glass touched his. She rested her head on his shoulder; pale silky hair brushed his neck. He didn't move.

'I should put a record on,' she said, and he could feel her smile. 'Do you remember how we used to dance, in Fitzroy Square?'

He closed his eyes. 'I do.'

*Missouri Waltz*, *That Naughty Waltz*, *Three O'clock in the Morning* . . .

Records from other rooms, winding up, winding down, in that great big house, with its shared bathroom, linoleum hall, cavernous moulded ceilings. Little Mr Schnecburger coming to the door of his dark, ground-floor rooms, every time anyone came in and out. Behind him, the mournful chirp of the canary. And in Nina's room the muslin curtains billowed in and out at the balcony doors, and shadowy screens surrounded her narrow bed, offering a glimpse of white pillow, a Japanese gown.

A painting: a corner, the edge of a life.

He had known nothing of Nina's life.

'I do have a gramophone,' she was saying now. 'I play it quite a lot, when I'm on my own.' He felt her soft hair on his cheek. 'Shall I put something on? Shall we dance?'

'Oh, Nina.' He opened his eyes, saw her looking into them. He put down his glass. 'I think I'd better go now.'

'I do wish you wouldn't, Walter. Won't you stay?'

'I can't.'

'For old times' sake?'

He gave a wry smile. 'There weren't any old times, were there? Not like that.'

'No, there weren't. What a waste.' She put both her hands on his shoulders, just as she used to do. She hadn't worn lipstick, then; now her little mouth, neat as a pencil drawing, was smudged with scarlet. It encircled her cigarette, burning into the room; it lay upon her glass, standing next to his on the table by the fire.

'Shall we make up for it now?' she asked softly, reaching out a finger, running it over his lips. 'Walter? Shall we go to bed together?'

'Oh, Nina,' he said again, and his arms went round her.

She lifted her mouth for his kiss.

Walter closed his eyes, shaking his head. He heard himself give a long, deep sigh.

'What? What is it? Aren't you going to kiss me?'

The fanlights lit up, all round the square. He drew her to him, her lips parted –

Now he tucked her head beneath his chin, he rested upon her silky hair. For a few moments neither of them spoke; they just stood there, arms round one another, still and quiet.

'Oh, it feels so lovely to be held,' she whispered against him.

He stroked her hair, he didn't answer. He thought, half-thought, filled with tenderness and desire, This quiet embrace is as if two people have come to rest. We are resting, before we begin. Down in the street – quite a long way down, she was high above everything, up here – cars drove past, pulled up; doors slammed, footsteps hurried home in the cold. All these lives, when he was so used to the silence of the countryside at night, the wind in the trees, the tick of a farmworker's bike, the church clock, chiming over the garden, the fields, the graveyard, where Geoffrey lay close to the wall.

'Walter?'

Nina drew away from their close embrace: she searched his face.

He heard, once again, in the distance, a train, pulling out of the station. Heading north? Heading south? Coming or going?

'Walter?' asked Nina again. 'Speak to me. What are you thinking?'

He thought, This sense of being at peace, at rest, before everything begins – this is how I felt with Sarah, in her kitchen in Shelton Street, the dark blind down against the sun, pigeons on the rooftops, our hands meeting, holding, never letting go. If we had known then, what darkness lay ahead . . . But that was the beginning of love, and this is – this is –

Nina's face had clouded.

He said, 'I'm thinking about my family.'

She bit her lip. Little smudge of scarlet, on small white teeth.

'Whom I love,' said Walter slowly. He thought of Meredith, looking up as he opened the kitchen door, her thin tense face relaxing into a smile, although she was never, ever, relaxed for long. He thought of Sarah, coming down from the studio, the heart of their life together, something that could sustain them to the end, in spite of that summer afternoon, the sudden, chilling awareness of silence, outside in the garden. She came up, she kissed him. Even though something, always, was held in reserve, she was there: first true love and last.

Nina was trembling. 'That feels rather cruel. I wouldn't want to take you away from them. You know I wouldn't.'

'But that's what would happen.'

'No, it wouldn't. Not just with one night, just tonight.'

'It would. I know that it would.'

They were still in each other's arms. He brushed back her hair from her face. 'I don't mean to be cruel. It's the last thing I'd want to be after everything you've been through.'

'Please don't try to be kind, either.' She moved her face aside. 'There, that's women for you. Exasperating, aren't we?'

He looked at her. 'What do you want me to say?'

She began to cry, all at once.

'Oh, Nina.' He tried to hold her, but she broke away.

'Don't, don't! Don't say any bloody thing at all, it's bound to be wrong.' She made for the sofa, fumbled in the box for a cigarette, sobbing. 'Why do men always make women cry? Always, always. Even when they're nice – that's what she says in *The Weather in the Streets*.' She lit up with a shaking hand. Beside her in the ashtray the last cigarette was still burning, a thread of smoke wavering into the air. She drew in a puff, then she cried and cried.

Walter stood watching her, feeling a wave of pity.

'Don't just stand there watching me.'

He crossed over, sat by her side. 'Dear, dear Nina, I'm so sorry.'

'And for God's sake don't pity me.'

What should he do?

'I told you,' she said bitterly, 'don't do anything.'

'Shall I go?'

'Yes. No. No, please don't go. Oh, Walter.' She buried her face in his shoulder, and his arms went round her again.

'Then let it all out,' he said quietly. 'I'm here.'

'You're not, you're not.'

'I am.' He leaned back and held her, stroking her hair again, watching the little blue gas flames burn and burn, and the fast, frantic tick of the clock.

Gradually Nina's sobs subsided. She fumbled behind one of the cushions, found a crumpled handkerchief. 'Always bloody crying on this sofa,' she said, blowing her nose. 'Always a hankie to hand. God Almighty, how pathetic.' She looked at him. Mascara was everywhere. 'Where's my compact? I must look a fright.'

'Never.' He took the soaking handkerchief and wiped some of the smudges of black away. He knew he had never done this before in his life; it felt extraordinarily intimate. 'There,' he said, and gave it back to her, touching her cheek. He thought, If I kissed you now, I would never want to stop, and he leaned back against the cushions again, suddenly overcome with longing. He closed his eyes and he saw them: naked in a white white bed, pale hair, pale skin like a flame in the darkness, the taste of cigarettes, and him plunging into her, into her, both crying out –

She took his hand. He held hers, he lifted it to his lips. He heard his great sigh fill the room. Then he got up.

'I must go.'

Nina said flatly, looking into the fire, 'I will only say this once, and please don't pity me. I am so, so lonely.' She shook her head. 'One should never, never say it.'

'Yes, you should,' said Walter, 'because it's the truth, and I know it, and I will tell you the truth about tonight. If I did what I wanted, I'd go to bed with you now and make love to you all night, and never want to stop. Please, please don't think I don't want to. But if I did, something would go for ever with Sarah, and we've lost too much. We're too vulnerable. If you knew what our lives have been like . . .' He stopped. Then he said, reaching out for her, taking her hands and lifting her to her feet, 'In the end, you might get horribly hurt again, because I shall never leave my home. I'm just not capable of it. And you've suffered enough. You deserve someone wonderful.'

'Stop it,' said Nina, starting to cry again. 'You're breaking my heart.'

He held her to him. 'You'll find somebody. Somebody will find you.'

She shook her head. 'No, they won't. Most of the good men were killed in the war. Or they've come back, and got married.' She drew away, she kissed his cheek, she wiped her eyes again. She walked across to the decanters. 'And now it looks as though we might have another war before too long. There's a cheering thought.' She unstoppered the whisky. 'If I were a man, I'd go to Spain now, and hope to get my head blown off.'

'Nina –'

'It's true,' she said, looking round for her glass, taking another one from the tray. 'But never mind. Perhaps I should go and drive an ambulance. Do ambulance drivers get killed?'

'Nina, please, please.'

'It's all right.' The last of the whisky trickled out. 'I won't do anything silly. You won't have to open the papers and think, Christ, she's done it. Not that I'd make the papers.' She turned to him, raising the glass. 'Cheers. Work tomorrow. Do you want to use the phone?'

'We're not on the phone. And they will be worried. I would like to use your bathroom, if I may.'

'You may, it's through there. But not on the phone – how on earth do you manage?'

'It isn't London,' he said. 'Lots of people aren't on the telephone yet.'

'Well,' said Nina, giving a thin little smile, 'at least that means I shan't have to sit waiting for it to ring.'

Out in the lamplit hall, she gave him his hat, and his bag.

'*Voilà*. Safe journey.'

'Thank you.' He looked at her, for what he knew would be the last time. He would never write, would never seek her out.

'Don't tell me to look after myself,' said Nina. 'I'm doing my best in that department.'

'I know,' he said, and leaned forward and kissed her tear-stained face, smelling the cigarettes, feeling her silky, silky hair against his cheek. 'You're wonderful.'

'I'm full of self-pity. I haven't even asked you about your work.'

'No.'

'Are you doing well?'

'Not really.'

'One day I'll see it all in a gallery. Or perhaps I'll go to Spain and do something useful, for once.' She held his hand against her cheek. 'I would say give my love to Sarah, I did like her so much. And I'm so, so sorry about your son.' She shook her head slowly. 'How I wish, how I wish . . .' A long sigh. 'Oh, well.' She kissed his hand, she gave it back to him. 'Let's not end on a sad note.' She went to the door. 'Do you know who I should have married?'

'Who?'

'Henry Marsh. He'd have made me laugh, we'd have had such fun.' And then her face clouded again. 'But still no babies. He might have found that—' She broke off, and pulled the door open. The shaft of light fell on the shadowy carpet. 'That's enough. That really is enough. Goodbye, Walter. I won't see you out, shipwreck that I am.'

'No, no, of course not. Stay in the warm.'

A last squeeze of the hand, then out, and along the carpeted corridor to the lift. Behind him the door clicked to, and the fall of light was gone.

Out in the street he turned and looked up. Was she there? Had she drawn the curtain back? He stood back on the pavement, trying to see which was her flat, her window, remembered standing below her balcony in Fitzroy Square, filled with anticipation, filled with nerves, the dance music flooding out into the gardens. Long moonlit nights, and the long walk back to Camden.

She was there. She was standing at the window with her glass, looking down at him, small and pale behind the darkened window. She gave a little wave, and he pressed his hand to his lips. Then the curtain fell back into place.

# 1937

## 1

Sleet blew over the fields and froze overnight. The lanes were glassy with puddles of ice; as the afternoons drew in, a hazy sun melted into a vaporous sky, smoky grey-pink over speckled-white land and bare trees. New Year. No classes. Walter chopped wood, and the sound of it rang in the frosty air.

Sarah and Meredith kept to the house, and the ground floor, oil stoves along the corridor, the range piled high and a fire in the dining room, crackling from mid-morning. Sarah brought down her drawing pad and pencils. She was planning a pair of engravings, frontispiece and endpiece, for a book about inland waterways. Something new. The work had been commissioned through a tutor at the Central School, who'd asked to see her work when Walter mentioned one day, over lunch in the autumn, that his wife was a wood-engraver. 'You're the one who should be teaching there,' he told her, on his return. 'It's much more arts and crafts than painting.'

'What's the name of this fellow?'

'Ashcroft. But it's a friend of his who's writing about the waterways.' He gave her the slip of paper, marking the place in his book.

'That's my book,' said Sarah, noticing. 'What are you doing, reading my Rosamund Lehmann?'

'Someone recommended it. Does anyone else want a bath?'

Nobody did. He made for the stairs.

'If you're reading *The Weather in the Streets*, you should read *Invitation to the Waltz*,' said Sarah, putting plates to warm. 'It's about the same couple, but when they're young and innocent.'

'Where is it?' asked Meredith.

'Somewhere in our room. You'd like it, you're just the right age.'

She went up to look for it; Walter went up with her, and ran a bath. He stood amidst the clouds of steam, the pipes coughing and banging, slowly undressing, his first lie by omission pulsing through him. And how would I ever have managed, he asked himself, dropping his clothes on the chair, if I had involved myself with Nina, and had to tell lie after lie? He knew that he never would have managed it; thought of the night of his late return, relief sweeping over Sarah and Meredith's anxious faces as he lifted the latch and came in, of his awkward explanation of people going for a drink after classes, quickly diverting into the account of the Tonks private view in the morning, seeing Steer again . . .

'Who else was there?'

'Oh, lots of people Henry knew. We saw Augustus John holding forth.'

'*Did* you?' said Meredith. 'What's he like?'

'I thought he looked like a crashing bore.'

'And Nina?' asked Sarah, as casually as he had used to try to ask her about Euan, but no longer ever did. 'Was she there?'

'Who's Nina?'

'Just an old girlfriend.'

Meredith looked at him. 'I didn't know you had an old girlfriend.'

'Well, I did. A long time ago, as old girlfriends tend to be.'

'What was she like?'

He didn't know how to answer that.

'What's she doing now?' asked Sarah.

'She's still working in Liberty's – I hardly spoke to her.' He was slicing bread, and nicked his finger. 'That's enough questions, now. The main thing is being in touch with Henry again – that's really very nice. He's invited us all to supper.'

'When?'

'One day. We must fix it up.' He sucked on his finger.

'I'll get you some cottonwool,' said Meredith.

The corner was turned, the moment past.

Walter lay in the bath, weeks later, a lie by omission – a borrowed book from Sarah's bedside table, an anonymous recommendation – ticking in his blood. How clumsy and innocent I still am, he thought. Plenty of men would think nothing of this. He recalled conversations overheard in the Central canteen, endless talk of affairs and much laughter. Look at Augustus John, for God's sake.

He thought, But it isn't just that I had such a sheltered beginning, that I shall never be sophisticated in that way. It's what happened to us: a dark drop through a summer's day that threw us all apart. Now it binds us. I never did take things lightly, but now – it's impossible not to be here.

He could hear Meredith coming back along the landing, going down into the warm. Could he ever have lied to her? The relief at the knowledge that he never would, nor ever again lie to Sarah, was as powerful as his feelings in 1920, when he stopped seeing Nina after months of misery. That was on Euan's advice, sitting by a half-dead fire in his digs in Euston, pigeons on the windowsill, smoke from the stations blackening the air, Euan's work on the table, all those fallen men.

*She must have her reasons, but it doesn't sound much fun.*

How I looked up to you, Walter thought, turning the taps on again with his feet. How much I cared for you then. Still do. And you?

*Have you never been in love?*

*I can't answer that.*

He turned off the taps, and lay back once again. Steam rose all round him, mysterious and cloudy. Euan would never compromise, it would have to be just the right person –

*This isn't the right time.*

And this is not the time for Nina, Walter thought, the water lapping round him, the steam dissolving into the cold high ceiling. Not then, for she did, indeed, have her reasons; not now, for I have mine.

Never, then.

And yet – and yet –

Pale silken hair, parted lips, welling up of desire in both of them.

He closed his eyes, he came with a groan into the water, clouds of milk in a river, washed and swept away.

Now, on a bitter January morning, in the first week of the year, Meredith sat curled in the basket chair by the fire and read, and Sarah worked on her illustrations. She had, within the light of the subject, been given free rein. Books were piled upon her studio table from the library in Ashford: canals, barges, locks and towpaths, the patient horse, the man at the tiller, puffs of smoke from the funnel, cargoes of coal and a little dog panting in the bows. She was lost in all this, was picking up on all of it for chapter headings and illustrations. But frontispiece and endpiece – what might she do?

The firewood snapped, Meredith turned a page, from out in the garden came the sound of the axe. Sarah looked through the window at the cold hard fields, the stumps of the pollarded willows. Everything frozen and still, not a sign of life anywhere. Then suddenly –

'There's the heron.'

'Where?' Meredith looked up from her book, and they watched him, huge and stark in the winter sky, flapping along the river, neck outstretched.

'He'll be hungry. Everything's buried so deep. I can remember thinking that when I was little. We were up in the studio . . .' Meredith frowned, and went back to her book.

That's what I'll do, thought Sarah, pencil upon the page. Water in winter: fish and rat and insect gone to ground, the bird passing slowly, far above, just a glimpse of a barge in the distance, the dark plume of smoke. I shall go beneath the water, that will open the book. And the endpiece will be lush, full summer, the barge slipping between tall banks of reeds, dragonfly and darting swallow, everything reflected.

She set to work.

The morning grew brighter. Walter came in from the garden, and took his boots off. He looked in on the two of them; neither looked up. Which is as it should be, he thought, making tea in the kitchen, climbing the stairs with it, walking along to the studio. A house in winter, a family absorbed in separate occupations, draughts filled, fresh firewood stored to dry.

The studio was washed with winter light. He took his tea to the churchyard window, looked out on to dense yew, grey tower, small stone by the wall.

Lunchtime, the clock striking once in the melting air, the three of them coming together again.

'May I see?' Meredith stood by her mother's shoulder, hearing Walter go past to the kitchen, opening the safe.

Sarah brushed crumbs of eraser off the page. 'It isn't finished, but what do you think?'

A frame, unadorned; within it all was under water, almost to the top of the page: a cold still place where everything lay dormant. Here and there a bubble rose to the surface, here and there an eye gleamed in the mud. A fin flicked amongst tangled roots, ice held sleek scales in its grip. How could anything live down there, in the dead of winter? Far above, on the dark cold surface, leaves drifted slowly downstream where the rudder of a barge broke the water; far above this, in the winter sky, the heron was searching, with outstretched wings.

Sarah looked up at her.

Meredith nodded.

Not a goose, not an angel come to herald or avenge a death, but a great bird out hunting: hungry, lonely, scanning the frozen world.

Meredith leaned against Sarah's head; Sarah put up an arm, and held her. Then they drew apart, and Sarah pushed her chair back, and went out along the passage to the kitchen, where Walter was getting out saucepans.

Meredith stood looking down at the drawing, unfinished but almost perfect. The wintry underwater world looked as though it would be like that for ever, as if the ice would never crack or melt, the water never start to rise, no fish come up to break the surface on a glinting afternoon.

She went to the window and leaned against the glass. The winter light was so pure and beautiful, over the empty fields.

Oh, I wish, I wish . . .

– What do you wish?

– You know.

She hardly ever saw him. When she did, he barely spoke. His card at Christmas had come with love to all of them; now he was up in London, visiting a stoneyard, visiting the Leicester Galleries, where Henry Moore and Epstein sometimes showed. He wanted to make a breakthrough, but everyone said that life was impossible now, for artists: no one had money to spend on pictures. Or sculpture – who bought sculpture? Rich private patrons, he'd said once, when they were all having supper, and she had asked him. That was a long time ago, before she had realised.

– Realised what?

– You know.

Rich private patrons, and galleries, and public places. *What are you working on now? Oh, just something for the Town Hall. A plaque. Nothing exciting.* He was like her father, unrecognised: two fine artists with nothing to show for it, not in the worldly sense. And he never had time for her now.

Her father said he'd been talking of going to Spain to fight against Franco; lots of writers and artists were doing that. If he went and got killed, and she had never told him . . .

Her breath had made a small misty cloud on the glass; she watched it shrink to nothing.

By Saturday, they had run out of everything.

'I'll go into Denham,' said Walter, looking in cupboards after breakfast, making a list. 'Does anyone want to come?'

'Not unless you really want me to,' said Sarah. 'I'm deep in this waterway now.'

'Meredith?'

She shook her head. 'What I want is exercise, and fresh air, and . . .' She stretched out her arms. 'Oh, I don't know.'

'Come in with me. Come in on the bus and we'll walk back.'

'With all the shopping?'

'Good point. We'll walk in, and get the bus back. Do come, I'd love to have you.'

'But I want to be by myself!'

They looked at her. She bit her lip.

'You can be by yourself,' said Walter gently. 'I don't mind at all, it was only a thought.'

She covered her face. Sarah put a hand on her arm. Meredith shook it off.

They left her to it, Sarah clearing away and going to light the fire in the dining room, Walter finishing his list.

'I'm going up to Grandad and Grandma,' he said, closing his notebook. 'To see if they want anything.'

Meredith nodded.

'I'll see you at lunchtime.'

No answer.

He fetched his things from the coat rack, and slipped out of the house.

'It's her age,' said his mother, over the shopping list. She licked her pencil. 'See if they've got any Bovril.'

Walter walked back down Mill Lane and saw Meredith, at the bottom, all wrapped up. She came slowly towards him.

'Changed your mind?'

She shook her head. 'I'm just going to see Grandma. Then I might go for a walk.'

'She'll be pleased.' He hesitated. 'You won't go on further, not up this way –'

She looked at him.

'Sorry. Of course you wouldn't.' They stood there in the cold, their breath streaming out before them. Meredith looked so pinched and drawn, her beret pulled down tight over her fringe, her scarf wound tight round her neck. He said, 'You do know we all love you.'

She covered her mouth, she shut her eyes, she stood there.

'What?' he asked, as carefully as he could. 'What is it?'

'Oh, Father.' An intake of breath in the sharp cold air. Then she shook her head. 'Nothing,' she said. 'Nothing, nothing, nothing.' And she walked on up the lane, beneath the smooth grave trunks of the beech, whose scattering of mast still lay on the verge.

Walter watched her go. It felt like moments since she was a baby, and they had walked up here with Euan, the first time he visited, she in her pram, clear-eyed and content. Euan had stopped, and picked up a hard spiny case, and prised it open, leaf by leaf, until he found the kernel at the heart, and Meredith had watched him doing it.

Why did he remember that so clearly?

Because there were so few of them here, and their relationships were so close and intense. And Meredith had lost the closest person in her life – had become, at a stroke, an only child again, as they had become the parents of an only child.

One two three.

Not just her age, but this enormous fact, this enclosure between two adults, with the yawning loss behind.

Walter heard the first bus of the morning approach from Hurst Green. He ran to flag it down.


Everyone was out and about in the village, walking carefully along the icy pavements where grit had been thrown down, but still missed patches.

'Morning, Mr Cox.'

'Good morning.'

'Keeping well?'

'Very well, thanks.'

In the shop, he queued behind housewives and scanned *The Times*. The Foreign Secretary had protested to France about the shelling of a British ship: Hitler had agreed to support a non-intervention pact on pain . . .

He flicked through, saw a familiar beaky profile, felt everything around him recede. He was on the Obituary page.

*Professor Henry Tonks, FRCS, formerly Slade Professor of Fine Art in the University of London, died at The Vale, Chelsea, yesterday.*

Walter put his hand to his mouth. Then he read on.

*The saying 'Out of the strong came forth sweetness' is very happily illustrated in the contrast between the personality and the work of Tonks. In appearance he was distinctly grim, and his speech was abrupt, but his work was full of the greatest tenderness . . .*

    *There can be no doubt that until they got to know him, his students at the Slade School found him rather terrifying . . . Together with P. Wilson Steer and C. Koe Child, who had been appointed assistants shortly before him . . . Tonks raised the Slade School to the highest pitch of efficiency . . . In spite of the awe he inspired, he maintained in private that he learnt more from his pupils than he taught them . . . some of his students would have been astonished at the affection with which he recalled their names . . .*

I was surprised, thought Walter. Tears pricked his eyes. *To lose your little son – my heart goes out to you . . . How strange and terrible life can be. I sense only that there is a curtain that blows between here and there, though none of us can know what lies beyond it . . .*

I hope it was peaceful, thought Walter, amongst the shopping bags. I hope that you died in your sleep, with the curtain blowing this way and that at an open window, letting in just enough winter air to keep the room fresh and the fire burning.

Isn't that how we all would wish to die?

The Obituary ran on for columns. He read on, miles and miles away.

'Mr Cox? Mr Cox? Was there anything you wanted?'

He pulled himself together, drew out his shopping list.

☆

'Tonks has died,' he told Sarah, going straight up to the studio as soon as he got home. 'It's in the paper – look.'

Sarah was stricken.

'I didn't realise,' she said, poring over the page beside him. 'I never thought I'd feel so . . .' She sat down, smoothing the paper. 'Father will be sad.'

Walter went to the window. 'Is Meredith back?'

'Not yet.'

He looked out down the empty lane. A flock of finches rose and dipped over the field; the cowls on Hobbs Farm were an aching white beneath a bruise-grey sky. The church clock struck twelve: it seemed to take for ever. Meredith, he thought, if anything happened to you, I'd die.

And then he saw her, rounding the bend, looking up towards the window, waving.

Term began again, for Meredith at school, and for Walter and Sarah, teaching in Ashford and London. Cold wet days and cold wet journeys: on the bus, swishing through rainswept lanes, and on the train, in unheated carriages. Walter packed a flask of hot tea in the mornings when he went up to the Central; he refilled it there, from the hissing urn in the canteen. Sometimes he had lunch with his students, or another member of staff; sometimes he went to the library, and took out books on engraving and carving for Sarah, and the new journals, to read on the return journey, when he stayed awake, or at home in the studio.

The mood of the art world had changed, and was changing still. Reading Nicholson and Hepworth in *Circle*, reading Moore and Coldstream, Walter tried to absorb some of what was going on, and to keep abreast of his brightest students, who attended debates and discussions, joined the Communist wing of the Artists International – one of them confided this over lunch and gave Walter a pamphlet – or left for Spain.

Art was no longer individual, as it had been after the war, when traumatised men had energy for little beyond their own work. Art was becoming politicised again. Everyone was looking to Europe, fearful and apprehensive. Within weeks of the International Surrealists opening at the New Burlington, Spain had begun to tear itself asunder, with Franco backed by German bombs. Those of Walter's students, and the scores of other young intellectuals who flocked to join the International Brigade, saw the spirit of internationalism within the arts as the only response to the growing threat of war.

In July, Walter on his journeys read in the paper that Hitler had opened an exhibition in the Haus der Kunst, in Munich. *Great German Artists* was a collection of neo-Romantic, mostly nineteenth-century paintings of youths and maidens, trailing clouds of glory. Next day, across the gardens in the Archaeological Institute, another show opened: *Degenerate Art*. Here was hung the work of the German modernists: Max Beckmann, stripped of his Frankfurt professorship; Emil Nolde, now banned from showing anywhere; Ludwig Kirchner, exiled in Paris; the gentle, dream-coloured horses of Franz Marc; cartoons by George Grosz, now fled to America; Kokoschka and Otto Dix, whose anti-war painting *The Trench* had him sacked from the Dresden Academy.

'We had Futurism, Expressionism, Realism, Cubism, even Dadaism,' Hitler thundered. 'Could insanity go further? Those who see things in this way can live and work where they like, but not in Germany.'

Refugee artists fled to New York and London. In Paris, where *Guernica*, Picasso's anguished response to the Spanish Civil War, was exhibited and seen by thousands, Kirchner shot himself. In London, a little circle of emigrés formed near Henry Moore's Hampstead studio, near Nicholson and Hepworth: Naum Gabo, Moholy-Nagy, Walter Gropius, Mondrian all came to live nearby.

Meanwhile, tensions were growing between irrational, subversive Surrealism, and the idealism of abstraction; between the formal purity of abstraction and a return to realism and representation.

For Nicholson, painting was spiritual. For Moore, sculpture was human – and for Moore the violent quarrel between the abstraction-ists and Surrealists was in some sense perverse, for these oppositions were reconcilable.

'All good art contains abstract and surrealist elements, classic and romantic, order and surprise, intellect and imagination, conscious and unconscious . . .' he had written. Not only art, but a full human being – in a way, that was what he was describing. Reconciling opposites: intellect and imagination, classic and romantic, the physi-cal and the spiritual.

Summer rain trickled down the grimy carriage window. Walter

folded his journals as the train pulled into Ashford, and fastened his bag. He paced about on the wet platform, thinking of two huge canvases up on the studio wall at home, *The Trinity of Women* and the ice-white angel of *Preparing for Bed*, the footfall along the landing, about to enter their lives.

Where, amidst schism and division, did his own work lie?

And Euan? He was easier to place – he belonged with Moore, you could feel it. He must be aware of that. His lettering lay with Gill, but in his sculpture, in spirit, he walked with Moore: human and profound.

Walter walked up and down on the platform, seeing the track stretch away in the drifts of rain, between the banks of pink willowherb and creamy wild lupin, remembering, all at once, another summer evening in 1922. He had gone down into the sculpture studios at the Slade for the first time, looking for Euan, and heard from behind a partition the ringing of chisel on stone. He came upon him, lost in his work, hammering in a rhythm which Walter, then, had been too young and inexperienced to recognise as having a deep, sexual power, but which, he realised now, contained profoundly that.

He had felt, in the aftermath of his painful months with Nina, as though he were stepping into a circle of light.

And now? What was Euan working on now? Where did he want his life to go?

The train was approaching, in Turner's rain and steam and speed, which he had made his own. Walter watched it, hardly seeing it, thinking of Euan, reconciling opposites: intellect and imagination, artist and artisan, a man who cared for people deeply, but who chose to live alone.

# 2

The path to his house; the sea, the sea. School broken up and the holidays stretching ahead like an empty road, the sun beating down and she –

What should she do?

'I'm going out,' she said to Sarah at breakfast, and went to the sink to fill her father's flask.

Sarah was looking through the post, which came early in summer. 'Where?' she asked, opening an envelope.

Water gushed into the flask and overflowed. 'I'm not sure yet.' Meredith turned the tap off. She screwed on the top of the flask and shook it. Drops flew everywhere. Through the open window she could hear the men out in the fields, bringing in the last of the harvest: her grandfather was there, and her father, helping out again now term had ended. Every couple of days Mr Monkton came down, to see how they were getting on, his dog nosing happily along the stubble, putting up trembling rabbits and racing after them. He lifted his gun and potted them, one two three, walked back to the car with them bumping against his side, glassy-eyed and faintly bloodied. Sometimes he gave them to the men; Walter had brought one home two days ago, and hung it in the pantry, where it dripped from its tender mouth on to a piece of newspaper, and was stiff within an hour. Meredith drew it, and then it became rabbit pie, and her grandparents came on Sunday to share it.

'Used to be rook pie, when we were young,' said her grandfather, pulling his chair out. 'Pigeon pie, rook pie . . .'

'I never had rook,' said her grandmother, unfolding her napkin. 'You'll be telling us you had four-and-twenty blackbirds next.'

'We had that on Saturday nights,' said her grandfather, winking at Meredith. 'And how are you, my lass?'

'Very well, thank you.'

'Looking forward to the holidays?'

'Sort of.'

'You and your sort ofs,' said her grandmother.

' "Time you were out to work, young lady," ' said Meredith. 'I know.'

'Know what you might want to do when you grow up?' asked her grandfather, as Sarah broke open the pastry crust and the kitchen was filled with a heavenly smell.

'Not yet.'

'Plenty of time.'

Walter passed the plates; they all tucked in.

'Want to be thinking about it, though, don't you?' Her grandmother was waving a hand to cool her burning mouth. 'Is there a glass of water?'

Meredith fetched her one. 'I think of it all the time.'

'What's that?'

'The future.'

'Do you now?' Her grandmother drained the glass. 'That's better. And what do you see, my duck?'

'Oh, I don't know.'

'We none of us can see that,' said her grandfather. 'You enjoy the summer while you can. And pass those potatoes, if you don't mind.'

Now Meredith stood by the cool stone sink, shaking drops off the flask, filled with nerves and excitement and –

Sarah looked up at her. 'Where did you say you were going?'

'I didn't.' She felt a blush rise. 'I'm going out, that's all. I'll be back by –'

Perhaps she would never come back.

'By teatime?' she said. 'Is that all right?'

The kitchen was filled with a pause that said everything: If anything happened to you – it won't, it won't – it so nearly did – I know better, now – I don't want to clip your wings – then don't, don't, don't – you're only fifteen – I'm *fifteen*! Let me go!

'You'd better take a sandwich,' said Sarah, pushing her chair back, and came across and kissed her.

Meredith kissed her back, and went out to the coat hooks, and took down her knapsack and sun hat.

The sun was climbing, and the sky was almost cloudless, just a wisp here and there in the blue. She rounded the bend in the lane, passing the churchyard wall, and then she felt she had left it all: the house, the harvest, parents and grandparents, everyone who knew her.

And then here was Fred Eaves on his bike. He touched his cap. 'Lovely morning.'

'Isn't it?'

– He might not even be there.

– I think he will be.

– So do I.

She walked on, hearing Fred's bike creak away behind her, seeing the cowls on Hobbs Farm so white above the mellow brick, so white against the blue. Another couple of weeks, and the pickers would be down, the fields full of all that activity and the smell of the drying hops drifting across the farm. Now they were empty, the bines full and heavy, stirring just a little in the lightest summer breeze. Mr Burridge had been spraying: a coppery iridescent green shone here and there on the leaves. Meredith walked on, down the lane of her childhood, every hedge and ditch and field and farm building known to her, every gate and every turning. Somewhere a hen had laid an egg, and her triumphant cackle rang through the morning air. This, too, Meredith had known all her life. And all her life she had been coming down this lane on visits: on the bus, when it was cold and wet, walking when it was fine: between hedge and field, on through Darwell, on towards Hurst Green, with the stretch of the marshes falling away towards the sea.

– And I came with you.

– Yes. Climbing every gate we passed, trailing behind, being called and waited for.

– It got on your nerves.

– No, it didn't.

– Yes, it did. Then it was only you, hand in hand between them.

The heat in the lane began to shimmer. Today, thought Meredith, hearing a motorcar behind her, I shall go a different way. She stopped at a gate on the left, and climbed it. The motorcar sped past. So many more now, that was something else everyone worried about – coming out of nowhere, townies on country lanes, taking the bends too fast. A cloud of dust went up; she leaned on the top of the gate and looked out over the field. A few cows were grazing in the sun, flicking away flies. One or two raised their heads, and stared at her. Water boatmen skimmed over the water in the drinking trough by the gate. If she climbed over here, and crossed to the stile on the right, she could go in a long diagonal all the way, and never need to mind about motorcars, or the hardness of the lane beneath her sandals, or anyone coming along to look for her.

The grass was lush, and full of buttercups; the air was full of birdsong. I'll go as the crow flies, she thought, just as I always wanted, and she swung her legs over the gate and dropped down.

The grass was cool beneath her feet; she kept to the line of the hedge, in the shade, a good distance from the cows, with a ditch alongside, thick with dandelion and hogweed. Honeysuckle and dog rose clambered over the hedge above; she stopped and picked some, tugging at tough stems, pricking her fingers. She mixed in tall buttercups, broke off a leaf of hogweed to keep it all cool, unfastened her knapsack and laid it carefully within. Then she walked on, and climbed on to the stile, remembering that on his very first visit here, when she was still a baby, he'd arrived with eggs and honey in his knapsack for her parents: Walter had told her that once, ages and ages ago. Now she was taking flowers to him.

The top of the stile was smooth and worn and comfortable. Meredith sat on it and looked out across the view. Farmland lay for mile upon mile: pasture broken by orchard and hopfield and barn and oasthouse. If she stood up, she could see the river, winding peacefully away in the distance, between the soft willows, beneath the wooded hills.

There was a cuckoo, from deep within the woods.

Meredith shut her eyes.

She thought, This is going to be all right. A flutter of nerves came deep in her stomach, but then, It's all right.

– I think he wants you to come.

She opened her eyes, she climbed down into the long grass, put on her straw hat and set out across the field.

If the crow had flown, he would have winged his way over the common and come to rest on an elm, skimmed down to perch on the barn roof, or alighted on the grass and looked about him, his head on one side, his eyes bright and fierce and his plumage gleaming in the sun.

Meredith came walking up the lane, for she had seen that to come down through the fields behind the common would have meant crossing cottage back gardens. She came down along a cart track – perhaps the old haycart he'd found in the barn, and kept in a corner, had travelled along here once – and walked the last quarter-mile between the dense hedges, as she had done all her life.

And that's what I want to do, she thought, smelling the sea, her heart beating hard. I want to walk as we've always done it, but this time it's me, and it's different. She could hear sheep cropping the grass, she could hear the gulls. She stopped, before she rounded the bend, and took her hat off, and smoothed her hair, damp from the heat. Her dress clung to her, her sandals were dark with sweat. She opened the knapsack, and lifted out the flowers, in their great dark leaf. They needed a drink. So did she. She drained the flask, put everything carefully back, and put on her hat again. Then she walked on, very slowly. The ropes of the goats brushed the grass on the common, a few rooks cawed in the elms. She could hear this, but she could not hear the sound of chipping or hammering, and for a moment she felt almost sick with disappointment.

Then she rounded the bend, and the goats looked up at her footsteps, and she saw that the door of the barn was wide open, held back by the heavy old stone just as always, and he was moving about inside it, tall and unhurried, his footsteps firm on the earthen floor.

I like the way you occupy space.

A confirming moment. And I like the way you move, she thought now, standing stock still, and watching him, watching him. I always have done. I like your easy walk; I like the way you light your pipe, and shake the match out, and the way you pick things up and put them down again.

You used to pick me up. I used to lie in your lap.

She moved, and the kids began to bleat. He must be used to that, cottagers coming and going. No one was coming and going now.

Only me –

The common was baking, but there was always a hint of a breeze from the sea, even on hot still days like this, and it brushed her face as she walked, as slowly as if in a dream, and bore on it the seeds of a dandelion clock, drifting through the summer air. One two three four – where did the years go, when they had passed? All that time, tick tock, tick tock, and now . . .

A little white kid was bleating and bleating. Euan came to the door, and looked out.

Here I am. There you are. This is how things stand between us.

Was it him, was it her, thinking this?

He was in shade, framed by the great brick arch of the doorway, and the sun was in her eyes as she walked over the burning grass, so she couldn't see his expression, only that he was wearing an old blue collarless shirt, and standing absolutely still, not raising his hand, nor coming to greet her, just waiting, where the door had worn a deep perfect arc in the ground, opening and closing, all through the years.

She thought, If I were a painter, I'd paint you there.

She stopped, she stood before him.

The cries of sheep and goats, the calling of the rooks in the elms, dandelion clocks drifting past in the cloudless air.

'Meredith,' he said slowly, and now she could see his face, and so many different expressions seemed to move across it, like the shadows of clouds on a sunlit field. 'What are you doing here?'

'I came to see you.' All at once she was so nervous that her knees began to tremble. 'I hope I'm not disturbing you.'

'No, no, of course not. Have you walked all the way?'

'Yes.'

'Well.' He moved forward, put a hand on her shoulder, and smiled down at her. 'What a nice surprise. You must be very thirsty. Come up and get a drink.'

She walked beside him over the common, matching his long easy stride. The knapsack was heavy and hot against her side. She thought of the wilting flowers and wondered, Should I really give them? Supposing it looks – supposing it looks as if . . .

Was this what love did? Now she was here, she couldn't think of anything to say. In the past, in the old days, she'd have talked quite freely. In the past, when she was little, he had picked her up and hugged her. She thought, If you hugged me now, it would start to make everything all right. She thought, If I put my hand to yours . . . And then, But I couldn't, I couldn't. Not now.

It felt as if a door had swung shut between them, when she wanted it to stand wide open, so that they could look at each other properly, for the very first time.

But I can't open that door, she thought, walking beside him over the grass. I'm too young. You'll have to do it.

And perhaps you don't want to at all.

'How are your parents?' he asked her.

'Oh, they're very well. Father's out with the harvest.'

'They do know you're here?'

She bit her lip. 'I just said I was going for a walk.'

He looked down at her again, with a flicker of a frown. 'Why didn't you tell them?'

She swallowed. 'I don't know.'

'They might be worried.'

'I said I'd be back by teatime.'

They came to the little walled garden; he opened the gate. 'Well,' he said, standing aside from her, giving her a smile which went right through her, 'we must make sure that you are. Mustn't we?'

She nodded. She walked into the garden.

The door to the house stood open. She remembered, a long time ago, sitting on the step, soon after – soon after it happened, when they'd all walked over here, and her mother had fallen asleep on the rug beneath the lilac tree. There was no rug out here now, just a wooden chair near the door, with a book on the grass beside it, and an empty cup.

'Sit down,' said Euan. 'I'll bring you some water.'

How hot it was, out here. How cool and dark and inviting was the square of hall beyond the door. She took her knapsack off her shoulder, and put it down on the grass, where it lay among daisies and dandelions; she took off her sun hat and fanned herself, sitting on the hard wooden chair. This was where he sat in the mornings, drinking his tea. What was he reading? She bent to pick up the book on the grass. *To the Lighthouse*. The dust-jacket was striking: blue verticals, tumbling blue and black waves, stippled rays of light – the sort of thing her mother admired. Meredith frowned. Where had she seen this book before?

He came out with a jug on a tray and two glasses.

'Here we are.' He set it down on the step, poured her a glass. 'I need an ice box,' he said, passing it to her. 'I ran the tap until it was really cold.'

'Thank you.' She took it; she drank and drank.

'More?'

'Please.' She held out the glass and he poured water into it, slowly, as if it were a small ceremony. 'Thank you,' she said again, and looked up at him. He was looking down at her, holding the plain white jug, and again she could not read his expression, for his face seemed so full of so many things.

'Do you mind me being here?' she heard herself say, and it felt as if she were taking a step off a cliff.

'Oh, Meredith.' He took a deep breath, and shook his head. 'No. No, I don't mind at all.' He poured the last of the water into his own glass, and drained it.

'I thought you might be at Challocks.'

'But you came all this way.'

She nodded. She swallowed. 'I brought you some flowers. I'm afraid they're wilting now.' She leaned down for her knapsack, and unfastened it, feeling his eyes upon her. She pulled them all out, and pollen and petals spilled on the dry grass; she folded the huge leaf of hogweed round it all, and held it out to him.

'How lovely.' He took it with great care; the bunch lay within his hands, the drooping buttercups and papery dog roses, with their thorny stems. The honeysuckle had lasted best.

'They were lovely when I picked them.'

'I'll put them in this jug. They'll be all right soon. Thank you.' He carried them to the open door.

'Euan? I'm terribly hot and sticky. Do you mind if I come in and wash?'

He stopped. 'No, of course not. How thoughtless of me. You know where the bathroom is.'

She did: she'd been using it all her life.

'I'll bring you a clean towel.'

She followed him into the cool tiled hall, with its plain square rooms to right and left. She stood there and waited, at the bottom of the stairs. The first time she'd come here, they hadn't dared to put her down, in case of rats.

He was taking the flowers and jug into the kitchen; she heard him running the tap into the old stone sink, which was just like theirs at home. Then he came back, and put the jug on the sill, beneath the open window, where dandelion clocks were floating in, landing somewhere invisibly: on the flags, in the open hearth, on the horsehair chair which had been here when he took the lease, and which he had kept, and sat in, all this time. This was where he read, and smoked his pipe, and thought about – and thought about . . .

– I think he thinks about you.

'There. Now let me fetch you a towel.'

She waited again, as he went up the narrow stairs, and heard him go into his bedroom and pull open a chest of drawers. Then he was down again.

'Please – take as long as you like. I'll be in the garden.'

She took the worn white towel through the sitting room, into the kitchen and then through that, into the little plain bathroom which hadn't even been here when he moved in. There'd been only a privy, in the patch of garden. You'd never have been able to get a bath up those stairs, so he had built a lean-to, brick and tiles, replacing the old tin roof while he was at it, and plumbed in a cistern and an old iron bath from a builders' yard, and a basin. When they were little, and came here, they'd stood on a box to reach the taps, just like at home.

Meredith closed the door behind her. She hung the towel on the hook, next to his. She turned on the tap in the basin and splashed and splashed her face, and the back of her neck. Would he mind, if she ran a bath? Just a quick cold bath. She went over. A large spider clung to the side, but she was used to that. She turned on the cold tap and swished it away. Then she put in the plug, and let the water gush. She sat on the lavatory, peeing and waiting for the bath to fill. Perhaps she could just bathe her feet. She took off her damp leather sandals and shook grass out of the window. She stepped into the bath, and let the water swirl about her hot feet, and reached for the soap on the side. Then she thought, Oh, it doesn't matter, and she got out again, and peeled her dress off, and her brassière and knickers, and hung them on a hook on the back of the door.

She could hear her grandmother saying, This isn't proper at all. Whatever are you thinking of, young lady?

She thought, for a second, as she stepped back into the bath, and sank down with a gasp into the wonderful, cold, cold water, of what her grandfather might say if he knew, and she bit her lip, remembering his warnings when she was young, and how she had taken no notice, and walked last summer all the way up to Mill Farm, putting herself in mortal danger.

But Euan had been there, coming to look for her: that was when she knew.

Just for a moment, she realised: with any other man, and in any other place, you could be in great danger now.

But then she turned off the taps and lay down, and let the water cover her, and willed herself not to resist the cold but to let it soothe her hot sticky skin. She could hear the goats, bleating away on the other side of the house, and the rooks through the little open window, and she could just hear Euan, out in the garden, moving the chair and coming back in for another, which would be for her, and now she was cool, her nervousness and anxiety ebbed away, and it felt as if she had been doing this for a long time: being here in this house, while he got on with things and she had a bath, and she thought, Well. Yes. This is how it will be, because one day I shall live here with him, and it will be our house. We shall know each other through and through, and our children will run about on the common.

'Meredith?' He had come back inside. He was calling her, just as he always would, and she would answer, 'Yes?'

'Everything all right?'

'I'm having a bath,' she sang out, as if she had been doing this for years, and he said, 'Oh. All right,' and went back outside, to sit on his chair in the sun.

Meredith reached for the soap, and washed away every last trace of grass and dust and sweat. She held her head under the tap, and felt her scalp tingle. Then she got out, and let the water gurgle away, and swished the bath clean, and dried herself, rubbing at her hair. She looked about her. His comb was on the windowsill, next to a beaker with his toothbrush and Kolynos toothpaste. She ran it through the tangles, tugging until her hair was smooth and her fringe flat, and she shook out her dress and put her things on again, the wet towel on the hook, though really it should go out in the garden to dry in the sun. She looked out of the window. Yes, there was a line, strung between posts. She went back into the kitchen, and out of the back door, and draped the towel over. The sun warmed her cold skin like a caress. Oh, she felt so much better.

She went through the house again, and out to the front. He had moved the chairs nearer the lilac, so they were in the shade; he was smoking his pipe, and the air was full of the smell of his tobacco. He looked at her, fresh and clean, wet hair still clinging to her head.

'Better?'

'Much. Thank you. Have you got any clothes pegs?'

In the future, in all those years together that lay ahead, she'd just call out, 'Where have you put the clothes pegs?' But now . . .

But now she was back in the present, not knowing what he thought, really, about any of this, though she felt, as he smiled across the garden, the same calm certainty:

This is how it will be.

On one side of the door lay certainty. That was all ahead. Now it still stood closed between them, everything unspoken.

But before I go, she thought, sitting on the hard wooden chair beside him, looking out over the common, before I go today, you will have to open it.

They talked about school, and matriculation next summer, and then –

'And then?' he asked, turning to look at her. 'What do you want to do?'

'I don't know yet. I wish I did. Sometimes I think I'd like to go to art school, like all of you. It's in my blood, I think.'

'I'm sure it must be. Perhaps you'll go to the Slade.'

'No more terrible Tonks. Father was so sad when he died.'

Euan nodded. 'Of course I was in the sculpture school. I didn't really know Tonks. So. You might go to art school, or –'

'Or there might be a war,' said Meredith slowly. 'Mightn't there? Worse than Spain.' And if you went – if you went away, just as we're –

He leaned down to the grass, where he'd put his tin of tobacco. 'Yes,' he said, straightening up, and opening it. 'I'm afraid there might be.'

'Are you going to Spain?'

'No.' He filled up his pipe, and closed the tin again. 'No, I'm not.'

Relief washed through her. It felt as if a great dark bird had lifted his wings and flown away from her.

'Good,' she said quietly, and the word and all it stood for now rang like a bell between them.

'But if there is a war with Germany,' said Euan, 'then I shall have to go. We all will.'

'Even Father?' She was shocked. How had she never quite thought of that?

'Yes.'

'But he can't,' said Meredith. 'He couldn't.'

Euan put out a hand. For a moment it rested on her bare arm.

'It may not happen.'

The sun was high in the endless sky; a few summer clouds were gathering, white and full, sailing slowly in from the sea.

'It's certainly not going to happen today,' he said, 'and you must be hungry.'

She was. How hadn't she noticed?

'Let's have some lunch.'

Because he hadn't been expecting her, or anyone today, and would be shopping in Ashford tomorrow, there wasn't much food in the house.

'It doesn't matter at all,' she said, watching him from the kitchen doorway, opening a rickety cupboard.

I like the way you open and close things. I like the way you're putting those plates on a tray, and looking in the drawer for knives and forks, and I like that shirt.

'Can I do anything to help?'

He glanced across, put the last of a loaf on a board, and gave it to her. 'You could take that into the garden, perhaps. And there's a rug in the sitting room – would you like to put it out?'

So she did these things, spreading out the rug beneath the lilac tree, where she had often sat as a child, with Geoffrey and then without him. Her mother had lain here, after his death, and she, on the step, had sat watching Euan arrange all the cushions, and make her comfortable, while her father sat on the grass, a little distance from them.

Meredith stood up. She looked across to where Euan's book still lay on the grass, the edges of the dust-jacket curling in the heat, and she thought:

I know where I've seen that book before. On my mother's bedside table. *To the Lighthouse* – she was reading it last year.

And all at once she was filled with unimagined feelings, so dark, so powerful, that for a moment it was as if she'd been hit.

She thought, This is how it must feel after a motorcar crash.

She thought, The last time I can ever remember feeling like this was when I came home from school and they told me that Geoffrey had fallen.

She thought; I am no longer a child. I shall never, ever, be a child again. I have crossed a divide, I can feel it.

The sunlit garden went black; she crumpled.


She opened her eyes. Euan was kneeling over her, sponging her face with an icy wet flannel.

'Meredith.' His face was full of tenderness and concern.

She shut her eyes again, and felt tears rise and fill them, and trickle beneath her lids.

'You've caught the sun,' he said gently. 'I'm so sorry.'

He squeezed out the flannel, and folded it. She felt him wipe her tears away, and then he laid the cool wet cloth across her eyes, and said, 'Rest. Just lie there and rest. We have all the time in the world.'

He was so nice. He was so, so nice, and now . . .

She felt too weak to move, and she lay there, feeling the softness of the rug against her bare limbs, feeling how close he was. She knew if she tried to speak she would cry and cry. She shook her head in misery, and the flannel slipped, and he replaced it, and smoothed back her fringe.

His touch felt perfect. Then he stopped, but she could still sense him beside her.

She thought, Now I know the meaning of desire. Now I know how she felt, in *The Weather in the Streets* – wanting and wanting him.

And now it will never happen.

The darkness of the cloth upon her eyelids made her feel as if the whole world had gone dark, and she behind it might never see colour or brightness again, only be able to feel, and long for a touch, and seek it blindly.

I know what this is. This is the painting I saw him gazing at in London: two shrouded lovers, kissing and kissing, in that blind and hopeless passion.

And now I know who he was thinking about, as he stood there and stood there. We came out into the sun, and he looked at me just for a moment, and then he saw my mother and his eyes were all for her. It wasn't me, it never will be me, and how shall I ever, ever be able to look at her again?

And then she did begin to cry, and pulled off the flannel and sat up, hunched over her knees, and sobs tore through her, as they had done last summer, racing away from Mill Farm, from those glittering eyes

362

and arms stretched out like beating wings before her, and found him there, running up the lane towards her.

He was holding her so close, as he'd held her then, but now it was different, now everything was different.

'What is it? What is it?'

She shook her head. How could she possibly say?

'You can tell me.'

'I can't, I can't!' The words broke from her. So many things she could never tell anyone.

– You can tell him about me. He'll understand.

'Oh, Geoffrey, Geoffrey, Geoffrey.'

He rocked her and rocked her. 'Is that what this is? All that sadness, all locked away?'

She nodded, weeping. 'But it's not just sadness – I can't explain. And it's not only that –' And then she stopped, and pulled herself back from the brink, and pulled away from him, and just sat there, her head on her knees, watching through swollen eyelids a tiny little insect, labouring through the grass, up one stem and down again, on and on and on.

That's me. That's me, going on and on by myself.

She shook her head, her hands to her mouth.

And now I shall never do anything again. I've come to a stop.

'Meredith?'

He said her name as if he had always been meant to say it. It sounded just right. But it wasn't, and that was the end of that.

'I must go,' she said dully. 'I shouldn't have come.'

'But why? Why do you say that?'

She shook her head again, looking up from the grass, with its intense and half-glimpsed life, and out through the wicket gate to the common, where the goats had moved into the shade of the barn, and were lying up against it, white against black, resting against its great solidity. She gave a long deep sigh, and reached for the flannel, and pressed it against her eyes. It was warm, now, but she held it there anyway, feeling faintly comforted.

Euan said slowly, 'Something's happened. Something has happened here, to make you feel like this.' She heard him get up from the rug, and come round in front of her, and he put his hands on her shoulders. 'Meredith? Look at me.'

She swallowed; she took away the flannel, and let it fall on to the grass. She looked.

He was kneeling before her, and his gaze was deep and full.

'Please tell me. Tell me, so I can put it right.'

'No,' said Meredith.

The sun was slipping low towards the river, and it made a path of flame. Walter stood in the studio and watched it, and the slow gathering of cloud beneath the gold. Birds were winging their way across the field, making for ash and elm and willow, making their way to the woods on the hills, already dusky and still. The cows were moving out of the shallows, walking slowly back towards their pasture, in the steady unhurried way he had known all his life. All this went on, as every evening, as every year. The empty quiet lane wound away.

Where was she?

He looked out of the window, he craned his neck.

What time was teatime? Where had she gone? Which way had she set out? he'd asked Sarah, coming in from the dusty cornfields, hanging up his hat and going to wash, but she didn't know.

How could she not have known that?

He went to the churchyard window, and leaned right out. Fred Eaves had been cutting the grass: Walter had come back at lunchtime and seen him, the cuttings flying up before the machine, the air full of the smell of it, sweet and fresh, petrol smoke puffing up in blue clouds, mingling with the hot dusty smell of the corn, cut down, drying in the sun. As last year, Fred getting on, but keeping going.

'Keeps me busy,' he'd called out to Walter, stopping to unclip the box, and Walter had leaned on the wall between the churchyard and Mill Lane, beneath the line of beech trees, where this time last summer, when Meredith had gone missing, Euan had gone up to look for her, and brought her safely home.

Where was she now?

All at once, he knew.

He leaned on the sill and the scent of cut grass hung in the cooling evening air, and he knew.

Not Sarah. How could he ever have doubted her?

Not Sarah.

Meredith. Euan and Meredith.

*Haven't you ever been in love?*

*I can't answer that.*
*But why? Why?*
Now he knew.
*One day perhaps I'll tell you. Not yet.*
At last he understood.

He put his head in his hands. He thought, I must go to her. And then he heard her footsteps, and quickly went to the window at the front, and leaned out and saw her, approaching so slowly, so horribly slowly, her head hung low.

'Meredith?'

She looked up and saw him, and nodded. Then she walked on. Walter went out, and along the landing, lit by the sun streaming in through the windows of the bedroom, his and Sarah's bedroom, where a long time ago, on a cold spring evening, he had gathered his wife and daughter, and painted their bereavement. He went down the stairs, and out through the front door into the garden, where Sarah was trimming the borders: clip clip clip, to keep away anxiety, all through the long afternoon.

He said, 'She's here.'

She put down the clippers. 'Thank God.'

He said, 'I must talk to you later,' and she looked at him, puzzled, and then they both went to the gate, and opened it, and stood there waiting, as Meredith came slowly towards them.

'You've been crying,' said Sarah, and put out her hand.

Meredith said, 'I don't want to talk. Please don't ask me anything.' She brushed past them, went into the house and closed the door.

Late evening, the garden thick with shadow. Sarah and Walter walked over the cool dry grass, up and down beneath the trees. The door to the kitchen stood open; the glow from the lamps lit the path, the curve of the water butt and the grey-green leaves of the sage bush, which Meredith, when she was little, used to tug at, stopping and sniffing as she ran in and out, in and out, all through the long summer days. Upstairs, the house was in darkness, her bedroom door closed, not a chink at the drawn curtains.

'Meredith?' Sarah had tapped, and waited.

Silence.

'Meredith? Darling?'

'Go away. Go *away*!'

Bats flitted in and out of the trees, the scent of the mown grass still hung in the air.

'Tell me,' said Sarah, taking Walter's hand.

He told her, and saw her go pale in the dusk.

'Then we mustn't see him again.'

# 1939

## 1

Dark January days. Franco's troops were closing in on Barcelona. Mussolini's bombers came roaring over the city. Beneath its fallen buildings, rubble-strewn roads and boarded-up shops and cafés, people crowded into Underground stations, huddled in cellars, starving. In Madrid, they were still fighting in the streets. In London, at the Whitechapel Gallery, they were showing Picasso's *Guernica*, brought over from Paris. The queue on the East End pavements stretched for hundreds of yards, umbrellas up against driving rain.

'We should go,' said Walter. 'This is important.' He looked at Meredith, across the breakfast table. 'Will you come?'

'It's term time,' she said, looking at the clock. 'How can I?'

'It's only on for a week,' said Sarah.

Meredith pushed her chair back. 'Then you go up to London and see it – I've far too much work.'

She went out to the passage. Walter followed. He found her amongst the coat hooks with her face pressed into his jacket. She didn't move. They heard Sarah get up to switch on the kitchen wireless, just as the church clock struck the hour.

'This is the Home Service . . .

'In Berlin, Chancellor Hitler will today re-open the Reichstag, refurbished after the fire of 1933 . . .'

'I must go.' Meredith drew away. She reached for her school hat and scarf.

'I'm coming with you,' said Walter.

'Why?'

'It's Tuesday. It's the first day of classes.'

'Soon there won't be any classes,' said Meredith, as the wireless went on and on. 'Soon there won't be anything.'

'Is that really how you feel?'

'Doesn't everyone?'

On the bus he said to her, 'I'd like us to go up to London together. The three of us. We might not be able to go again for a while.'

'Why not?'

'All sorts of reasons.'

'Because it might not be safe.' She looked out of the window at the endless winter rain.

'I'd like us to go,' said Walter again, 'and see the Picasso, and visit the Slade. After all these years, I've never taken you. I want to walk into the quadrangle with you and Sarah, and show you the studios where we used to work.'

A motorcar overtook them, its headlights caught in the rain. Then the morning, once again, was dark around them.

'You mean in case anything happens to us,' said Meredith. 'In case there really is a war.'

He put his arm round her shoulders. She leaned her head against his.

They moved into the gallery with the crowds. The painting filled half the far wall: they glimpsed a dragging foot, an outstretched hand, and moved through the crush towards it, waiting their turn. The room was hushed: a murmur of voices as visitors came and went; footsteps across the boards. Meredith looked carefully about her. Was he here? Had he come to see the war picture which everyone had come to see? It felt as if half of London were pressing into the room.

There were smaller works, by other Spanish artists: waiting to reach the Picasso, people were going to look at them. She saw a tall man with a beard reach into his jacket pocket – for his pipe? She froze. No, for a pair of glasses. He put them on, stood back, looked carefully, as Euan looked at things. But he did not have that presence, that air entire and of itself, of being a little apart and yet quite self-possessed: moving so easily, standing so still, absorbed. It wasn't him.

And what would she have done if it was him?

Turned away, flooded with feeling?

Gone quietly up to him, stood beside him, waiting and waiting until he turned and saw her?

Meredith –

His face lighting up in the way it used to, looking at her with such . . .

She closed her eyes, saw lovers kiss beneath the shroud of a cloth, as he had seen them, in another, much grander gallery, and stood gazing and gazing, filled with intensity and longing.

She'd sensed that, right across the room.

'Meredith?'

Her eyes flew open. Her father was shepherding her towards the great length of the painting; people were turning away in silence.

She accompanied her parents. The phrase rang in her head. *I am accompanying my parents*, like a child from another age.

'It's medieval – like a Bosch, or like Brueghel,' Walter and Sarah were saying quietly to one another, and then they all fell silent, as everyone else had done, looking up at the vast, dismembered images, collage of horror, beneath the falling German bombs: arms thrust towards the sky, mouths gaping, flames and a mighty rushing wind driving across the canvas, through the limping wounded, the shrieking horse, the trampled corpse and wailing, wailing mother. Above it all, the great bull of Spain stood with his teeth bared, tail smoking, implacable.

They walked slowly along the length, trying to take it all in: its scale, its howl of fury. Sarah remembered the first time she'd seen Picasso: an only child, accompanying her parents on another January afternoon, before the last world war. Walter saw himself climbing the steps of the Royal Academy, taken by David Wicks to see the War Artists, gazing at the wounded, gasping in churned-up mud, taking in for the first time how John William might have died.

Meredith stood between them, her hand to her mouth.

*Are you going to go to Spain?*

*No. But if there's another war – if we go to war with Germany, then I shall have to go. We all will . . .*

'Meredith?' Her father touched her arm.

She shook her head, she turned and pushed her way through the crowd, not looking at anyone, coming out of the gallery rooms to the foyer, and out to the street, with its winding queue and shining pavements, wet from the morning rain. She stood breathing in the smell of the city, as trolley-buses hummed along the main road, trying to steady herself.

'Darling.' Her parents were beside her, as they always, always were.

She looked at her father. 'If there's a war, I don't want you to go.'

She sat on the Underground train between them, as they rattled through the tunnels, catching sight of their reflections in the glass: three serious people, who did not speak. That's what they were like, now. Her mother wore a trim little hat, and her one suit, a good soft tweed from Simpsons. She herself was in the dark winter coat which her Wimbledon grandmother had given her the Christmas before last, and her grandmother at home had let down for her, tugging at the sleeves and hem. 'Growing up and up – time you filled out, my lass.' Her navy felt hat was pulled down above her fringe. She looked neither London nor country: they all had that in-between look. Her father caught her eye as the train slowed, approaching Euston Square. He put his hand on hers, on the red leather armrest.

'It was too much for you – I'm sorry.'

'It doesn't matter.'

'You know I won't go unless I have to. And it might not happen.'

She nodded. The train squealed to a halt.

'One more stop. We won't stay there long.'

When they came out of the station the rain had cleared in a gust of cold wind, blowing up Euston Road. Sarah and Meredith held on to their hats.

'That's where I used to cycle in from Camden,' said Walter, pointing across through the traffic. 'All through Mornington Crescent, down Hampstead Road. And Euan's digs –' He stopped.

'Euan's digs,' said Meredith steadily. 'Where did he live?'

'In a back street behind the station, down towards King's Cross.'

'But my little flat,' said Sarah, taking Meredith's arm, 'my little flat was in the heart of Covent Garden, right by the vegetable market and the Opera House. I loved it.'

Meredith drew her arm away. Sarah bit her lip. They all walked on up Gower Street. Buses roared past. The trunks of the trees were black with soot; white-coated medics hurried through gaps in the traffic, up the steps of University College Hospital, in through the glass swing doors.

Walter slowed down. 'Let me just have a moment.'

They stopped, and he stood on the crowded pavement, amongst all the passers-by, and he saw himself, so young and nervous, coming down on the tram from Camden on a foggy January morning in 1920, looking out of the window; glimpsing Sickert's melancholy women in ill-lit upper rooms and thinking, One day all this will be just a moment in my children's past – a moment in their father's past, long before they were born.

Now he looked at Meredith, waiting patiently while he relived his memories, grave and withdrawn. Who knew what was making war within her?

The wind was icy; they all began to shiver.

'Come on.'

They hurried up the street, and in through the gates by the porter's lodge. Bicycles were fastened to the railings in the quad. Students were walking along the paths to the refectory for lunch.

'You can still pick out the ones from the Slade,' said Sarah, watching them, and it was true. Not a suit in sight, and many were older than the medics: they were post-graduates, with something of an air.

They followed them all, going into the smell of hot lunch and the banging of aluminium lids beneath the portraits. This was where Walter had invited Sarah for lunch, on a pouring wet winter's day; this was where he had watched Nina, laughing and flirting with everyone, as if she hadn't a care in the world; this was where he had first had lunch with Euan, his overalls flecked with plaster, his hands shaking, and thought, You're someone I'd like to get to know.

And now they never met. Euan had not called at the house again, and they had not been to see him. All those years of friendship, swept away.

My love, my love, he thought now, watching his daughter as she looked about her, taking it all in. How can I help you? What should I do?

Barcelona was taken. In March, the last Republicans surrendered in Madrid. People came clambering out of the cellars, waving the Nationalist flag. Franco's triumph was complete.

☆

April: the first week of the Easter holidays, a cool wet dawn. It had rained in the night and the smells of earth and grass, manure and blossom and daffodils blew over the soaking fields, and in through the open windows of the house, where Meredith lay in her bedroom, watching the curtains stir in this sweet movement of air.

Today I am seventeen.

Up at Hobbs Farm the cock was crowing in the morning. Lambs cried, and deep answering calls of the ewes came back to them. The church clock chimed six, and the last stroke faded. Through the open door of her parents' bedroom, and their open window, Meredith could hear footsteps walking down the lane: the farm boy from Middle Yalding, coming to let the cows out. She heard him unlatch the gate and push it across the grass, she heard the slow file of the herd, stopping to tear at young grass on the verges as they made their way down for the milking.

'G'arn! Move along!'

He'd be running alongside, whacking huge hindquarters.

– I used to want to do that.

– I know. I remember.

She hardly ever heard him now.

*Today I am seventeen.*

The curtains at the window, half-drawn back, blew into the room and blew out again.

What shall I do with my life?

Her parents' door was opening further. She heard her father's footsteps along the landing, passing her door, going down, as always, to make tea and bring it up to her mother, still sleeping. A gesture that had lasted all through their marriage, something that had happened every morning for as long as she could remember. She lay there listening to him go down the winding dark stair, along to the kitchen, the gush of water into the kettle, his raking and filling the range, opening the back door and letting the morning wash in. She knew he'd be standing there on the step, taking in the wet grass, the first light. When they were small, he used to go out painting, even earlier.

She thought, This is what I wanted with Euan – for our lives to intertwine. I wanted our house to have just this deep rhythm, with things we did together, and things we did apart, but always, always, coming together again, talking things through, lying together all night.

I was too young for a long time to know that's what I wanted. Then I did, and then –

It was like a great dark blade, slamming down right through the sun.

– Like my death.

– Yes.

And like the war will be, if there is a war. Everyone says it may not happen, but everyone knows it will.

The curtain blew in and the curtain blew out; the birdsong was ecstatic.

I live in the most beautiful place on earth, and all these terrible things . . .

Footsteps up the stairs and along the landing; a tap at the door.

'Yes?'

Walter looked in. 'Tea?'

'Please.'

He came in with the tray; he set it down on her desk.

'Happy birthday, my darling.'

'Thank you.' She sat up against the pillows, watching him pour two cups. 'What about Mother?'

'Let's leave her to sleep a bit longer.' He came over, gave her the yellow cup and saucer, with its hairline crack. She'd been drinking out of it for as long as she could remember, just as Sarah, somehow, had managed to keep her own blue cup unbroken, all through the years. China lasted, people were broken in two.

'Now, Meredith.' Walter stopped.

He was going to try to talk to her, he was going to try to get her to say things.

He looked at her from the chair. 'You're nearly grown-up.'

'I am grown-up.'

'Very well. You're grown-up, and something is terribly wrong.'

Oh, please, please. She pulled in the shutters, she barred and bolted them, one two.

He leaned over, he touched her hands, clasping the yellow cup.

'How can I help you?'

'You can't.'

He was stroking the back of her hands with a finger, so loving and kind. Like Euan, out in the little walled garden, the sun beating down beyond the shade of the lilac, the goats resting against the side of the barn. His hands were on her shoulders, his gaze went right through her.

But she wouldn't let it, she would never let anyone in again.

'Meredith,' said Walter.

'Stop it. Please, Father, please don't.' She moved her hands away, and tea spilled on the covers.

'But if I don't, who will? You won't talk to Sarah.'

'I can't.'

'But why? She feels it terribly.'

Meredith looked down.

'Something happened between you and Euan,' said Walter slowly, and the words, spoken aloud at last, filled the room, for both of them. 'The summer you were fifteen. Isn't that so? Isn't that where this all began?'

She put down her empty cup, shaking.

'Listen to me,' he said. 'We want only what is best for you. You're still so young, you must understand that. Will you tell me what happened that day?'

'No.'

'Did Euan hurt you? Did he . . .' He could not bring himself to say it. He could, still, hardly bring himself to think it.

'He didn't do anything!' Meredith's face was burning.

'Then what? What upset you so dreadfully?'

'Stop it!' She pushed the wet covers away.

He tried to steady himself. He said, 'Meredith, I only want your happiness. I can't bear to see you suffer. But Euan is old enough to be your father – he's older than I am. How can we not be concerned?'

Meredith said, and her voice was shaking, 'You don't know what you're talking about.'

Walter frowned. 'Then tell me.'

'I can't. I can't. If I do, if I did –' She could feel the blood rushing through her, her heart hammering. And she could hear her mother, the springs creaking in the high iron bed as she got out of it, pulling on her dressing gown.

Walter took her hands again, determined.

Meredith looked at him, full in the eye. 'If I tell you,' she said, 'your life will be ruined.'

'What?'

'I don't want *you* to suffer any more. There's been enough suffering in this house.'

Walter was silent. Then he said slowly, 'There has been a dreadful misunderstanding. Meredith, please believe me. I don't know what has led you to think as you do, but I'm certain you're wrong.'

'I know that I'm right,' said Meredith bitterly as her mother came along the landing. She drew an enormous breath. 'It's my birthday. Please can we stop?'

May, rustling and perfect. The corn standing warm and tall in the sun, threaded with poppies, young hops racing up the bines, pigeon and cuckoo calling. The trees in the lane cast a deep shade; the first green fruit were forming on damson and plum and apple tree.

On just such a day, just such an afternoon, Geoffrey had climbed a ladder that needed mending.

Ten years had passed.

Sarah and Walter stood in the studio, with its three windows open to the sun and air, as they had stood there then, working at the table, looking through Walter's pictures and preparing a portfolio, pre-occupied and content.

Outside, now, both pairs of grandparents were gathered in the garden, on the church side of the house, straightening hats and ties, talking of this and that, four people who had lived such different lives but had been drawn together: by their children, who had fallen in love at an art school; by their grandchildren, one of whom had died. Meredith was looking after everyone: from the churchyard window, Sarah and Walter could hear them all talking in low voices, waiting for them to come down when they were ready.

'Such a pity the girls can't be here.' Sarah's mother gave a little laugh. 'Why do I always call them that?' She was eighty, a reed bent in the wind, but her voice was still as clear as water.

'I always call them that myself,' said Agnes Cox. 'They'll always be the girls to me. Like you, Meredith. Your mum and dad will be calling you a girl when you're old and married.'

Meredith didn't answer.

'Annie finds it too upsetting,' Agnes went on. 'She's tender-hearted, and I think it's having no children of her own. Makes it worse, somehow. She knows she ought to come, but I told her not to mind.'

'I'm sure that was best,' said Geoffrey Lewis. He was eighty-two, stooping over his stick.

'You look so handsome in that panama,' said Meredith.

'I don't notice you saying that to me, young lady,' said William Cox.

'You're not wearing a panama.'

Walter and Sarah could hear them all, making an effort, doing it so well.

'Elsie would have come,' said Alice. 'She wouldn't have missed being here for anything, but Jim's done his back in so bad with the lifting – there was no one to mind the children.'

'Where's he working now?' asked Sarah's father.

'He's down in the docks, down in Dover. Good job, but it's not doing him much good. Be terrible if they laid him off.'

A bee sailed into the studio, from the window on to the back. Walter's window. It landed on his easel, where a blank canvas waited. Then it took off. He went to wave it out again, with a piece of paper, and stood looking down on the stretch of grass where Geoffrey used to stand, and listen to the bells, and conduct them.

'There was a bee in here then,' said Sarah, at the table.

'That day?'

'Yes. I remember noticing.'

'I can hardly remember anything. Not like that. Not before we realised . . .' He looked at the grass, where Geoffrey's shadow used to fall so long behind him, as the sun went down on the other side of the house.

'Walter?'

'Yes?'

'Come here.'

He turned from the window, and saw her, very still.

She said, 'I have something to tell you.'

'What?' he asked, and was pierced by a sliver of fear.

'About that day – about everything since. I haven't been able to forgive you. I have held it against you, all this time. For not being careful enough – for looking after everything, mending everything, except the ladder. For leaving it up against a tree, where any child –' She stopped and bit her lip. How like Meredith she looked, when she did that.

Walter said, 'Do you think I have ever forgiven myself – even for a moment? Don't you think it hasn't haunted me, all these years?'

'I know, I know. That's what I wanted to say, now: that I'm sorry. I forgive you. Anyone might have done the same.' She came across the floorboards and put her arms round him. 'I should have been down in the garden myself. One of us should have been. Or he should have been in here with us.'

'Most of the time he was.'

'I know. But not then.'

She gave a long sigh. Then they stood very close, not speaking, his head against her head, like two horses who had long shared the same field, and then been parted, and now were leaning over the gate between them, sharing the warmth of the sun.

'And do you still love me?' Walter asked her.

'Yes. Yes, I do.'

'You haven't said so for such a long time.'

'I know. I'll say it now. I love you. I'm sorry I've been so . . .'

'It doesn't matter.' He kissed her soft springy hair, which when she unknotted it made a cloud around her shoulders. 'And I have something to tell you,' he said, remembering pale silky strands against his cheek, and the smell of tears and lipstick and cigarette smoke, so close, so close.

It had been Geoffrey, the thought of him out there beneath the wall on a winter night, out there always, which had brought him home. And Sarah. And Meredith, so thin and tense and troubled.

'What do you have to tell me?' Sarah asked now.

'I'll tell you tonight,' he said. 'But first I have to ask you something. Even if it makes you angry, even if this is the wrong time.' He hesitated. 'Meredith believes – I think she believes – that you and Euan are lovers.' Sarah's eyes widened. 'Or have been lovers,' Walter said carefully. 'For the last time, tell me it isn't true.'

'It isn't true,' she said slowly. 'Of course it isn't true.' She shook her head. 'How could she possibly think it?'

'I used to think it myself,' said Walter, remembering glances, conversations which seemed so close. 'You know I did. Was it really so foolish?' He searched her face; she looked back at him steadily.

'I liked him very much. How could anyone not? When I was younger, sometimes I used to daydream . . . But that was all.' She took his hand again. 'I give you my word.'

Walter closed his eyes, feeling the doubts of years slip away, and leave a great peace within him.

'But then how could Meredith think it?' he asked at last, as Sarah's arms went round him.

'I have no idea. Who knows what children see, or really think about?'

From outside the open window, they could hear their parents walking about the garden with their daughter, an only child, talking of this and that, waiting.

'We must go down.' They drew apart. He said, 'If Meredith really is in love with Euan – if he really is in love with her – what should we do?'

'I don't know,' said Sarah. 'Let's talk about it later. I don't want to think about it any more. Not today.'

He kissed her again. And then they went out, past the great paintings of his life, and her pure and fine engravings, walking, his arm around her, along the sunlit landing, where ten years ago they had run in sudden terror.

They walked through the gate to the churchyard, and along the grey path between grass and gravestone. Sheep slept beneath the trees, too hot to get up.

Walter and Sarah, with Meredith between them, one two three. Then Geoffrey and Jane, and William and Agnes, up to the little mound beneath its headstone, with its simple, perfect lettering.

*In loving memory of Geoffrey William Cox.*

They laid their summer flowers beneath it. Then they stood in silence, surrounding him.

Pigeons were murmuring, the beech trees in Mill Lane rustled in the soft summer air, somewhere a tractor was chugging along, and a motorcar went past, slowing at the bend and going off into the distance. Then it was quiet again, with only the misty call of the cuckoo, deep in the woods, deep in the blue and gold afternoon.

And footsteps, in a long steady stride, coming along the lane.

Meredith stood quite still.

She heard him come up to the gate, and stop, and wait, and then unlatch it, and walk quietly into the churchyard, and close it again, and come up the path and then stop, keeping his distance.

After a while, they all went back to the house.

'You came,' said Walter, holding the gate to the garden open.

'He was my godson,' said Euan. 'How could I not?'

Meredith heard this, and went inside, leaving them all to sit down in the shade. She came out with the tea tray, and served every one of them, not looking at him once. When she had finished, she sat on the rug, listening to everyone talking about Geoffrey, how he would have been fifteen this year, and who he might have taken after, and where he might have gone to study music.

One by one, they stopped, and she knew that each one of them was picturing a laughing, fair-haired boy, for he had looked like a Lewis, not really a Cox: sitting beside them all now, in a shirt with the sleeves rolled up in the heat, helping Walter and his grandfather with the harvest, playing the piano on long afternoons, Chopin and Schubert floating out through open windows.

Is that what it would have been like?

– Something like that.

Meredith felt herself give a little shiver. He only ever spoke to her when they were alone.

Her father put down his tea and stretched. 'You know what I want to do now?'

'What?' asked Sarah.

'Go for a walk by the river. Would anyone else like to come?'

'I'm not going anywhere,' said his mother, deep in an unaccustomed deckchair, brought down from Wimbledon in the motorcar parked on the verge.

'I think we're a little too old now for walks in the fields,' said Jane Lewis, in her clear, musical voice. She touched Sarah's arm. 'But you go, darling, it will do you good.'

Sarah looked at Walter. 'Would you like me to come?'

'Yes, but you don't see your parents often.'

'You mustn't mind us,' said Geoffrey Lewis, from beneath his panama hat.

'Nor me,' said Walter's father, from beneath his old felt.

They were all falling asleep.

Walter got up. Meredith saw her parents' long exchange of glances. Then, 'Euan? Meredith?'

She felt their two names blazing in the silence.

'Yes,' said Euan. 'I'll come.' He came across the grass and stood beside her. 'We haven't seen each other for such a long time.'

She didn't answer.

'How are you?'

'All right.'

'Will you come with us, Meredith?'

– Oh, go on, you goose.

Not Geoffrey as she remembered him, as she had always, always talked to him, a little ghost lying deep within her, but as he would have become, a teasing brother, whom she had to keep in check, who made her laugh.

She got to her feet.

They all walked out across the fields together, over the tussocky grass, past the grazing cows, who started to follow, then stopped, as Walter waved them back. Finch and fieldfare darted in and out of the hedges; they walked through the far gate, which stood open, and saw some of the cattle moving towards the willows, where one or two were already drinking, swishing their tails in the shade.

Walter said, leading them all in a diagonal, so they could go downstream, away from the animals, 'I haven't told anyone this, but I had a letter this morning from Henry Marsh.'

'And?' asked Sarah.

'He said if we do go to war – if – I should apply for a commission as an artist.'

'You mean –' Meredith stepped over a cowpat, caking in the heat. 'You mean you might not have to go?'

'We'll see.'

He held out a hand. She took it, and held it, and let it go.

'What about Euan?' asked Sarah.

Euan gave a rueful smile. 'Sculptors are generally called in when wars are over.'

'Oh, Euan.'

'Let's not talk about it now.' He glanced at Meredith. She glanced away.

They all walked on, coming at last to the shade of the willows, overhanging the riverbanks, trailing deep into the water.

'Oh, that's better.'

They stood in the cool and the shade, watching the slow steady current flow on and on.

There was the kingfisher! He flashed downstream, glinting.

'I wonder if we'll see the heron.'

'We used to have such nice times here, when you were both little,' said Walter to Meredith. 'Didn't we?'

'I remember mostly you and Geoffrey. You used to fish.'

'And I used to fish here when I was a boy.'

They moved slowly on. Dragonflies shimmered above the water, a coot beneath the far bank sat on her nest of twigs and watched them, her white bony head the only thing that told them she was there amongst the reeds. Then they saw her darting chicks, as she stepped off the nest, and into the water. They all stood and watched them for ages.

'This makes me think of your waterways book,' said Meredith to Sarah, after a while, but there was no answer. She turned and looked round. Where were her parents?

'They're just round the corner,' said Euan.

She stopped, and looked. She could hear them, walking and talking, further downstream. Their voices grew fainter.

Euan said, 'Meredith, I want to talk to you.'

She didn't answer. A fish broke the surface of the water with a tiny sound, and she stood there, watching the ripples spread.

'Shall we walk, or shall we sit down?'

Warblers flew in and out of the reeds. Everything was about to happen: she knew.

He put out his hand, and it rested upon her shoulder. She didn't move away, she couldn't. She just let the weight of his hand sink into her bones, and waited.

He said, 'The last time I saw you, when you came over that summer, you were a child.'

She shook her head.

That was the day I left childhood for ever.

'Well, not a child. But still very young.' He put his other hand on her shoulder, as he had done that burning day, kneeling before her as she gazed into blackness. 'I couldn't say to you then, all the things that I wanted to say. And something had happened to you, hadn't it? Something that upset you deeply. Will you tell me what it was?'

The water flowed past them, over the stony bed, and amongst the reeds.

'Meredith?'

She looked up at him, and met his gaze, so serious and beautiful and intent upon her.

'Oh, Euan.'

I will take this leap, and the water will carry me.

'Tell me. Whatever it is. Tell me, so I can put it right. After all this time.'

She said, shaking, 'If what I think happened, happened, then there can never be anything between us.'

'Would you like there to be something between us?'

His touch on her shoulders was coursing through her. She couldn't speak. Then she made herself.

'Did my mother ever lend you a book?'

'What?'

'Did my mother ever lend you a book?'

He looked bemused. 'Yes. Your parents and I have often lent each other books. Why do you ask?'

She felt herself go scarlet. Had she really, really been so foolish?

'Which book?' he asked her, and he lifted his hand and began to stroke her hair. 'Which book has troubled you so much?' She saw him trying to understand.

She said, feeling hot embarrassment rise, 'The day I came over to see you, there was a book on the grass. The last time I saw it was at my mother's bedside.'

He looked at her so intently that she thought she would stop breathing. Then at last he understood.

'You thought that I and your mother . . .'

'Yes.'

'Oh, my dear God.' There was a silence. Then he took her face in his hands. 'For two years you have thought this?'

'Yes.'

He gave a long deep sigh. Then his hand ran over her face, over and over it, warm and tender and loving. 'What was the book?' he asked her, and then, 'No, wait, I'll remember. I remember every single thing about that day. I've gone over and over it.'

Like his hand, running over her face. She reached up and took it, and held it to her lips, and closed her eyes again, feeling him stand very still.

'*To the Lighthouse*,' he said slowly. 'I can see it now, on the grass. And who would have believed . . .' He was cupping her face in both hands again. 'Look at me.'

She looked, and felt love pour over her, like light, like water, endless.

'What a long time it has taken us, and how much you must have felt that day.'

'Yes.' She couldn't stop looking at him, now; she wanted to look at him for ever.

Her parents were coming back along the riverbank. She could hear them, talking quietly, and the clip-clip talk of the coot and her young, sailing downstream.

'Will you come and see me?'

'Yes,' she said, filled with happiness. 'Yes, yes, I will.'

'Do you know that I love you?'

'Yes.'

'That I always have done?'

'Yes.'

'And no one else,' he said, and now the door between them had swung right open, and they were looking at each other properly, for the very first time.

She wanted to say that she loved him, too, but he knew that she did, and she wanted to wait.

He lifted her face: at last he kissed her.

They all walked home together, across the fields. No one talked about what had happened, but everyone knew, and unexpected happiness was everywhere between them. It was growing cooler, the sun beginning to dissolve into gathering cloud, mellow here and there on dock and sorrel. The gate to the lane stood open, the cows gone out to milking. Euan had lit his pipe, and the early evening air was filled with the smell of his tobacco. Meredith thought, For the whole of my life I shall remember this: everything come right between us, and everything ahead.

They crossed to the house, saw the grandparents, still in their chairs beneath the trees, and waving. The first moths were out, flitting like ghosts above the flowers.

'I'm going to say goodbye now,' said Euan, and he came in and made his farewells to them all. Then Meredith followed him out to the front garden gate. No one could see them here.

He took her hand, he drew her to him. They stood in the lane in a long and perfect silence, their arms round one another, her head against his chest.

'Come and see me,' he said at last, and she leaned back in his arms and looked up at him.

'I will, I will.'

'Would you like to come tomorrow? I'm not going into Ashford.'

She hesitated. Did this sound strange? 'I think I need a day by myself first.'

'Because?'

'Because – because I have been so unhappy here, for such a long time. I want to – to collect myself, I suppose. Just to be here, and think about you, and look forward . . .'

'I understand that perfectly. And I shall do the same.' He traced her mouth with his finger, he traced each eyebrow, as if he were smoothing clay.

'The day after that?' she asked him, filled with longing.

'I think I'm meant to be at Challocks. I'll rearrange it. Yes – come then, come early.'

'I will,' she said again, and then, 'I don't know how I shall wait.'

'That's what tomorrow is for,' he said, with his beautiful, piercing smile. 'Isn't it?'

And then, and then –

She covered her face.

'Goodbye, my darling.' He took her hands away from her face, he bent to kiss her. And then he released her, and walked away.

She leaned on the wall, feeling the long summer grass on the verge brush her ankles. The sun was sinking low now, and his shadow on the lane behind him went on and on. The church clock struck the half-hour, a single pure note, and he reached the corner, and turned, and stretched out his hand towards her. Then he walked on.

Meredith leaned on the wall's old coping stone, with its patterns of lichen, pale in the gathering dusk. She could hear them all getting up in the garden, the two sets of grandparents saying goodbye, her name mentioned between them all. What were they saying? Her London grandparents were staying the night. Tomorrow she would play Patience with her London grandmother, and show her drawings to her grandfather, and watch him lift them one by one with his old mottled hands, and tell her they were rather good. And all the time she'd be thinking . . .

Her other grandparents – her real grandparents, as she always, always thought of them – were coming out now, through the end gate. She went on leaning on the wall, seeing beyond the parked motorcar the first cows start to walk up the lane from Middle Yalding, heavy with calf.

'Well now, my girl,' said her grandmother, coming along in her hat. 'And what have you been up to?'

'Nothing,' said Meredith, blushing.

Her grandmother gave her a look. Here was her grandfather, lighting his pipe. He shook out the match, and dropped it in his pocket.

'You just be careful, young lady,' he said.

'I am,' said Meredith, feeling the blush deepen. 'I will be.'

'I mean it. You're still a lass. He's old enough –'

'To be my father,' she said, running her finger along the wall, not looking at them now. 'I know.'

The cows were drawing closer, swaying towards them, and the open gate. They turned to stare at the motorcar, up on the verge.

'You keep away from that,' said her grandfather, moving towards them, and they swung their heads away and went on through the gate.

Meredith watched them. What could she say? She thought, This is how it's always going to be for us. People will look, and wonder. They'll say things. They won't understand.

She put out a hand to her grandmother. She said, 'I've known him all my life.'

'I know.' Her grandmother squeezed the hand. 'I know you have. And he's a good man, we can see that. But you mustn't mind us worrying. We've known you all your life, too, remember.'

'But when you were my age . . .'

'When I was your age, we'd been courting a year.' She turned to her husband. 'Isn't that right, William?'

'We were the same age, I seem to remember.' He drew on his pipe and it glowed in the dusk. The last of the cows was gone through the gate; here was the farmboy, banging it to.

'Evening.'

'Nice evening.'

He nodded, and turned back, tapping his stick all along the lane, breaking into a run as he reached the corner.

'Just like your dad,' said Meredith's grandmother. 'Well now.' She looked at Meredith again. 'I don't suppose you'll be wanting to take too much notice of us.'

'I do,' said Meredith. 'I do take notice. But . . .'

'I know.' Her grandmother squeezed her hand again. 'It's not as if we don't want you to be happy.'

'Thank you. I will be.' And she felt joy coursing through her once more.

Her grandfather was smoking and listening. He looked at Meredith, softening a little, she could tell.

'Just remember,' he said.

'I will,' she said again, and then she stepped off the grass and kissed them.

'That's a good girl.'

And then they were walking away to the turning, walking side by side, talking about shutting up the hens, she could hear them, as the moon began to rise.

Meredith walked up to the end gate. The garden was empty, the lamplight from the open kitchen door spilling out on to the brick path, touching sage and lavender. She could hear the chink of plates and glasses, see them all moving about, sitting down at the table. She heard her name, and Euan's name, but she didn't want to listen to them worrying. She closed the gate behind her and walked across the shadowy grass, beneath the apple trees.

– This is the one.

– Yes.

She stood beside it.

– If I had lived, I'd be taller than you are now.

She shut her eyes.

Little boy, buried deep inside her.

Tall laughing brother, pulling out the piano stool, resting his hands upon the keys, beginning to play.

– You know I shall always be part of you –

– Yes.

Something was moving over the grass. She stood there like stone.

A footfall – the brush of a garment – the brush of a wing. Cold as winter, stern and unforgiving.

Meredith's eyes flew open. The garden was empty, but something stirred.

There were always creatures moving about in the fields and gardens at night, just as there were always sounds and creaks in the house. A fox, his long brush parting the undergrowth – a hedgehog, nosing about.

She knew this. And yet, and yet –

He was still there, still waiting for her, cold as starlight, cold as death.

'Meredith?'

Her mother was in the open doorway, looking out. 'There you are.' She came down the path, and Meredith walked towards her. They stopped, they embraced, as they had not done for two whole years.

'You're shivering. Come inside.'

Inside, her father was fiddling with the controls on the wireless. The church clock sounded, the pips came on, through a faint crackle. Her London grandparents were sitting at the table, listening.

'This is the seven o'clock news, and this is John Snagge, reading it. His Majesty the King has today given the Royal Assent to the government's plans for conscription.'

Meredith, two days later, set out early in the morning, leaving a note in the kitchen. She opened the front door, saw the grass and the stone wall wet with dew; she closed the door quietly behind her. Out through the front gate, on to the lane. Shreds of mist clung to the hedges; she saw the ewes in the churchyard look up as she walked past them, as her father had always said they did for him.

First light, first up.

Today I shall tell him everything. I shall try to.

Today she wouldn't walk across the fields, as the crow flew. The crow took no time at all, but last time she had made this journey it had taken her all morning. She walked down the lane, past the misty hopfields, hearing the cockerel greet the day. How full of joy he sounded. She quickened her pace.

She came up the road to the common just after nine. The mist was rolling away across the marshes; she saw the goats, and the door of the barn drawn back and she stopped, hearing a cottage door open. Someone came out, and walked down to wait for the first bus – a woman with a shopping basket.

'Nice morning.'

'Isn't it?'

Meredith walked up over the grass, still wet, and now her heart was hammering once again. She stopped and stroked the goats, letting them nuzzle against her bare legs, waiting for him to realise, and come out.

If anything goes wrong this time –

Movement in the deep interior of the barn. Then he was at the door, coming to look for her. He saw her and he waited, just as she wanted him to do.

She walked towards him, slowly; she stopped, and stood before him.

How should they begin?

'There's someone out here.'

He looked. 'So there is.'

He drew her into the barn, as airy and cool and high as a cathedral. She drank in the smell of it all, the clay, the plaster, the earthen floor, beaten down by generations. There was the haycart, resting in its corner, filled with bags of clay, and sacks of plaster. There were the shelves of the things he'd collected, all down the years: driftwood and stones and bones and branches, and some of them were from her. There were the shelves of the things he'd been making, all this time: little maquettes, little models and carvings, for much larger work. Slabs of stone leaned against the wall, figures stood here and there in the shadows.

She'd been coming in here all her life. It was as it should be: like coming home.

'What are you working on now?'

'I'll show you.' He took her hand and led her to the table.

A group of small marble forms stood at one end: monoliths, placed here and there like stones in a field. She could see he was trying things out. And, at the other end, there was a bust, with a damp cloth over it. He lifted it carefully: she could smell the wet clay.

There was a girl with a fringe, her hair thumbed over and over. There was her face, or something like it, looking across the barn to the open door.

She put her hand to her own face, feeling it, as someone else might do, as a sculptor might, measuring bone and plane and contour.

'That's me.' She looked at him. 'You've been modelling me.'

'Trying to. Not very well, I'm afraid. I need the real thing to work from.'

She reached out a finger. How cool clay was, how good it must be to work with.

'What I should really like to do,' he said, standing beside her, resting his hand on her shoulder, as if they came in here every day, to talk about their work, 'what I should really like is to do it properly.'

'How?'

He turned her to him: he ran his hands over her face, as he had done by the river, smoothing and smoothing it, then feeling every little place. 'I'd have to cover your head in plaster, and wait until it dried.' The tips of his fingers were upon her brow, her temples, feeling everywhere, all down the line of each cheek, and across her mouth. Her eyes were closed, she felt every nerve in her body alive, waiting for his touch.

'How would I breathe?' she whispered.

He put a finger on each nostril. 'I'd have to put a straw in here, and here. For a while you'd look rather strange.'

She felt the smile in his voice, and she smiled back, feeling happiness once again begin, to well up within her.

'And then?'

'And then I would read to you, while the plaster dried, and now and then come and check it, and then, when it was absolutely dry, I'd cut it open, very carefully, and put it on this table, in two halves, and then you'd be free.' He drew her to him; she leaned against his tall warm body, smelling tobacco and cotton, hearing his heartbeat. 'And what would you do then?' he asked her, drawing her closer still.

'I'd do this,' she said, holding him. 'And I'd never go away.'

He cradled her head in his hands, she felt his caress on her hair, over and over.

She heard through the open door the bus come rumbling along the lane and pull up for the woman off to do her shopping. Then it was rumbling away again, and everything was quiet, with only the sound of the goats cropping the grass, and the rooks feeding their young in the elms.

'Shall we go up to the house?' asked Euan, and his voice, and his question, filled the world.


Meredith lay naked in her lover's arms and the sounds of her childhood were borne through the open window: the sigh of the wind in the elms, the creaking branches, the plaintive thin call of the goats, the door of a cottage opening, somebody working in the garden.

'Euan, Euan.'

He moved to lie on her, holding her face in his hands. 'My love, my love.'

They could not stop looking at one another.

'I love you,' said Meredith. 'I have always loved you.'

'Is that true?'

'For as long as I can ever remember.'

'And I you,' he said. 'From the first moment I saw you.'

'I was a baby.'

'I know.'

They lay there in silence, she beneath him, loving his weight upon her.

'I'm so old, now,' he said. 'You're still so young.'

'It doesn't matter. We belong. I belong here with you, in this house.'

'Yes.'

His mouth covered hers. They kissed and kissed.

'Come into me,' whispered Meredith.

He parted and opened her, moved his beautiful fingers inside her, over and over, everywhere. 'Meredith. My own true love.' Then he sank deep within. They lay still.

The wind touched the curtains, they billowed out into the room.

'Go on,' whispered Meredith, her hands all over him.

He began to move and she flung out her arms in abandon.

'Euan, Euan, Euan—'

She was three, she was six, she was seven, she was racing across the garden towards him, she was caught in his arms and held high and put down again.

'No, no – no – don't ever leave me. Don't ever stop –'

'I love you, I love you.'

He pounded deep into her, surf upon the shore. And then she wept and wept.

'What is it? What is it? I love you, tell me.'

'I can't, I can't.'

'You can tell me.'

'I can't tell anyone, not even you.' She sobbed into the pillow.

'You must,' he said gravely, naked against her. 'If we are to be together, you must.'

She lay in his arms, in his narrow bed which faced the window, across on the other side of the room. The curtains, in the summer wind, blew in and blew out, between here and there.

She said, 'I don't deserve such happiness.'

'Why not?'

'Because . . .'

'Go on.'

She felt as though she were walking on broken glass, down a long dark corridor, which stretched ahead for ever, and stretched back as far as she could ever remember.

She said, 'You are the only person I could ever tell this to. You are the one person who knew both of us, I mean other than my family, and I can't tell them.'

He lay there, listening, her hand in his.

'When I was young,' she began, 'when I was very young, I had violent fantasies.' She began to cry again, and he held her.

'Go on.'

She tried. 'You know my father's painting –'

'There are many paintings.'

'The one of my mother and me. At night. With the angel.' She covered her face. 'That painting was like a bird, rising from the ashes. It was great, and important, I know that. It probably saved my father.'

'But for you? Meredith? Darling. Look at me, tell me.'

'It's followed me all my life – the angel – as if he knew, and had come to claim me.' Tears were pouring out of her.

'To claim you because?'

'I used to think all these terrible thoughts. I couldn't help it, they came and came. Violent fantasies. Somebody falling. And then, when it happened . . .' She began to howl.

At last she had stopped, and had told him everything.

'And you've carried this all your life,' he said, lying there with her head on his chest, smoothing her hair, which now was so tousled and wet.

She nodded, quite drained.

'And I've talked to him all my life. Ever since he died. And he has talked to me.' She stopped.

'Go on.'

'I think that started here,' she said slowly, remembering herself, down on the step to the garden, watching her mother fall asleep, and her father and Euan walk into the barn, and her life stretch before her, without a brother. 'Yes. Soon after he died. And it feels –'

'It feels?'

'As if I'm betraying him now – by telling you how he and I have always talked, have always been together.' She shut her eyes, beginning to cry again. 'I don't want to let him go. I don't want to leave him behind.'

'You don't have to,' said Euan. 'Why should you?' He lay there, feeling her heart beneath his hand. 'I was an only child,' he said. 'Have I told you that?'

'No.' She opened her eyes and turned to look at him. 'Like my mother.'

'And like you,' he said. 'As you became. I do remember what it was like. Of course you must keep him alive.'

Meredith drew away. She sat up, and knelt before him; she let her eyes run over his long naked body. She ached with how beautiful he was. She took his hand.

'You have made everything right.'

'And you for me.'

They searched each other's gaze.

'This is it,' he said simply, at last. 'Isn't it? This is for ever.'

'Yes.'


June, and the harvest almost ready. It had rained in the second week, and everyone was ready for that, the long sweet soak into the earth, the pattering in the trees at night. Then the sun came out again, and the corn reached up towards it.

They were married right at the end of the month, the first date possible, in the church of Meredith's childhood, where her brother had been christened, and from where he had been buried. On the day of her wedding, it was filled with roses. Her father gave her away, and gave the ring to Euan.

# 2

Three trees stood in a field. Walter, his canvas bag bumping against his side, took note of them. It was mid-morning, hazy, and he was out far from the house, walking over the land behind Hobbs Farm, which stretched for a long way on the other side of the river, and began to rise towards the wooded hills. Behind him were the hopfields, acre upon acre; here he was in an open meadow, a field left fallow this year. He could hear cattle grazing on the other side of the hedge; sheep dotted the lower slopes of the hills.

Here were three trees. He stopped, and looked at them.

They were oaks, well spaced, nicely planted, still with a long growth ahead, but full and leafy. He could remember them from when he was a boy, and he and John William and Eddie Pierce used to come out on rambles, bringing sandwiches. Sometimes they fished, and sometimes they didn't. They'd come all the way up here and go nesting in the woods, then they'd come back and lie down in the shade. Three boys, two of them older than him, with a tree each, lying beneath, looking up. In autumn, acorns dropped on their heads.

'Somebody threw that.'

'Not me.'

'Our dad'll be wanting them, for the pigs.' That was Eddie, who'd joined up the same day as John William.

'Bit of a lark, with the two of us.'

Smoking their Woodbines, outside the Drill Hall, stubbing them out, going in.

Walter stood before the trees now, still at some distance, remembering it all.

Three trees, three boys, and one too young to go.

Three trees: himself, and Sarah, and Meredith. Three, where there should have been four. He unfolded his canvas stool and sat down. He opened his bag. A small oil sketch on a board: that was what he liked. Then he would work it up in the studio, then he would make something of it.

The letter from Henry lay amongst the brushes: he took it out, and re-read it.

*. . .I wish I'd been able to get you a show. But the main thing now is to put yourself down for an artist's commission – I'll give you a reference. I know a chap who knows a chap – you know how these things go.*

No, thought Walter, turning the page. I never did know, and I never tried to; that's been the trouble, no doubt.

*. . .Fellow called Muirhead Bone – he used to commission Spencer and Nash – been helping refugee artists, knows Kenneth Clark, who knows everyone. I'll give you the low-down – promise you'll apply. If it happens, they'll want people at home, as well as abroad, I'm sure of that, document-ing everything. There's a great feeling about the artists from the last war; people keep talking about them . . .*

Walter folded the letter. High above came the sound of an engine. He looked up, saw an aeroplane travelling slowly through the blue haze of the morning, over the fields and the winding river, over the oak trees of his boyhood, his family of three, and out above the wooded hills, leaving a long white vapour trail.

He sat there, thinking, getting his things out. From a long time ago, all at once, came a line from Roger Fry, read in Regent's Park on a summer afternoon not long after the last war. *For me it is of no consequence whether I paint Christ or a saucepan. What has significance is only the form . . .*

But it is of consequence to me, thought Walter now, as he had then. The subject matters. It has to. He unscrewed a half-used tube of Prussian green, and then a viridian, mixing them on the palette, looking up at the trees. He thought of all those articles in *Circle*, read coming home on the train. Nicholson and Hepworth had picked up on Fry, in their way; so had Moore: they wanted to look for what lay beneath, the essence. He'd seen some of that in Euan's abstract work, and understood it.

But for me, he thought, settling down to it, the board upon his lap, for me the thing itself has significance: those trees, these fields in Kent, that trail in the hazy sky above them, in the summer of 1939.

He set to work.

Meredith drew a map. She sat at her desk, brought over in the Challocks van from her bedroom in the house of her childhood, and set down before a different window.

'I never knew what to do with this room,' said Euan, watching her settle in.

'That's because it was waiting for me.' Meredith set out her pencils and paper. She stacked up her notebooks and sketchbooks, put her pens in a pot. She looked out across the garden through the open window, smelled the sea in the wind. 'This is my studio now.'

He came up behind her, put his hands on her breasts. She turned in his arms; they climbed the narrow stairs.

'My love, my darling.'

Never had anything felt so right.

Later, he lay in bed listening to her move about the house, as the afternoon light grew deeper. He heard her fill the kettle, and set it on the range; he heard her open the front door, and knew she was standing there, on the step where she used to sit as a child. He heard her go into the room of her own, and the scrape of the chair on the flags.

Meredith drew a map. She put in the house by the church, the weather vane high on the tower pointing east, towards this house. She drew in the lanes which lay between the two, and marked in the villages she had always known: Denham and Darwell and Parsonage Wood, Hawkhurst and Goudhurst; she marked in the hamlets: Asham's Mill, Hurst Green. She drew in fine pen the buildings and oasthouses of the farms, and named them, and then she drew a crow, flying over them, beating his way over farmland and hopfield, between that place and this place, where she had come to rest.

She sat looking out of the open window, at the little walled garden, the stretch of grassy common beyond the gate, the grazing goats and great barn and elms which overlooked it all.

'Geoffrey?'

There was no answer.

But you know you will always be with me, she said, deep inside her. Even now.

She looked back at the map; she drew, in the churchyard, a little grave beneath the long stone wall, beneath the yew. Then she pinned up the map beside her studio window, as her father had done with his.

There.

Upstairs, getting dressed, Euan heard the sound of an aeroplane. He went to the window and watched it circle, and fly inland.

☆

August, parched and burning. Then a light wind, and more rain, and September began, with the first hint of autumn, just in the early morning, the first leaves falling.

Sunday, and everyone out in the garden, then going inside to turn on the wireless, and listen to the lunchtime news, and Chamberlain.

Road blocks. Barbed wire, rolled out all along the coast. Everyone looking up at the sky. In Ashford they were selling blackout fabric, scissors slicing through yards of it, all along the counter, over and over again. Conscription notices were everywhere.

Outside the Drill Hall, The Buffs were lining up.

Inside, Walter drew them: the men coming in, taking off shirts and jackets, dropping braces, dropping trousers, passed as fit by the officers at the desk.

He thought, I know about this.

At home, in the studio, he put some of it in boxes, sent some up to London, waited.

Without Meredith, the house felt as empty as a field in winter.

Euan received his papers. He went down to the recruiting station in the Drill Hall, and told them his age, just two years off forty-five, the cut-off point. He said that he had served in the last war, and been invalided out, that now he had only just married, that his wife was very young. He told them that he was a sculptor, applying for a commission from the War Artists Advisory Committee.

They listened. He knew he would have to go.

# Epilogue

In London, two major exhibitions. The first, in the winter of 1945, Walter went to with Sarah alone. Smoky clouds blew over a bombed city; on the roof of the Royal Academy the flags snapped in the wind. They hurried down Piccadilly, and into the shelter of the courtyard.

'Stop,' said Walter. He turned Sarah to him, he lifted her chin with his gloved hand. Beneath her winter hat her face was bright with the cold. He kissed her frozen mouth.

'Twenty-six years since I came up here for an exhibition and noticed a girl in the queue.'

'And now we're coming to see you.' Sarah was shivering.

'And you.'

'Quick, let's go in.'

*The War Paintings*: a corner of the poster tore in the wind. They ran up the steps; Walter held the door wide. The foyer was packed. They watched people greeting one another, went to pick up their catalogues, waited for Henry.

'Ah, there you are!'

Here he was, in long coat and scarf, peeling off his gloves. 'Wonderful to see you both.'

They climbed the broad stone stairs.

A different war, and different artists: Bawden, Ardizzone, Moore. They stood before pastels of Londoners huddled in the Underground, sleeping like Dante's dead beneath the Blitz.

Only Spencer and Nash had been recommissioned: the furnaces of the shipbuilders on the Clyde burned through a whole gallery; Walter paced up and down before Nash's frozen seas and tumbling spitfires, remembering churned-up mud, and another desolation.

'Don't you want to see your own work?' Henry was taking his arm, leading him through to a smaller gallery. People were crowding in, peering at the small printed cards alongside his paintings, standing back to take in the rolls of barbed wire, all along Dover beach, the vapour trail of the plane above the trees. They looked at the men lining up for enlistment in the Ashford Drill Hall, the Land Girls milking, along at Middle Yalding, and up at Hobbs Farm; the wartime hop-pickers and wartime ploughmen, bundled up in their celluloid tractor cabs, the gulls screaming behind them – men like his father, too old to go. White cowls of the oasthouse beneath a gun-metal sky; swede and potato cast up on frozen furrow; the church tower grey beneath the clouds; an oil of his parents, listening to the wireless in the lamplit kitchen; a little oil of Meredith, reading a wartime letter.

Walter looked round the room, saw people turning the pages of the catalogue, searching for his name.

Well. So this was how it felt.

He looked at the gathering visitors, saw a familiar, much older figure, one shoulder a little lower than the other, still moving awkwardly through the crush.

'David Wicks.'

'Walter.'

They embraced in the crowded room.

Sarah's woodcuts and engravings had been hung on the two walls framing the doorway: black and white, night and day, each with the studio mark: Three Windows. Kent in winter, Kent in the war; blackout across a farmhouse window, plane against moonlit cloud, little heap of letters on a desk.

'We mustn't stay too long,' said Walter.

Before they went, Henry said in the foyer, 'This will lead to more. I'm sure of it.'


Rain fell on the Thames; wet leaves clung to the Embankment. People arriving for the private view at the Tate shook out their umbrellas on the steps, and moved quickly through the revolving doors. *English Painting and Sculpture Between the Wars*: the glass on the posters on the railings glistened; rain trickled over the names. Nash and Nicholson, Spencer and Smith, Bell and Fry and Grant and Coldstream; Epstein and Gill and Moore and Hepworth.

Meredith looked, and frowned. 'Father? Why aren't you there? And where's Euan's name?'

'I'm in a minor key,' said Euan, climbing the steps beside her. 'They can't list everyone.'

'How can you say that?' She looked at his grave gentle face beneath the umbrella, his hair and beard gone grey. 'Don't ever say that.'

Inside, they left their wet coats.

'Now,' said Meredith, turning the pages of the catalogue. The paper was thin and the print small. It was 1949; everything still had that rationed, wartime feel to it.

Beside her, Euan's long finger ran down the column of names. Hitchens and Wallis and Jones and Wood.

'There,' he said at last.


They were hung side by side: two great framed canvases, taking half a wall. Meredith saw her parents stand before them, saw people stop, and stand back.

131 *The Trinity of Women* 1923 Walter Cox

It blazed from the wall in blue and gold and scarlet: Renaissance colours, Gauguin's colours, the women like Gauguin's women – mythical, modern, timeless. Figures in an orchard garden, figures in a dream. Beside them, the wings of the great goose beat through the summer air, as they had beaten through Walter's childhood, and through her own.

132 *Preparing for Bed* 1930 Walter Cox

Huge and sombre as a Rembrandt, mysterious as Magritte. A dark interior, curtain, bed and blanket deep in shadow; firelight and starlight glinting on satin and brass. A pale, grieving woman at the window; a girl taking off black stockings. And there, at the door, an unearthly whiteness.

'Like *The Light of the World*,' said Euan quietly.

Meredith looked at him. 'You know that isn't true.'

His arm went round her. She slipped her own beneath his jacket; her fingers touched thin ribs.

Around them people were murmuring; someone was coming towards them.

'Walter.' Henry was beside him, shaking his hand. 'Many congratulations. I want to introduce you to Dudley Tooth.'

Meredith stood watching it all: her father's shy smile, her mother's look of delight, a tall man crossing the gallery floor towards them.

'And where are you, my love?' she asked her husband.

'Let's go and see.'

The sculptures were placed all through the exhibition. Euan and Meredith drew apart now and then, he to look at the Moore and Epstein, she at the paintings.

Nash's *Landscape from a Dream*, bird and boulder lit by a fiery sun; Nash's *Harbour and Room*, where a wall was missing, and sea washed into it, black and glittering.

I remember that, thought Meredith, recalling the tide of loneliness that had flooded her, a girl in a London gallery, in 1936. An only child, up with her parents and a man she was falling in love with – too young to know that then, thinking only: I like the way you occupy space. Knowing only her own restlessness and sadness, and wondering at the rush of feeling when he walked away from her.

I remember that.

'Euan?' She turned in the crowd; she felt her eyes fill with tears.

'I'm here.'

He was here; he'd come back. She gave thanks every day.

In the house on Hurst Green the box of his letters from Burma was locked away. She had read them so often they'd come to bits.

'Euan?'

His arm was tight around her. They walked from room to room.

There. There they were.

On plinths in the centre of the room stood two little Hepworths: spheres white and perfect, perfectly placed. And in each corner, the Harrisons:

146 *In Memoriam* Clay 1920

148 *Figure I* Hopton stone 1926

150 *Figure II* Elmwood 1935

152 *Meredith* Bronze 1946

They stood watching strangers look at his work: the great abstract figures; the dead from another, long distant war; the young wife gazing at him on his return from the last – the first real work he'd done after coming home, out in the barn again, in early spring, hearing the creak of the elms, the plaintive cry of the goats which had haunted her, all through the years when he'd been away.

He said, as people came and went around them, 'I thought of you every single day.'

'And I you.' She leaned against him.

'You know how I wish I could give you a child.'

'Don't. It doesn't matter.'

He knew it wasn't true.


A morning in early November, the air cold and still, leaves dropping into the quietness. Walter was out in the garden, raking the grass. He piled the leaves into the barrow, and wheeled it across to the bonfire, smoking beside the long line of the ditch; he went back and began again, raking and sweeping beneath the apple trees. Sarah was working upstairs; after lunch, he would go up and join her. The letter from Dudley Tooth was pinned up by his window, next to the curling postcards and the faded map. Tooth represented Spencer. Now he wanted to represent him.

He had a gallery, he had someone waiting to see Walter's new work.

What should he do?

Walter swept up the last of the damp dark leaves, and tipped them out of the barrow. The clock in the church tower struck the hour, ringing out over the empty fields. Eleven strokes. Soon it would be the Armistice.

He stood in the quiet garden, bordered by the lanes where he and his brother had run as boys, beneath the tree where his little son had fallen. Across on the other side of the grass, up the path to the kitchen door, stood the water butt, where Geoffrey and Meredith used to play. They'd played all through the garden: he used to listen through the open studio windows, hearing them call, and race in and out of the house, Geoffrey with his jar of creatures, setting them down, wandering into the playroom, picking out a tune; Meredith running upstairs with her doll – 'I'm having a baby!'

Walter walked over to the water butt, and tapped on the side, as he used to do when they were little, holding them up to see the surface of the water break, and the light break into pieces.

He tapped, he looked down. On the dark curve of the wood a little pulse of reflected light was leaping: up and down, up and down. He stood there and watched it, remembering a morning in boyhood when he had woken to some sense of how beautiful that was; thinking now, as a man, of life rushing through us, caught in a moment, gleaming on water, gone.

# Acknowledgements and Author's Note

I am grateful to Faber and Faber Ltd for permission to reproduce lines from 'The Waste Land' from *Collected Poems 1909–1962* by T.S. Eliot.

Less formally, I should like now to express my gratitude to the many people who during the research and writing of *Earth and Heaven* gave generously of their expertise: in advice, the loan of books, copying of maps, reading of the manuscript, illuminating conversation and remarks. Chief amongst these was the artist Stephen Chaplin, Archivist at the Slade School of Art from 1990–1997, who in two afternoons lit up period and place, and thereafter made invaluable corrections and suggestions. I should also particularly like to thank the wood engraver Simon Brett, who so generously took up the tools of Sarah Cox to provide the exquisite part-title illustrations; the painter Patrick Cullen, to whom I gave the manuscript too late, alas, to make proper use of his wise suggestions, but who earlier gave eloquent insights into the dialogue between landscape and canvas; and Nigel Haigh, who conducted me in kind and painterly fashion through rooms of the National Gallery, imparting expert knowledge of school and technique.

I am also especially indebted to Lynette Levine, who tirelessly typed and re-typed the manuscript: as I cling to my corner of the past by continuing to write on a manual typewriter, and correct in a barely decipherable hand, I could not possibly manage without her.

In addition, I am very grateful to the following: John Aiken, Head of Sculpture at the Slade, for a tour and conversation; Steve Alwyn, for insights into bell-ringing; C.P. Atkins, Librarian at the Nation Railway Museum, for Kent-London routes during the period; the sculptor Brenda Berman for books, conversation and the image of a quarry; Sally Brooks, Library Officer at the Museum of London, for period maps and guidebooks; Martin Crowther, Assistant Curator of the Royal Museum and Art Gallery in Canterbury; Krzysztof Cieskowski of the Tate Gallery Library for detailed information and cuttings on artists, galleries and exhibitions; Felicity Edholm and Sharon Finmark for books and conversation; Michael Freeman, for painstaking references relating to the First Battalion of the East Kent Regiment, 'The Buffs'; Tom Hall, of the Ashford Borough Museum Society; Charlotte Halliday, Keeper of the Archive of the New English Art Club, for books, conversation and invitations; the fashion and social historian Rosemary Hawthorne; Janine Haythorne-Thwaite, Archivist of the Whitechapel Art Gallery; David Hepher, Professor of Painting at the Slade, for a tour, conversation and a sandwich; Nick Hewitt, Project Coordinator, National Inventory of War Memorials at the Imperial War Museum; staff of the London Transport Museum Resource Centre; the poet Peter Daniels Luczinski for 'Some account of the needful', a poem which reminded me that writing needs to interweave a vision with good plain sewing; David McLachlin of the British Library Music Collections for help in trying to trace copyright; James Mayor and Andrew Murray of the Mayor Gallery, London, for access to archives; Michael Moody, Research and Information Officer, Department of Art, the Imperial War Museum; Justin and Franny Owen, the best of neighbours, for letting me write in their empty house at a crucial time; Emma Pearce, Educational and Technical Services Advisor at Winsor & Newton; Richard Pitkin, Librarian in the archive of the *Illustrated London News*; Mark Pomeroy, Archivist of the Royal Academy of Arts; Philip Poole, 'His Nibs', latterly of the staff of Cornelissen's, for letters, conversation and a remarkable memory; Professor Lorna Sage, my academic supervisor at the University of East Anglia, for continual encouragement, wisdom and kindness; Frances Spalding for a valuable conversation and *British Art since 1900*, on which, with much more of her work, I drew with real enjoyment; Judy Spours, for encyclopaedic knowledge of period and artefact; Nicholas Walt, Director of L. Cornelissen & Son Ltd, for an inspiring interview; John Windsor, of Nostalgia Cassettes, Leominster, who offers a marvellous resource in tracing recordings of twentieth-century popular music.

Finally, I should like to express my heartfelt thanks to two groups of people whose help has been much more than professional: first, my agents Laura Longrigg, Gill McNeil and Diana Tyler at MBA, and my fine new editor Marion Donaldson of Headline Review: all combine loyalty and enthusiasm with a clear head and a sharp eye, and without them I should be quite adrift. Secondly, I thank my good friends and colleagues at Middlesex University: for the long quiet weeks of a sabbatical, and for their kindness and tolerance of a team-member at its official close whose mind is often elsewhere: to Maggie Butt, Juliet Gardiner, Susanna Gladwin and Carl Miller, may I raise a glass, or at least a cup of coffee in the kitchen.

And, at the very end, my thanks go to Marek: with, as so often, just the right word.

Any mistakes and errors which remain here are mine alone. There is one deliberate and I trust forgivable anachronism in the description of an unattributed painting: this I will leave the sharp-eyed reader to discover.

I should add that the painter Walter Cox; his wife, the wood engraver Sarah Cox; and their friend, the sculptor Euan Harrison, all have their own fictional lives and locations, and, like everyone else in these pages, are quite unrelated to any person known to me, living or dead. The only real people to inhabit the novel are Henry Tonks, Professor of Fine Art at the Slade from 1918–1930, and the painter, Philip Wilson Steer, who also taught alongside him for thirty years. And also Dudley Tooth, managing director of Arthur Tooth and Sons, the gallery which long represented Stanley Spencer.

I should also add that every exhibition described in the novel took place, except the last.

Sue Gee
London, 2000

SARA GEORGE

# The Journal of
# Mrs Pepys
# Portrait of a Marriage

The highly acclaimed, bestselling fictional journal of
the wife of our most celebrated diarist.

'An altogether enchanting novel . . . sheds a brilliant
beam into the dark interior of this 17th-century
household and with compassion elegantly scripts a
couple's most intimate moments' *Scotland on Sunday*

'Sara George has succeeded admirably in finding a
voice – and a sweet, innocent but intelligent and
warm voice it is – for one of the many women half-
hidden from history by their dominant menfolk'
Margaret Foster

'Pepys's wife finds her voice . . . all the more powerful
for being partial' *Daily Telegraph*

'Anyone who thinks that Bridget Jones epitomises
an existence turbulent with trials and tribulations
should take a look at Elizabeth Pepys's journal . . . The
minutiae of daily life against the huge events of fire and
plague echo Pepys but in a far more accessible form;
Elizabeth is an attractive creation and this piece of
"faction" makes a spirited tale' *Independent on Sunday*

0 7472 5761 2

review

JENNIFER JOHNSTON

# Two Moons

In a house overlooking Dublin Bay, Mimi and her daughter Grace are disturbed by the unexpected arrival of Grace's daughter Polly and her striking new boyfriend. The events of the next few days will move both of them to reassess the shape of their lives. For while Grace's visitors lead her to consider an uncertain future, Mimi, who receives a messenger of a very different kind, must begin to set herself to rights with the betrayals and disappointments of the past.

'Superbly executed . . . both enchanted and enchanting' *Daily Telegraph*

'A marvellously affirmative and exhilarating novel which satisfies like a gorgeous piece of music. More please' Clare Boylan, *Image Magazine*

'Mesmerising . . . a richly atmospheric coupling of fairy-tale conceit and raw emotional urgency' *Daily Express*

0 7472 5932 1

review

*If you enjoyed this book here is a selection of other bestselling titles from Review*

| | | |
|---|---|---|
| MY FIRST SONY | Benny Barbash | £6.99 ☐ |
| THE CATASTROPHIST | Ronan Bennett | £6.99 ☐ |
| WRACK | James Bradley | £6.99 ☐ |
| IT COULD HAPPEN TO YOU | Isla Dewar | £6.99 ☐ |
| ITCHYCOOBLUE | Des Dillon | £6.99 ☐ |
| MAN OR MANGO | Lucy Ellmann | £6.99 ☐ |
| THE JOURNAL OF MRS PEPYS | Sara George | £6.99 ☐ |
| THE MANY LIVES & SECRET SORROWS OF JOSÉPHINE B. | Sandra Gulland | £6.99 ☐ |
| TWO MOONS | Jennifer Johnston | £6.99 ☐ |
| NOISE | Jonathan Myerson | £6.99 ☐ |
| UNDERTOW | Emlyn Rees | £6.99 ☐ |
| THE SILVER RIVER | Ben Richards | £6.99 ☐ |
| BREAKUP | Catherine Texier | £6.99 ☐ |

Headline books are available at your local bookshop or newsagent. Alternatively, books can be ordered direct from the publisher. Just tick the titles you want and fill in the form below. Prices and availability subject to change without notice.

Buy four books from the selection above and get free postage and packaging and delivery within 48 hours. Just send a cheque or postal order made payable to Bookpoint Ltd to the value of the total cover price of the four books. Alternatively, if you wish to buy fewer than four books the following postage and packaging applies:

UK and BFPO £4.30 for one book; £6.30 for two books; £8.30 for three books.

Overseas and Eire: £4.80 for one book; £7.10 for 2 or 3 books (surface mail).

Please enclose a cheque or postal order made payable to *Bookpoint Limited*, and send to: Headline Publishing Ltd, 39 Milton Park, Abingdon, OXON OX14 4TD, UK.
Email Address: orders@bookpoint.co.uk

If you would prefer to pay by credit card, our call team would be delighted to take your order by telephone. Our direct line is 01235 400 414 (lines open 9.00 am–6.00 pm Monday to Saturday 24 hour message answering service). Alternatively you can send a fax on 01235 400 454.

Name .......................................................................................

Address ....................................................................................

...............................................................................................

...............................................................................................

If you would prefer to pay by credit card, please complete:
Please debit my Visa/Access/Diner's Card/American Express (delete as applicable) card number:

| | | | | | | | | | | | | | | | | | | |
|---|---|---|---|---|---|---|---|---|---|---|---|---|---|---|---|---|---|---|

Signature .................................................... Expiry Date ..............